CIRCLE OF WOMEN

CIRCLE OF
WOMEN

An Anthology of

Contemporary Western

Women Writers

EDITED BY

Kim Barnes and Mary Clearman Blew

RedRiver
books

University of Oklahoma Press : Norman

for Philip, Rachel, Jordan, Jace, and Evan

LIBRARY OF CONGRESS CATALOGING IN PUBLICATION DATA

Circle of women : an anthology of contemporary western women writers / edited by Kim Barnes and Mary Clearman Blew.
   p.   cm.
 Includes bibliographical references.
 ISBN 0-8061-3367-8 (paper)
  1. American literature—West (U.S.)   2. Women—West (U.S.)—
Literary collections.   3. American literature—Women authors.
4. American literature—20th century.   5. West (U.S.)—Literary
collections.   I. Barnes, Kim.   II. Blew, Mary Clearman, 1939–

PS561 .C57   2001
810.8'09287'097809045—dc21

                                                    2001027726

Pages 412–414 constitute an extension of this copyright page.

The paper in this book meets the guidelines for permanence and durability of the Committee on Production Guidelines for Book Longevity of the Council on Library Resources, Inc. ∞

1 2 3 4 5 6 7 8 9 10

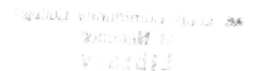

CONTENTS

INTRODUCTION   ix

MARY CLEARMAN BLEW
"THE SOW IN THE RIVER"   1

TESS GALLAGHER
"WOODCUTTING ON LOST MOUNTAIN"   10

PATRICIA HENLEY
"THE SECRET OF CARTWHEELS"   17

MELANIE RAE THON
"IONA MOON"   35

MARY ANN WATERS
"WHEN I WAS TEN, AT NIGHT"   53
"LUCK"   54

Contents

DEBRA EARLING

"THE JUST REWARDS" 56

"CHANGING" 58

MARILYNNE ROBINSON

FROM *HOUSEKEEPING* 62

RIPLEY SCHEMM

"RULES" 74

"SONGS WERE HORSES I RODE" 78

"THEY KEEP THEIR STORY" 79

"FOR MARY, ON THE SNAKE" 80

IRENE WANNER

"VISITING THE HUTTERITES" 83

DIANE RAPTOSH

"SCALE" 101

INEZ PETERSEN

FROM "MISSING YOU" 103

JANET CAMPBELL HALE

FROM *THE JAILING OF CECELIA CAPTURE* . . . 108

MADELINE DEFREES

"IN THE HELLGATE WIND" 133

DENNICE SCANLON

"THE DIFFERENCE IN EFFECTS OF TEMPERATURE
DEPENDING ON GEOGRAPHICAL LOCATION
EAST OR WEST OF THE CONTINENTAL DIVIDE:
A LETTER" 135

ANNICK SMITH

"IT'S COME TO THIS" 137

Contents

MOLLY GLOSS
FROM *THE JUMP-OFF CREEK*   158

TERESA JORDAN
"BONES"   168

JUDY BLUNT
"LEAVING HOME"   180
"WHAT COMES OF WINTER"   181
"AT THE STOCKMAN BAR, WHERE THE MEN
FALL IN LOVE, AND THE WOMEN JUST FALL" . .   183

CYRA MCFADDEN
FROM *RAIN OR SHINE: A FAMILY MEMOIR* . . .   186

DIXIE PARTRIDGE
"ENTERING SMOOT, WYOMING POP. 239" . . .   197

RUTH MCLAUGHLIN
"SEASONS"   199

SANDRA ALCOSSER
"CRY"   212
"TRACKS"   214
"THE SAWYER'S WIFE"   215

CHRISTINA ADAM
"FIRES"   219

PAM HOUSTON
"IN MY NEXT LIFE"   242

ANITA ENDREZZE
"RED ROCK CEREMONIES"   258
"CLAIMING LIVES"   259
"MOVING DAY AT THE WIDOW CAIN'S"   262

Contents

GRETEL EHRLICH
"ISLAND" 264

NEIDY MESSER
"THE FORCE OF ONE VOICE" 268
"LEGEND IN A SMALL TOWN" 269

VICTORIA JENKINS
FROM RELATIVE DISTANCES 271

LESLIE RYAN
"THE OTHER SIDE OF FIRE" 278

MARY GOLDEN
"A COYOTE IS LOPING ACROSS THE WATER" . . 300

PAULINE MORTENSON
"THE HUNSAKER BLOOD" 315

ALISON BAKER
"HOW I CAME WEST, AND WHY I STAYED" . . 326

DEIRDRE McNAMER
FROM RIMA IN THE WEEDS 341

KIM BARNES
"CIRCLE OF WOMEN" 356
"CALLING THE COYOTES IN" 358
"THE SMELL OF RAIN" 359

TERRY TEMPEST WILLIAMS
"THE CLAN OF ONE-BREASTED WOMEN" . . . 362

CLAIRE DAVIS
"BREATHING THE SNAKE" 372

NOTES ON THE CONTRIBUTORS 387

We are two women whose friendship deepened as we came to understand how our childhoods and comings of age in different pockets of the Rocky Mountain West shaped, scarred, and strengthened our lives in similar ways. Mary was raised on a cattle ranch in central Montana in the twilight of the range tradition of cowboy style—silence and toughness. For Kim, growing up in the logging camps of northern Idaho twenty years later, the tradition was eerily the same: isolation, absolute self-reliance, and a fierce devotion to a rugged and precarious way of life that hastened its own end with every tree that was felled.

As children, we heard stories about the hardships of coming to live in the West and the sacrifices of staying here. Devotion to landscape and lifestyle, we understood, counted for more than comfort or security. As a young man traveling from Oklahoma into the great forests of northern Idaho, Kim's father could not have foreseen an end to timbering, any more than

Mary's father, approaching old age, could accept a world where the old customs of ranching and his homestead boyhood had been replaced by the bottom lines of agribusiness.

"Working in the timber gets into your blood," Kim's father told her. But he stopped working as a logger after a spiritual crisis. Mary's father died of exposure after a lone and inexplicable odyssey into the plains of eastern Montana. Separately each of us tried to come to terms with the end of a mythology. Shorn of glamour, of idealized individualism, of the romantic despair of the logger's last stand or the cowboy's last ride into the sunset, what were the implications of the past? What had really happened? What had gone wrong?

The end of the myth of the West is where we began. And we are still drawn to the values of that myth: the courage, the self-reliance, the toughness. But if we no longer believe the old narratives that told us how our perseverance and our endurance of hardships led to the settlement of the West, or even wholeheartedly in the settlement itself, knowing what we do about its cost in bloodshed, bankruptcy, and destruction of the natural environment, then what of our present and future? How are we to understand our lives, and the place where we live, and how are we to bring up our children—for we both have children—without the support and connection and meaning of stories? Where do we turn?

As CHILDREN, we could easily have believed that our mothers had no stories. What we discovered as we grew older was that the women had kept their stories secret. Sometimes they were only whispered between generations, sometimes not even that. And so our task as writers, as daughters, as mothers ourselves, became a search for a more complete tradition than the one that had been handed down to us through family history, popular culture, or even the literature written in our region. Ferreting out the secrets that had been withheld, speculating, listening to the alternative voices that have been growing in strength over the past twenty years in the West, we began to understand that our lives were not anomalies but rather a part of a vast web of common experience.

Stories, poems, and personal essays are being written today in the Rocky Mountain West by women whose voices could not have been heard twenty years ago. For, as the women of our generations have begun to talk to one another, a radically new way of perceiving the western experience has emerged. This vision draws on the self-reliance and courage of the old western mythology but sees greater strength in community, in making connections, in interdependence. Often it is stark, often it reveals unspeakable brutalities within families or between cultures or against the environment. Sometimes it offers healing and love.

We want readers to share our excitement and pleasure at the commonalities of experience and perception that we have found in these selections. Rather than string together these poems, stories, and personal essays chronologically or alphabetically, we have tried to make this anthology function as a whole, to read almost as a novel would; or as pages from a communal diary—a section of the "text" of the lives of women who came to an awareness of themselves as writers while living in the West during the past few decades.

Landscape has had an enormous effect upon the literature being written today by women living in the West. A sense of isolation stemming from gender and physical environment, from being part of the frontier in any number of ways—politically, ethnically, sexually—lends a strong unity to otherwise divergent literary styles. Our common geography is one circle that draws us together, whether, as with us and the many other born westerners in this collection, because it is familiar, or whether, as with Pam Houston, Annick Smith, and others who came from elsewhere to live in the West, because it is—or was—novel. Using the geography of the Rocky Mountain West as a point of departure was a way to draw attention to the centrality of landscape and to create a manageable anthology out of the wealth of available literature.

We believe that this book creates a sense of events, time, and place that is not predominantly linear or narrative, but spatial. Another word that describes the structure of this collection is "quilted." It seems fitting that a book by and about women should have the feel of pieces sewn together to form a whole.

One "patch" in the quilt is Terry Tempest Williams recounting her discovery that her dreams of a stunning light were in fact a reality—the incandescence of nuclear testing witnessed by her and her family. Another is Tess Gallagher, raised in a family of loggers, wondering at the truths she and her brother have learned since their father's death. Judy Blunt steels herself to escape the ranch, her husband, and the only life she knows to enroll at the University of Montana and save herself. Madeline DeFrees must redefine herself after leaving the convent. Anita Endrezze awakens to the poetry of ceremony and the strength of her elders. Annick Smith tells us that life is motion, and that we should choose love.

Kinship is another matter of intensity for these writers. "Once there was a family: one mother, five sons, six daughters, and ten fathers." For Mary Golden, for Leslie Ryan, for Victoria Jenkins, for Patricia Henley, the circle of kinship has been battered by alcoholism, by the insatiable drive for acquisition, by displacement and fragmentation and despair. And yet the circle of life offers hope and spiritual regeneration even against these terrible odds.

Recognizing our mixed heritage, we wonder what to keep in our lives, what to discard. For all of us are concerned with change. Water imagery occurs again and again in these selections, implying change and changelessness, flux and permanence. Ripley Schemm writes,

> *I know what you're seeing, Mary,*
> *I know how it is for me, denying*
> *the present, wanting the past,*
> *longing to retrace each stone, to be*
> *quick, clear, sun reaching my depth.*
> *But too much has happened, hasn't it.*
> . . .
> *Only, Mary, the mean current is there,*
> *down under the surface. Not so far*
> *down. Remember the Judith, clear*
> *and fast where you grew up. For me,*
> *the Teton, racing out of the Rockies.*
> *Neither river hits the swollen Missouri*
> *till it's run a hundred miles. We are*
> *both, Mary. That early mean current*
> *carved out the course, and heads*
> *the placid surface where we're going,*
> *even now.*

There is a way in which the western writers of our time have lived on the cusp of the western experience, have not only suffered and benefited from the myth, but have been a part of the process of demythologizing as well. Some of the circle of women represented in this anthology were both repressed by landscape and instructed by it in the very survival skills they needed to break away from it intellectually and often physically. Others, traveling here from afar, found healing in landscape itself. In background they are urban as well as rural, newcomers and native Americans. Some are well known. Some are previously unpublished. Taken together, they present an intriguing and multidimensional profile of the Rocky Mountain West and the women who live and write there.

MANY WOMEN sent poems, short stories, and essays that we were unable to include in *Circle of Women*. We thank them all; we believe that many of these voices will be heard soon, and we know that already they are part of the circle that enables us all to hear and be heard.

Thanks are due to any number of friends who generously advised and assisted us in the process of creating *Circle of Women*. We particularly want to thank Hugh Nichols and Roger Johnson of Lewis-Clark State College for their assistance and encouragement. That Keith and Shirley Browning are friends unparalleled, we think they know. And we do not know what we would do without the quiet support and wisdom of Robert Wrigley.

Kim Barnes

Mary Clearman Blew

CIRCLE OF

WOMEN

MARY CLEARMAN BLEW

THE SOW IN THE RIVER

≈≈≈≈≈≈≈

In the sagebrush to the north of the mountains in central Montana, where the Judith River deepens its channel and threads a slow, treacherous current between the cutbanks, a cottonwood log house still stands. It is in sight of the highway, about a mile downriver on a gravel road. From where I have turned off and stopped my car on the sunlit shoulder of the highway, I can see the house, a distant and solitary dark interruption of the sagebrush. I can even see the lone box elder tree, a dusty green shade over what used to be the yard.

I know from experience that if I were to keep driving over the cattle guard and follow the gravel road through the sage and alkali to the log house, I would find the windows gone and the door sagging and the floor rotting away. But from here the house looks hardly changed from the summer of my earliest memories, the summer before I was three, when I lived in that log house on the lower Judith with my mother and father and grandmother and my grandmother's boyfriend, Bill.

My memories seem to me as treacherous as the river. Is it possible, sitting here on this dry shoulder of a secondary highway in the middle of Montana where the brittle weeds of August scratch at the sides of the car, watching the narrow blue Judith take its time to thread and wind through the bluffs on its way to a distant northern blur, to believe in anything but today? The past eases away with the current. I cannot watch a single drop of water out of sight. How can I trust memory, which slips and wobbles and grinds its erratic furrows like a bald-tired truck fighting for traction on a wet gumbo road?

≈

Light flickers. A kerosene lamp in the middle of the table has driven the shadows back into the corners of the kitchen. Faces and hands emerge in a circle. Bill has brought apples from the box in the dark closet. The coil of peel follows his pocketknife. I bite into the piece of quartered apple he hands me. I hear its snap, taste the juice. The shadows hold threats: mice and the shape of nameless things. But in the circle around the lamp, in the certainty of apples, I am safe.

The last of the kerosene tilts and glitters around the wick. I cower behind Grammy on the stairs, but she boldly walks into the shadows, which reel and retreat from her and her lamp. In her bedroom the window reflects large pale her and timorous me. She undresses herself, undresses me; she piles my pants and stockings on the chair with her dress and corset. After she uses it, her pot is warm for me. Her bed is cold, then warm. I burrow against her back and smell the smoke from the wick she has pinched out. Bill blows his nose from his bedroom on the other side of the landing. Beyond the eaves the shapeless creatures of sound, owls and coyotes, have taken the night. But I am here, safe in the center.

I am in the center again on the day we look for Bill's pigs. I am sitting between him and Grammy in the cab of the old Ford truck while the rain sheets on the windshield. Bill found the pigpen gate open when he went to feed the pigs this morning, their pen empty, and now they are nowhere to be found. He has driven and driven through the sagebrush and around the gulches, peering out through the endless gray rain as the truck spins and growls on the gumbo in low gear. But no pigs. He and Grammy do not speak. The cab is cold, but I am bundled well between them with my feet on the clammy assortment of tools and nails and chains on the floorboards and my nose just dashboard level, and I am at home with the smell of wet wool and metal and the feel of a broken spring in the seat.

But now Bill tramps on the brakes, and he and Grammy and I gaze through the streaming windshield at the river. The Judith has risen up its cutbanks, and its angry gray current races the rain. I have never seen such a Judith, such a tumult of water. But what transfixes me and Grammy and Bill behind our teeming glass is not the ruthless condition of the river—no, for on a bare ait at midcurrent, completely surrounded and only inches above that muddy roiling water, huddle the pigs.

The flat top of the ait is so small that the old sow takes up most of it by herself. The river divides and rushes around her, rising, practically at her hooves. Surrounding her, trying to crawl under her, snorting in apprehension at the water, are her little pigs. Watching spellbound from the cab of the truck, I can feel their small terrified rumps burrowing against her sides, drawing warmth from her center even as more dirt crumbles under their hooves. My surge of understanding arcs across the current, and my flesh shrivels in the icy sheets of rain. Like the pigs I cringe at the roar of the river, although behind the insulated walls of the cab I can hear and feel nothing. I am in my center and they are in theirs. The current separates us irrevocably, and suddenly I understand that my center is as precarious as theirs, that the chill metal cab of the old truck is almost as fragile as their ring of crumbling sod.

And then the scene darkens and I see no more.

≈

For years I would watch for the ait. When I was five my family moved, but I learned to snatch a glimpse whenever we drove past our old turnoff on the road from Lewistown to Denton. The ait was in plain view, just a hundred yards downriver from the highway, as it is today. *Ait* was a fancy word I learned afterward. It was a fifteen-foot-high steep-sided, flat-topped pinnacle of dirt left standing in the bed of the river after years of wind and water erosion. And I never caught sight of it without the same small thrill of memory: that's where the pigs were.

One day I said it out loud. I was grown by then. "That's where the pigs were."

My father was driving. We would have crossed the Judith River bridge, and I would have turned my head to keep sight of the ait and the lazy blue threads of water around the sandbars.

My father said, "What pigs?"

"The old sow and her pigs," I said, surprised. "The time the river flooded. I remember how the water rose right up to their feet."

My father said, "The Judith never got that high, and there never was any pigs up there."

"Yes there were! I remember!" I could see the little pigs as clearly as I could see my father, and I could remember exactly how my own skin had shriveled as they cringed back from the water and butted the sow for cold comfort.

My father shook his head. "How did you think pigs would get up there?" he asked.

Of course they couldn't.

His logic settled on me like an awakening in ordinary daylight. Of course a sow could not lead nine or ten suckling pigs up those sheer fifteen-foot crumbling dirt sides, even for fear of their lives. And why, after all, would pigs even try to scramble to the top of such a precarious perch when they could escape a cloudburst by following any one of the cattle trails or deer trails that webbed the cutbanks on both sides of the river?

Had there been a cloudburst at all? Had there been pigs?

No, my father repeated. The Judith had never flooded anywhere near that high in our time. Bill Hafer had always raised a few pigs when we lived down there on the river, but he kept them penned up. No.

≈

Today I lean on the open window of my car and yawn and listen to the sounds of late summer. The snapping of grasshoppers. Another car approaching on the highway, roaring past my shoulder of the road, then fading away until I can hear the faint scratches of some small hidden creature in the weeds. I am bone-deep in landscape. In this dome of sky and river and undeflected sunlight, in this illusion of timelessness, I can almost feel my body, blood, and breath in the broken line of the bluffs and the pervasive scent of ripening sweet clover and dust, almost feel the sagging fence line of ancient cedar posts stapled across my vitals.

The only shade in sight is across the river where box elders lean over a low white frame house with a big modern house trailer parked behind it. Downstream, far away, a man works along a ditch. I think he might be the husband of a second cousin of mine who still lives on her old family place. My cousins wouldn't know me if they stopped and asked me what I was doing here.

Across the highway, a trace of a road leads through a barbed-wire gate and sharply up the bluff. It is the old cutoff to Danvers, a town that has dried up and blown away. I have heard that the cutoff has washed out, further up the river, but down here it still holds a little bleached gravel. Almost as though my father might turn off in his battered truck at fifteen miles an hour, careful of his bald wartime tires, while I lie on the seat with my head on his thigh and take my nap. Almost as though at the end of that road will be the two grain elevators pointing sharply out of the hazy olives and ochers of the grass into the rolling cumulus, and two or three graveled streets with traffic moving past the pool hall and post office and dug-out store where, when I wake from my nap and scramble down from the high seat of the truck, Old Man Longin will be waiting behind his single glass display case with my precious wartime candy bar.

Yes, that little girl was me, I guess. A three-year-old standing on the unswept board floor, looking up at rows of canned goods on shelves that were nailed against the logs in the 1880s, when Montana was still a territory. The dust smelled the same to her as it does to me now.

Across the river, that low white frame house where my cousin still lives is the old Sample place. Ninety years ago a man named Sample fell in love with a woman named Carrie. Further up the bottom—you can't see it from here because of the cottonwoods—stands Carrie's deserted house in what used to be a fenced yard. Forty years ago Carrie's house was full of three generations of her family, and the yard was full of cousins at play. Sixty years ago the young man who would be my father rode on horseback down that long hill to Carrie's house, and Sample said to Carrie, *Did your brother Albert ever have a son? From the way the kid sits his horse, he must be your brother's son.*

Or so the story goes. Sample was murdered. Carrie died in her sleep. My father died of exposure.

≈

The Judith winds toward its mouth. Its current seems hardly to move. Seeing it in August, so blue and unhurried, it is difficult to believe how many drownings or near drownings the Judith has counted over the years. To a stranger it surely must look insignificant, hardly worth calling a river.

In 1805 the explorers Lewis and Clark, pausing in their quest for the Pacific, saw the mountains and the prairies of central Montana and the wild game beyond reckoning. They also noted this river, which they named after a girl. Lewis and Clark were the first white recorders of this place. In recording it, they altered it. However indifferent to the historical record, those who see this river and hear its name, *Judith*, see it in a slightly different way because Lewis and Clark saw it and wrote about it.

In naming the river, Lewis and Clark claimed it for a system of governance that required a wrenching of the fundamental connections between landscape and its inhabitants. This particular drab sagebrush pocket of the West was never, perhaps, holy ground. None of the landmarks here is invested with the significance of the sacred buttes to the north. For the Indian tribes that hunted here, central Montana must have been commonplace, a familiar stretch of their lives, a place to ride and breathe and be alive.

But even this drab pocket is now a part of the history of the West, which, through a hundred and fifty years of white settlement and economic development, of rapid depletion of water and coal and timber and topsoil, of dependence upon military escalation and federal subsidies, has been a history of the transformation of landscape from a place to be alive in into a place to own. This is a transformation that breaks connections, that holds little in common. My deepest associations with this sunlit river are private. Without a connection between outer and inner landscape, I cannot tell my father what I saw. "There never was a sow in the river," he said, embarrassed at my notion. And yet I know there was a sow in the river.

≈

All who come and go bring along their own context, leave their mark, however faint. If the driver glanced out the window of that car that just roared past, what did he see? Tidy irrigated alfalfa fields, a small green respite from the dryland miles? That foreshortened man who works along the ditch, does he straighten his back from his labors and see his debts spread out in irrigation pipes and electric pumps?

It occurs to me that I dreamed the sow in the river at a time when I was too young to sort out dreams from daylight reality or to question why they should be sorted out and dismissed. As I think about it, the episode does contain some of the characteristics of a dream. That futile, endless, convoluted search in the rain, for example. The absence of sound in the cab of the truck, and the paralysis of the onlookers on the brink of that churning current. For now that I know she never existed outside my imagination, I think I do recognize that sow on her slippery pinnacle.

Memory lights upon a dream as readily as an external event, upon a set of rusty irrigation pipes and a historian's carefully detailed context through which she recalls the collective memory of the past. As memory saves, discards, retrieves, fails to retrieve, its logic may well be analogous to the river's inexorable search for the lowest ground. The trivial and the profound roll like leaves to the surface. Every ripple is suspect.

Today the Judith River spreads out in the full sunlight of August, oblivious of me and my precious associations, indifferent to the emotional context I have framed it with. My memory seems less a record of landscape and event than a superimposition upon what otherwise would continue to flow, leaf out, or crumble according to its lot. What I remember is far less trustworthy than the story I tell about it. The possibility for connection lies in story.

Whether or not I dreamed her, the sow in the river is my story. She is what I have saved, up there on her pinnacle where the river roils.

TESS GALLAGHER

WOODCUTTING ON LOST MOUNTAIN

for LESLIE *and for* MORRIS

Our father is three months dead
from lung cancer and you light another Camel,
ease the chainsaw into the log. You
don't need habits to tell us
you're the one most like him.
Maybe the least loved
carries injury farther into tenderness
for having first to pass through
forgiveness. You
passed through. "I think he respected me
at the end," as if you'd waited a lifetime
to offer yourself that in my listening.

"Top of the mountain!" your daughter cries.
She's ten, taking swigs with us
from the beer can in the January sun. We see
other mountain tops and trees forever.

A mountain *could* get lost in all this, right
enough, even standing on it, thinking this
is where you are.

"Remember the cabins we built when we were
kids? The folks logging Deer Park and
Black Diamond." My brother, Morris, nods,
pulls the nose of the saw into the air as a chunk
falls. "We built one good one. They
brought their lunches and sat with us
inside—Spam sandwiches on white bread,
bananas for dessert and Mountain Bars, white
on the inside, pure sugar on
the inside—the way they hurt your teeth."

Sawdust sprays across his knee, his face
closes in thought. "Those whippings." He
cuts the motor, wipes his forehead with an arm.
"They'd have him in jail today. I used to beg
and run circles. You got it worse because you
never cried. It's a wonder we didn't
run away." "Away to where?" I say. "There's no
away when you're a kid. Before you can get there
you're home."

"Once he took you fishing and left me
behind," my brother says.
"I drew pictures of you sinking
all over the chicken house. I gave you a head
but no arms. We
could go back today and there
they'd be, boats
sinking all down the walls."

{ *11* }

His daughter is Leslie, named after our father.
Then I think—"She's a logger's daughter,
just like me"—and the thought pleases as if
the past had intended this present. "You
didn't know you were doing it," I tell him,
"but you figured how to stay
in our childhood." "I guess I did. There's
nothing I'd rather do," he says, "than cut wood.
Look at that—" he points to stacks of logs
high as a house he's thinned from timber—
"they're going to burn them. Afraid
somebody might take a good tree
for firewood, so they'll burn half a forest.
Damn, that's the Forest Service for you. Me—
I work here, they'll have to stop me."

Leslie carries split wood to the tailgate
and I toss it into the truck. We make
a game of it, trying to stack as fast
as her father cuts. "She's a worker,"
Morris says. "Look at that girl go.
Sonofagun, I wouldn't trade four boys for her.
No sir." He picks up the maul, gives a yell
and whacks down through the center of a block
thick as a man. It falls neatly into
halves. "Look at that! Now *that's* good wood.
That's beautiful wood," he says, like he
made it himself.

I tell him how the cells of trees
are like the blood cells of people, how trees
are the oldest organisms on the earth. Before
the English cut the trees off Ireland, the Irish

had three dozen words for green. He's impressed,
mildly, has his own way of thinking about trees.

Tomorrow a log pile will collapse
on him and he will just get out alive.

"Remember the time Dad felled the tree on us
and Momma saved us, pushed us into a ditch? It's
a wonder we ever grew up."

"One of the horses they logged with, Dick
was his name, Old Dick. They gave him
to Oney Brown and Dick got into the house
while everyone was gone and broke
all the dishes. Dishes—what could they mean
to a horse? Still, I think he knew
what he was doing."

Oney's wife, Sarah, had fifteen kids. She's
the prettiest woman I'll ever see. Her son,
Lloyd, took me down to the railroad tracks
to show me the dead hounds. "We had too many
so they had to shoot some." The hounds were
skeletons by then, but they haven't moved
all these years from the memory
of that dark underneath of boughs.
I look at them, stretched on their sides, twin
arches of bones leaping with beetles and
crawlers into the bark-rich earth. Skipper
and Captain—Cappy for short. Their names
and what seemed incomprehensible—a betrayal
which meant those who had care of you
might, without warning, make an end of you

in some godforsaken, heartless place. Lloyd spat
like a father between the tracks, took
my hand and led me back to the others.

Twenty years settles on the boys
of my childhood. Some of them loggers.
"It's gone," they tell me. "The Boom Days
are gone. We thought
they'd never end, there were
that many trees. But it's finished,
or nearly. Nothing but stumps
and fireweed now."

"Alaska," Morris says, "that's where the trees
are," and I think of them, like some lost tribe
of wanderers, their spires and bloodless blood
climbing cathedral-high into the moss-light
of days on all the lost mountains of
our childhoods.

Coming into the town we see the blue smoke
of the trees streaming like a mystery
the houses hold in common.
"Doesn't seem possible—," he says, "a tree
nothing but a haze you could
put your hand through."

"What'll you do next, after the trees are gone?"

"Pack dudes in for elk."

"Then what?"

"Die, I guess. Hell, I don't know, ask
a shoemaker, ask a salmon. . . .
Remember that time I was hunting and got lost,
forgot about the dark and me with no coat, no
compass? You and Dad fired rifles from the road
until I stumbled out. It
was midnight. But I got out. It's a wonder
I could tell an echo from a shot, I was so cold,
so lost. Stop cussing, I told the old man, I'm
home, ain't I? 'You're grown,' he kept saying,
'you're a grown man.'
I must be part wild. I must be part tree or part
deer. I got on the track and I was lost
but it didn't matter. I had to go where it led.
I must be part bobcat."

Leslie is curled under my arm, asleep.

"Truck rocks them to sleep," Morris says.
"Reminds me, I don't have a license for this
piece of junk. I hope I don't get stopped. Look
at her sleep! right in the middle of the day.
Watch this: 'Wake up honey, we're lost. Help me
get home. You went to sleep and got us lost.'
She must be part butterfly, just look at those eyes.
There—she's gone again. I'll have to carry
her into the house. Happens every time.
Watch her, we'll go up the steps and she'll be
wide awake the minute I open the door.
Hard to believe, we had to be carried into houses
once, you and me. It's a wonder we ever
grew up."

Tomorrow a log pile will collapse
and he'll just get out alive.

He opens the door. Her eyes start,
suddenly awake.

"See, what'd I tell you. Wide awake. Butterfly,
you nearly got us lost, sleeping so long.
Here, walk for yourself. We're home."

PATRICIA HENLEY

THE SECRET OF CARTWHEELS

≈≈≈≈≈≈≈

The winesap trees along the road were skeletal in the early-evening light. I stared out the school-bus window and cupped like a baby chick the news I looked forward to telling Mother: I'd decided on my confirmation name.

"What's nine times seven?" Jan Mary said.

"Sixty-three," I said. *Joan*. That was Mother's confirmation name, and I wanted it to be mine as well. She'd told me it was a name of strength, a name to carry you into battle.

"I tore my cords," Christopher said. He stood in the aisle, bracing himself with one hand on the chrome pole beside the driver, who wore a baseball cap and a big plaid mackinaw.

The bus driver sang, "Don't sit under the apple tree with anyone else but me." I knew we were nearing our stop, the end of the route, whenever the driver sang this song. We were the last ones on the bus. Although the heater was chuffing hard, frost in the shape of flames curled along the edges of the windows.

"Sweet dreams," the driver said, as we plodded down the slippery steps of the school bus.

Aunt Opal's pale green Cadillac was parked at an odd angle near the woodshed. I knew something was wrong—she never drove out from Wenatchee to visit in the winter. I remembered what our mother had told me the night before. Before bedtime we all lined up to kiss her good night, and when my turn came, she'd said, "There are signs in life. Signs that tell you what you have to do." Her voice had frightened me. I didn't want to hear what she had to say.

Jan Mary said, "Who's that?" Her knit gloves were soggy, her knees chapped above slipping-down socks.

"Aunt Opal," Christopher said. His voice was dead and I knew he knew and understood.

Our breath came in blue blossoms in the cold, cutting air, and a light went on in the living room. I didn't want to go in, but I kept trudging through the snow.

Inside, everything was in its place, but our mother was gone, which made the house seem cold and empty. Four-year-old Suzanne stood on the heat register, her grubby chenille blanket a cape around her shoulders. Her hair had been recently brushed, and she wore plastic barrettes, a duck on one side, a bow on the other. When I remember those years at home, this is one of the things I focus on, how nothing ever matched, not sheets, not barrettes, not cups and saucers, not socks. And sometimes I think the sad and petty effort to have matching things has been one of the chief concerns of my adult life. Aunt Opal perched uneasily on a ladder-back chair with the baby, Laura Jean, on her lap. Laura Jean, eyes roving, held her own bottle of milk, and when she saw me, her look latched on to me and she stopped sucking and squirmed and kicked. Her plastic bottle clunked onto the floor. Aunt Opal's white wool pantsuit stretched tightly across her fat thighs. Her teased hair stood hard and swirled. Ill at ease, she shifted her weight gingerly as though she might get dirty. I thought I saw pity in her eyes, and I looked away. Christopher and Jan Mary hung back by the kitchen door, Christopher banging his metal lunch box softly against his leg.

"Where's our mother?" I said, scooping Laura Jean away from Aunt Opal.

"Now I hate to have to be the bearer of bad tidings," she began. "I know this will be hard on you children. I don't know what your mother was thinking of." She got up and stalked over to Suzanne, her spike heels dragging on the linoleum.

"Just tell me where she is." The baby stiffened in my arms. This was the first time I'd ever issued a command to a grownup, and I felt both powerful and worried. Without our mother there, I was suddenly older.

Aunt Opal took a few seconds to adjust one of Suzanne's barrettes. "At the VA hospital," she said. "She's sick. Surely you must have known? She needs a rest. She's gone away and left you."

Christopher and Jan Mary went meek as old dogs into the living room and turned on the television. I snugged the baby into her high chair, wrapped a receiving blanket around her bare legs, and began peeling potatoes for supper. Suzanne sat in her miniature rocker, holding a Dr. Seuss book upside down and mouthing the words she knew by heart. I remember thinking if we could just have an ordinary supper, do our homework, fold the laundry, say our prayers, then it would be all right with mother away. We might feel as though she'd just gone through the orchard to visit a neighbor, and that she might return at any moment.

"You'll have places to go, of course," Aunt Opal said, lighting the gas under the stale morning coffee. The sulfurous smell of the match lingered.

"Places?"

"Christopher can stay with Grandma and Grandpa. Janice will take the baby."

"We'll stay here together," I said.

"Roxanne," she said, pouring coffee into a flowered teacup. "You can't stay here alone with all these children."

I remember feeling small and powerless then, and I saw that I still needed to be taken care of—in fact, wanted to be taken care of—but I did not think I would be. I had no trust in anyone, and when you are a child feeling this way, every day becomes a swim through white water with no life jacket. Many years went by before I allowed myself to wonder where my father was during this time.

"How long will we be gone?" I said.

"It's hard to say," Aunt Opal said, sighing. "It's really hard to say."

I was thirteen, Christopher twelve, and Jan Mary eight. We went to St. Martin's and rode the public school bus home, aware of our oddity—Christopher's salt-and-pepper cords instead of jeans, the scratchy scapulars against our chests, the memorization of saints' names and days and deeds. The week before our mother went away, I had stayed home from school twice, missing play auditions and report-card day. She had written excuses on foolscap: *Please excuse Roxanne from school yesterday. I needed her at home.*

Our father worked in another state. The house was isolated, out in the country; our nearest neighbor lived a mile away. During the summer I loved where we lived—the ocean of apple blooms, the muted voices of the Spanish-speaking orchard workers, the wild berries, like deep black fleece along the railroad tracks. Winters were another story. We heated with wood, and the fine wood ash smudged our schoolbooks, our clothes and linens, our wrists and necks. The well was running dry, and we children shared our bathwater. By my turn the water was tepid and gray. Our mother fed the fire, waking sometimes twice in the night to keep it going, and her hands and fingers were cracked, swollen. I wanted to cry whenever I looked at them. The loneliness was like a bad smell in the house.

In the evening while the others, the younger ones, watched "I Love Lucy," she sipped Jack Daniel's from a jelly glass and told me her secrets, plucking me from childhood's shore. Very late, when the others had gone to bed, she'd curse our father in a whisper. One night, when she had filled that jelly glass for the third time, and wanted company, she told me about her true love, a woman she'd known in the WACS during the war when they worked together in the motor pool in Dayton, Ohio. You can learn too much too soon about your mother's past. The weight of her concerns made me turn from her and wish that something would save us from the life we shared with her. I couldn't make the wish while watching her split and bleeding hands light a cigarette. But later, lying confused and rigid in the double bed I shared with cuddling Jan Mary and Suzanne, I wished that our mother would go away.

ALL OF THE MOVING took place at night. Aunt Opal drove Suzanne, Jan Mary, and me up the Entiat River to Entiat Home, a place local people called the orphans' home, but in truth the children there were not orphans but children whose parents could not care for them. The frozen river glittered in the moonlight. The fir trees rode in dark procession along the far bank. I sat in the front seat, a privilege of the oldest. The car was vast and luxurious and foreign. Most of the way, no one spoke.

Finally, from the cavernous backseat, Suzanne said, "Where's the baby?"

Don't ask, I thought, don't ask. I tried to send this silent message to Suzanne, but she didn't get it. Blood beat in my head.

"Laura Jean might need us," she said.

"Laura will be fine. Fine, fine," Aunt Opal said. "She's with your cousin Janice, who has another baby for her to play with."

Her jolly voice made me feel as though someone was hugging me too hard, painfully. When we'd left Christopher at Grandma and Grandpa Swanson's I'd felt sick to my stomach, not because I would be separated from him—no—but because I wanted to stay there too. I wanted to cling to Grandma Swanson and say, Take me, keep me. But I was the oldest. I didn't cling and cry.

I would miss Christopher. We had fallen into the habit of sitting in the unfinished knotty-pine pantry, after our baths and the dishes were done, listening to the high school basketball games on the staticky radio. We knew the players' names and numbers. Together we had anticipated the mystery of going to high school.

Aunt Opal turned slowly into the uphill drive, which was lined with billows of snow. The dark was my comfort—I didn't want to see everything at once. We parked in front of a red brick house with two wrought-iron lamps beside the neatly shoveled steps. Silence leaped at us when Aunt Opal shut off the engine. The place seemed a last outpost before the black and convoluted mountains, the Cascades, which, I imagined, went slanted and ragged to the sea. Then quickly, nimbly, a man and woman came coatless down the steps and opened the car doors, greeting us as though we were their own children returning home. The woman was thin and wore pearls and a skirt and sweater. The man had hair as black as an eggplant. Their voices were cheerful, but they kept their hands to themselves, as though they knew we would not want to be touched by strangers.

One moment we were in the dark, the car, the winter mountain air; the next, all three of us were ushered into the blinding white room, which was like a hospital room, with white metal cupboards, white metal cots, and everything amazingly clean and shiny under the fluorescent lights, cleaner even than Grandma Swanson's house.

We sat on the edge of one cot without speaking to one another. Snow dripped in dirty puddles from our saddle oxfords. The floor was black and white like a checkerboard. In the hallway, out of sight, Aunt Opal spoke with the man and woman—"Well behaved," I heard her say—and then she departed with all the speed and indifference of a UPS driver. Through a tall window in the room I watched her headlights sweep across the cinnamon bark of a ponderosa pine. From someplace far away in the house came Christmas carols, wreathed in pure recorded voices. My body played tricks on me; my head hurt; my stomach knotted in an acid snarl.

Suzanne growled in a baby way she had when she was tired or angry. I pulled her onto my lap and she sucked her thumb. Consoling her was my only source of reassurance.

Jan Mary stamped the dirty puddles with the toe of her shoe. "How will we get to school?" she said.

"We'll go to a different school."

"I don't want to."

"We don't always get to do what we want," I said, shocked at the way I parroted our mother.

The woman in the pearls came into the bright room and leaned over us, one arm around Jan Mary's back.

"I'm Mrs. Thompson," she said. Her words were stout with kindness, which seemed a warning to me, as though she could hurt me, and she smelled good, like flowery cologne. She's someone's perfect mother, I thought.

"You'll need baths before bedtime, girls," she said. She strode to the oak door across the room and opened it, then switched on the bathroom light. "You have your own pajamas?"

"Yes," I said, nodding in the direction of the cardboard Cream of Wheat carton, which held my clothes. Each of us had packed a carton with our best things.

"You can help your sisters bathe, Roxanne," she said. "Then I'll check your heads for lice."

"Our mother wouldn't allow that," I said.

"What did you say?"

"Our mother wouldn't allow us to have lice," I said. My voice seemed inordinately loud.

"It's just our policy," she said. "Now get moving. It's late."

We bedded down the first night in that same room, on the single cots made up with coarse cotton sheets and cream-colored wool blankets with a navy stripe around the edge. The light from the hallway bridged the high transom of the closed door, and I didn't sleep for a long time. Our presence there rebuked our mother, and I felt that humiliation as keenly as though I were she. I kept thinking, We'll be better when we go home —we'll work harder, knock down the cobwebs more often, check Jan Mary's homework, throw out the mismatched socks. Keeping domestic order was, inexplicably, bound up with being good, blessed. The fantasies that lulled me to sleep were of cupboards packed with thick folded towels, full cookie jars, an orderly abundance like perpetual fire against the night.

The next morning I lay there, warm but wet, with the covers up to my neck. Suzanne and Jan Mary were still asleep. A cat meowed urgently in the hallway. The windows were long and divided into panes of wavery old glass. Outside it was snow-

in her fifties and smelled of gardenias and cigarette smoke. Her lipstick was thick and cakey, the color of clay flower pots. She prided herself on her hair—it was coppery and resembled scrubbing pads we used in the kitchen. If someone broke the rules, she would announce to the group at large, "That's not allowed here." The chill in her voice always arrested the deviant.

Life in the Little Girls' House was orderly, neat, regulated. Before school in the morning we did our chores, young ones polishing the wooden stairs, older ones carting the laundry in duffle bags to the laundry building. Some were assigned kitchen duty, others bathrooms. Everyone, down to the four-year-olds, had work to do. I was impressed with the efficiency and equanimity with which work was accomplished. I wrote letters to our mother, in my experimental loopy left-hand slant, suggesting job charts on the refrigerator, new systems we could invent to relieve her of her crushing burden.

There were twenty-three of us. Jan Mary and Suzanne naturally gravitated toward others their age. They slept away from the oldest girls, in a drafty long hall near Mrs. Hayes's apartment. Our family ties were frayed, and I was genuinely surprised when I met Jan Mary's musing blue eyes in recognition across the dinner table. She seemed to be saying, How in the world did we arrive here?

The first day at the new school I was issued a faded blue cotton bloomer for PE. At St. Martin's, PE had meant softball on the playground. At the new school the locker room was my personal hell: the body smells, the safety-pinned bras, the stained slips, the hickeys, the pubic hair growing wild down our thighs. Sister Michael had always told us not to look at ourselves when we bathed, to be ashamed and vigilant. In the locker room we girls were elbow to elbow in the narrow aisle beside the dented pink lockers.

"What is your *prob*lem?"

"The F word. That's all he knows these days."

"My mother won't let me."

"Bud's getting a car for his birthday."

Their conversations shimmered around me like a beaded curtain. We couldn't help but see one another—our new breasts, our worn underwear—but the talk kept us on another plane, a place above the locker room, where we could pretend we weren't totally vulnerable, absolutely displayed.

Georgia Cowley, a squat freckled woman, ruled that class with a cruel hand. When I entered the gym for the first time, she waved sharply in my direction and I went over to her.

"Name?"

"Roxanne Miller."

"We're tumbling, Roxanne Miller," she said, writing something on her clipboard. "You ever tumbled?"

"No, ma'am." I looked at the girls casually turning cartwheels, blue blurs, on the hardwood floor. My hope of fading into the wrestling mats for the hour fluttered like a candle in a storm.

"Come out here with me," she said.

I followed her to the sweaty red mat in front of the stage.

"We start with forward rolls. Squat down."

I squatted, glancing desperately around to see if there was someone I could imitate. All motion had wound down, and the girls were gathered in gossip knots, chattering and watching me with slitted eyes. I remember staring at Miss Cowley's gym shoes; there were dried tomato seeds on the toes.

"Tuck your head. Now one foot forward, hands on the mat."

She gave me a little shove to propel me forward. I fell sideways, my pale thigh plopping fishlike on the floor. The girls giggled and hot tears swelled in my head. The seconds on the floor expanded, seemed to go on forever.

"Get up," she said. "Sit over there on the bleachers for a while and watch. You'll get the hang of it." Then she blew her chrome whistle, and the girls lined up to do their forward rolls.

On the bleachers, a Negro girl from Entiat, Nadine, slid next to me, sighing hard. "Got the curse," she said. "I'm sitting out."

"You can sit out?"

"Sure 'nough." She scratched her skinny calf. "You know the secret of cartwheels, Roxanne?"

"No," I said, interested, thinking there might be some secret I could learn from her, some intellectual knowledge that I could translate into body knowledge.

"Catch yourself before you kill yourself," she whispered, as she retied her sneaker. "Catch yo-*self*." And then she leaped up and turned a few, flinging herself into them with her own peculiar flick of her pink palms above her nappy head.

"Jefferson," Cowley barked. "Sit down and keep quiet."

For the rest of gym period, Nadine and I wrote messages on each other's backs, using our index fingers like pencils through the scratchy blue bloomer blouses.

AT CHRISTMAS we were farmed out. I do not know how these decisions were made. Certainly I don't remember being asked where I would like to go for Christmas. Suzanne went with Mr. and Mrs. Thompson. Jan Mary was taken by Aunt Opal. I went to stay with the family of Darla Reamer, who had been our neighbor for five years. Darla was two years older than I was. When I'd been in fifth grade and Darla in seventh, we rode the school bus together and wrote love notes to one another using a special language we'd developed, a lispish baby talk in writing. Later that year she chose another girl as her best friend and left me miserable. Going to spend Christmas with her and her family, enduring their charity, was like an arduous school assignment I had to survive to attain the next grade. Her mother gave me a Shetland sweater and a jar of Pacquin's hand cream. Her father took me out in the wind-crusted snowy field to see his apiary. We went to church, and those brief moments kneeling in the oak pew and at the altar, with its starlike poinsettias, were the only familiarity and peace I experienced. Darla spent many hours on the telephone with Julia, the one who'd taken my place. I was relieved when Mr. Reamer drove me back to Entiat on Christmas night. Many girls were still away and Mrs. Hayes let me stay up late. I drank hot chocolate alone in the dining room and wrote our mother a letter of false cheer and fantasy about the future.

In the older girls' sleeping quarters, after lights out, under cover of dark, some girls took turns revealing fears, shames, wishes expressed as truth. When this talk began, their voices shifted from the usual shrill razzmatazz repartee about hairstyles, boys at school, and who'd been caught smoking. They spoke in church whispers.

"My mother tore my lip once. I have five stitches."

"My father's coming to get me on my birthday."

I didn't participate in this round robin, but instead lay on my stomach, my pillow buckled under my chest, and watched the occasional gossamer thread of headlights on the river road. It seemed there was so much freedom and purpose—a will at work—in night travel. Their talk was sad and low, and I, in my isolation, dreamed of going away, of having the power, the inestimable power, to say *I'm leaving*. Boys could somehow run away and make it, survive. But everyone knew that a girl's life was over if she ran away from home, or whatever had become home, whatever sheltered her from ruin.

Some nights, if we heard the rush of Mrs. Hayes's shower, we would sing in our thin voices a maudlin song that was popular at the time—"Teen Angel." One night the community of singing gave me courage, and after the song faded, I said, "I saw my mother hit my father with a belt."

As one they sucked in their breath. Then Nadine said, "No *wonder* your mama in the hospital, girl."

And the others laughed, a false, tentative snicker. I hated Nadine at that moment and felt heartbroken in my hate. I'd always tried to be nice to her, because our mother had said they were just like everyone else inside.

On Valentine's Day, we received a crumpled package wrapped in a brown grocery sack and tied with butcher twine. Inside was a cellophane bag of hard candy hearts stamped BE MINE and I LOVE YOU. Our mother had enclosed three penny valentines and on mine she wrote, "I'm home now with Laura Jean and Christopher. See you soon." She was home! I'd given up on mail from her, but I'd kept writing. I tried to imagine her there with Christopher and the baby, without me to help her, and the thought made me feel invisible, unnecessary in the world. Don't think about it, I said to myself, and I began then the habit of blocking my thoughts with that simple chant. *Don't think about it.*

IN APRIL we were allowed to go home for a weekend.

"Your neighbor's here," Mrs. Hayes whispered in my ear, early that Saturday morning. "Help your sisters dress. I'll give him a tour while he's waiting."

I had a great deal to be excited about: seeing Christopher, going to our old church, being with our mother. Our mother.

Her life without me was a puzzle, with crucial pieces missing. I had high hopes about going home. Our mother was well; everyone—Mrs. Hayes, Mr. Reamer—said so.

We met him by his pickup truck. His khakis were spattered with pastel paint; he said he'd been painting his bee boxes. We fell into silence on the drive home. The thought surfaced, like the devil's tempting forefinger, that though we were only an hour's drive from our mother, we hadn't seen her since that morning in December when we went to school not knowing life would be irrevocably changed by the time we returned home. Did she know that morning that she wouldn't see us for four months?

Spring was alive down in the valley. The daffodil leaves were up along the driveway, though the flowers were still just pale shadows of memory, curled tightly and green. Mr. Reamer parked his pickup truck and sat hunched, arms folded across the steering wheel, waiting for us to get out.

We were all shy, bashful, and I hung back, urging Jan Mary and Suzanne forward with little pushes on their shoulder blades.

Jan Mary flinched and said meanly, "Don't push."

"Don't spoil it now," I said.

And we three walked forward in a solemn row down the gravel drive toward the house. We wore our next-best dresses. Mine was a taffeta plaid with a smocked bodice and a sash, and I'd worn my cream-colored knee highs, saving my one pair of nylons for Sunday morning. I hadn't wanted to go home in nylons—they were a new addition to my sock drawer and I was afraid our mother would say I was growing up too fast. The house looked the same, sagging at the roof corners, the gray paint blistering along the bottom of the door. It was a sunny day. Darla Reamer's cocker spaniel came yapping out the drive, flipping and bouncing the way cockers do. As we drew near the house, I saw that Darla was sitting with our mother in that small patch of grass in front of the house. Someone had put a wooden cable spool there for a table, and Darla and Mother sat near each other in lawn chairs. Darla was painting Mother's fingernails.

"Here come my girls," Mother said, waving her free hand.

Music was on inside the house and we could hear it through the open window: *you made me love you.* I didn't know what to do with Darla there. I'd imagined our mother embracing us, welcoming us, with significance. My heart shrank in disappointment, a rancid feeling, everything going sour at once. Suzanne, being only four, went right up to our mother and slipped her little arms around her neck and kissed her cheek. Jan Mary said, "Will you do mine, too, Darla?"

Laura Jean started crying from somewhere in the house. Mother, startled, rose partway from her chair and then sank back, waving her wet fingernails and looking helplessly at Darla. There was a raw, clean smell about the yard, like cornsilk when you go outside to shuck corn in the summer dusk. Darla looked older, in a straight linen skirt with a kick pleat in the back. She had on slim flats and tan-tinted nylons. Her hair was in a French roll.

"I'll get her," Darla said, and she went in the house, letting the screen door slam. Suzanne was close on her heels.

Mother pulled me near, her arm around my waist. "How's my big girl?" she asked. She'd had her black hair frizzed in a permanent wave and her nails were painted fire-engine red. With one hand she shook a Lucky from the pack on the table. A glass of whiskey and melting ice was on the ground beside her chair. Her knuckles looked pink, but the cuts and splits were healed.

"Fine," I said.

"Darla's been helping me," she said.

I held my breath to keep from crying.

I felt exhausted, not the clean exhaustion of after-dark soft-ball but a kind of weariness; I was worn out with the knowledge that life would be different, but not in the way I had imagined or hoped. I didn't want to forgive her for being the way she was, but you have to forgive your mother. She searched my eyes and tried to make some long-ago connection, sweet scrutiny, perhaps the way she'd looked at me when I was a new baby, her first baby. I looked away. Jan Mary gnawed delicately at her cuticles. Christopher came around the corner of the house swinging his Mickey Mantle bat, his leather mitt looped on his belt. The new spring leaves were so bright they hurt my eyes.

MELANIE RAE THON

IONA MOON

≈≈≈≈≈≈≈≈

W illy Hamilton never did like Iona Moon. He said country girls always had shit on their shoes and he could smell her after she'd been in his car. Jay Tyler said his choice of women was nobody's business, and if Willy didn't like it, he should keep his backdoors locked.

Choice of women, Jay said that so nice. He thought Iona was a woman because the first night they were together he put his hand under her shirt and she didn't stop kissing him. He inched his fingers under her brassiere, like some five-legged animal, until his wrist was caught by the elastic and his hand was squished against her breast. She said, "Here, baby, let me help you," and she reached around behind her back and released the hooks. One hand on each breast, Jay Tyler whistled through his teeth. "Sweet Jesus," he said, and unbuttoned her blouse, his fingers clumsy and stiff with the fear that she might change her mind. Jay Tyler had known plenty of girls, girls who let him do whatever he wanted as long as he could take what he was after without any assistance on their part, without ever saying, "Yes, Jay," the way Iona did, just a murmur, "Yes," soft as snow on water.

In the moonlight, her skin was pale, her breasts small but warm, something a boy couldn't resist. Jay cupped them in his palms, touching the nipples with the very tips of his fingers, as if they were precious and alive, something separate from the girl, something that could still be frightened and disappear. He pressed his lips to the hard bones of Iona Moon's chest, rested his head in the hollow between her breasts and whispered words no boy had ever spoken to her.

He said, "Thank you, oh God, thank you." His voice was hushed and amazed, the voice of a drowning man just pulled from the river. As his mouth found her nipple, Jay Tyler closed his eyes tight, as if he wanted to be blind, and Iona Moon almost laughed to see his sweet face wrinkle that way; she couldn't help thinking of the newborn pigs, their little eyes glued shut, scrambling for a place at their mother's teats.

IONA SUPPOSED Willy Hamilton was right about her shoes, but she was past noticing it herself. Every morning, she got up early to milk the four cows. Mama had always done it before Iona and her brothers were awake. Even in the winter, Hannah Moon had trudged to the barn while it was still dark, slogged through the mud and slush, wearing her rubber boots and Daddy's fur-lined coat that she could have wrapped around herself twice. The waves of blue snow across the fields fluttered, each drift a breast heaving, giving up its last breath.

Mama said she liked starting the day that way, in the lightless peace God made before he made the day, sitting with your cheek pressed against the cow's warm flank, your hands on her udder, understanding your pull has to be strong and steady but not too hard, knowing she likes you there and she feels grateful in the way cows do, so she makes a sleepy sound like a moan or a hum, the same sound Iona heard herself make at the edge of a dream.

WILLY HAD A GIRL, Belinda Beller. She wore braces, and after gym class, Iona saw her stuff her bra with toilet paper. Willy and Belinda, Iona and Jay, parked down by the river in Willy's Chevy. Belinda kept saying, "No, honey, please, I don't want to." Jay panted over Iona, licking her neck, slipping his tongue as far in her ear as it would go; her bare back stuck to the vinyl seat, and Willy said, "I'm sorry." His voice was serious and small. "I'm sorry." He said it again, like a six-year-old who had killed his own gerbil by mistake.

Willy thought of his father handcuffing that boy who stole the floodlights from the funeral home. Willy was twelve and liked cruising with his dad, pretending they might get lucky and find some trouble. They caught up with the boy down by the old Miller Creek bridge. His white face rose like a moon above his dark clothes, his eyes enchanted to stone by the twin beams of the headlights.

Horton Hamilton climbed out of the patrol car, one hand on his hip. The thick fingers unsnapped the leather band that held the pistol safe in the holster. Willy's father said, "Don't you be gettin' any ideas of makin' like a jackrabbit, boy; I got a gun." He padded toward the skittery, long-legged kid, talking all the time, using the low rumble of his voice to hold the boy in one place, like a farmer trying to mesmerize a dog that's gone mad, so he can put a bullet through its head.

Willy recognized the kid. His name was Matt Fry and he lived out west of town on the Kila Flats, a country boy. Horton Hamilton believed you could scare the mischief out of a child. He cuffed Matt Fry as if he were a grown man who'd done a lot worse. He said stealing those lights was no petty crime: they were worth a lot of money, enough to make the theft a felony even though Matt Fry was only fifteen years old.

A policeman didn't get much action in White Falls, Idaho, so Horton Hamilton took what business he had seriously. He'd drawn his gun any number of times, or put his hand on it at least, but he'd had cause to shoot only once in nineteen years, and that was to kill a badger that had taken up residence on poor Mrs. Griswold's porch and refused to be driven away by more peaceable means.

Fear of God, fear of the devil, that was good for a boy, but Willy heard later that Matt Fry's parents had had enough of his shenanigans and that a felony was the limit, the very limit. They told the county judge they'd lost control of their boy and it would be best for everyone to lock him up and set him straight. Until then, Willy didn't know that if you did a bad enough thing, your parents could decide they didn't want you anymore.

When Matt Fry came back from the boys' home, he smelled like he forgot sometimes and pissed his own pants; he didn't look at you if you saw him on the street and said, "Hey." His parents still wouldn't let him come home and he slept in a burned-out barn down in the gully. People said Matt Fry got caught fighting his first day at the state home. They threw him in the hole for eighteen days, all by himself, without any light, and when they dragged him out he was like this: lame in one foot, mumbling syllables that didn't add up to words, skinny as a coyote at the end of winter.

WILLY STOPPED pawing at Belinda and sat with his hands in his lap until she leaned over to peck his cheek and say, "It's all right now, honey." Iona Moon had no sympathy for Belinda Beller's point of view. What sense was there in saving everything up for some special occasion that might not ever come?

How do you hold a boy back if it feels good when he slides his knee between your legs? How do you say *no* when his tongue in your ear makes you arch your back and grab his hair?

Willy liked nice girls, girls who accidentally brushed their hands against a guy's crotch, girls who wiggled their butts when they walked past you in the hall, threw their shoulders back and almost closed their eyes when they said hello. Girls who could pull you right up to the edge and still always, always say no.

Iona thought, you hang on to something too long, you start to think it's worth more than it is. She was never that way on account of having three brothers and being the youngest. When she was nine, her oldest brother gave her a penny to dance for him. Before long, they made it regular. Night after night Iona twirled around the barn for Leon, spun in the circle of light from the lantern hanging off the rafter. Dale and Rafe started coming too; she earned three cents a night from her brothers and saved every penny till she had more than four dollars. Later they gave her nickels for lifting her shirt and letting them touch the buds that weren't breasts yet. And one time, when Leon and Iona were alone in the loft, he paid her a dime for lying down and letting him rub against her. She was scared, all that grunting and groaning, and when she looked down she saw that his little prick wasn't little anymore: it was swollen and dark and she yelled, "You're hurting yourself." He clamped his dirty hand over her mouth and hissed. Finally he made a terrible sound, like the wail a cow makes when her calf is halfway out of her; his mouth twisted and his face turned red, as if Iona had choked him. But she hadn't; her arms were flung straight out from her sides; her hands clutched fistfuls of straw. Leon collapsed on his sister like a dead man, and she lay there wondering how she was going to explain to Mama and Daddy that she'd killed him. He crushed the breath out of her; sweat from his face trickled onto hers, and she felt something damp and sticky soaking through her jeans. When she tried to wriggle out from under him, he sprang back to life. He pinched her face with one hand. Squeezing her cheeks with his big fingers, he said, "Don't you ever tell, Iona. Mama will hate you if you ever tell."

After that her brothers stopped paying her to dance for them, and Leon made Rafe and Dale cut their thumbs with his hunting knife and swear by their own blood that they'd never tell anyone what they did in the barn that year.

YOU CAN'T MAKE my brothers do much of anything unless you force them to swear in blood, Iona thought.

One morning after a storm, she tramped out to the barn to do her milking. The wind howled, cutting through her jeans. Snow had drifted against the door; she bent over and dug like a dog. The first stall was empty. She ran to the next, shining her flashlight in every corner, trying to believe a cow could hide in a shadow like a cat, but she knew, even as she ran in circles, she knew that all four cows were out in the fields, that her brothers had just assumed an animal will head for shelter on its own. They didn't know cows the way Iona and her mama did. A cow's hardly any smarter than a chicken; a cow has half the brains of a pig; a cow's like an overgrown child, like the Wilkerson boy who grew tall and fat but never got smart.

She heard them. As she ran across the fields, stumbling in the snow, falling on her face more than once and snorting ice through her nose, she heard them crying like old women. The four of them huddled together, standing up past their knees in the drifts. Snow had piled in ridges down their backs; they hadn't moved all night. They let out that sound, that awful wail, like their souls were being torn out of them. Iona had to whip them with her belt to get them going; that's how cows are: they'll drop to their knees and freeze to death with their eyes wide open and the barn door barely a hundred feet in front of them.

Later, Iona took Mama her aspirin and hot milk, sat on the edge of her bed and moaned like the cows, closing her eyes and stretching her mouth wide as it would go. Mama breathed deep with laughter, holding her stomach; the milk sloshed in the cup and Iona had to hold it. Mama had a bad time holding on to things. Her fingers were stiff and twisted, and that winter, her knees swelled up so big she couldn't walk.

IONA MOON told Jay Tyler how it was in the winter on the Kila Flats, how the wind had nothing to stand in its way, how the water froze in the pipes and you had to use the outhouse, how you held it just as long as you could because the snow didn't fall, it blew straight in your face; splinters of ice pierced your skin and you could go blind or lose your way just walking to that little hut twenty-five yards behind the house. She told him she kept a thundermug under her bed in case she had to pee in the night. But she didn't tell him her mama had to use a bedpan all the time, and Iona was the one who slid it under her bony butt because Mama said it wasn't right for the man you love to see you that way.

MAMA knew Iona had a guy. She made Iona tell her that Jay Tyler was on the diving team in the summer. He could fly off the high board backwards, do two somersaults and half a twist; he seemed to open the water with his hands, and his body made a sound like a flat stone you spin sideways so it cuts without a splash: blurp, that's all. Mama worked the rest of it out of Iona too. Jay's father was a dentist with a pointed gray beard and no hair. Jay was going to college so he could come back to White Falls and go into business with his dad. Iona said it like she was proud, but Mama shook her head and blinked hard at her gnarled hands, trying to make something go away. She said, "If I was a strong woman, Iona, I'd lock you in this house till you got over that boy. I'd rather have you hate me than see your heart be broke."

"Jay's not like that," Iona said.

"Every boy's like that in the end. Dentists don't marry the daughters of potato farmers. He'll be lookin' for a girl with an education." She didn't talk that way to be mean. Iona knew Mama loved her more than anyone alive.

WILLY THOUGHT that just listening to Jay Tyler and his father might be dangerous, a bad thing that made his stomach thump like a second heart. Horton Hamilton had raised his son to believe there was one way that was right and one way that was wrong and nothing, absolutely nothing, in between. Willy said, "What if someone steals food because he's hungry?" And his father said, "Stealing's wrong." Willy said, "If a man's dying, if he feels his whole body filling up with pain, would the Lord blame him for taking his own life?" Horton Hamilton rubbed his chin. "The Lord would *forgive* him, Willy, because that's the good Lord's way, but no man has the right to choose his time of death, or any other man's time of death." Willy thought he had him now: "Why do you carry a gun?" His father said his gun was to warn and to wound, but only if there was no other way. He liked talking better.

Willy remembered the way his father talked to Matt Fry. He saw Matt Fry hobbling down the middle of the street, his head bobbing, his pants crusted with dirt, smelling of piss. He thought maybe Matt Fry would have been better off if his father had shot him dead at Miller Creek. And he bowed his head with the shame of letting himself think it.

Jay Tyler's dad wanted to be a lawyer but became a dentist

like his own father instead. He taught Jay to argue both sides of every question with equal passion. When Willy told him there was one right and one wrong and all you had to do was look in the Bible to see which was which, Andrew Johnson Tyler scratched his bald head and said, "Well, Willy, I tell you, it's hard for a *medical man* to believe in God." Willy couldn't figure out why, but there was something about the way Dr. Tyler said "medical man," some secret reverence, that made Willy afraid to question him.

Jay's mother floated across the veranda, her footsteps so soft that Willy glanced at her feet to be sure they touched wood. The folds of her speckled dress fell forward and back; Willy saw the outline of her thighs and had to look away. "All this talk, all this talk," she said. "How about some lemonade? I'm so dry I could choke." Everything about her was pale: her cheeks, flushed from the heat; the sweep of yellow hair, wound in a bun but not too tight; a few blond tendrils swirling at the nape of her neck, damp with her own sweat; the white dress with tiny pink roses, cut low in front so that when she leaned forward and said, "Why don't you help me, Willy," he saw the curve of her breasts.

In the kitchen she brushed his hair from his eyes, touched his hand, almost as if she didn't mean to do it, but he knew. He scurried out to the porch with the lemonade on a tray, ice rattling against glass. From the cool shadows of the house, he swore he heard a woman holding her laughter in her throat.

WILLY LOST HIS WAY on the Kila Flats. All those dirt roads looked the same. Jay told him: "Turn left, turn right, take another right at the fork"; he sent Willy halfway around the county so he'd have time in the backseat with Iona Moon, time to unhook her bra, time to unzip his pants. Willy kept looking in the rearview mirror; he'd dropped Belinda Beller off hours ago. He imagined his father cruising Main and Woodvale Park, looking for him. He imagined his mother at the window, parting the drapes with one hand, pressing her nose to the glass. She worried. She saw a metal bumper twisted around a tree, a wheel spinning a foot above the ground, headlights blasting into the black woods. She washed the blood off the faces of the four teenagers, combed their hair, dabbed their bruises with flesh-colored powder, painted their blue lips a fresh, bright pink. That was back in '57, but she saw their open eyes and surprised mouths every time Willy was late. "Forgive me, Lord, for not trusting you. I know my thoughts are a curse. I know he's safe with you, Lord, and he's a good boy, a careful boy, but I can't help my worrying, Lord: he's my only son. I love my girls, but he's special, you see, in that way." She unlaced her fingers and hissed, "I'll thrash his hide when he walks in that door." She said it out loud because God only listened to prayers and silence. He was too busy to pay attention to all the clatter of words spoken in ordinary tones.

Jay said, "Shit, Willy, you took the wrong turn back there. I told you *right* at the fork." And Willy said he did go right, and Jay answered, "We'd be in front of Iona's house if you went right." There was something in Jay's voice, a creak or a gurgle in the throat, that gave him away. Willy slammed the brakes; his Chevy did a quarter spin that threw Jay and Iona against the door. "What the hell?" said Jay.

"Get out," Willy said.

"What?"

"You heard me. Get out of my car."

Jay zipped his pants and opened the door; Iona started to climb out after him. "Just Jay," Willy said, and he got out too. The front window was cracked open enough for Iona to hear Willy say, "You're gonna get me grounded because you wanna fool around with that little slut." Jay shoved Willy over the hood of the car, and Iona watched the dust curl in the streams of yellow light, waiting for the blow. But Jay didn't hit him; he held him there, leaning on top of him, ten seconds, twenty; and when he let Willy up, Jay clapped him on the shoulder, said, "Sorry, buddy, I'll make it up to you."

JAY STOOD ON the diving board, lean and tan, unbeatable. Willy was almost as good, some days better; but next to Jay he was pale and scrawny, unconvincing. Jay rolled off the balls of his feet, muscles flexing from his calves to his thighs. He threw an easy one first, a single somersault in lay-out position. As he opened up above the water, Iona gasped, expecting him to swoop back into the air.

Willy did the same dive, nearly as well. All day they went on this way, first one, then the other; Jay led Willy by a point and a half; the rest of the field dropped by ten.

Jay saved the backward double somersault with a twist for last. He climbed the ladder slowly, as if he had to think about the dive rung by rung. His buttocks bunched up tight, clenched like fists. On the board, he rolled his shoulders, shook his hands, his feet. He strutted to the end, raised his arms, and spun on his toes. Every muscle frozen, he grit his teeth and leaped, clamped his knees to his chest and heaved head over heel, once, twice, opened up and twisted, his limbs straight as a drill.

But in that last moment, Jay Tyler's concentration snapped. By some fluke, some sudden weakness, his knees bent and his feet slapped the water.

Iona thought she'd see Jay spit with disgust as he gripped the gutter of the pool, but he came up grinning, flashing his straight, white teeth, his father's best work. Willy offered his hand. "I threw it too hard, buddy," Jay said. *Buddy.* Iona stood outside the chain-link fence; she barely heard it, but it made her think of that dusty road; stars flung in the cool black sky by a careless hand; Willy pinned to the hood of the car; and Jay saying: *Sorry, buddy, I'll make it up to you*. Only this way Willy would never know. It was just like Jay not to give a damn about blame or forgiveness.

Willy's dive was easier, two somersaults without a twist, but flawless. He crept ahead of Jay and no one else touched their scores. They sauntered to the bathhouse with their arms around each other's shoulders, knowing they'd won the day.

Standing in the dappled light beneath an oak, Jay Tyler's mother hugged Willy and Jay, and his father pumped their hands. Willy wished his parents could have seen him, this day above all others, but his father was on duty; and old lady Griswold had died, so his mother was busy making her look prettier than she ever was.

Iona Moon shuffled toward them, head down, eyes on the ground. Willy nudged Jay. In a single motion, graceful as the dive he almost hit, Jay turned, smiled, winked, and flicked his wrist near his thigh, a wave that said everything: go away, Iona; can't you see I'm with *my parents?* Willy felt the empty pit of his stomach, a throb of blood in his temples that made him dizzy, as if he were the one shooed away, as if he slunk in the shadows and disappeared behind the thick trunk of the tired tree, its limbs drooping with their own weight.

He was ashamed, like the small boy squinting under the fluorescent lights of the bathroom. His mother stripped his flannel pajamas off him with quick, hard strokes and said, "You're *soaked*, Willy; you're absolutely *drowned*."

UPSTAIRS THE AIR was still and hot, but Hannah Moon couldn't stand the noise of the fan and told Iona, no, please, don't turn it on. Iona said, "I'm going to town tonight, Mama. You want anything?"

"Why don't you just stay here and read to me till I fall asleep? What are you planning in town?"

"Nothing, nothing at all in particular. I get this desire, you know. It's so dark out here at night, just our little lights and the black fields and the blacker hills. I want to see a whole blaze of lights, all the streetlamps going on at once, all the houses burning—like something's about to happen. You have to believe something's going to happen."

"Don't you go looking for him," Mama said. "Don't you go looking for that boy. I know he hasn't called you once since school got out. Bad enough what he did, but don't you go making it worse by being a fool."

"He's nothing to me, Mama. You want a treat or something, maybe a magazine?"

"Take a dollar from my jewelry box and get me as much chocolate as that'll buy. And don't you tell your daddy, promise?"

"Promise."

"He thinks it's not good for me; I think I've got to have some pleasure."

Daddy sat on the porch with Leon and Rafe and Dale. They rocked in the great silence of men, each with his pipe, each with the same tilt of the head as if a single thought wove through their minds. A breeze high in the pines made the tops sway so the limbs rubbed up against one another. The sound they made was less than a breath, a whisper in a dream or the last thing your mother said before she kissed you good night. You were too small to understand the words, but you knew from her voice that you were loved and safe; the kiss on your forehead was a whisper too, a promise no one could keep.

Iona buzzed up and down Main, feeling strong riding up high in the cab of Daddy's red truck, looking down on cars and rumbling over potholes too fast. Daddy kept a coil of rope, a hacksaw and a rifle in the back behind the seat. She had no intention, no intention at all, but she swung down Willow Glen Road, past Jay Tyler's house. She honked her horn at imaginary children in the street, stomped on her brakes and laid rubber to avoid a cat that wasn't there; but all that noise didn't lure anyone out of the Tyler house, and no lights popped on upstairs or down. In the green light of dusk, the house looked gray and cool, a huge lifeless thing waiting to crumble.

She sped toward Seventh, Willy Hamilton's street. She might just happen to roll by, and maybe in the course of conversation she'd say, "Are the Tylers out of town?" Not that she cared; she was only mildly curious. "The house looks absolutely deserted," she'd say. "I don't know why anyone would want to live in that big old thing."

Sure enough, Willy stood in the driveway, hosing down his sky-blue Chevrolet. Iona leaned out the window. "Hey, Willy," she said. He wrinkled up his forehead and didn't say anything. Iona was undaunted. "You wanna go get an ice cream with me?" she said. The spray from the hose made a clear arc before it spattered on the cement and trickled toward the gutter in thick muddy rivulets.

Willy was feeling sorry for her in a way. But he still didn't like her, and he didn't think he could stand the smell of her truck. He told himself to be brave; it wouldn't last long, and it was such a small thing to do, such a small, kind gesture; then he felt very proud, overcome with the realization that he was going to do this good thing.

He was still thinking how generous he was when they finished their cones and Iona jolted out along the river road instead of heading toward his house. He said, "Where are you going?" And she said, "The river." He told her he needed to get home; it was almost dark. Iona said, "I know." He told her he meant it, but his voice was feeble, and she kept plowing through the haze of dusk, faster and faster, till the whole seat was shaking.

She swerved down to the bank of the river, where all the kids came to park; but it was too early for that, so they were alone. Willy stared at the water, at the beer bottles bobbing near the shore, and the torn-off limb of a tree being dragged downstream. "I'm sorry about Jay," he said.

"Why're you sorry? He's not dead."

"He didn't treat you right."

Iona slid across the seat so her thigh pressed against Willy's thigh. "Would you treat me right?" she said. He tried to inch away, but there was nowhere to go. Iona's hand rested on his knee, then started moving up his leg, real slow. Willy swatted it away. "You still think I'm a slut?" Iona said. She touched his thigh again, lightly, higher than before. "I'm not a slut, Willy; I'm just more *generous* than most girls you know." She clutched his wrist and tried to pull his closed hand to her breast. "Don't be afraid," she said. "You won't be fingering Kleenex when you get a grip on my titties." Willy looked so confused that Iona blew a snort of laughter out her nose, right in his face. "You don't know, do you, sweetheart? You don't know Belinda Beller's boobs are made of paper."

"I don't want to hear you say her name," Willy said.

"Fine," said Iona, breathing in his ear, "I don't wanna talk about her either."

Willy felt the pressure in his crotch, his penis rising against his will. He thought of his mother putting lipstick and rouge on old Mrs. Griswold after she died, but even that didn't help this time.

Iona Moon pounced on top of him, kissing his mouth and

locking the door at the same time. She fumbled with his belt, clawed at his zipper. He mumbled *no*, but she smothered the word, swallowed it up in her own mouth.

When Willy wrestled his sisters, his father told him to be careful. The strong have to look out for the weak, he said. It didn't matter that his sisters were older. Even if they jumped him two at a time, Willy was the one who had to go easy. He wasn't strong enough to win a fight without hurting them, without kicking and wrenching and taking a few blind swings, so he had to hold back. Most times he was lucky just to get away.

Willy clamped Iona's arms, but she twisted free. "You know you want it, Willy," she said. "Everybody wants it." But he didn't, not like this, not with Iona Moon. She bit at his lips and his ears, sharp little nips; her fingers between his legs cupped his balls dangerously tight.

With his hands on her shoulders, he shoved her back, flung her against the dashboard so hard it stunned her, and he had time to unlock the door, leap, and flee. But he didn't get far before he heard the unmistakable sputter of tires in mud, an engine revving, going nowhere. Slowing to a trot, he listened. Rock it, he thought, first to reverse, first to reverse.

He heard her grind through the gears, imagined her slamming the stick, stamping the clutch, thought that by now tears streamed down her hot cheeks. Finally he heard the engine idle down, a pitiful, defeated sound in the near darkness.

Slowly he turned, knowing what he had to do, hearing his father's voice: *A gentleman always helps a lady in distress.* She's no lady. *Who are you to judge?*

He found small dead branches and laid them under the tires in two-foot rows. One steady push, his feet braced against a tree, one more, almost, third time's charm, and the front tires caught the sticks, spun, spat up mud all the way to his mouth, and heaved the truck backward onto solid ground. He wiped his hands on his jeans and clumped toward the road.

"Hey," said Iona, "don't you want a ride?" He kept marching. "Hey, Willy, get in. I won't bite." She pulled up right beside him. "It'll take you more than an hour to get home. Your mama will skin you. Now get in. I won't lay a hand on you." He didn't dare look at her. His face felt swollen, about to explode. "What I did before, I didn't mean anything by it. I never would have tried anything if I thought you wouldn't like it. Willy?" He glanced up at her; she seemed no bigger than a child, hanging on to that huge steering wheel. "Willy, I got a gun. Right here behind the seat, I got my daddy's gun." *Don't you be gettin' any ideas of makin' like a jackrabbit, boy.* Willy didn't know if Iona meant it as a warning or a threat, but he knew there was nothing real behind her words, no reason not to get in the truck, no reason except his pride, and that seemed like a small thing when he weighed it against the five-mile trek along the winding road, his mother's pinched face, and the spot of grease from her nose on the windowpane.

White Falls sat in a hollow, a fearful cluster of lights drawn up in a circle for the night, a town closed in on itself. Iona said, "I almost died once. My brother Leon and I started back from town in a storm that turned to a blizzard. Everything was white, like there was nothing in the world besides us and the inside of this truck. Leon drove straight into a six-foot drift; it looked just the same as the sky and the road. We had to get out and walk, or sit there and freeze like the damn cows. We stumbled, breaking the wind with our hands; then we crawled because the gusts were less wild near the ground. I saw the shadows of houses wavering in the snow, right in front of us, but they were never there. A sheet of ice built up around my cheek and chin, and I kept stopping to shatter it with my fist, but it took too long; Leon said, leave it, it will stop the wind.

I thought they'd find me that way, the girl in glass, and they'd keep me frozen in a special truck, take me from town to town along with the nineteen-inch man and the two-headed calf. But Leon, Leon never thought for a minute we were going to die on that road. When I dropped to my belly and said I was warm now, he swatted my butt. Not this way, he said, not this way, God. And then I wondered if he'd whispered it or if I heard what he was thinking. Leon talking to God, I thought; that was more of a miracle than surviving, and I scrambled back to my knees and lunged forward.

"Just like a dog, Leon knew his way. I forgave him for everything. I swore in my heart I'd never hold a harsh thought against him, not for anything in the past or anything he might do later on, because right there in that moment, he was saving our lives.

"When Mama wrapped my hands in warm rags and my daddy pulled off my boots to rub my toes as hard as he could, I knew that nothing, nothing in the world was ever going to matter so much again." She punched the clutch and shifted into fourth. "Do you know why I'm telling you this?" Willy nodded, but he didn't know; he didn't know at all.

It wasn't until Iona Moon eased into her driveway and shut off the engine that she remembered her mother's chocolate and the ragged dollar bill still crumpled in her pocket. *I think I've got to have some pleasure*, that was the last thing Mama said. She rested her head on the steering wheel. A single sob erupted, burst from between her ribs as if someone had pounded his fist against her chest. She fought her own cry, choked it dry, and was silent.

WHEN I WAS TEN, AT NIGHT

while the family slept, unable to stay with them inside,
I would raise the bedroom window, would slide out

pajama-clad, drop the uncertain space from the sill
to the flowers below, and, witless, wild, run past houses

lost in shadow, past the houses of sleeping friends, down
Madison Street to the ice house, to the black river

held in place by moonlight there below the Van Buren Bridge
where the Rattlesnake entered the Clark Fork,

and I would make faces at the water, wanting, unable,
to let out what needed out. Then, giddy with the roar

of the river, I'd run back up the street to the grocery.
I imagined, inside, the soft drink machine parked

near the bread rack, and the handle which lifted the lid
like a car trunk, and, inside, the slick, wet bottles

of too-sweet coca-cola chilled in the humming black water,
the shaped green glass, the fluted, cork-lined bottlecaps

caught in the bin below the opener, and I remembered
what I know now must have been an accident, one

August afternoon when I was even younger, another
bottle of coca-cola, a bottle brush, perhaps, broken off

and trapped inside, alive with a hundred bright eyes
like a stalk of sea anemone wavering in the liquid,

purposeful, almost, and I cried for the unaccountable
thing inside the bottle, and for my unaccountable thirst.

LUCK

Now there is no house, mother,
or if there is we can't find it
though God knows we have looked,
stopping to measure ourselves
against each abandoned farm
on this hard prairie ground
from the Bear Paws to the Sweet Grass,
the wind blowing our failure
through someone else's wheat.

From the Winnemucca casinos
to the racetrack in Spokane
it's been a summer of no luck,
or else the luck we thought
would whistle in singing yes,
or amen, has been disguised
as love, this blood between us
that outlasts land, that makes
even time look simple.

To walk backwards is to take risks,
is to invent your photograph
beneath the photograph of your sisters
staring hard at the camera
as if there were no sun
and no remembering.

Mother, it is to tell me
how your own mother gambled
and lost, and to forgive her
and to forgive my curiosity.

It is, finally, to hold yourself
carefully to the light,
golden now over the wheat
here where there should be a house
and isn't, and then to forgive
yourself, knowing luck always waits
for that forgiveness.

DEBRA EARLING

THE JUST REWARDS

Myra

≈≈≈≈≈≈≈≈

Mama likes to say we get what we deserve. She likes this saying best when she is polishing her salt-and-pepper-shaker collection. And maybe it's true in a way. When Dad and I are fishing Dog Lake in lazy circles and the sky above us is pink with dusk, we deserve not to get a bite. We deserve the dream of fish. And my brother, he's done enough things good and bad to deserve his wife Maureen. I think Mama has gotten what she deserves: a house that in any other place but a reservation would be considered small but here it's considered big, and a salt-and-pepper-shaker collection that could serve the whole state of Montana that she washes twice a month and dusts every day. I'd say getting what you deserve is sometimes justice.

I have a hard time believing Louise gets what she deserves. I once heard Mr. Mellman saying to my father when it got around that Lester had almost broken Louise's leg that she deserved it for behaving the way she does. And I sat there in the compost spread with Mama's special planting spoon, wondering what I deserved.

TWO OR THREE SUMMERS AGO Louise talked me into walking to Dixon and sharing a pop. It took us a long while to get there. I remember because we weren't lucky enough to hitch a ride. It was just after she started going with Lester. I called Lester a wee wee to her face and she knocked me down so hard I couldn't catch my breath for a whole minute. Then it was forgotten. I like that about Louise. I can never quite figure out what she's going to do next. I don't understand the way she feels about Lester even now but I know what loyalty means. And Louise is loyal.

We sat outside the Dixon bar with the screen open. The talk inside was easy, friendly as a good wind coming at our backs. Harvey Nielson was talking to Eddie the bartender and June Murdock Joyce. Harvey was drunk, I think. He's always drunk. And he started talking about seeing Louise's sister Florence. How one morning he'd seen Florence bathing on the front porch of their grandmother's house. How Florence was really going to be the looker in the family.

"Those girls are asking for it," he said, "believe you me."

Louise got up then and put her pop down carefully on the porch step next to me. She stood up and stretched and I had a mind to stand myself. I didn't know there was going to be trouble by the way Louise acted but I sensed a new wind blowing. And I liked it.

Louise entered the bar and the slap of the screen door sent a sharp puff of wind my way that smelled like Purex and beer foam. I pressed my face to the musty screen to see in. Louise was dusk-colored in the coolness of the bar. She leaned up close to Harvey and pulled back her thick hair with her fist.

"See what I mean?" Harvey said to Eddie. But I don't

think Eddie heard him. Eddie was standing at the jukebox, picking songs.

I noticed the line of Louise's arm, admired the dense slender swell of muscle. Strong. Harvey pulled her close to him and kissed her along the pulse of her neck as if she had offered it to him. I felt my ribs tighten my breath. My scalp itched. Louise spoke low to him and there was a depth to her voice that rolled along my back. She lifted a smooth hand to the back of his fat head and in slow circles twirled whatever hair he had left. He pressed his round fringed head into her palm. He closed his eyes. Ernie Tubb was singing on the jukebox. She twisted his hair tighter and I saw his right foot point toward the bar floor rest. She jerked his head back and jabbed a fast fist to his nose, kicking his barstool out from beneath him. He landed with a floor-shuddering boom flat on his wide ass. Breathless. And Louise walked out. Just like that. And I loved her then.

CHANGING

Louise and Myra

September 1941

Louise dunked a deep tin pan in the spring and carried cold water into the house to the room upstairs where her mother used to sleep. I was feeling good, real good. It was warm for September and the window was open and the breeze smelled good. I was glad to be away from my mama. I saw a pale, wrinkled dress draped over the back of a pink, chipped chair.

"That what you're wearing?" I asked.

"Don't know," she said. "I guess."

I held up the flowerprint dress and I felt sorry for Louise. I saw a pair of shoes under the chair, toes puckered from tired glue, too many times being mended.

Louise didn't seem to care. She pulled her dress off over her head and dropped it to the floor. I talked about my new clothes, tried not to mention Jules Bart, looked out the window, tried not to watch her standing naked in the middle of the room. But when she kicked off her shoes, I couldn't help but notice that her toenails were painted desert red. The same red polish my mother wouldn't let me wear. I sat down on the bed. The room was almost dark with dust but I could see the curve of her shoulder, the smooth cup of her breasts lavender-edged. The dim light coming in through the window. I looked at my dry, wide hands, black-pored and short-fingered. I listened to the sound of water and soap smile on Louise's thigh. She put her foot on the chair and washed the inside of her legs, from the hollow of her foot up a long length of calf. She didn't use a wash cloth, only her hands shining like oil. I stared. There was a good smell in the room like my mama's clean sheets, like Fels Naphtha and cold water. I felt funny. I felt lonesome. I stood up and looked out the window. I thought I was lonesome for the cowboy. But all I was really lonesome for was myself. Lonesome for all the things in so many small ways I would never be a part of, silly things, like my mother's clean sheets, nail polish, perfume, and the smell of Louise's skin. All these things were connected somehow like a mystery some women shared. I felt sick because even my mother was part of it, but not me.

I saw Louise's breasts turn gooseflesh. Her nipples grew dark and tight. I wished my breasts weren't encircled with dark hair. Louise unclipped her braid and picked up a small mirror. The mirror caught a flash of light that lit her face. I saw her eyes and she looked back at me. I looked away, but I felt she kept right on looking at me. I looked at my hands like I was wearing rings. I swallowed. I'd been caught watching her.

I sat back down on the bed. My mother had shaved off the shadow over my mouth and I couldn't stop touching the bristle on my upper lip. She had also suggested I tweeze the hair around my nipples. I half took her advice and I hated myself. I had tried to shave my breasts and now they itched in my stiff bra. My face was hot. My mascara felt tacky as road tar. Every time I blinked, my eyelashes stuck together. When I looked back up, Louise had turned from me. I saw the small laddered muscles in her brown back, the thumb-print dimples above her lean rump. She pulled on a pair of underpants the color of her flesh. And they had little roses and a few glass beads up each side that caught the smallest light like water.

"Where did you get those?" I asked.

"You never know what kind of situation you might get in," she said. And she told me about a man in Missoula who had bought her breakfast and a room in return for a look at her naked.

"Happened a while after Lester cracked my leg," she said. "He saw I had holes in my underwear."

"With your cast on?"

I must have looked at her the way my mother looks at me sometimes because she gathered her dress up over her head and stopped talking. For a moment Louise couldn't see me watching her. I wondered who else had seen her in her nakedness besides me. I had a tightness in my stomach I didn't understand. I leaned back on the palm of my hands.

"You sure are slow," I said.

I felt a little bad because I was lucky my parents could afford the things she would never have. I could have pretty much what I wanted. I tipped my head back. I could feel the new cut of my hair stiff and thick on my neck.

Louise slid her dress down just below her knees. It was a yardage dress. The worn fabric hung in soft pleats. She brushed her hair once with her fingers and turned to me. The dress moved like spring grass in wind. The light touched her red hair. The ugly dress on the chair seemed to have changed. I thought it must be the light or something to do with Louise. Even though the dress was worn, it showed up vines of morning glories the color of dawn clouds, poppies were melon-colored. The dress had faded in the way a flower garden fades in a photograph. It had only become more beautiful, something you couldn't buy in a store. Louise didn't wear a slip and even in the shifting window light I could see her changing shadow. She could have gone barefoot or worn an Indian braid. No one would notice or would care. And even my hair, the most beautiful hair, my mother had said, could not console me. I felt sick with ugliness.

≈≈≈≈≈≈≈≈

The summer that followed was summer indeed. In spring I had begun to sense that Lucille's loyalties were with the other world. With fall began her tense and passionate campaign to naturalize herself to it. The months that intervened were certainly the last and perhaps the first true summer of my life.

It was very long. Lucille and I stopped going to school at the end of March, as soon as the weather relented enough to make truancy possible. As a courtesy to Sylvie we put on our school clothes every morning and walked a block in the direction of school. Where the train tracks intersected the road we followed the tracks, which led to the lake and the railroad bridge. The hoboes built on the shore in the bridge's very shadows. Our grandmother, to instill caution in us, had told us that a child who came too near a train was liable to be scalded to death where she stood by a sudden blast of steam, and that hoboes made a practice of whisking children under their coats and carrying them off. So we simply looked at the hoboes, who rarely looked at us.

We in our plaid dresses and Orlon sweaters and velveteen shoes and they in their suit coats with the vestigial collars turned up and the lapels closed might have been marooned survivors of some lost pleasure craft. We and they alone might have escaped the destruction of some sleek train, some flying shuttle of business or commerce. Lucille and I might have been two of a numerous family, off to visit a grandmother in Lapwai. And they might have been touring legislators or members of a dance band. Then our being there on a bitter morning in ruined and unsuitable clothes, wordlessly looking at the water, would be entirely understandable. As it was, I thought of telling them that our grandfather still lay in a train that had slid to the lake floor long before we were born. Perhaps we all awaited a resurrection. Perhaps we expected a train to leap out of the water, caboose foremost, as if in a movie run backward, and then to continue across the bridge. The passengers would arrive, sounder than they departed, accustomed to the depths, serene about their restoration to the light, disembarking at the station in Fingerbone with a calm that quieted the astonishment of friends. Say that this resurrection was general enough to include my grandmother, and Helen, my mother. Say that Helen lifted our hair from our napes with her cold hands and gave us strawberries from her purse. Say that my grandmother pecked our brows with her whiskery lips, and then all of them went down the road to our house, my grandfather youngish and high-pocketed, just outside their conversation, like a difficult memory, or a ghost. Then Lucille and I could run off to the woods, leaving them to talk of old times, and make sandwiches for lunch and show each other snapshots.

WHEN LETTERS were sent to Sylvie about our days and weeks out of school, Sylvie would compose little notes to the effect that the trouble lay with the discomforts of female adolescence. Some of these notes she mailed and some she did not. At the time I thought she lied very blandly about this, considering that she was, much of the time, wholly without guile. But perhaps what she told them was only what she forgot to tell us. Lucille was, often enough, a touchy, achy, tearful creature. Her clothes began to bind and pull, to irk and exasperate her. Her tiny, child-nippled breasts filled her with shame and me with alarm. Sylvie did tell me once that Lucille would mature before I did because she had red hair, and so it transpired. While she became a small woman, I became a towering child. What twinges, what aches I felt, what gathering toward fecundity, what novel and inevitable rhythms, were the work of my strenuous imagining.

We went up into the woods. Deep between two hills was an old quarry, which we were fond of pretending we had discovered. In places the stone stood in vertical shafts, six-sided or eight-sided, the height of stools or pillars. At the center of each of them was a sunburst, a few concentric circles, faint lines the color of rust. These we took to be the ruins of an ancient civilization. If we went up to the top of the quarry, we could ease ourselves a quarter of the way down its face on our toes along a diagonal cranny, till we came to a shallow cave, just deep enough for the two of us to sit in. There was a thick tuft of grass between us, always weathered, always coarse, that we stroked and plucked as if it were the pelt of an old dog. If we fell down here, who would find us? The hoboes would find us. The bears would find us. No one would find us. The robin so red brought strawberry leaves, Lucille would sing. There was an old mine at the foot of the quarry, where someone had looked for gold or silver. It was just a round black hole, an opening no bigger than a small well, so overgrown and rounded by grass that we could not tell just where the verge was. The mine (which we only looked at and threw things into) and the cave were a great and attractive terror.

The woods themselves disturbed us. We liked the little clearings, the burned-off places where wild strawberries grew. Buttercups are the materialization of the humid yellow light one finds in such places. (Buttercups in those mountains are rare and delicate, bright, lacquered, and big on short stems. People delve them up, earth and all, and bring them home like trophies. Newspapers give prizes for the earliest ones. In gardens they perish.) But the deep woods are as dark and stiff and as full of their own odors as the parlor of an old house. We would walk among those great legs, hearing the enthralled and incessant murmurings far above our heads, like children at a funeral.

We—in recollection I feel no reluctance to speak of Lucille and myself almost as a single consciousness even through the course of that summer, though often enough she was restless and morose—we always stayed in the woods until it was evening, and when it was not bitterly cold we stayed on the shore throwing rocks into the water until it was dark. Sometimes we left when we smelled the hoboes' supper—a little like fish, a little like rubber, a little like rust—but it was not the pleasures of home at suppertime that lured us back to Sylvie's house. Say rather that the cold forced me home, and that the dark allowed Lucille to pass through the tattered peripheries of Fingerbone unobserved. It is accurate to say that Lucille went to the woods with me to escape observation. I myself felt the gaze of the world as a distorting mirror that squashed her plump and stretched me narrow. I, too, thought it was just as well to walk away from a joke so rudely persisted in. But I went to the woods for the woods' own sake, while, increasingly, Lucille seemed to be enduring a banishment there.

When we did come home Sylvie would certainly be home,

too, enjoying the evening, for so she described her habit of sitting in the dark. Evening was her special time of day. She gave the word three syllables, and indeed I think she liked it so well for its tendency to smooth, to soften. She seemed to dislike the disequilibrium of counterpoising a roomful of light against a worldful of darkness. Sylvie in a house was more or less like a mermaid in a ship's cabin. She preferred it sunk in the very element it was meant to exclude. We had crickets in the pantry, squirrels in the eaves, sparrows in the attic. Lucille and I stepped through the door from sheer night to sheer night.

If the weather was cold Sylvie always had a fire in the kitchen stove when we came home. She would switch on the radio and hum domestically while she heated our soup and toasted our sandwiches. It was pleasant when she scolded us for coming in late, for playing in our school clothes, for staying out in the cold without our coats on.

ONE EVENING that summer we came into the kitchen and Sylvie was sitting in the moonlight, waiting for us. The table was already set, and we could smell that bacon had already been fried. Sylvie went to the stove and began cracking eggs on the edge of the frying pan and dropping them *shoosh* into the fat. I knew what the silence meant, and so did Lucille. It meant that on an evening so calm, so iridescently blue, so full of the chink and chafe of insects and fat old dogs dragging their chains and belling in the neighbors' dooryards—in such a boundless and luminous evening, we would feel our proximity with our finer senses. As, for example, one of two, lying still in a dark room, knows when the other is awake.

We sat listening to the rasp of the knife as Sylvie buttered and stacked the toast, bumping our heels with a soft, slow rhythm against the legs of our chairs, staring through the warped and bubbled window at the brighter darkness. Then

Lucille began to scratch fiercely at her arms and her knees. "I must have got into something," she said, and she stood up and pulled the chain of the overhead light. The window went black and the cluttered kitchen leaped, so it seemed, into being, as remote from what had gone before as this world from the primal darkness. We saw that we ate from plates that came in detergent boxes, and we drank from jelly glasses. (Sylvie had put her mother's china in boxes and stacked them in the corner by the stove—in case, she said, we should ever need it.) Lucille had startled us all, flooding the room so suddenly with light, exposing heaps of pots and dishes, the two cupboard doors which had come unhinged and were propped against the boxes of china. The tables and chairs and cupboards and doors had been painted a rich white, layer on layer, year after year, but now the last layer had ripened to the yellow of turning cream. Everywhere the paint was chipped and marred. A great shadow of soot loomed up the wall and across the ceiling above the stove, and the stove pipe and the cupboard tops were thickly felted with dust. Most dispiriting, perhaps, was the curtain on Lucille's side of the table, which had been half consumed by fire once when a birthday cake had been set too close to it. Sylvie had beaten out the flames with a back issue of *Good Housekeeping*, but she had never replaced the curtain. It had been my birthday, and the cake was a surprise, as were the pink Orlon cardigan with the imitation seed pearls in the yoke and the ceramic kangaroo with the air fern in its pouch. Sylvie's pleasure in this event had been intense, and perhaps the curtain reminded her of it.

In the light we were startled and uncomfortable. Lucille yanked the chain again, so hard that the little bell at the end of it struck the ceiling, and then we sat uncomfortably in an exaggerated darkness. Lucille began swinging her legs. "Where's your husband, Sylvie?"

There was a silence a little longer than a shrug. "I doubt that *he* knows where *I* am."

"How long were you married?"

Sylvie seemed a little shocked by the question. "Why, I'm married now, Lucille."

"But then where *is* he? Is he a sailor? Is he in jail?"

Sylvie laughed. "You make him sound very mysterious."

"So he isn't in jail."

"We've been out of touch for some time."

Lucille sighed noisily and swung her legs. "I don't think you've ever *had* a husband."

Sylvie replied serenely, "Think what you like, Lucille."

By that time the crickets in the pantry were singing again, the window was luminous, the battered table and the clutter that lay on it were one chill ultramarine, the clutter of ordinary life on the deck of a drowned ship. Lucille sighed again and consented to the darkness. Sylvie was relieved and so was I. "My husband," Sylvie said, as a gesture of reconciliation, "was a soldier when I met him. He fought in the Pacific. Actually he repaired motors and things. I'll find a picture . . ."

At first Lucille imagined that our uncle had died or disappeared in the war, and that Sylvie had been deranged by grief. She forgave Sylvie everything for a while, until Sylvie, pressed repeatedly for a picture of her husband, finally produced a photograph, clipped from a magazine, of a sailor. After that Lucille forgave her nothing. She insisted on a light at suppertime. She found three place settings of china and began demanding meat and vegetables. Sylvie gave her the grocery money. For herself Sylvie stashed saltines in her pockets, which she ate as she walked in the evening, leaving Lucille and me alone in the lighted kitchen with its blind black window.

There were other things about Sylvie's housekeeping that

bothered Lucille. For example, Sylvie's room was just as my grandmother had left it, but the closet and the drawers were mostly empty, since Sylvie kept her clothes and even her hairbrush and toothpowder in a cardboard box under the bed. She slept on top of the covers, with a quilt over her, which during the daytime she pushed under the bed also. Such habits (she always slept clothed, at first with her shoes on, and then, after a month or two, with her shoes under her pillow) were clearly the habits of a transient. They offended Lucille's sense of propriety. She would imagine what some of the sleek and well-tended girls at school, whom she knew only by name and whom no possible combination of circumstances could make privy to such details of our lives, would think if they saw our aunt's feet on the pillow (for she often slept head downward as a cure for insomnia). Lucille had a familiar, Rosette Browne, whom she feared and admired, and through whose eyes she continually imagined she saw. Lucille was galled and wounded by her imagined disapprobation. Once, because it was warm, Sylvie took her quilt and her pillow outside, to sleep on the lawn. Lucille's face flushed, and her eyes brimmed. "Rosette Browne's mother takes her to Spokane for ballet lessons," she told me. "Her mother sews all the costumes. Now she's taking her to Naples for baton." Sylvie suffered in such comparisons, it was true, and yet I was reassured by her sleeping on the lawn, and now and then in the car, and by her interest in all newspapers, irrespective of their dates, and by her pork-and-bean sandwiches. It seemed to me that if she could remain transient here, she would not have to leave.

Lucille hated everything that had to do with transience. Once Sylvie came home with newspapers she had collected at the train station. At dinner she told us she had had a very nice conversation with a lady who had ridden the rods from South Dakota, en route to Portland to see her cousin hanged.

Lucille put down her fork. "Why do you get involved with such trashy people? It's embarrassing!"

Sylvie shrugged. "I didn't get involved. She couldn't even come for supper."

"You asked her?"

"She was worried that she'd miss her connection. They're always prompt about hanging people." Lucille laid her head on her arms and said nothing. "She's his only relative," Sylvie explained, "except for his father, and he's the one that was strangled . . . I thought it was kind of her to come." There was a silence. "I wouldn't say 'trashy,' Lucille. *She* didn't strangle anyone."

Lucille said nothing. Sylvie had missed the point. She could not know that Rosette Browne's mother had looked up from her sewing (Lucille told me she was embroidering dish towels for Rosette's hope chest) startled and nonplussed. How could people of reasonableness and solidity respond to such tales? Lucille was at this time an intermediary between Sylvie and those demure but absolute arbiters who continually sat in judgment of our lives. Lucille might say, "Sylvie doesn't know that you don't make friends with people who fly on their backs a thousand miles, twelve inches from the ground, even to see a hanging." Rosette Browne's mother might say, "Ignorance of the law is no excuse," and Rosette Browne might say, "Ignorance of the law is the crime, Mother!" Sometimes I think Lucille tried to approach our judges as an intercessor, saying perhaps, "Sylvie means no harm." Or "Sylvie resembles our mother." Or "Sylvie's very pretty, when she combs her hair." Or "Sylvie's our only relative. We thought that it was kind of her to come." Even as she offered them, Lucille must have known that such arguments were extraneous. She herself regarded Sylvie with sympathy, but no mercy, and no tolerance. Once Lucille and I were on our way to the Post Office when we saw, in the fallow little park that memorialized war dead, Sylvie lying on a bench, her ankles and her arms crossed and a newspaper tented over her face. Lucille stepped into the lilacs. "What should we do?" She was white with chagrin.

"Wake her up, I guess."

"*You* wake her up. Hurry!" Lucille took off, running toward home. I went over to the bench and lifted the newspaper. Sylvie smiled. "What a pleasant surprise," she said. "And I have a surprise." She sat up, groped in her trench-coat pocket, and pulled out a Mountain Bar. "Is that still your favorite? Look at this," Sylvie said, spreading the paper in her lap. "There's an article here about a woman in Oklahoma who lost an arm in an aircraft factory, but who still manages to support six children by giving piano lessons." Sylvie's interest in this woman struck me as generous. "Where's Lucille?"

"Home."

"Well, that's fine," Sylvie said. "I'm glad to have a chance to talk to you. You're so quiet, it's hard to know what you think." Sylvie had stood up, and we began to walk toward home.

"I suppose I don't know what I think." This confession embarrassed me. It was a source of both terror and comfort to me then that I often seemed invisible—incompletely and minimally existent, in fact. It seemed to me that I made no impact on the world, and that in exchange I was privileged to watch it unawares. But my allusion to this feeling of ghostliness sounded peculiar, and sweat started all over my body, convicting me on the spot of gross corporeality.

"Well, maybe that will change," Sylvie said. We walked a while without speaking. "Maybe it won't." I dropped a step behind and watched her face. She always spoke to me in the voice of an adult dispensing wisdom. I wanted to ask her if she knew what she thought, and if so, what the experience of that sort of knowledge was like, and if not, whether she, too, felt ghostly, as I imagined she must. I waited for Sylvie to say, "You're like me." I thought she might say, "You're like your mother." I feared and suspected that Sylvie and I were of a kind, and waited for her to claim me, but she would not. "You miss too much school," she said. "Childhood doesn't last forever. You'll be sorry someday. Pretty soon you'll be as tall as I am."

Most of the way home was along First Street, a row of cottages and bungalows with swings on their porches and shady lawns. The sidewalk on First Street was heaved and buckled like a suspended bridge in a high wind. It was shadowed by lilac and crab and pine trees that grew so near the walk that we had to bend to pass under some of them. I fell farther behind Sylvie, relieved that her thoughts seemed to have moved on to other things. Her advice to me never held her attention even as long as it held mine. We turned onto Sycamore Street, where there was no sidewalk. Sylvie walked in the road, and I followed her. This was our street. The houses were set back from the road and widely spaced. Dogs trotted out growling to sniff our ankles as we passed. Sylvie had a transient's dislike of watchdogs, and tossed sticks after them. She stood still in the road to watch a long train pass. She stripped a willow switch and broke the necks of dandelions and Queen Anne's lace that bloomed near the road. When finally we came to our house we found Lucille in the kitchen, in a tumult of cleaning, with the lights on, although it was not evening yet. "Now we find you asleep on a *bench!*" she shouted, and was unmollified by Sylvie's assurances that she had not been asleep. "Probably nobody saw her," I said.

"In the middle of town? In the middle of the afternoon?"

"I mean, *recognized* her."

"But who else—Ruthie, who else would—" Lucille threw

her dish towel at the cupboards. I heard Sylvie open the front door.

"She's leaving," I said.

"She always does that. She just wanders away." Lucille picked up her dish towel and threw it at the front door.

"But what if she really leaves?"

"It couldn't be worse." Clearly Rosette Browne's mother had had Lucille on the rack that afternoon. In such cases the advocate will merge with the accused. "I don't know what keeps her here. I think she'd really rather jump on a train."

We did not know where to look for her, so Lucille turned out the lights and we sat at the kitchen table, trying to name the states of the union, and then the capitals of the states, in alphabetical order. Finally we heard her quiet steps and her tentative opening of the kitchen door. "I was afraid you'd have gone to bed. I left these on the bench today. They were too nice to waste." She opened a newspaper parcel, and we smelled huckleberries. "They're all over by the station. I had an idea about pancakes." She made Bisquick batter, and stirred the berries into it while we attempted to list all the nations of the world. "Your mother and I used to make these. We used to go to that same place when we were little girls. Liberia. We were close then, like you two."

"We always forget Latvia," Lucille said.

Sylvie said, "We always forgot Liechtenstein. Or Andorra. Or San Marino."

Ripley Schemm

Rules

1. SCHOOL BUS

I wait in the frozen rut
by the gate, huddled
in a red scarf wound tight
around my chin. My breath
wets the wool, wind stiffens the wool.
I figure by the shadow I stand in
how sun could reach over the rimrock
before the bus, in time
to warm my nose. I wait
for the thing to happen, the thing
I'm reaching for. I have a lot
to figure with. Whether the cow
will calve before I'm back home,
whether the hollow-cheeked kids
from Hound Creek had breakfast,

and if I can toss
my fresh-made curls
when I pass the seat
where Jim Johnson sits.

2. SPEECH

To have speech perfect
rising in pitch
leading the way to my mind,
I take the pipe, the iron pipe
that shuts the corral gate
after we've milked. I take
the iron pipe in my mouth.
Thirty below and I am eight.
My brother is so afraid for me
he grabs the pipe, yanks it
out of my mouth,
the lining with it.
Then to have pain and no words
hurts less. My bloody mouth
is a kind of speech
the whole school understands.

3. SCALES

Only 10 lbs. of cracked corn
I ask the old man for.
Even wait while he takes my time
to shift the wad and spit.

It's to finish my 4-H calf
for the Fair. Well, he might not
sell off any unless I'm willing
to pay the going rate. I know
I'm a tall girl in tight jeans,
small breasts bearing July sun,
eyes level with the old man's.
I can't stay always a 4-H'er
hand heart head home. He hooks
two fingers over his edge
of the heaped scale. My thumb
pushes up my side.

4. FIRE ON THE NORTH FORK

Eighteen singed men slouched
at the pine table, too tired
to lift their hands when I set down
the full plates, so tired
they shove their forearms out,
breaststroking smoke.
I slide between them,
thin Help in braids, glide back
and forth from the kitchen,
carry how they've been recruited
hopeless from 2nd Street South,
their burnt out lives just right
to save a canyon, a forest,
game they'll never hunt.
When their forks clank
the emptied plates, I'm glad

my belt lies flat on my hips,
glad my mouth knows the rules.

5. LEAVING

One spring I leave for town,
I leave for love,
for learning, for all
the lives I want.
Town brings a bigger town,
after that cities too big
to beg. I live all the lives
I pass on the stairs,
in the street, in the park.
I hardly know which of the women
is pushing this child in a swing.
My own life gets along at home
by itself. Stubs its toe
on a willow root,
coils old rope in the shed,
cuts the engine when a quail's
limp feathers fly up with the hay,
races against my heart
to the house to save the nest
of hatchlings. I leave
the morning to mould in the field.

SONGS WERE HORSES I RODE

for MATTHEW

One more stride east, one last push
over the ridge, the mountain at our back.
Dawn swims blue in the prairie grass,
new every spring we've known.
We walk into sun, warm in our throats,
and those great gray stones asleep in the grass,
horses asleep in my dream.

This year you slow your pace
to mine, your sight quicker for lift
of plover, for broken-wing ploy
of curlew. My fearful watch, constant
since you first belonged to me,
loses to wind, to crushed wild mint.
We stop by the nearest stone down the slope,
smooth, gray, curved as a horse
asleep in my dream.

There were songs that could comfort
when you were small. You grew
in your sleep. When I was a child,
songs were horses I rode
to this foothill spring, safe in the lore
of a man kneeling to drink,
the reins still held in his hand.
Our boots bend the grass again
and again where those stones lie
sleeping. We belong here, prairie mornings,

walking for sun in our throats,
in the hollows our hands form, suppliants
on all fours to water soaking our knees,
running down our chins.

I know those stones asleep in my dream
of prairie sky. Ice of a million winds ago
melted down their flanks, left them
roaming wild bunchgrass, some turned
piebald with lichen, some scarred by storm.
Let it be danger of rattler
or rusted tine near your foot
that wakes them. Horses watch in their sleep.
They rise and bolt for the ridge.

THEY KEEP THEIR STORY

Tall smooth lavender hills
I live with now, keep
their story from me. I thought
great light off grassland meant
clear sighting, a strong cut against sky.
Here, land gathers mass to anchor sky.
No trees tell water in this land
except dark brush hidden in draws.

Like that last run of the day
cross country. My skis slowed
at the hunting shack—that quick motion
in the strung deer, cavity open to dusk.

A steady pulse where the heart should be.
And I who beg life again, and again
where it can't be, my eyes catch
light shade, light shade, light—
a pulse where there can't be. What I
see is the small bird working inside
a dark hollow the ribs form, wings
keeping beak steady at a dark source of food.

That was my other country.
Not this one—the great slide of hills
dropped to water where I live now.
This country's great heart—its history—
beats like that small bird, keeps pulsing
out of sight of my life, inside
these steep folded hills.

FOR MARY, ON THE SNAKE

Two years ago, you on the east bluff,
I on the west, watched over the Snake
swinging north down there between us
out of its cliff-bound canyon.
A massive river, taught a man-made role,
swollen from below by dams. How was it
before, we asked, before the dams. Now,
just today, your letter about the drawdown.

"So amazing," you write, "I kept
wanting you to see it." I *do* see it,
Mary, the Snake you give me, your list

of what's been uncovered, becoming
a wonderful river poem.

"But the most amazing thing of all,"
you continue, "was the reappearance
of the river itself." I write it back
to you so you hear the poem your words
sing: "Underneath has been a tough
western river all along with sandbars
and a real current. Day by day
it emerged, and it was like gradually
recognizing a lost part of myself."
But then you tell how they closed
the gates, how you saw the river widen,
hardly stirring again. "Apparently,"
you end, "it's not possible to have both
placid surface and mean current."

I have to write you back, Mary. Think how
the mean current works, always there,
deceptive, below the surface.

Think of the Missouri back home,
once another "tough western river."
All those dams drowned its story, but
the mean current's always there.
We called it the undertow, exhausted
unwary swimmers pulled under by it
if they didn't float till the surface
carried them to shore. And horses
we swam across, their churning legs fighting
that current. If we clung to their manes,
swimming hard beside them, they'd turn back,

sure we were on high ground. So we'd slide
down, hang on their tails until
they hit the far bank, rising free
of the current. Then we'd slide
up fast onto their backs, ride
mounted out of the water. We'd
started them way up river to allow
for that current.

I know what you're seeing, Mary,
I know how it is for me, denying
the present, wanting the past,
longing to retrace each stone, to be
quick, clear, sun reaching my depth.
But too much has happened, hasn't it.

So I claim the hardly stirring placid
surface, too, maneuver between dikes,
sullenly allow commerce, reflect
sunlight, moonlight, off the mass
of silt I carry.

Only, Mary, the mean current is there,
down under the surface. Not so far
down. Remember the Judith, clear
and fast where you grew up. For me,
the Teton, racing out of the Rockies.
Neither river hits the swollen Missouri
till it's run a hundred miles. We are
both, Mary. That early mean current
carved out the course, and heads
the placid surface where we're going,
even now.

IRENE WANNER

VISITING THE HUTTERITES

≈≈≈≈≈≈≈≈

In the wide lot fronting Route 2, trucks idle, shimmering red and blue and black, their chrome and glossy paint wavering in the summer heat. Judy and I linger in the truckstop's air-conditioned restaurant. Past the partition—"Professional Truckers Only," a sign says—men laugh, coffee cups clink, the juke plays on. Across the highway and rising to the horizon, the rich green of the earth has burned brown, a lifeless contrast to the new green of Glacier Park farther west. Here, fields of wheat and corn die under a rainless sky.

I wish we could spend these last few hours relaxing, perhaps sharing a pitcher of Margaritas and swapping stories, but in such small-town surroundings, Judy would become the hottest item of idle talk if she were seen drinking away an afternoon. We finish cheeseburgers with fries and Cokes. Judy indulges her sweet tooth with a slice of apple pie à la mode. Touched by her efforts to entertain me, I've tried to appear enthusiastic about visiting the Hutterites.

"They're a German-speaking Anabaptist sect," she says, "and pacifists. They live on large communal farms called a Bruderhof. It's like a monastery, except they emphasize married life."

I take down the facts in the reporter's notebook that my husband, Adam, calls part of my Lois Lane kit. It's my hope Judy won't realize that after several weeks on the road covering assigned stories, another excursion to another attraction is the last thing I want.

"Their preacher is called a teacher," she says, "and they have daily evening prayer—twice on Sunday—in their school-house, which is private. Their children don't learn English until they start school."

"How many times have you visited?"

"Maybe half a dozen. I wrote a couple of pieces about them when I was still a stringer for a few papers."

"Don't you file stories anymore?"

"When the kids get older," she says, "there'll be time again."

"Adam and I keep talking about having a child."

Judy winks. "If you only talk, you don't have to worry."

"Are you glad, Judy? Having children?"

"When they first sent me home from the hospital with Laura, I just burst into tears. Then when I brought Red home, Laura couldn't stop crying. The thing is," Judy says, and as she smiles, she looks at something distant or within, "the thing I keep telling myself is: Every day that passes means we won't have to go through *that* again."

"It's difficult, you mean?"

Judy touches my arm. For a moment, I expect her to give me the bottom line, the scoop, as she used to in her news stories, which always seemed more insightful and concise than mine.

Instead, she resorts to generalities: She's happy to have the children. Mixed blessings, she says. Never a dull moment.

"You miss going after stories, don't you?" I ask.

Judy says only, "End of interview."

Sam, Judy's husband, was transferred here by the Department of Agriculture. From what I've seen, they're making the best of it, but they don't really fit in with the overweight men, pregnant women, large families, diaper talk, failed crops.

Clearly, times are tough in north central Montana. Hope and hard work can't control drought, blizzards, or falling beef and oil prices. Judy and Sam will move in two years to a bigger city, with libraries, better schools, art and music and museums. This town, they've shown me without having to say so, is trapped between a past that didn't pan out and a dead-end future.

"Was everything all right today?" the waitress asks, clearing our plates.

Judy nods. "Want anything else, Abby?"

"I'm fine. Thanks."

We have a brief tug-of-war for the check.

"Let me pay," I tell Judy. "I didn't get to take you and Sam out for a special dinner."

At the cash register, the waitress is posting a sign that says: SORRY, CHECKS NO LONGER ACCEPTED. She rings up our lunch and, as she writes me a receipt in the loopy back-slanting script of a lefty, asks, "Hot enough for you, Judy?"

"Hot enough we pig-shaved the dog."

The waitress grins. She counts change into my hand and eyes the two cameras I brought inside so the heat in the truck wouldn't ruin the film. At Judy's house, my film bag is stowed in the refrigerator beside the eggs and cheese. We've been pulling the children's legs about cooking an Agfachrome omelet.

"Just visiting?"

"Carol, this is my good friend, Abby Lyons. In college, we were the inseparable, disastrous duo." Judy introduces us, then tells me, "Carol and I sometimes look after each other's kids."

"Pleased to meet you."

Every woman I've met here does duty minding children. Jobs, from what I've seen, are limited to waitress, grocery clerk, secretary, librarian. I feel like I've stepped into the twilight zone.

"What could you find to report on around here?" Carol asks.

Judy says, "We're going to visit the Hutterites."

"The hoots? Again? What on earth do you see in them, Judy?" Carol shakes her head. "Listen, I heard there's a woman left them. Do you know anything about it?"

"No," Judy says.

For a moment, no one speaks. My curiosity gets the better of me.

"Why would she leave?"

"It's very rare," Judy tells me.

"Maybe so," Carol says, "but *I* wouldn't want to be stuck way out there, no TV, no movies, never a trip to Hawaii or anything, having a baby every year."

When we step outside, the heat almost takes my breath away. I wish I could tell Judy she needn't go to the trouble of making this trip, but she's looking forward to it so much I don't say a thing.

"I hope Carol didn't spoil it for you," Judy says. She starts the engine. "The Hutterites are different, sure, but they're very kind."

The seat of the pickup burns and my shoulders stick to the vinyl upholstery. We head north into the empty countryside.

"I think you'll be surprised, Abby."

"Surprised? Why?"

"They live peacefully. They choose an old tradition, but they make it work." On down the road a bit, Judy adds, "And in hard times, they have each other."

I have vague notions about monastic people—icons, beads, rules and formula phrases, riddles and ghosts—that don't square with the businesslike facts Judy now gives. There are only four families, she explains, but they're quite large. They work hard and save money; when colonies grow big and wealthy enough, they buy more land in a separate location and a new group goes off on its own.

"They sent out a community just recently," Judy says.

"How do they decide who goes?"

"I'm not sure. You're told, I guess."

I load a roll of Plus-X—a slow film for this bright light —into the black-and-white camera. Although I can't imagine wanting to take many pictures of the Hutterites, the photographers at the paper always say it's better to waste the last few exposures on the end of an unfinished roll than to start a shoot and run out just as things get interesting.

The film I remove was shot during a week-long river rafting trip on the Colorado. I felt fortunate to get that assignment, because Adam and I could also make a vacation of it. He said someone had to stay home "to feed the garden and water the cat," though, and claimed he was prone to motion sickness. In fact, he becomes a couch potato during the baseball season. When he volunteered to hold the fort, he'd already made up his mind. Neither of us could manage to admit some time apart would be a good idea. We've been fighting lately.

AFTER JUDY turns off the pavement, the truck kicks up billowing clouds of dust that rise behind us like smoke signals.

We follow the contour of wind-scoured ridges past dry ponds, then crest a hill, which opens above a broad swale protecting an isolated cluster of barracks-like houses, barns, and sheds.

"It's so *far* from anything," I say.

"Yes." Judy smiles. "So peaceful."

Peaceful isn't what I meant. Judy remarks how clear the stars are away from streetlights, how once she was here after dark and heard coyotes singing. Their voices carried from all around, making Judy realize she was surrounded by invisible lives, something she'd never thought about when she lived in the city.

A hot wind lifts dust from the barren ground, swirling into a tan funnel that spins and spreads away in a wavering path. Far above, the straight white trail of a jet crosses the sky.

"I should have called," Judy says.

"They have phones?"

"Sure. And tractors and milking machines and computers. People confuse them with the Amish, but Hutterite agricultural methods are very progressive."

The compound is spare and efficient, sectioned by paved walkways and close-cut lawns gone brown. Fences are straight and mended. Ribbed silver silos stand shimmering before a distant hill. The dark earth is streaked dun gray—clay from ancient glacial lake bottoms—and has hardened to hold the tracks of heavy farm equipment.

Judy pulls into the yard and parks. We hear nothing once she turns off the engine. Hot and anxious to get into shade, I reach for the door handle.

"Just a sec, Abby." Judy waits for someone to greet us. "I *should* have called first."

"I thought they knew you."

"I guess I meant they know who I am." Hesitant, she blows

her bangs off her forehead, then brushes away the sweat. "Sometimes I think they invite me in just from courtesy."

We sit a few moments longer, watching a black-and-white magpie lift across the hillside in its dip-and-rise flight of flutter and glide. Then a girl, maybe twelve or thirteen years old, appears at a shed doorway. She wears a long plaid cotton skirt under a white apron, an elbow-length blouse buttoned at the neck and covered by an embroidered black vest, and a spotted kerchief tied at her chin.

"That's Lydia," Judy says.

"Judy!" Lydia waves and runs across the yard. "Welcome."

"I should have called," Judy repeats, allowing Lydia to open her door. "Will it be all right?"

"Yes."

Lydia's white apron lifts on the wind, as white as her teeth, as white the plain bleached sheets drying on a laundry line near the houses. She squeezes Judy's hands.

"I have a friend with me. This is Abby Lyons."

"Bring her in," Lydia says, glancing at me briefly. "We're cutting radish tops."

Lydia goes ahead, walking briskly. Her black oxfords shine fleetingly beneath the rippling skirt. From the back, I notice her hair is confined in a cap of stiff white mesh.

"Mother," Lydia calls, "Judy's come with a friend."

As one, the women look up. There are no men among them. They continue trimming greens, tossing plump radishes into plastic buckets. A beam of sunlight widens across the concrete floor, where a child manages to sweep the floor clean with a broom taller than she.

"My," Judy says, "what happens to so many radishes?"

"The men take them to the grocery in town."

My cameras feel strange and heavy on my hip. Standing

in the doorway, my shadow stretches toward the women, each with covered head and shoulders, floor-length skirts, aprons and fingers stained from work. My face burns with embarrassment. I notice Judy's long-sleeved blouse that buttons at her wrists and wonder why she didn't tell me to wear something more modest.

"Come," one of the women says. "Sit."

"We'd be happy to help," Judy tells her. "Do you have two more knives?"

An old woman pauses, then she, too—softly but firmly—tells us to make ourselves comfortable. We cross into the shade and slip onto a metal-top utility table. Someone speaks quietly, in German, and the women all laugh.

"Judy," I whisper, "maybe I should go outside."

"It's okay."

We watch the women slicing against their fingers. They speak among themselves. The pleasing flash of silver blades is rhythmic and unhurried but steady. Buckets fill. Greens are carried away—for the pigs and chickens or compost, Judy explains, so nothing's wasted—the floor is swept, and more radishes are brought.

In the banded light by a window, Lydia works. Her eyelashes brush her smooth cheeks. She turns. A downy curl of dark hair at her temple frames her face. Then she looks up with wide green eyes, which are strikingly unlike the women's dark brown. Perhaps the cameras interest Lydia, or my bare shoulders. Her curiosity, it seems to me, betrays a longing to know things that the rest of the women have no interest in.

"Judy?"

"What."

I indicate the cameras. "I don't know their customs." The women work as though unaware of us. I'm afraid I've insulted them, coming dressed in a tank top. "Do they mind if I take pictures?"

"Abby says can she take your pictures," Judy says, amused as though I had asked if they believed I'd be stealing their souls.

The women laugh. They want us to feel at home, which only emphasizes we're strangers here.

"Relax, Abby. They'd love it."

The ease of their work and talk goes on unchanged. I take a deep breath, retreating to my equipment. A long lens on the black-and-white camera, a wide-angle for color. I slide from the steel table. My hands work. The women keep at their jobs. I focus, concentrate on the light and composition, at home only with the complexity of cameras.

Lydia, looking west as though she might see mountains and the world beyond the farm's surrounding hills, bares a neck as white as a cloud. A wisp of hair has escaped from her cap. I photograph this: the curving line of cheekbone and eyelash, cap and curl, the rising earth and sky beyond.

"Go and get our guests lemonade," the old woman says.

Judy speaks quickly. "Oh, no. Please. We're fine."

When Lydia smiles, her dreams show. I steal the image.

I hasten to take more pictures: a weathered face, a girl of four or five tending a baby boy in a little black suit, this sunlit room of women in their uniform clothing.

Even though they wear the same things, the fabrics of each woman's colors and patterns clash: green plaid with Day-Glo pink flowers, blue paisley with orange stripes. I wonder if they've ever seen fashion magazines. Then, looking through the lens at the blanched land, I focus on infinity. The women become colorful moving blurs against the still and vacant land, only shades of tan and brown, buff and rust and umber.

A girl brings a pitcher of lemonade and plastic cups. When she hands me a filled glass, she asks, "Is that real?"

"Is what real?"

"Your hair."

Once more, the women laugh. They all have black hair pulled straight back and rolled at the sides of their faces. Most wear glasses. I lift the pale blond braid that hangs to my waist, the thick plaited rope Adam loves. For him, I don't cut it.

"Here. Tug it."

To my surprise, she does. I accept the cold juice and, drinking gratefully, notice Lydia has finished her pile of radishes. She stares at me. The point of her knife is poised at her lower lip.

My hair has become sunbleached from working outside and from the salt of skin diving. Brain coral and butterflyfish, string bikinis and scuba gear seem less foreign than the here and now. I check around the room and am relieved to see that at least these women all wear watches.

KATE, AGE TEN, and Becky, eight, join us on Lydia's guided tour of the farm. We see eight hundred ducks and two thousand geese. Hundreds of huge, fat sows lie nursing piglets kept warm under heat lamps indoors. The pens' cement floor and heavy metal bars are designed for easy cleaning and optimal use of space: the pigs haven't room to turn. A mouser cat works the pig barn. Eight hundred chickens, in tiered cages and living in the dark, lay five hundred eggs daily. The forty-two cows can be milked in half an hour; a Vitamilk tanker takes delivery every other day.

Judy walks ahead, talking quietly with the younger girls. I follow, writing down these facts Lydia gives me. We stop to see their oven, as large as a pottery kiln, where twice a week all the bread is baked. Kate shows us temperature-controlled storerooms stacked high with fifty-pound flour sacks, the Hutterites' own grain milled in Great Falls, then we continue toward the schoolhouse. We make sure all's well in the fenced yard where babies and toddlers play, supervised by little girls.

I ask Judy—in a whisper, I realize—whether she thinks the Hutterites enjoy having visitors.

"It's hard to tell," she says, "isn't it?"

We look past the freshly painted buildings, whose simple façades shelter such sophisticated equipment and efficient production. Lydia and her sisters appear not uncomfortable in their well-defined roles, and I wonder if I have insinuated my own restless sadness on them.

"Do you think they're happy?" I ask Judy.

"I don't know, Abby. I guess that's why I keep coming back."

"Sing for us," Kate says.

"Yes," Becky agrees. "Please?"

Lydia tells me, "It's a tradition. Visitors sing for us. Then we'll sing for you."

We're sitting in their schoolhouse. The benches and tables are handmade. Like the floors, they're highly finished and spotless. The walls are white, mostly glass on the south and east, and the one room's high ceiling lends the feeling of a church consciously made utilitarian.

"I have the worst voice," I say.

The girls tell me it doesn't matter. Judy has sung for them every time, they giggle, even though a duck sounds better.

"I can't think of any songs," I lie.

Becky says, "Judy always sings 'Happy Birthday.' "

So we sing "Happy Birthday." And the sound, in that clean, sunny room, reverberates. The girls then sing a hymn in three-part harmony. I shiver. Their young voices rise and meld. I close my eyes. The girls' song seems so at peace, so full and loving, that I am surprised by Lydia's remark later when we stroll back toward the row of houses.

"I wish I had your blue eyes," she says, "and I wish I had your hair."

No one has ever said anything like this to me. I'm both embarrassed and puzzled, understanding she means something more or different from mere appearance.

"Lydia," I tell her, "you're very beautiful."

She shakes her head and holds the screen door open. As I step inside, Lydia murmurs, "I'm supposed to be like all the rest."

"ARE YOU MARRIED?" Mr. Wurz asks.

I say yes.

"And how is it your husband lets you go so far from home?"

"Well," I tell him, enforcing a patient smile, "it's my job, you see?"

"He lets you go so far, *alone?*"

The patriarch, Mr. Wurz has put aside his week-old newspaper to question me. His immense stomach is coming free from a too-small shirt. His house is immaculate. Judy and I have been given warm dumplings that taste a bit like onions, and weak coffee. Kate sets a plate of chocolate chip cookies on the table.

I'm thinking: a month on the road, four thousand miles of open road, changing landscapes and new friends, satisfying work and unexpected pleasures—it's turned out to be not so far for all this, half a dozen stories, and getting paid besides.

"And you have children?"

I say no, then sensing Mr. Wurz's disapproval, I add, "Not yet."

"But your parents live with you?"

"My husband's father is still alive," I tell him, "but he wants to stay in his own home."

In fact, Adam's father insists he's fine alone in a big house, content with his gardening and power tools. His dog, Beau, is sixteen. The two of them have arthritis. They both have trouble getting up and down the stairs and neither sees well. Beau's cat-chasing days are over, Adam's dad said recently, and so I guess I'll have to give up chasing cats, too. What Adam and I worry about most are his father's saws and drills, all those sharp steel edges he can't really see and won't quit using.

"How old are you?" Becky asks me.

Lydia steps up behind her sister, laying her hands gently on Becky's shoulders. "Don't ask so many questions, Beck."

"It's like the singing," Becky goes on. "We always guess."

"Guess, then," I say.

Kate says twenty-five. I shake my head. Becky guesses twenty-two.

"You're way off. I'm thirty-three."

"You're not," Lydia says.

"It's that Oregon rain," Judy tells them. "And the moisture from the ocean. Everyone there looks younger than they are."

"You should have brought us some rain, then," Mr. Wurz jokes.

"I wish I could have."

In the west, a few high cumulus clouds have gathered. They drift slowly. By dinnertime, they will have thinned under the heat and moved on.

Judy and I accept another cup of coffee. The Wurz boys —tall and gangly and fit, like any high school kids except for the black suits and felt hats and starched white shirts—return from town. They greet Judy, shake my hand, and sit down to lunch. I'm told the women and small children eat later, separately from the men.

"I wish you'd let me go to town, too," Lydia whispers to one of her brothers.

"Lydia?" Mr. Wurz says.

She turns. "Yes, Papa?"

"Enough of that."

"I wish I could go with you," Lydia says. "Can't you take me?"

We're walking to the pickup to get a jar of chokecherry jam Judy brought. She looks at me and shakes her head, then wags a finger and tells Lydia not to be silly. We act as though she were joking. Our hearts would break otherwise.

I say, "I'll send you a photograph. I think I got a really good one."

"Of me?"

"Yes, of you."

"The boys get to go to town," Lydia says, glancing back at the house.

She is intelligent and quite beautiful and could have been anything. A model. Or rather, not just a model. She could have been a dancer, an artist, a woman in business, a teacher or doctor.

"Look," Lydia says.

Touching my arm with one hand, she points toward a small group of pronghorn antelope making their way timidly across the upper pasture.

"Pronghorns usually keep away from people," Lydia tells us. "In some parts of their range, they're endangered because they're too frightened to compete with mustangs and burros for feed and water, even though it's the antelope who are indigenous. But now with the drought, they have to come right up close. They have to trust us for water."

"Where did you learn so much about the antelope, Lydia?" Judy asks.

"Books."

Judy hugs herself as though she were chilled. There are a few gestures she makes—this tightening against someone's hurt, for instance—that I've known since school days. I believe it must be the first time Judy has seen discontent here, the first time she's seen traditions questioned.

A tractor starts. Lydia turns and shields her eyes. One of the men drives the tractor through an open gate, heading out to move the beef calves to graze on what's left of another dead cornfield. The wind lifts dust in an opaque sheet. When it settles, the antelope have disappeared.

"Thanks for showing us around," Judy says, suddenly ready to leave.

Lydia nods. "Any time."

Judy gives Lydia a hug and the jar of homemade jam. When it's my turn, I squeeze Lydia, too. I touch her slender shoulders. She holds me a moment and whispers something I can't make out.

But once more, when Judy and I are seated in the truck, she says, "I wish I could go with you."

Before she can ask again, Judy puts the truck in gear. We start uphill, leaving Lydia alone in the yard. Whenever I look back, she waves. At last, we pass over the ridge and out of sight.

"Did she really mean that?" I ask. "About wanting to come?"

"Yes." Judy holds her left hand out the window, cupping her hand against the invisible strength of the wind. "She's never done that before."

"Wouldn't it be wonderful if we *could* have brought her?"

"I don't know, Abby."

And for a time, we don't speak. I look at the wide sky, which is so pale it's almost white. In every direction, the land's horizon is clean and unbroken, changing subtly with each mile we go.

When I had arrived three days before, I found Sam and Judy's house with its little fenced yard that kept the kids and dog safe. Judy and I sat on a porch swing after gathering beans and lettuce, and digging potatoes, then picking berries for dessert. Sam cooked. We ate at a Formica-top table flanked by two highchairs and restless, crying children. After the dishes were stacked to soak in the sink, we all set off for the country.

"You've got to see the Minuteman missile silos," Sam had said.

We drove east from town, parked in a wheatfield, and walked right up to a circular fenced enclosure posted with government signs listing penalties for breaking and entering. The high chain-link barrier was topped by rolls of barbed wire. A huge reinforced concrete portal lay flush with the earth. Overhead, the sky flared gold and rose and blue. Meadowlarks sang.

"If a missile were launched," Sam said, testing the gate's padlock, "that hatch would blow off automatically. It weighs several tons. It could come down anywhere within a five-mile radius."

"Town's within five miles," Judy told me, "and they can't predict where the hatch would fall."

Later, we drove to a ghost town. We saw quail and ring-necked pheasants and a red fox, the first evening star and a gleaming planet. Since it was just past the solstice, we had late light that threw long shadows across the golden land as we walked. Below a bright orange waxing moon, we crossed a road into sweetgrass and prickly pear to look at the old wooden buildings. Crickets chirred.

In one room, there were horse collars and brittle leather harnesses. Long since, glass had been broken from the windows. Bright green June bugs nestled on the sills. The faded sign on the Ford dealership read 1915. Above the old gas station, we could distinguish a faded flying red horse. To have taken Lydia along, to have had her visit us, seemed such a small and harmless pleasure.

"I'm glad we went, Judy. Thank you."

"It wasn't what you expected, was it?"

"I don't know what I expected, but no, it wasn't."

"Abby?"

"Yes?"

Judy pauses, then says, "I won't go back. I could never just drive away again."

Judy says nothing more. She watches for potholes. We breeze on toward the highway, bouncing on bad shocks over rough road, startling three white-tailed deer feeding in the tall dead reeds at the roadside. Red-winged blackbirds circle and sing and land as soon as we pass.

"Will you go talk with the woman who left?" I ask.

"Yes." Judy glances in the rearview, at me, ahead. "Now I'll have to."

"When I spoke with Adam last night, Judy, I told him I'd start home this evening. That way I can avoid another day of this heat."

"Okay. You can stay for supper or I'll pack you something."

"Thanks."

"Listen, are things okay with you and Adam?"

"Things," I say now, "look better with time and distance."

"Meaning?"

"Mixed blessings."

"I see." Judy nods. She grins. "End of interview."

Last night, I suddenly missed Adam. I told him so. He said at first he'd enjoyed having the house to himself, but now he was lonely. I realized that although the trip had been nice, going away made going home possible.

Adam suggested I camp by his dad's old trout fishing

stream southwest of Missoula. It was right on my way, he said, and to make sure I could find it, he'd marked the map.

"Dad would really like that, Abs, if you could tell him it's still as pretty as ever. That'd be such a treat for him."

Curious about what spot his X marked, I had passed there on the way to visit Judy. A narrow road opened onto a meadow edged by cottonwoods. It was peaceful, protected by pines and bedded with their rich-scented needles. Nearby, boulders edged a deep pool so sheltered you could strip and jump into chilly fresh water up over your head. When you'd fished and eaten and slept and decided to leave, a little dirt path gave access to the highway. There you had your choice whether to take the road home.

DIANE RAPTOSH

SCALE

for MY BROTHER

The strong pitch of roof over the shed,
launchpad to the green swath just past
our yard: the best jump for the neighborhood's
longest legs. Mr Swindell's red
mower ran meanwhile; only you knew it did
in the key of A. You memorized the two

steps and the half-step, found the best way home
the long way around: thirty-three strides crossing
our lot, over Old Man Glee's, a stop
at Wheeler's, into the mouth of Lion's
Park. Then the straight shot—you first—
out of the state of childhood, to Moscow,

New York. Me, odd posts in the midwest.
Now you're back near home
making a life, maintaining the place

is as you'd remembered it, the roof hard
pressed to hold its own, the familial
rasp lifting to your hands at the cornet.

Now what past to set store by, or at rest?
And on whose word? Yours—you aiming for the next
bent note, mementos close as numberless
stuck valves? Or my word, from a looking
back that overshoots the mark? I see
your point about the down side

of being at the place from which we'd no choice
but to fall ahead. I nearly see *you* there,
standing as you look now on the diamond
shaped boulder in the rock garden
in the old back yard, deciding what
stone or spot of dirt should hold you up

next. Or am I saying it's you only
to keep things on the up and up here?
Maybe we've both been too long in one place.
What say we each throw a handsized
stone then go where it lands? Or plan
on meeting halfway between here and

Idaho some time ahead. Try a foothill
in one of the Dakotas. Maybe then let it suffice
we shared a small wedge of land
shored up by a long-held A and a man
who looked to have lived eons, and that we,
too, grew to be old starting from there.

INEZ PETERSEN

FROM "Missing You"

≈≈≈≈≈≈≈≈

Once there was a family: one mother, five sons, six daughters, and ten fathers. The mother's beauty was legendary. Even today people sigh at the mention of her name: Amelia Lucille. When she was young, one man had steamshipped halfway around the world to find her, then left the makings of the first son in her fifteen-year-old beauty.

Already it was too late to remember the ways of her tribe, the Quinault. Only one tradition came easily—the tradition of running away from Indian boarding school. Her mother had run away, and so had her mother's mother before her. Back then, dances were danced and songs were sung in a language that was not English. This language was spoken to the children who ran away, back home to Taholah.

One day, the grandmothers who had run away remembered carrying rocks in their mouths when they attended Chemawa Indian Boarding School. This reminded them of the importance of speaking English. They did not remember other punishments for speaking their own tongue; they did not remember the welts puffed tender on their arms.

These women loved their children and wanted a better life for them, as mothers do. They imagined all the trouble their children would be facing once they left the village. Before that could happen, the mothers decided to speak only English.

It was hard. Love-names cried to escape. Mother-lips pulled firm. Nowadays only the very old trees in Taholah remember Quinault names.

The beautiful Quinault ran back home to a mother who spoke only English. Away from the school, she learned a new tradition. She learned to drink and pretended she was not able to read the signs nailed to the entrances of all the bars in town: NO DOGS OR INDIANS.

A flurry of children gusted behind, like the changeling leaves of autumn. In naming her children, she took care to honor her family: Frank Lee, Robert Henry, William, Violet Rose, Tina Marie, Almeta Marie, Jule Roger, Edna Marie, Pierre Jon. Mama gave me the name of her mother's sister: Inez. There was another brother whose name I have never known, a son she gave to some local church people while in the hospital after giving birth to Robert. They would take care of him, they said. She signed the papers, and the church people moved off the reservation, away from Taholah, taking the nameless boy with them.

Used to be, these names felt like family. But after the foster homes, my feelings emptied out, like a gurgling tub of bathwater. I remember sitting in the back seat of an old Dodge Dart, my arms full of little sisters. Violet was three and Tina almost two. At five, I was the oldest, and they snuggled in close. All I could see was the back of Miss Wendell's bouffant hairdo. Miss Wendell was the caseworker. Three-month-old Pierre Jon, Pear-pear we called him, slept on the seat next to her, too young to understand what was happening.

We stopped in front of an unfamiliar house and Miss Wendell lifted Tina from my arms. Tina whimpered, but I had to be stern. *Go on*, I said. *Don't make trouble.* Her chubby hands clung to my shirt. I willed her to let go. When Miss Wendell came back to the car, she was alone.

We drove for what seemed like a very long time. It was getting dark. The intricate stitching of the seat covers faded as the light diminished around us. When Miss Wendell finally braked to a stop, I knelt on the seat and peeked out the side window.

The house was squat, with a flat roof. Everything—the walls, the trees, the bushes—seemed gray.

"Do you want to live here or over there?" Miss Wendell asked, nodding toward another house across the pasture.

"Here," I answered.

It was that simple. Miss Wendell sent Violet shuffling across the field toward the two-story house whose silhouette I could see against the darkening sky. I watched her small body disappear into the shadows.

I dragged the worn toes of my favorite pair of Keds through the sandy soil. As we stepped toward the porch of my house, an outside light came on and the door opened. A large, plain-faced woman greeted us.

"Come on in. We were just sitting down for supper."

"This will only take a minute," said Miss Wendell. "Charlene Hubbard, this is Inez, and this is Pierre Jon." She spoke rapidly, at the same time pushing my sleeping brother into the big woman's arms.

I listened to the crunching gravel as the Dodge backed out of the driveway. Headlights swept over the patchy lawn where we stood shivering, and for a moment the three of us were caught in the startling brightness.

I could see the goosebumps on Charlene's fleshy arms. The

thin cotton shift she wore was little protection from the cold. When she looked down at me, I saw the dark circles beneath her eyes.

"Come on in, honey," she said.

"You are not my mama. Only my mama can call me that name." I held my head high, resisting her kindness.

Still holding Pear-pear in one arm, she reached out with the other and touched my shoulder.

"Come inside. I've fried some trout."

I loved fried fish. Fish would taste like home, like the reservation. I followed Charlene into the house, noticing how carefully she carried herself, as if her feet hurt.

The light inside glowed warm against the wood paneling. A worn couch and an easy chair were turned toward a console television. Richard Hubbard, Jr., already sat at the dining room table, dressed in jeans and a white T-shirt, a pack of Marlboros rolled in the right sleeve. A father at the dinner table—another new thing in my world.

"D-d-dinner's guh-gettin' cold," he stuttered. His florid complexion contrasted with the tight curls of his cropped hair. He reached over one of the three children seated next to him —his, I supposed—and grabbed a bottle of ketchup. Great blotches of red covered the beautiful trout.

I didn't move. "You don't *do* that," I whispered. "You *don't*."

≈

Later that night, I sat huddled on the portable bed Charlene had made up for me, watching her large form shifting above the crib. She held my brother in her arms.

"Pee-air," she said, wrinkling her nose. "That's just too

much name for this baby boy." She peered down at his brown limbs.

"We call him Pear-pear," I said.

"Pierre Jon Petersen. Might go over in Paris, but not here. How come an Indian mama would name her kid that anyway?"

I glared at her broad back. "We're French too. *And* Quinault." My voice seemed small, not big enough to reach as high as Charlene's ears.

"Pee-air," she repeated, looking at the baby. "Your little neck don't even hold up your head. How can you possibly handle a name bigger than you?"

"He'll grow and fill it up," I answered.

Charlene let the sounds of my brother's name roll around in her mouth.

"Too foreign. How about John, plain and simple." She turned to look at me. "And we'll spell it your mama's way, all right?" She repeated the name. "Jon. Jon. Jonny. That fits just fine."

"His name is Pierre Jon," I said. "You can't do that. You can't just take his name."

She laid Pear-pear in the crib. "Go to sleep," she said. "It's been a day."

I lay in the dark room and made a promise—*I'll remember for you, little brother*. I curled tight around my bunched heart, in this new bed with two sheets. I dreamed the heaviness of rocks on my tongue. I dreamed the names of my grandmothers.

≈≈≈≈≈≈≈

It was April of 1962 and though no snow had fallen in six weeks, the spring was cold and dry, and melting, dirtied patches remained on the ground here and there, in ditches and gullies, in the densely forested areas, in the shadows of mountains, where the sun seldom shone.

It was just daybreak now; the sky, dark and overcast, had been threatening rain since the afternoon before. In her room in the small wooden frame house twelve-year-old Cecelia Capture prepared for the day. She was running a race today at the St. Mary's track meet. Two races, actually, the 660 and the Girl's Relay. The Girl's Relay was not that important, but the 660 was. She was representing Lodi Junior High School.

Cecelia stood in front of the dresser mirror and brushed her hair, which was only somewhat long, an inch or two past her shoulders, not the long, long, past-the-waist length she would have liked it to be.

Her mother nagged her about even this length: "Long and

straight and stringy. Why don't you get it cut and put in a good perm? You look just like some old witch. You look like Geronimo. You look like some damned reservation kid" (which her mother knew that she was but did not like to recognize).

Cecelia brushed and brushed her straight black hair, brushed it smooth and shiny as glass.

Am I attractive? Beautiful? Plain? Just okay? It might depend, she thought, on who her audience was and maybe, too, on what she did.

Surely, if she became an ace runner and won gold medals at the Olympic Games, the sportswriters would describe her as "the beautiful, raven-haired Indian maiden who won all the medals Jim Thorpe had won and then some, who, amazingly, broke records set by Jesse Owens even though her legs were not quite so long."

On the other hand, if she went down to southern Idaho and became a potato-picker, or if she waited table at the truck stop in Bonner's, probably nobody would be moved to write about or even comment upon her remarkable beauty. Unless it was some truck driver.

Cecelia lined her eyes, shadowed them in Midnight Blue, coated her lashes with mascara. She stepped back to admire her handiwork.

Liz Taylor, eat your heart out, she thought. She looked glamorous, like an ancient Egyptian princess. Her parents would not tolerate lipstick, but she had no trouble getting away with Egyptian-princess eyes. They never seemed to look at her eyes.

Cecelia emerged from her room at a quarter to seven, carrying her school books and a bundle of running clothes.

Will Capture sat drinking the coffee he had made himself. He was going over his notes and the agenda for the open meeting of the tribal council. The meeting would begin in the late morning and go on into the late afternoon. He had gone over these things before. He wanted to do it again, just one more time. He wanted to be thoroughly prepared.

Will Capture was an ex-prizefighter and he worked to keep himself in shape. He looked ten years younger than his age, which was sixty-seven. He was proud of his youthful appearance.

He always got to the meetings early so he could get together with some people beforehand and talk over the issues. His reading glasses kept getting fogged over by the steam from his coffee, and he had to stop and remove his glasses and wipe the steam away with an old once-white handkerchief.

Cecelia tried to slink past her father quietly without being noticed. She had made it to the door before he saw her.

"Hey, you," he called, "get back in here right now." She was so close to freedom she could reach down and grasp the knob of the door. She didn't move. "I have to catch the bus," she said without even turning around. "No time to get back. It's almost seven."

"Get back here, I said." His voice was flat and not very loud. He looked up at her over the tops of his bifocals. "You have to eat some breakfast," he said. "Go cook yourself a couple of eggs."

"Oh, Dad, for Pete's sake. I'm going to miss the school bus, and there's a track meet today," and besides, she didn't say, she was trying to become as thin as a cracker, as thin as a fashion model.

She would have liked to have a figure like her two oldest sisters, who lived on the coast; they were built the way their mother had been as a young woman, petite with no bones to be seen, just soft, rounded curves. But Cecelia and Andrea, the third sister, were built differently. They were tall and sturdy and had prominent bones.

Cecelia was already five feet seven inches tall. She would soon reach what would turn out to be her full adult height of five feet nine inches, but at twelve she worried that she might keep on growing taller and taller until she was an incredible seven-foot-tall woman, and no boy would even want to dance with her unless he was a Watusi or something on that order.

Since she had to be tall, she wanted to be thin, like a model, with hollow cheeks and hip bones that protruded and ribs you could count when she wore a clingy bathing suit, and just the slightest suggestion of a bosom. Sleek and streamlined like a greyhound, built for speed. Only she already had, young as she was, more than just the suggestion of a bosom.

"You're not getting out of here without eating some breakfast," her father said, "so you might as well relax. I'll drive you to school in the pickup. I'm going to the agency to a meeting today anyway, and to the dump. I think your mom wants me to do some grocery shopping, too. So just put your things down, take off your coat and fix yourself some eggs."

She did as she was told, but not without glaring her resentment. She wondered how he had such command, although he was so easygoing in his manner. He never used a cuss word, except maybe a "damn" now and then, and she had never heard him really raise his voice in anger. It was hard for her to imagine him as the fierce opponent he was supposed to have been back in his prizefighting days.

Cecelia stood at the wood-burning stove and cracked eggs into the frying pan. She discovered she was hungry. Maybe she would even make herself some toast. No, too much trouble. Eggs were enough.

"Dad, do you want some eggs?"

"No, thanks. I already ate. But bring me some coffee, will you?"

She poured his coffee. He looked up and noticed the bright

red sweater she was wearing. She hoped that for once he wouldn't say anything. She was back at the stove when he spoke.

"I don't like that red thing you're wearing." She didn't say a word. "No, I sure don't like it. None but a certain kind of woman wears red."

She knew what he meant, the kind of woman he had in mind. He was so out of step it was pathetic. He was born in 1895, after all. Probably no one else in the whole world who was Cecelia's age had to put up with such an old person for a father. "Grandchild" his friends jokingly called her; she didn't think they even knew her real name.

Cecelia was the child of her parents' old age, twelve years younger than her nearest sister. Odder still, she was not the only old-age child, simply the only one who had survived.

Cecelia didn't know then, as a child of twelve, but she would understand later that she must have been Will Capture's last attempt to have a son, a son who would maybe be the athlete he had always thought he had the potential to become but never was, a son who would become the lawyer he had wanted to be but had failed to become.

Probably he could imagine his son in this big court battle and that one, winning land-claim cases and other sorts, and people saying, "Did you read in the paper about the big water-rights case? The attorney was young Capture, you know, old Will's boy." Will would teach his son from the very beginning the importance of academic discipline. Will's son would form his very thoughts in English. Will's son would provide the Indian people with quality legal representation.

In fact, there were two sons. One was stillborn two years before Cecelia's birth. The other, born a year later, had lived just a few minutes. He was undersized, born too early, and he had managed only a few weak cries, had thrashed his little limbs about weakly, and then had died in his father's arms.

Will Capture had no son in his old age to guide toward the ambitions he had once had for himself. He had only Cecelia, and for a few years he treated her almost as if she were the son that he wanted.

He taught her to excel in school. He taught her the importance of academic discipline. He wouldn't allow her to go to the mission school, where he had gone, where her sisters had gone, because it was not academically sound. He helped her with her homework, drilled her over and over again, listened to her read. When she was home sick, she would get ahead of her classmates because of his coaching.

She was the only Indian child in the town school, and she longed to go to mission school with all the other Indian children, but he said no. He said if you were going to compete successfully in a white man's world, you had to learn to play the white man's game. It was not enough that an Indian be *as good as;* an Indian had to be *better than*.

When Cecelia was eight years old, she skipped third grade, and this made her father proud. Years later he was still finding ways of mentioning this to people, of working it into his conversations. His pride in her was what made going to school in Lodi, which she hated, bearable.

This past year, though, he hadn't seemed at all interested in her studies. He still wanted to look at her report card, and he seemed pleased with her grades, but he was no longer intensely interested. He no longer tested her and drilled her and gave her pep talks about school. She didn't know why he had turned away from her this way. She supposed it was because he took less of an interest in almost everything since his drinking had increased.

"No, Cecelia, I sure don't like to see you wearing that getup." He could be so aggravating. "Getup." Did she wear "getups"?

Of course he would notice that red sweater, which was perfectly respectable, but he would not notice the tight jeans and the eyeliner and shadow and the thick coats of mascara that stuck her lashes together in clumps. Lipstick and rouge and anything red he would notice.

"And another thing," he went on, "you know what they used to say in the old days, when I was a boy? They used to say you could always tell Indians because of the color red. When they saw a rig coming or people riding horses in the distance, they would say, 'Just look for the color red, and you'll know if they're white or Indian.'"

You *had* to say that, didn't you, Cecelia thought, scooping her eggs onto her plate and carrying the plate to the table, clutching a fork in one hand. It was fully light now, so she turned off the kerosene lamp, even though her father was still reading and it would have been more considerate to have let it burn. She sat herself across the table from him and began eating her eggs.

Red was always going to be her favorite color when she grew up, she thought vindictively. Her whole wardrobe would consist of nothing but red. Red coats and red dresses and red high-heeled shoes, red jeans and red nylon stockings. Even red underwear.

Like many Indian people of his generation, her father seemed to Cecelia in some curious way ashamed of being Indian, although he would have denied it vehemently. He spoke the native language, hadn't even begun to learn English until he was twelve and went to mission school.

Cecelia could not help wondering how her father had managed to feel patriotic, why he had enlisted when his father had been defeated in the Indian wars and he himself was not even a U.S. citizen at the time. Her father had taught her a little Indian history when she was small. She knew Indians weren't granted citizenship until 1924. But both of the Capture boys made it over to France to fight Germans on behalf of the United States, as did many, many Indian men, *none* of whom was a U.S. citizen.

She finished eating her fried eggs and poured herself some coffee. Her father continued studying his papers.

He was preparing to argue his liberal political views with the tribal council, that "damned bunch of BIA puppets," as he called them. He had been on the tribal council for a while but was impeached because he was caught sneaking outside for a quick shot of whiskey during a meeting.

Drinking was not allowed on the agency grounds. That was a law first established by his father, Eagle Capture, who had served as tribal judge for many years and who believed that alcohol was the single greatest enemy of the Indian people.

"Those damned BIA puppets would drive Jesus Christ to drink," Will had said when they impeached him, but he still headed up committees and went out and argued his views and got people to vote, and he always took an active role in tribal politics.

He was so absorbed now, she knew he would have to be reminded of the time. She took another sip of coffee. Will's coffee was always strong. It made Cecelia feel grown-up to drink her father's coffee.

She looked out the window. It was a dark, dismal day, and the air felt close. She hoped it wouldn't rain until after the track meet, at least until after the 660. It would be a shame to get rained out.

Cecelia was aware of the beauty of the scene, and when she looked out over the countryside from the kitchen window she thought of the things she had so often heard her father say: that this land belonged to him and he belonged to it, and that he would never leave it again, never, no matter what might happen.

She saw the school bus rumble along the highway and pass the Capture mailbox.

"Dad, the bus."

No response. "Dad, Dad." He looked up from his papers. "The school bus just went by." He glanced down at his wristwatch. It was an old, handsome one, given to him by his father when he graduated from Jesuit High School, before he went away to college.

"We still have a few minutes. Why don't you go put on something else."

Cecelia sat still a few minutes, ready to stand her ground, ready for a fight, she told herself, if it came to that. Her inalienable right to wear what she felt like wearing was at issue here. But now she would feel self-conscious wearing it, anyway. She went to her room and changed to a long-sleeved, crisp white cotton blouse. There, she thought, looking in the mirror, I don't look like a floozy anymore, and nobody can tell that I'm an Indian from a mile away. I hope he's satisfied. He's in for a surprise when he sees all the red I'll wear when I grow up.

Her mother was up making more coffee when Cecelia returned to the kitchen. Her father was outside. He had turned on the engine of the pickup to warm it up and was loading the bed with plastic sacks filled with garbage.

Her mother was a light-skinned, green-eyed half-breed who didn't show her Indian blood at all. When she was young, she had had auburn hair, but it was gone completely gray now, and she had worn it in a short, squarely cut style for as long as Cecelia could remember.

Her mother hadn't put in her false teeth yet. She was short

and overweight, and had a double chin, a great sagging bosom and thick ankles. She wore a faded flower-print muumuu. People often said that Mary Theresa Capture had been very pretty once, when Will first married her and brought her to the reservation. Her mother's prettiness was hard for Cecelia to imagine. She had never been pretty in Cecelia's memory.

"Missed your bus, I see," Mary Theresa said without looking at her, the chronic frown tightening her face, as Cecelia put on her sweater. The sweater, she decided, would be better than a coat today. It wasn't really that cold anymore.

"But you've got your dad to drive you, don't you? Your very own private chauffeur. Aren't you the lucky one?"

God, Cecelia thought, how can a person be that way so early in the morning? Didn't even need to warm up first; she was a champion nagger.

Will came in the door, leaving the truck with its engine idling in the yard. At six feet he towered over his wife.

"I'm going into town and to take the garbage to the dump," he told her. "I'll be home sometime in the afternoon, say four or five."

She nodded. She took a piece of folded paper from the pocket of her muumuu and handed it to him. Her grocery list.

He unfolded the list, took his bifocals from his shirt pocket and read it. "What's this," he said in mock alarm, "toilet paper? We're not that fancy around here, not as long as we still have the trusty Sears catalogue."

Mary Theresa smiled slightly at his joke and said, "Then pick up a Ward's catalogue. I'm sick and tired of Sears."

He laughed and replaced the bifocals in his pocket along with the grocery list.

Mary Theresa went to the washstand and tried to lift a dipper of water from the bucket to pour into the white enamel basin to wash her face, but even a dipperful was too much for her to manage with her aching, arthritic hands. Will took the dipper and filled the basin.

Mary Theresa's condition hadn't ever before been as bad as it was this year. Though she had often complained of aching hands and shoulders and knees, still she got around well enough. The arthritis hadn't affected her walk before. Now she walked in a slow, stiff manner that showed she was in pain, not always but sometimes, like today. Cecelia remembered that just summer before last her mother had been strong enough to chop wood and to help carry the washtub full of water outside to empty it. Cecelia knew that her mother's condition was worsening. Anyone could see that.

"It would be nice," Mary Theresa said as her husband performed the task of filling the basin, "to have running water, wouldn't it? Then I wouldn't be such a nuisance. Then I could take care of myself."

He said nothing. Before, when she campaigned to move away, Will always made speeches about how he would never leave. This time he said nothing.

The mention of leaving made Cecelia feel uneasy. This was home in a way no other place could ever be. Yet the idea of leaving was an enticing one, too. The hard part about them all leaving together to live somewhere else was that then there would be no going back, no home to return to.

The road from the house to the highway was rough, and the old Ford pickup rattled and rattled and shook its way along. They had a car, too, a two-door Chevy sedan, which Mary Theresa said looked "undignified" for old people to drive because it was a bright banana-yellow. She would have preferred gray or a nice sedate blue. The Chevy sat all by itself in the yard of the Capture place. Mary Theresa had never learned to drive and was therefore effectively stranded when Will was gone.

When Will and Cecelia came to the highway, Cecelia reached to turn on the radio, but her father signaled her to wait by holding up one finger. He said, "Don't even try to run a race without eating. That's no good. All your energy could leave you all of a sudden. Just like that"—he snapped his fingers—"and you wouldn't be able to take another step. Or you might faint. How would you like that, eh? How would you like to fall on your face in front of all those yahoos at the track meet?"

"Not much," Cecelia said, a vision flashing before her of herself lying in her red gym shorts and white T-shirt, passed out, face down in the dust, while everyone else ran past her. It would be, as he said, "no good."

"All right, then," he said, watching for cars before pulling out onto the narrow ribbon of concrete.

Cecelia would have liked to tune in some rock and roll, to hear a little Chuck Berry or maybe Buddy Holly, but she knew that her father had a strong dislike for music of that sort, and she did like country music. She dialed the country station.

Hank Williams was singing about "Pore Ole Kawliga." A country classic. Kawliga was a wooden cigar-store Indian who fell in love with the statue of an Indian maid but was unable to take any action, given that he was what he was.

> *Pore ole Kawliga,*
> *He never had a kiss.*
> *Pore ole Kawliga,*
> *He don't know what*
> *He missed.*
> *Is it any wonder*
> *That his face is red?*
> *Kawliga, that pore ole*
> *Wooden head.*

Will Capture sang the last chorus of the song along with Hank Williams: "Kawliga, that pore ole wooden head."

They passed a mile-long row of skinny foreign-looking trees growing alongside the highway. Will had planted those trees. That was what he told her once when she was a little girl, and she believed him. She imagined her father out there all alone, à la Johnny Appleseed, personally planting each and every one of those trees.

Actually, he had been part of the highway beautification crew, a WPA program, during the Roosevelt administration, and the crew had planted those trees.

She remembered, too, how she used to think that he had built Grand Coulee Dam, because he had worked there. She could remember taking in the awesome sight of the dam, the tons of white water thundering over it, and thinking that her father had built it, probably with a little help from his friends, just as he had built their house and painted it himself.

Once she had thought nothing was beyond his powers. It was while he was working at Grand Coulee, though, staying in a hotel, that he was robbed and beaten. Two young men, he said later, were waiting for him inside his darkened room and jumped him. They took all his money and beat him badly, broke a rib and an arm.

One of Mary Theresa's sisters and her brother-in-law had driven Cecelia and her mother to Okanogan, where Will had been taken to the hospital. They brought him home with them. His arm was in a cast and a sling. His ribs were taped. Cecelia had never felt quite so secure after that. He was the one who was in charge of keeping her safe. Certainly Mary Theresa could not. If *he* could be beaten up and robbed, rendered helpless by a couple of punks, his bones broken, his money taken, what sort of dangers might befall Cecelia? She was just a little girl.

She knew then that even her big, strong, tough father was not capable of keeping her safe always.

They passed the fenced-in Indian property leased by Triangle Cattle Company, where cows grazed, alone and in clumps. They entered the densely forested area, where the road twisted and turned, and came to the place where there was sheer cliff on one side. When Cecelia's sister Andrea was a teenager, she had had a bad accident here in the family car. It was a gray Studebaker, and the insurance had lapsed just the week before. Andrea had had a passenger, one of her friends from mission school. They were coming home from an Audie Murphy movie. It had been raining. The car skidded on the slick road and dropped off down the side of the cliff. Andrea's friend was killed, and Andrea herself badly hurt. The car, of course, was demolished. These were dangerous roads, out on the reservation near Lodi.

"You know," Will said, "it might not be so bad at that, moving away. Your mom's getting so crippled up now I hate to leave her alone, and she's got it so hard out here. Always did. Maybe it's time to move. Your mom and I, we're not getting any younger. We have so little time left now, Mary Theresa and I, just a few more years, and then it will all be over for us."

That was true, but she didn't like to hear it, and it seemed to her he had said it too often this past year.

"And you know something else? I think it would be a good thing if we could live nearer the grandchildren."

They drove through the forested area.

Cecelia nodded, though he wasn't paying any attention to her. She nodded because she was thinking that maybe it wouldn't be so bad, moving away from Route 1, Lodi, Idaho. It was an exciting notion, but a frightening one, too.

Mary Theresa had been a grown woman before she even saw this place, and Will had gone to college in Indiana and done basic training in North Carolina and gone to France and then, when he was in the ring, had spent years roaming far and wide across the country. Cecelia had never been anywhere but Lodi, except to visit her married sisters.

When Will spoke again it was more to himself than to her. "We could make it. I know we could. I'm still strong and able. I could get carpentry jobs working for other old people who can't afford to pay union scale, little jobs on the sly. And with army pension and wheat income, hell, we could manage." Sure, but then he would have to leave his ancestors' bones, wouldn't he, and the land that was his, the house he had built with his own hands, for which he need not pay taxes or rent or utility bills. Cecelia was glad of the sound of the twangy country-western guitar in the cab of the little pickup truck.

Just before reaching town, they came to a green meadow surrounded by forest. This land, meadow and timber, also belonged to Will Capture. It was only ten acres, and it produced no income. It had been Eagle Capture's favorite place to go in the old days, to be alone and to think of things. Sometimes, Will said, his father would go there and stay for three or four days at a time. He liked being there. It was easy to think while he was on that land.

A deer dashed seemingly out of nowhere onto the road in front of them and froze, its dumb face gazing at them. Will applied the brakes and came to a sudden jolting stop. A second passed. Then the deer dashed off to safety, disappearing into the forest on the other side of the road.

The sudden stop dislodged a flask of Jack Daniel's whiskey, which now lay on the floor against Cecelia's feet. She reached down and picked it up. Will put out his hand and drove on, his eyes watching the road straight ahead, and she laid the flask in the palm of his hand. He grasped it and stuck it somewhere inside his heavy overcoat.

She hoped that it was just part of his emergency stash and not intended for today. She had to turn her thoughts toward school now. No. No school. Just the track meet today. She had to get in a running mood. She had to put herself in a competing frame of mind.

Will let her off in front of the school, barely in time for the bell. She ran up the walk and the five steps of the red brick building. She turned to wave to him from the top of the steps, but he had already pulled away and wasn't looking back.

In the rear of the truck she could see the boxes of garbage and a big stack of books. She hadn't noticed the books before now. Law books. He was going to get rid of his law books, she thought; he was taking them to the dump. Or did he have them with him because he was going to need them at the meeting? No, that couldn't be it. He wouldn't need all of them. Old, out-of-date law books. He had been given those law books by his dad, Eagle Capture, when he went away to college. Eagle Capture had wanted his son to be a lawyer, and he had jumped the gun a little, going out and buying him a set of law books for a going-away-to-college present along with the gold watch, which was the graduating-from-high-school present. But Eagle Capture didn't know. He was just an old Indian. Eagle Capture didn't even speak English, let alone read or write or know anything about schooling, or much about schooling, even if he was a tribal judge. He didn't know how great the distance was between graduating from high school and practicing law.

Will Capture had told his daughter a lot about old Eagle Capture, how much he had admired his father and wanted to please him. He was the one who had brought the white man's system of justice to the tribe. He believed that the key to survival was legal representation. If the Indian people had had adequate legal representation, there would have been no Little Bighorn or Wounded Knee. It wouldn't have been possible for the white-eyes to steal land and murder Indians. Legal representation was the key. Through the orderly system of laws the Indian people could regain much of what they had lost; they could make sure that treaties were kept, that no more land was stolen and that water rights belonged to the rightful owners. Eagle Capture could not read or write. He could understand English, but he almost never spoke it, Will said, probably because he spoke it so poorly and did not want to appear stupid.

Will had told her how once, when he was a schoolboy, he was with Eagle Capture and they found a gate on their property left open by Grady, a white man whom Eagle Capture permitted to use his land to move cattle across.

Eagle Capture asked Will to write a note to Grady, which he dictated: "Mr. Grady, You keep um gate closed. Me no like um like this. Next time me say you no more use um Eagle Capture's gate." Will had known that his father was speaking improper English, but he had not dared to change one word. He wrote down what his father had dictated and attached the note to the gate. Mr. Grady was never again so careless as to leave the gate open.

Years and years ago, Will's becoming a lawyer had been his and his father's dream. His brother, Mike, wouldn't have been able to do it, and that was okay, because Eagle Capture had two sons. Mike learned English and how to read and write well enough to get by, but not well enough to go on to high school, let alone to college to study law. So Eagle Capture sent Will to Spokane to board with a white family and go to Jesuit High School and prepare for college.

At Jesuit High School Will studied hard and played some good football, helping his school to win the state championship.

In those days, Indians didn't go to high school very often,

and the idea of one's going to college was practically unheard of. But Will won a football scholarship to Notre Dame, and he was on his way.

When Will first told this story to Cecelia, when she was a little fourth-grade girl, he said that the short time just before he went away to college must have been the very happiest period of his whole life. It looked as if everything was going to work out right, exactly as he had hoped.

But then there was the game in which he hurt his knee. Just one more game after that, and football was over for him. And he couldn't keep up with those smart white boys at college. He couldn't, no matter how hard he tried. English was not his native language, and he had to stop and translate where they did not. They knew more. Their minds were nimbler than his, and he could not compete. No amount of study helped, and he flunked out. But Cecelia, he told her, was going to be different; she was not even going to learn to speak the native tongue, although all her sisters knew it. Then she would have to look at the world and see it as any English-speaking person does, would be forced to form her thoughts in English, and would be able to keep up with any white person. Work, work, work. Study, study, study. It wasn't enough, he told her, to be okay, to hold her own; she had to do better, much better, if she was going to survive in a white man's world.

Cecelia had heard the story many, many times about her father's wanting to be a lawyer, and how the Indian people had a great, great need for high-quality legal representation, and why it was the duty of any Indian person able to become a lawyer to become one and then dedicate his professional life to helping his people obtain justice. No father could be prouder than her father was of how well she did in school, and once or twice he kidded her in a way that she didn't like, that she wouldn't like even when she was a grown woman and he was dead and she was remembering him. She would think that it was no way for a father to kid a daughter. He would tell her, "It's too bad that you're a girl, Cece, because, you know, men just don't like smart women. When you grow up, you are going to have to pretend to be dumb or else you're never going to get a husband."

The part of her father's life that followed the war was not told to her when she was a young child, but she knew it very well by the time she was twelve. It had caused her a lot of pain. Her mother was the first one to tell her, and her motive was unclear. It probably came up on one of those occasions when her mother was telling her how she was just like her father and would grow up to be just like him, and he was no damned good. The story involved his near-murder of a white man and the subsequent time he had spent in the Colorado State Penitentiary. Her father was an ex-convict.

That story had haunted her from the time her mother first told it to her when she was nine or ten. Then her father told her about it himself. He said he was telling her because it was well known and he was afraid she might hear it from some gossip and it would hurt her, so he wanted her to hear it from him. It made a little more sense when her father told the story, but it was essentially the same. Many years later, when she was twenty-nine and living in Spokane and her father was long dead, a drunk woman from her tribe came up to Cecelia in a bar, where Cecelia was herself attempting to get drunk, and said she knew her father, Will Capture, had known him very well, in fact, and she told the story a third time, beginning, "I remember when that incident in Colorado happened. Everyone was talking about it. When he went to trial, it was written up in the tribal newspaper. It wasn't his fault, the way it happened. Not all of it, the way he told it, anyway, but then nobody really knows who wasn't there . . . but this is how I heard it . . ."

And so she had to hear the tale a third time, had to endure it again when she least expected it, from a drunken, foolish source.

The story went like this: After the war was over, Will did not return to Idaho. He didn't feel like going back. Eagle Capture was dead. There was nothing there for him, and he felt restless. He hadn't expected to survive the war—that was why he had been so decorated, because he thought he was going to die, and it didn't matter. It wasn't really that he was so awfully brave. But he did survive, and then he didn't know quite what to do with himself.

He entered the ring professionally, and he roamed the country, prizefighting and boozing. There was a law in effect then, repealed only in 1954, against selling alcoholic beverages to Indians, but those laws were enforced only in dumb little reservation towns. In the places he traveled—Chicago, L.A., San Francisco, New Orleans—nobody knew of such a law, or if they did, they didn't care. Fighting, boozing, barroom brawling, that was the life of the war hero after the war was over.

He was in Denver once, and he was in a tavern, and he was drunk. A white man called him chief. He thought he was being chummy by calling him that. "Chief," he said in a friendly, familiar way. Will Capture didn't like it when white men called him chief. His comrades-in-arms had called him chief, and he hadn't minded it then, at least not at first. He had taken it as a show of respect: a chief, which he certainly was not, was accorded great respect. But he came to understand it as a mockery when they called him that, a mockery of him and of his people and of what it meant to be a chief.

And he would hear it said time and time again, in that humorous, mocking tone, even at times when he was really down and out, penniless because he'd blown all his money on a binge, and was panhandling in the street in his dirty, rumpled clothing. Some benevolent passerby would drop a dime or a quarter into his outstretched, begging palm and say, "Here, chief, get yourself a cup of coffee," and he would fight down the bitter bile taste in his mouth and smile his thanks.

Except that last time with the poor stupid white-eyes in the tavern in Denver, who testified in court that he had only wanted to buy him a beer, that he had no idea the big Indian would get insulted, why, he called all Indians "chief"—didn't everybody? All nigger men were "boy" and all Indian men were "chief." That was the way it was. He didn't mean anything by it.

Only that wasn't all he had said. If he had let it go at that, it might have been all right. That particular white man, though, had a taste for Indian women. Will had heard him tell another man in the bar that he had a taste for squaws, for "dark meat," acquired when he worked for a time in Nevada.

He bought Will Capture a beer, made some "friendly" small talk, addressing him as "chief" all the while. Will was good and drunk by then. He sat there on his barstool with his head down, his body all hunched over.

The white man leaned his face closer to Will and lowered his voice to an intimate level. He said he sure would like to get himself a hot little squaw for the night and could the chief help him find one? There would be a little something in it for him.

The white man, whose name turned out to be Russell, testified in court: "Then, for the first time, he turned and looked into my face."

It was a smiling, leering face Will Capture looked into, and Russell's breath reeked of garlic and beer.

"I hadn't realized, not until that moment, how drunk he really was. He was sitting up straight and looking at me, and his eyes were narrow, evil-looking slits." But Russell didn't move. He sat there, that stupid grin on his face, waiting for a reply to his question about the "hot little squaw" he hoped to find to spend the night with.

"Then," Russell continued, "the first blow landed, breaking my jaw. God, I didn't even see it coming."

What Will Capture would remember about that moment he looked into the white man's face was that he could hardly make out the features at all. The rage was blinding him, blotting out visual images.

The rage was horrible and violent. *Blind* rage, taking possession of him, of his body and his mind and his very spirit. He beat that white man down in Denver, who was clearly no match for him, beat him senseless, beat him unconscious, beat him to within a bloody inch of his death. And that was why Will ended up spending a year in the Colorado State pen and why he could never fight in the ring again.

He prayed to have that taken from him, that awful anger, and it was. The rage would never overtake him that way again. In time he would, like his brother, Mike, become known as "an easygoing fellow." He decided that he would rid himself of alcohol, too. He would stay at home in Idaho from then on, and he would lead a simple, clean life. He wouldn't drink, and he wouldn't fight. It worked for a time. He stayed sober for a number of years. He was still off the bottle when he met and married Mary Theresa.

Cecelia didn't know why her father started drinking again, but he did, and her mother grew bitter with the passing years as her condition became worse and worse.

Cecelia hoped her father would not drink that day, that her mother would have a good day and not suffer too much. She would like to come home to them and have them be some kind of company for her. She tried not to think of her father and his drinking or her mother and her craziness and her suffering. She had to get herself prepared to race.

At the St. Mary's track meet, Cecelia fought menstrual cramps as she warmed up, got herself ready for the competition. She hated getting periods. It wasn't fair. She was glad that her shorts were red. She wouldn't have to worry about stains.

Damn cramps. They were very painful; they made her feel queasy, almost like throwing up. It had been like that every time she got her period, ever since she had begun to menstruate six months ago.

The school nurse had given her some Midol tablets before they left Lodi. The school nurse, who was also the "hygiene" teacher, said that menstrual cramps weren't real, though they felt as if they were. They were just imaginary pain. Psychosomatic. It was all in her head—she was resisting becoming a woman. Maybe it was because she didn't want to grow up. She would certainly have resisted if she had thought that it would do her any good. She would have written letters, the way her father did when he ran across situations he didn't like, to her congressman and to editors of newspapers. But there was just no way a person could get out of menstruation, at least none that she knew of or could dream up.

As far as not wanting to be a woman . . . well, if this pain and distasteful messiness were a sample of what being a woman meant (along with being neat, virtuous, and hard-working, as her mother said women should be, were expected to be, *were*, if they were normal), then she could certainly live without being a woman. She would be perfectly content to go through life as a preadolescent girl. She would even like it. She could picture herself at seventy-five, white-haired and stooped, but still preadolescent.

Cecelia did push-ups, deep knee-bends, stretching exercises from side to side. She had to loosen those muscles up, get the blood flowing and forget about that awful aching down low in her belly.

She wasn't the tallest, longest-legged one in this competition, although she *was* tall for her age. There was one girl from Coeur d'Alene who looked like some sort of giraffe, tall and skinny and raw-boned, all legs, arms, and neck. Cecelia felt afraid. She had to win this damned race. She just *had* to win. All that training was going to pay off. It would, wouldn't it? Otherwise it would all have been for nothing. Wasted effort. Like her mother's life. Like what her mother always said her life had been.

Cecelia tried to push thoughts of her mother out of her mind, but they kept pushing themselves back in. Mary Theresa had stayed there and lived that hard life because she was the mother of three little girls. That was all. The only reason. Because she had grown to hate her husband. Those girls had one sorry excuse for a father, and she couldn't very well leave them with him. So she was a prisoner until they grew up. She was their mother; she had to be a prisoner.

Mary Theresa told Cecelia that she had lived only for the day when the three little girls were grown-up, and she would be free to leave Will Capture and get away on her own. But just when the last one was nearly grown, when Mary Theresa was forty-three years old and, God knows, older than her years, Cecelia was born.

"And just when I thought I was going to be free, I found out that *you* were on the way." A condemned woman then. Of course, one discrepancy in the story was the boys' births. What about them? She had them one and two years before Cecelia's birth, yet they were always conveniently left out of the story. Mary Theresa had a way, it seemed, of rearranging her memories of how things had been to suit her interpretation of the way things were.

Well, Cecelia was not going to be like that. Never. She didn't know how she would ever manage it, but for certain her life wasn't going to overtake her that way and make her a prisoner and a cripple, miserable, mean and bitter. She would not wind up like her mother. Her life was going to be her own.

MADELINE DEFREES

IN THE HELLGATE WIND

January ice drifts downriver
thirty years below the dizzy bridge. Careening traffic
past my narrow walk
tells me warm news of disaster. Sun lies
low, can't thaw my lips. I know
a hand's breadth farther down could freeze me solid
or dissolve me beyond reassembling.
Experts jostle my elbow.
They call my name.
My sleeves wear out from too much heart.

When I went back to pick up my life
the habit fit strangely. My hair escaped.
The Frigidaire worked hard while I slept my night
before the cold trip home.
Roots of that passage go deeper than a razor
can reach. Dead lights

in the station end access by rail.
I could stand still to fail the danger,
freeze a slash at a time, altitude for anaesthetic.
Could follow my feet in the Hellgate wind
wherever the dance invites them.

The pure leap I cannot take stiffens downstream,
a millrace churned to murder.
The siren cries
at my wrist, flicks my throat, routine
as the river I cross over.

DENNICE SCANLON

THE DIFFERENCE IN EFFECTS OF TEMPERATURE DEPENDING ON GEOGRAPHICAL LOCATION EAST OR WEST OF THE CONTINENTAL DIVIDE: A LETTER

I had a mind to begin by scraping April
from the ridge. When in doubt, the saying
goes, dwell on weather. Haven't we been blessed
with dusk, a thousand ways to grieve the sun
receding? You must find spring a welcome
change where little changes. It's easy
to spot along valley fencelines—the new
calves, Hawn's mended coop, snake-edged
alfalfa oddly whipped against the wind.
Rain doesn't mean as much here. Pigeons
clutter the eaves, softball's late
starting but words wear thin for clouds
in season, the sting of long drives home.

At fifty-two hundred feet, torn buildings
soar. You left before mines with names
dull as Alice closed Butte. The big strike

settled like copper rings on branches.
Cottonwoods wrapped around sewerlines to pop
them at the joints and dusted days took
root. I only mention it because land to us
is personal as choice, whether it swells
in bluffs, plateaus or Indian corn,
we both know what's enough. Yours gives back
what you put in—grain, slim tops
of asparagus, early beets. Mine demands
something hard to thrive, a red metal core.
When it's gone, dying's less complicated,
slow, as one house at a time boards up,
another promise of work falls through, ground
that's left overlaps its people and keeps
them from the boundary of their dreams.

It weighs my mind to write this way
with sky in doubt, bringing April when gray birds
sulk in the eaves. There was more to say
but news is smaller on the page, neighbors
nice to lunch with, the friends we knew
still close. I wanted to tell you nights
are filmy and alive with bugs, invite you
for Shakespeare in the Park beneath a peeling
signboard, find a part for your eyes to play
out in stages or fold you like a paper star.
But I know what mountains divide, some
common ground unsettled. The best country
is one we can sow and leave with fewer words.
And the best letter brief, seasonal as wheat
or old town affairs. One that closes before
weather wilts ridges between with love.

IT's COME TO THIS

≈≈≈≈≈≈≈

No horses. That's how it always starts. I am coming down the meadow, the first snow of September whipping around my boots, and there are no horses to greet me. The first thing I did after Caleb died was get rid of the horses.

"I don't care how much," I told the auctioneer at the Missoula Livestock Company. He looked at me slant-eyed from under his Stetson. "Just don't let the canneries take them." Then I walked away.

What I did not tell him was I couldn't stand the sight of those horses on our meadow, so heedless, grown fat and un-tended. They reminded me of days when Montana seemed open as the sky.

Now that the horses are gone I am more desolate than ever. If you add one loss to another, what you have is double zip. I am wet to the waist, water sloshing ankle-deep inside my irrigating boots. My toes are numb, my chapped hands are burning from the cold, and down by the gate my dogs are barking at a strange man in a red log truck.

That's how I meet Frank. He is hauling logs down from the Champion timberlands above my place, across the right-of-way I sold to the company after my husband's death. The taxes were piling up. I sold the right-of-way because I would not sell my land. Kids will grow up and leave you, but land is something a woman can hold on to.

I don't like those log trucks rumbling by my house, scattering chickens, tempting my dogs to chase behind their wheels, kicking clouds of dust so thick the grass looks brown and dead. There's nothing I like about logging. It breaks my heart to walk among newly cut limbs, to be enveloped in the sharp odor of sap running like blood. After twenty years on this place, I still cringe at the snap and crash of five-hundred-year-old pines and the far-off screaming of saws.

Anyway, Frank pulls his Gyppo logging rig to a stop just past my house in order to open the blue metal gate that separates our outbuildings from the pasture, and while he is at it, he adjusts the chains holding his load. My three mutts take after him as if they are real watchdogs and he stands at the door of the battered red cab holding his hands to his face and pretending to be scared.

"I would surely appreciate it if you'd call off them dogs," says Frank, as if those puppies weren't wagging their tails and jumping up to be patted.

He can see I am shivering and soaked. And I am mad. If I had a gun, I might shoot him.

"You ought to be ashamed . . . a man like you."

"Frank Bowman," he says, grinning and holding out his large thick hand. "From Bowman Corners." Bowman Corners is just down the road.

"What happened to you?" He grins. "Take a shower in your boots?"

How can you stay mad at that man? A man who looks at you and makes you look at yourself. I should have known better. I should have waited for my boys to come home from football practice and help me lift the heavy wet boards in our diversion dam. But my old wooden flume was running full and I was determined to do what had to be done before dark, to be a true country woman like the pioneers I read about as a daydreaming child in Chicago, so long ago it seems another person's life.

"I had to shut off the water," I say. "Before it freezes." Frank nods, as if this explanation explains everything.

Months later I would tell him about Caleb. How he took care of the wooden flume, which was built almost one hundred years ago by his Swedish ancestors. The snaking plank trough crawls up and around a steep slope of igneous rock. It has been patched and rebuilt by generations of hard-handed, blue-eyed Petersons until it reached its present state of tenuous mortality. We open the floodgate in June when Bear Creek is high with snowmelt, and the flume runs full all summer, irrigating our hay meadow of timothy and wild mountain grasses. Each fall, before the first hard freeze, we close the diversion gates and the creek flows in its natural bed down to the Big Blackfoot River.

That's why I'd been standing in the icy creek, hefting six-foot two-by-twelves into the slotted brace that forms the dam. The bottom board was waterlogged and coated with green slime. It slipped in my bare hands and I sat down with a splash, the plank in my lap and the creek surging around me.

"Goddamn it to fucking hell!" I yelled. I was astonished to find tears streaming down my face, for I have always prided myself on my ability to bear hardship. Here is a lesson I've learned. There is no glory in pure backbreaking labor.

Frank would agree. He is wide like his log truck and thick-skinned as a yellow pine, and believes neighbors should be friendly. At five o'clock sharp each workday, on his last run, he would stop at my blue gate and yell, "Call off your beasts," and I would stop whatever I was doing and go down for our friendly chat.

"How can you stand it?" I'd say, referring to the cutting of trees.

"It's a pinprick on the skin of the earth," replies Frank. "God doesn't know the difference."

"Well, I'm not God," I say. "Not on my place. Never."

So Frank would switch to safer topics such as new people moving in like knapweed, or where to find morels, or how the junior high basketball team was doing. One day in October, when red-tails screamed and hoarfrost tipped the meadow grass, the world gone crystal and glowing, he asked could I use some firewood.

"A person can always use firewood," I snapped.

The next day, when I came home from teaching, there was a pickup load by the woodshed—larch and fir, cut to stove size and split.

"Taking care of the widow." Frank grinned when I tried to thank him. I laughed, but that is exactly what he was up to. In this part of the country, a man still takes pains.

WHEN I FIRST CAME to Montana I was slim as a fashion model and my hair was black and curly. I had met my husband, Caleb, at the University of Chicago, where a city girl and a raw ranch boy could be equally enthralled by Gothic halls, the great libraries, and gray old Nobel laureates who gathered in the Faculty Club, where no student dared enter.

But after our first two sons were born, after the disillusionments of Vietnam and the cloistered grind of academic life, we decided to break away from Chicago and a life of mind preeminent, and we came to live on the quarter section of land Caleb had inherited from his Swedish grandmother. We would make a new start by raising purebred quarter horses.

For Caleb it was coming home. He had grown up in Sunset, forty miles northeast of Missoula, on his family's homestead ranch. For me it was romance. Caleb had carried the romance of the West for me in the way he walked on high-heeled cowboy boots, and the world he told stories about. It was a world I had imagined from books and movies, a paradise of the shining mountains, clean rivers, and running horses.

I loved the idea of horses. In grade school, I sketched black stallions, white mares, rainbow-spotted Appaloosas. My bedroom was hung with horses running, horses jumping, horses rolling in clover. At thirteen I hung around the stables in Lincoln Park and flirted with the stable boys, hoping to charm them into riding lessons my mother could not afford. Sometimes it worked, and I would bounce down the bridle path, free as a princess, never thinking of the payoff that would come at dusk. Pimply-faced boys. Groping and French kisses behind the dark barn that reeked of manure.

For Caleb horses meant honorable outdoor work and a way to make money, work being the prime factor. Horses were history to be reclaimed, identity. It was my turn to bring in the monthly check, so I began teaching at the Sunset school as a stopgap measure to keep our family solvent until the horse-business dream paid off. I am still filling that gap.

We rebuilt the log barn and the corrals, and cross-fenced our one hundred acres of cleared meadowland. I loved my upland meadow from the first day. As I walked through tall grasses heavy with seed, they moved to the wind, and the undulations were not like water. Now, when I look down from our cliffs, I see the meadow as a handmade thing—a rolling swatch of green hemmed with a stitchery of rocks and trees. The old Swedes who were Caleb's ancestors cleared that meadow with axes and cross-cut saws, and I still trip over sawed-off stumps of virgin larch, sawed level to the ground, too large to pull out with a team of horses—decaying, but not yet dirt.

We knew land was a way to save your life. Leave the city and city ambitions, and get back to basics. Roots and dirt and horse pucky (Caleb's word for horseshit). Bob Dylan and the rest were all singing about the land, and every stoned, long-haired mother's child was heading for country.

My poor mother, with her Hungarian dreams and Hebrew upbringing, would turn in her grave to know I'm still teaching in a three-room school with no library or gymnasium, Caleb ten years dead, our youngest boy packed off to the state university, the ranch not even paying its taxes, and me, her only child, keeping company with a two-hundred-and-thirty-pound logger who lives in a trailer.

"Marry a doctor," she used to say, "or better, a concert pianist," and she was not joking. She invented middle-class stories for me from our walk-up flat on the South Side of Chicago: I would live in a white house in the suburbs like she had always wanted; my neighbors would be rich and cultured; the air itself, fragrant with lilacs in May and heady with burning oak leaves in October, could lift us out of the city's grime right into her American dream. My mother would smile with secret intentions. "You will send your children to Harvard."

FRANK'S BEEN MARRIED twice. "Twice-burned" is how he names it, and there are Bowman kids scattered up and down the Blackfoot Valley. Some of them are his. I met his first wife, Fay Dell, before I ever met Frank. That was eighteen years ago. It was Easter vacation, and I had taken two hundred dollars out of our meager savings to buy a horse for our brand-new herd. I remember the day clear as any picture. I remember mud and Blackfoot clay.

Fay Dell is standing in a pasture above Monture Creek. She wears faded brown Carhartt coveralls, as they do up here in the winters, and her irrigating boots are crusted with yellow mud. March runoff has every patch of bare ground spitting streams, trickles, and puddles of brackish water. Two dozen horses circle around her. Their ears are laid back and they eye me, ready for flight. She calls them by name, her voice low, sugary as the carrots she holds in her rough hands.

"Take your pick," she says.

I stroke the velvet muzzle of a two-year-old sorrel, a pure-bred quarter horse with a white blaze on her forehead.

"Sweet Baby," she says. "You got an eye for the good ones."

"How much?"

"Sorry. That baby is promised."

I walk over to a long-legged bay. There's a smile on Fay Dell's lips, but her eyes give another message.

"Marigold," she says, rubbing the mare's swollen belly. "She's in foal. Can't sell my brood mare."

So I try my luck on a pint-sized roan with a high-flying tail. A good kids' horse. A dandy.

"You can't have Lollipop neither. I'm breaking her for my own little gal."

I can see we're not getting anywhere when she heads me in the direction of a pair of wild-eyed geldings.

"Twins," says Fay Dell proudly. "Ruckus and Buckus."

You can tell by the name of a thing if it's any good. These two were out of the question, coming four and never halter broke.

"Come on back in May." We walk toward the ranch house

and a hot cup of coffee. "I'll have 'em tamed good as any sheep-dog. Two for the price of one. Can't say that ain't a bargain!"

Her two-story frame house sat high above the creek, some Iowa farmer's dream of the West. The ground, brown with stubble of last year's grass, was littered with old tennis shoes, broken windshields, rusting cars, shards of aluminum siding. Cast-iron tractor parts emerged like mushrooms from soot-crusted heaps of melting snow. I wondered why Fay Dell had posted that ad on the Sunset school bulletin board: "Good horses for sale. Real cheap." Why did she bother with such make-believe?

Eighteen years later I am sleeping with her ex-husband, and the question is answered.

"All my wages gone for hay," says Frank. "The kids in hand-me-downs . . . the house a goddamn mess. I'll tell you I had a bellyful!"

Frank had issued an ultimatum on Easter Sunday, deter-mined never to be ashamed again of his bedraggled wife and children among the slicked-up families in the Blackfoot Com-munity Church.

"Get rid of them two-year-olds," he warned, "or . . ."

No wonder it took Fay Dell so long to tell me no. What she was doing that runoff afternoon, seesawing back and forth, was making a choice between her horses and her husband. If Fay Dell had confessed to me that day, I would not have believed such choices are possible. Horses, no matter how well you loved them, seemed mere animal possessions to be bought and sold. I was so young then, a city girl with no roots at all, and I had grown up Jewish, where family seemed the only choice.

"Horse poor," Frank says. "That woman wouldn't get rid of her horses. Not for God, Himself."

March in Montana is a desperate season. You have to know what you want, and hang on.

FRANK'S SECOND WIFE was tall, blond, and young. He won't talk about her much, just shakes his head when her name comes up and says, "Guess she couldn't stand the winters." I heard she ran away to San Luis Obispo with a long-haired carpenter named Ralph.

"Cleaned me out," Frank says, referring to his brand-new stereo and the golden retriever. She left the double-wide empty, and the only evidence she had been there at all was the white picket fence Frank built to make her feel safe. And a heap of green tomatoes in the weed thicket he calls a garden.

"I told her," he says with a wistful look, "I told that woman you can't grow red tomatoes in this climate."

As for me, I love winter. Maybe that's why Frank and I can stand each other. Maybe that's how come we've been keeping company for five years and marriage is a subject that has never crossed our lips except once. He's got his place near the highway, and I've got mine at the end of the dirt road, where the sign reads, COUNTY MAINTENANCE ENDS HERE. To all eyes but our own, we have always been a queer, mismatched pair.

After we began neighboring, I would ask Frank in for a cup of coffee. Before long, it was a beer or two. Soon, my boys were taking the old McCulloch chain saw to Frank's to be sharpened, or he was teaching them how to tune up Caleb's ancient Case tractor. We kept our distance until one thirty-below evening in January when my Blazer wouldn't start, even though its oil-pan heater was plugged in. Frank came up to jump it.

The index finger on my right hand was frostbit from trying to turn the metal ignition key bare-handed. Frostbite is like getting burned, extreme cold acting like fire, and my finger was swollen along the third joint, just below its tip, growing the biggest blister I had ever seen.

"Dumb," Frank says, holding my hand between his large mitts and blowing on the blister. "Don't you have gloves?"

"Couldn't feel the key to turn it with gloves on."

He lifts my egg-size finger to his face and bows down, like a chevalier, to kiss it. I learn the meaning of dumbfounded. I feel the warmth of his lips tracing from my hand down through my privates. I like it. A widow begins to forget how good a man's warmth can be.

"I would like to take you dancing," says Frank.

"It's too damn cold."

"Tomorrow," he says, "the Big Sky Boys are playing at the Awful Burger Bar."

I suck at my finger.

"You're a fine dancer."

"How in God's name would you know?"

"Easy," Frank smiles. "I been watching your moves."

I admit I was scared. I felt like the little girl I had been, so long ago. A thumb-sucker. If I said yes, I knew there would be no saying no.

THE AWFUL BURGER Bar is like the Red Cross, you can go there for first aid. It is as great an institution as the Sunset school. The white bungalow sits alone just off the two-lane on a jack-pine flat facing south across irrigated hay meadows to where what's left of the town of Sunset clusters around the school. Friday evenings after Caleb passed away, when I felt too weary to cook and too jumpy to stand the silence of another Blackfoot night, I'd haul the boys up those five miles of asphalt and we'd eat Molly Fry's awful burgers, stacked high with Bermuda onions, lettuce and tomato, hot jo-jos on the side, Millers for me, root beer for them. That's how those kids came to be experts at shooting pool.

The ranching and logging families in this valley had no difficulty understanding why their schoolteacher hung out in a bar and passed the time with hired hands and old-timers. We were all alike in this one thing. Each was drawn from starvation farms in the rock and clay foothills or grassland ranches on the floodplain, down some winding dirt road to the red neon and yellow lights glowing at the dark edge of chance. You could call it home, as they do in the country-and-western songs on the jukebox.

I came to know those songs like a second language. Most, it seemed, written just for me. I longed to sing them out loud, but God or genes or whatever determines what you can be never gave me a singing voice. In my second life I will be a white Billie Holiday with a gardenia stuck behind my ear, belting out songs to make you dance and cry at the same time.

My husband, Caleb, could sing like the choirboy he had been before he went off to Chicago on a scholarship and lost his religion. He taught himself to play harmonica and wrote songs about lost lives. There's one I can't forget:

> *Scattered pieces, scattered pieces,*
> *Come apart for all the world to see.*
>
> *Scattered pieces, lonely pieces,*
> *That's how yours truly came to be.*

When he sang that song, my eyes filled with tears.

"How can you feel that way, and never tell me except in a song?"

"There's lots I don't tell you," he said.

We didn't go to bars much, Caleb and me. First of all we were poor. Then too busy building our log house, taking care of the boys, tending horses. And finally, when the angina pains struck, and the shortness of breath, and we knew that at the age of thirty-seven Caleb had come down with an inherited disease that would choke his arteries and starve his heart, it was too sad, you know, having to sit out the jitterbugs and dance only to slow music. But even then, in those worst of bad times, when the Big Sky Boys came through, we'd hire a sitter and put on our good boots and head for the Awful Burger.

There was one Fourth of July. All the regulars were there, and families from the valley. Frank says he was there, but I didn't know him. Kids were running in and out like they do in Montana, where a country bar is your local community center. Firecrackers exploded in the gravel parking lot. Show-off college students from town were dancing cowboy boogie as if they knew what they were doing, and sunburned tourists exuding auras of campfires and native cutthroat trout kept coming in from motor homes. This was a far way from Connecticut.

We were sitting up close to the band. Caleb was showing our boys how he could juggle peanuts in time to the music. The boys tried to copy him, and peanuts fell like confetti to be crunched under the boots of sweating dancers. The sun streamed in through open doors and windows, even though it was nine at night, and we were flushed from too many beers, too much sun and music.

"Stand up, Caleb. Stand up so's the rest of us can see."

That was our neighbor Melvin Godfrey calling from the next table. Then his wife, Stella, takes up the chant.

"Come on, Caleb. Give us the old one-two-three."

The next thing, Molly Fry is passing lemons from the kitchen where she cooks the awful burgers, and Caleb is standing in front of the Big Sky Boys, the dancers all stopped and watching. Caleb is juggling those lemons to the tune of "Mommas, Don't Let Your Babies Grow Up to Be Cowboys," and he does not miss a beat.

It is a picture in my mind—framed in gold leaf—Caleb on that bandstand, legs straddled, deep-set eyes looking out at no one or nothing, the tip of his tongue between clenched teeth in some kind of frozen smile, his faded blue shirt stained in half-moons under the arms, and three bright yellow lemons rising and falling in perfect synchronicity. I see the picture in stop-action, like the end of a movie. Two shiny lemons in mid-air, the third in his palm. Caleb juggling.

IT'S BEEN A LONG TIME coming, the crying. You think there's no pity left, but the sadness is waiting, like a barrel gathering rain, until one sunny day, out of the blue, it just boils over and you've got a flood on your hands. That's what happened one Saturday last January, when Frank took me to celebrate the fifth anniversary of our first night together. The Big Sky Boys were back, and we were at the Awful Burger Bar.

"Look," I say, first thing. "The lead guitar has lost his hair. Those boys are boys no longer."

Frank laughs and points to the bass man. Damned if he isn't wearing a corset to hold his beer belly inside those slick red-satin cowboy shirts the boys have worn all these years.

And Indian Willie is gone. He played steel guitar so blue it broke your heart. Gone back to Oklahoma.

"Heard Willie found Jesus in Tulsa," says Melvin Godfrey, who has joined us at the bar.

"They've replaced him with a child," I say, referring to the pimply, long-legged kid who must be someone's son. "He hits all the right notes, but he'll never break your heart."

We're sitting on high stools, and I'm all dressed up in the long burgundy skirt Frank gave me for Christmas. My frizzy gray hair is swept back in a chignon, and Mother's amethyst earrings catch the light from the revolving Budweiser clock. It is a new me, matronly and going to fat, a stranger I turn away from in the mirror above the bar.

When the band played "Waltz Across Texas" early in the night, Frank led me to the dance floor and we waltzed through to the end, swaying and dipping, laughing in each other's ears. But now he is downing his third Beam ditch and pays no attention to my tapping feet.

I watch the young people boogie. A plain fat girl with long red hair is dressed in worn denim overalls, but she moves like a queen among frogs. In the dim, multicolored light, she is delicate, delicious.

"Who is that girl?" I ask Frank.

"What girl?"

"The redhead."

"How should I know?" he says. "Besides, she's fat."

"Want to dance?"

Frank looks at me as if I were crazy. "You know I can't dance to this fast stuff. I'm too old to jump around and make a fool of myself. You want to dance, you got to find yourself another cowboy."

The attractive men have girls of their own or are looking to nab some hot young dish. Melvin is dancing with Stella, "showing off" as Frank would say, but to me they are a fine-tuned duo who know each move before they take it, like a team of matched circus ponies, or those fancy ice skaters in the Olympics. They dance only with each other, and they dance all night long.

I'm getting bored, tired of whiskey and talk about cows and spotted owls and who's gone broke this week. I can hear all that on the five o'clock news. I'm beginning to feel like a wallflower at a high school sock hop (feelings I don't relish reliving). I'm making plans about going home when a tall, narrow-hipped old geezer in a flowered rayon cowboy shirt taps me on the shoulder.

"May I have this dance, ma'am?"

I look over to Frank, who is deep in conversation with Ed Snow, a logger from Seeley Lake.

"If your husband objects . . ."

"He's not my husband."

The old man is clearly drunk, but he has the courtly manner of an old-time cowboy, and he is a live and willing body.

"Sure," I say. As we head for the dance floor, I see Frank turn his head. He is watching me with a bemused and superior smile. "I'll show that bastard," I say to myself.

The loudspeaker crackles as the lead guitarist announces a medley—"A tribute to our old buddy, Ernest Tubb." The Big Sky Boys launch into "I'm Walking the Floor Over You," and the old man grabs me around the waist.

Our hands meet for the first time. I could die on the spot. If I hadn't been so mad, I would have run back to Frank because that old man's left hand was not a hand, but a claw—all shriveled up from a stroke or some birth defect, the bones dry and brittle, frozen half-shut, the skin white, flaky, and surprisingly soft, like a baby's.

His good right arm is around my waist, guiding me light but firm, and I respond as if it doesn't matter who's in the saddle. But my mind is on that hand. It twirls me and pulls me. We glide. We swing. He draws me close, and I come willingly. His whiskey breath tickles at my ear in a gasping wheeze. We spin one last time, and dip. I wonder if he will die on the spot, like Caleb. Die in midmotion, alive one minute, dead the next.

I see Caleb in the kitchen that sunstruck evening in May, come in from irrigating the east meadow and washing his hands at the kitchen sink. Stew simmers on the stove, the littlest boys play with English toy soldiers, Mozart on the stereo, a soft breeze blowing through open windows, Caleb turns to me. I will always see him turning. A shadow crosses his face. "Oh dear," he says. And Caleb falls to the maple floor, in one motion a tree cut down. He does not put out his hands to break his fall. Gone. Blood dribbles from his broken nose.

THERE IS NO going back now. We dance two numbers, the old cowboy and me, each step smoother and more carefree. We are breathing hard, beginning to sweat. The claw-hand holds me in fear and love. This high-stepping old boy is surely alive. He asks my name.

"Mady."

"Bob," he says. "Bob Beamer. They call me Old Beam." He laughs like this is a good joke. "Never knowed a Mady before. That's a new one on me."

"Hungarian," I say, wishing the subject had not come up, not mentioning the Jewish part for fear of complications. And I talk to Mother, as I do when feelings get too deep.

"Are you watching me now?" I say to the ghost of her. "It's come to this, Momushka. Are you watching me now?"

It's odd how you can talk to the ghost of someone more casually and honestly than you ever communicated when they were alive. When I talk to Caleb's ghost it is usually about work or the boys or a glimpse of beauty in nature or books. I'll spot a bluebird hovering, or young elk playing tag where our meadow joins the woods, or horses running (I always talk to Caleb about any experience I have with horses), and the words leap from my mouth, simple as pie. But when I think of my deep ecology, as the environmentalists describe it, I speak only to Mother.

I never converse with my father. He is a faded memory of heavy eyebrows, Chesterfield straights, whiskery kisses. He was a sculptor and died when I was six. Mother was five feet one, compact and full of energy as a firecracker. Every morning, in our Chicago apartment lined with books, she wove my tangled bush of black hair into French braids that pulled so tight my eyes seemed slanted. Every morning she tried to yank me into shape, and every morning I screamed so loud Mother was embarrassed to look our downstairs neighbors in the eyes.

"Be quiet," she commanded. "They will think I am a Nazi."

And there was Grandma, who lived with us and wouldn't learn English because it was a barbaric language. She would polish our upright Steinway until the piano shone like ebony. I remember endless piano lessons, Bach and Liszt. "A woman of culture," Mother said, sure of this one thing. "You will have everything."

"You sure dance American," the old cowboy says, and we are waltzing to the last dance, a song even older than my memories.

"I was in that war," he says. "Old Tubb must of been on the same troopship. We was steaming into New York and it was raining in front of us and full moon behind and I saw a rainbow at midnight like the song says, 'Out on the ocean blue!'"

Frank has moved to the edge of the floor. I see him out of the corner of my eye. We should be dancing this last one, I think, me and Frank and Old Beam. I close my eyes and all of us are dancing, like in the end of a Fellini movie—Stella and Marvin, the slick young men and blue-eyed girls, the fat red-head in her overalls, Mother, Caleb. Like Indians in a circle. Like Swede farmers, Hungarian gypsies.

Tears gather behind my closed lids. I open my eyes and rain is falling. The song goes on, sentimental and pointless. But the tears don't stop.

"It's not your fault," I say, trying to smile, choking and sputtering, laughing at the confounded way both these men are looking at me. "Thank you for a very nice dance."

I CRIED FOR MONTHS, off and on. The school board made me take sick leave and see a psychiatrist in Missoula. He gave me drugs. The pills put me to sleep and I could not think straight, just walked around like a zombie. I told the shrink I'd rather cry. "It's good for you," I said. "Cleans out the system."

I would think the spell was done and over, and then I'd see the first red-winged blackbird in February or snow melting off the meadow, or a silly tulip coming up before its time, and the water level in my head would rise, and I'd be at it again.

"Runoff fever" is what Frank calls it. The junk of your life is laid bare, locked in ice and muck, just where you left it before the first blizzard buried the whole damned mess under three feet of pure white. I can't tell you why the crying ended, but I can tell you precisely when. Perhaps one grief replaces another and the second grief is something you can fix. Or maybe it's just a change of internal weather.

Frank and I are walking along Bear Creek on a fine breezy day in April, grass coming green and thousands of the yellow glacier lilies we call dogtooth violets lighting the woods. I am picking a bouquet and bend to smell the flowers. Their scent is elusive, not sweet as roses or rank as marigolds, but a fine freshness you might want to drink. I breathe in the pleasure and suddenly I am weeping. A flash flood of tears.

Frank looks at me bewildered. He reaches for my hand. I pull away blindly, walking as fast as I can. He grabs my elbow.

"What the hell?" he says. I don't look at him.

"Would you like to get married?" He is almost shouting. "Is that what you want? Would that cure this goddamned crying?"

What can I say? I am amazed. Unaccountably frightened. "No," I blurt, shaking free of his grasp and preparing to run. "It's not you." I am sobbing now, gasping for breath.

Then he has hold of both my arms and is shaking me—a good-sized woman—as if I were a child. And that is how I feel, like a naughty girl. The yellow lilies fly from my hands.

"Stop it!" he yells. "Stop that damned bawling!"

Frank's eyes are wild. This is no proposal. I see my fear in his eyes and I am ashamed. Shame always makes me angry. I try to slap his face. He catches my hand and pulls me to his belly. It is warm. Big enough for the both of us. The anger has stopped my tears. The warmth has stopped my anger. When I raise my head to kiss Frank's mouth, I see his eyes brimming with salt.

I don't know why, but I am beginning to laugh through my tears. Laughing at last at myself.

"Will you marry me?" I stutter. "Will that cure you?"

Frank lets go of my arms. He is breathing hard and his face is flushed a deep red. He sits down on a log and wipes his eyes with the back of his sleeve. I rub at my arms.

"They're going to be black and blue."

"Sorry," he says.

I go over to Frank's log and sit at his feet, my head against his knees. He strokes my undone hair. "What about you?" he replies, question for question. "Do you want to do it?"

We are back to a form of discourse we both understand.

"I'm not sure."

"Me neither."

MAY HAS COME to Montana with a high-intensity green so rich you can't believe it is natural. I've burned the trash pile and I am done with crying. I'm back with my fifth-graders and struggling through aerobics classes three nights a week. I stand in the locker room naked and exhausted, my hips splayed wide and belly sagging as if to proclaim, Yes, I've borne four children.

A pubescent girl, thin as a knife, studies me as if I were a creature from another planet, but I don't care because one of these winters Frank and I are going to Hawaii. When I step out on those white beaches I want to look good in my bathing suit.

Fay Dell still lives up on Monture Creek. I see her out in her horse pasture winter and summer as I drive over the pass to Great Falls for a teachers' meeting or ride the school bus to basketball games in the one-room school in Ovando. Her ranch house is gone to hell, unpainted, weathered gray, patched with tarpaper. Her second husband left her, and the daughter she broke horses for is a beauty operator in Spokane. Still, there are over a dozen horses in the meadow and Fay Dell gone thin and unkempt in coveralls, tossing hay in February or fixing fence in May or just standing in the herd.

I imagine her low, sugary voice as if I were standing right by her. She is calling those horses by name. Names a child might invent.

"Sweet Baby."

"Marigold."

"Lollipop."

I want my meadow to be running with horses, as it was in the beginning—horses rolling in new grass, tails swatting at summer flies, huddled into a blizzard. I don't have to ride them. I just want their pea-brained beauty around me. I'm in the market for a quarter-horse stallion and a couple of mares. I'll need to repair my fences and build a new corral with poles cut from the woods.

My stallion will be named Rainbow at Midnight. Frank

laughs and says I should name him Beam, after my cowboy. For a minute I don't know what he's talking about, and then I remember the old man in the Awful Burger Bar. I think of Fay Dell and say, "Maybe I'll name him Frank."

Frank thinks Fay Dell is crazy as a loon. But Fay Dell knows our lives are delicate. Grief will come. Fay Dell knows you don't have to give in. Life is motion. Choose love. A person can fall in love with horses.

MOLLY GLOSS

FROM *The Jump-Off Creek*

≈≈≈≈≈≈≈

On the Fourth of July Lydia went down to Evelyn and Mike Walker's. The weather was hot and windless. She wrapped the jars of milk round with wet rags before setting them down in the hamper packed with saw chips, and wet the saw chips as well, with the clear, cold water from the Jump-Off Creek.

She had been months encountering people singly or by twos: her heart turned over when she saw there were already six men or seven standing about in the yard as she rode the mule slowly up the narrow track off the Oberfield Road. Gradually she saw among them Tim Whiteaker, Blue Odell, Mike Walker, and his hired man. The others she did not know.

It was Mr. Odell who came out to meet her. He held the mule and put a hand up for the hamper. "How are you, Mrs. Sanderson."

"Hello, Mr. Odell. This is heavy."

"I've got it."

She climbed off the mule and stiffly pulled down the skirt of her good blue dress without looking toward the several men watching her.

"I don't know if you've met all of us," Mr. Odell said gently. He was watching her as if he might be appraising her in some way.

She looked toward the others, stiffening her mouth in a deliberate smile. "No."

He pinched her elbow lightly in his hand and walked her over there. "Mrs. Sanderson," he said, gesturing vaguely. "We have a few for you to meet. This is Carroll Oberfield. He raises cattle down at the end of this road." She put her hand out and Mr. Oberfield shook it politely. He was a short man but thick-set, his hands thick from front to back and his head shaped quite round and placed solidly on the broad neck. She had it from Evelyn Walker that he was well-to-do, and that his wife lived in Maryland. They had met and married suddenly while Mr. Oberfield was on a tour East, calling on relatives. But she had been in delicate health, or of delicate constitution. She had lived with him briefly, in 1883 or '84, and not since. He spoke his wife's name occasionally. So far as anyone knew, they had never divorced.

The man who stood next to Carroll Oberfield put out his own hand abruptly. "I'm Jim Stallings, ma'am. I live over at the Goodman Station." He had a big rough face, reddish-skinned, large-featured, a smile that showed big teeth.

Beside him was an old thin bachelor, Herman Rooney. She remembered that he was the man who raised dogs. When Mr. Odell said his name, he nodded his head and took her hand lightly without shaking it. He was scrupulously clean, smelling of bath salts and shaving lotion, his mustache neatly waxed.

"You know Mike Walker, and Tim," Blue said. Neither of those two stepped up to shake her hand, they stood back and nodded. She had not seen Mr. Whiteaker since his proposal was made. She glanced toward him in stiff embarrassment. His own look was stiff too, his arm was stiff as he touched his hat.

"Do you know Otto Eckert?" That was Mike Walker's hired man. He was a bachelor, with a blond beard and pale eyes set deeply so that he seemed to peer out of the brush. He was excruciatingly shy, or he had taken a dislike of her, she could not tell which it was. She was always determinedly polite. "Hello, Mr. Eckert." He took a step backward and folded his arms up on his chest. Maybe he bobbed his head.

"Shall I bring this in the house now, ma'am?" Blue Odell lifted the hamper slightly.

"Yes. Thank you, Mr. Odell."

She followed him in, striding forthrightly while the men watched her from behind. The house was stifling hot inside. Evelyn Walker's face was scarlet and glossy.

"Oh, Mrs. Sanderson! There you are." Evelyn took hold of both her hands tightly. Her smile made a sweet bow in her wide face.

Lydia smiled herself. "I am here," she said, sighing.

The McAnallys came last, in the late morning, sitting up on a high wagon behind a pair of brown hinny mules. They lived almost to the Umatilla-Union county line. They had left there at six-forty by Avery McAnally's watch, and come the long way without stopping except as the mules required water.

Doris McAnally was fifty, her hair coarse and black, almost without gray, her face dark and creased as muslin. Three of her children were grown and married. Two were dead. Two were half-grown: a thin, shy girl, twelve; and a boy fourteen who rode Avery's horse ahead of the wagon. Doris, when she came in the hot little house, shook Lydia's hand strongly, as if she were a man, and then kissed her once firmly on a cheek. "There," she said. "That is for getting Avery to drive us here.

I haven't seen Evelyn in a year, and we wouldn't have come now, except he must get his look at the woman homesteader."

Lydia smiled briefly, sourly. "I am famous, then."

"Well, until they have all seen you once or twice, and made up their minds that you are bound to fail!" Doris McAnally's smile was sour also. She squeezed Lydia's hand in fierce, abrupt friendship.

There was no shade at all near the house. The men carried the sawhorses and the planks down under the pine trees a hundred yards away, and the food was all brought down there by slow, hot procession. Evelyn's shy boys were carried down on Mike Walker's shoulders, but they afterward hid under the sawhorse table and would not be coaxed out.

Lydia sat down too soon: the stationman, Jim Stallings, came and took up the bench next to her, where she had hoped Doris McAnally or Evelyn Walker might sit.

Mr. Stallings was talky company. Shortly she knew he was a widower twice, with eleven children farmed out to sisters-in-law in three different states. "I've lately been considering taking off the time and going round to see them all, see if they are growing up right," he said, smiling in a slow, contrite way. "I wouldn't mind marrying again," he told her, and smiled ruefully, so it was a joke, or anyway only half serious. "But you know I'd have to take all those offspring back again if I did that, so I figure I had best stay a bachelor until they are grown. There's no hope, anyway, of finding a woman who would marry a man with eleven offspring." He looked at her sidelong, with his brows pinched up in his reddish forehead.

She smiled slowly, stiffly. "Oh I'm afraid not, Mr. Stallings, no hope at all."

He nodded. "Well, I thought so," he said. "Here, Mrs. Sanderson, let's get the coffee down to our end here. I do like having the little cream to sweeten it, eh? Owing to you. I said to myself I'd got used to coffee without cream but now that I've had it again I see I was lying to myself all along." He flashed a cheerful grin.

She smiled faintly also. "I could not live long without milk," she agreed. "But I'm afraid it's sugar I miss. It is too dear for me. I have gone without for months."

"Well, sugar has gotten high right now, that's a fact. But I've heard they're going to grow it down on the Grande Ronde, and I wonder if the price of it won't come down on that account. Of course, not soon enough!"

"I don't suppose we could grow sugar beets up here."

"Oh no, ma'am, not a chance. They need those long hot summers, hot nights too. We've got but three seasons up in these mountains and that's Winter, Thaw, and August." He grinned again, enjoying what he had said. "But I guess you'd know about winters all right. It gets cold in the state of Pennsylvania, I hear."

"Yes, it's cold. But they have gotten hot long since, I imagine, and likely to stay so until October."

He smiled wider, as if he took a perverse pride in harsh weather. "Well, there's no telling here. We've had a hard frost in June and again by the end of August. Snowed once in June, I remember. There's just no telling. Soil is thin too. I don't believe it'll grow much besides tamaracks and pines and rocks."

She shook her head but she kept smiling too. She was not sure how serious he was, though the peas had not come up at all, the turnips were still small as marbles. "Oh, Mr. Stallings, I hope you're wrong. I've put so much work onto the garden."

He grinned and shook his head. "Well, I shouldn't have said it. The truth is, I've never tried to grow anything myself, except once I planted a squash and the seed rotted in the ground, but I haven't got the hand for it, I know that, and you shouldn't take me for a standard. Did you put in spuds? I believe they'll grow in rocky ground well as anything only their shapes will come out crooked. They'll stand some cold too."

"They are coming up for me."

"Well good. So you see I spoke too quick. You'll be roasting spuds on the stove next winter and I'll be eating rocks, and the needles off them tamaracks."

She laughed and sipped the sweet hot coffee. She would surely have found him wanting as a husband, or as a father, but she discovered she did not mind his company on the Fourth of July. He had an easy sociability—maybe it was the result of two wives and eleven children.

Beneath the table, one of Evelyn's boys sat on the toes of her boots, staring up under the edge of the cloth. She had not quite looked down at him. But in a while she lowered a spoon of yellow rice pudding, and when he had thought it over, he took the spoon in his own hand and licked it clean.

"Are you Junior or Charlie?" she asked him, whispering gravely.

He whispered, "Junior."

She fed him slowly, by spoonfuls, reaching below the table.

Afterward the three women walked back across the dry grass to the house, carrying up the platters and plates, and standing together in the stifling room doing up the dishes. Doris McAnally's daughter Catherine stayed in the shade under the pine trees, watching over the two Walker children, silently tempting them to play in the grass and the brush away from the benches.

Doris said in a low voice, looking out the window across the still, bright field to the trees, "Poor Catherine has got her friend already, she's not thirteen yet. I don't wonder she has turned as shy as those two little boys."

Lydia considered. Then she said, "I was twelve myself," with something like Mr. Stallings's perverse pride in bad weather.

Doris McAnally shook her head, made an unhappy clucking sound. "Well, I am over it myself, anyway, and not sorry to see it behind me."

Evelyn, in a low way, looking down at her hands wiping out bowls, told them, "I have heard if you get it early, you won't carry a baby well, but I don't know if that's true." Her eyes jumped to Lydia.

Doris shook her head again, thoughtfully. "My first girl, Muriel, was almost as early, she was thirteen, and she has two children already and never had any trouble carrying them." She looked at Lydia in her steady, unreserved manner. "Did you have that trouble, then, carrying babies?"

She liked Doris's plain straightforwardness. It made her feel steady, herself. She said, "Yes," and smiled firmly.

Doris nodded. "Do you miss having them?"

That surprised her. She looked away. "No!" Then she said slowly, stubbornly, "I am not inclined to loneliness."

"I guess I have been lonely, with five or six of my children in the same room with me," Doris said ruefully. In the moment afterward, Lydia saw the look that went between Doris and Evelyn, an understanding of something, from which she was unavoidably shut out.

Then Evelyn said suddenly, in a girlish way, impassioned, "I admire you so much, Lydia! You are brave as anyone!"

Lydia made a surprised, disbelieving sound that was not quite a laugh. But she felt better afterward. She knew there was a small, keen truth in it.

In the afternoon they lounged on the benches and on the grass in the stippled shade and listened drowsily while the men spoke of cattle prices and the progress of the depression, and the usefulness of putting up hay. Carroll Oberfield was the only one of them who had been doing it for long. He had no spring roundup to speak of. His cattle stayed all winter near the stack-yards where the hay was doled out to them on the snow. Then it was a simple matter to watch over the calving, and afterward to separate out the calves for branding. Mike Walker had bought a mower and sweep himself. The hired man, Otto, was not a range hand but a skilled hayer. The two of them had just begun to cut the wild grass hay on the big field the house sat in.

While they talked about cutting and raking and shocking hay, Tim Whiteaker sat on the grass glumly and stripped the stems of weeds with his fingers. "I guess we lost as many cows to wolfers, last winter, as to starving," he said finally, but there was little quarrel in it; it had a slow, thoughtful sound.

Carroll Oberfield scrubbed the top of his round, cropped head. "Tim," he said gently, "I suppose if most of your cows were kept down on your stackyards where you could keep an eye on them, there wouldn't be too many wolfers who would bother them." He looked faintly sorrowful. "The cattle business is bound to change, Tim. There's no stopping it, you know."

Mr. Whiteaker put his chin down. Then Blue Odell began to smile slowly without looking at Tim. "He knows it, Carroll. He just doesn't like it yet."

Mr. Whiteaker shifted his place on the grass and gave Blue a ducking look and finally he smiled a little, or grimaced—it was a deepening of the long creases that framed his mouth. "You know what they say about old dogs," he said unhappily.

The McAnallys left early in the afternoon. Doris gave Eve-lyn and then Lydia a short, strong hug and a sorry smile, and when her husband drove her off in the wagon she looked back without smiling or waving. Herman Rooney left too, and after that the spirit was gone out of the party. The men broke down the tables and benches and carried the planks up to Mike Walker's barn. Evelyn and Lydia waded in the creek with the two little boys, who were turning over rocks and undertaking to catch crawdads in a tin can. Blue Odell was the only one of the men who walked back down under the trees where they were.

"If you want company, Mrs. Sanderson, I can wait and ride you home."

"No. Thank you, Mr. Odell."

"Well, all right then. We'll go on. Tim has got to be back up to the log camp tonight." He had been squatting down along the muddy bank next to their shoes. He stood up and touched his hat. "Thanks, Mrs. Walker."

"You're welcome." Evelyn stood with the edge of her skirt floating out on the water, and the palms of her hands flat on her hips, smiling in a slightly shy way.

They watched him walk away. Then Lydia began again, turning over stones in the slow, cold creek.

"You know, Mr. Odell is Indian," Evelyn said softly.

In the evening, when the air cleared and became cool, Lydia walked out for Rollin and saddled him and led him back to the house. She was the last to leave. Mike Walker carried out the hamper and stood aside awkwardly while Evelyn came for a quick rigid embrace. When Lydia had climbed up on the saddle, he set the box in front of her. He was a big man, he reminded her in that way of Lars. But his face was strong and bony. He had a habit of looking at his wife, following her with his eyes. When he stood back from Lydia, he looked at Evelyn and seemed to wait.

Deliberately, Lydia said, "Thank you, Mr. Walker. I always enjoy our visits."

His big brows rose up into his forehead. "I do also, ma'am." He patted the shoulder of the mule.

"Good-by, Mrs. Sanderson," Evelyn said in a stout way,

smiling. She had her arms folded on her bosom. Her wide face looked girlish in the sunset light.

When Rollin had taken her a short way down the road, she turned and lifted a hand to Evelyn. Evelyn held one of the little boys up in her arms. She shifted his weight onto her hip and waved slowly. She was still holding her brave smile. There had been a flag hung down from the eave of their house, in front of the south-facing window. Mike Walker was taking it down, reaching up to get it off the nails.

TERESA JORDAN

BONES

At Laguna, when someone dies, you don't "get over it"
by forgetting; you "get over it" by remembering.

—*Leslie Marmon Silko*

≈≈≈≈≈≈≈≈

It is hot August, high noon under an airless sky, and my father and a hired hand have brought in a sick bull for doctoring. I am four years old, maybe five, and I sit on a corral rail to watch. I smell horse sweat and the black, watery manure that the bull swipes with his tail in an arc across his ass. Dust cakes in my nostrils and around the edges of my mouth. I want to go back to the coolness of the house, but I also want to watch. I rub my mouth with the back of my hand and stay.

The bull is on the fight and he paws the ground. His eyes are dull and green with sickness, and when he throws his head and bellers, long strands of snot stream from his mouth and fly back across his shoulders, raising a few of the flies that blanket his rump.

When my father rides into the corral, the bull tries to take him. My father pivots his horse out of the way and ropes the bull, pulls him up short to the snubbing post and dallies around. He passes the end of the rope to the hired man, who has come into the corral on foot. Once the bull is secure, my father dismounts, ties his horse to a fence post, and returns with boluses and a syringe full of antibiotic.

The bull grumbles, fights the rope, snorts. But he is sick and he grows calmer with fatigue. My father jabs the needle into the animal's thigh. The bull rears back against the rope. The wraps on the post slip. The bull breaks loose, snot flying in an arc, his beller blue and loud.

From the fence I watch as he takes my daddy down. The world erupts in dust and blood. The bull is roaring, groaning, grinding, someone is yelling, my father is a tiny spider of flailing arms and legs.

I hear the hired hand crying over and over, "Oh my God, oh my God, oh my God." He tries to snub the bull again but he might as well attempt to drag a mountain from its plain. Finally, he gains a wrap of rope and my father rolls free. I watch as he crawls across the corral, climbs the fence hand over hand, his heavy legs dangling uselessly beneath him. He casts himself over the top rail, crashes in a grunt of dust on the other side. The bull bellers and falls silent. The dust settles. Everything is perfectly still.

My father was loaded onto a door and taken to town in the back of a pickup. A few weeks later he came back, and though he walked with a limp, he took up his regular chores. The bull, too, recovered. He was a quality bull and we kept him until he was too old to service cows. Then we shipped him to the packers.

We. A few weeks ago, I learned that this happened before I was born. I have carried it like a memory, but it's not a memory; it's a story I've heard, fleshed out by details told down through the years. I'm amazed. I cannot imagine this event without also imagining myself within it, watching.

FEW OCCUPATIONS are as physically threatening as arid-country cattle ranching. Professional football is; roughnecking on an oil rig; logging. And like other occupations that depend on the body yet place it constantly in peril, cattle ranching breeds an attitude toward danger of both reverence and disdain.

Our neighbor Buddy Hirsig always helped us brand. One time his horse fell on him and broke his ankle as we brought cattle into the corral. "Do you mind if I rope today?" he asked my father. "I can't walk so good and I'd rather stay horseback."

"Oh hell," my father answered. "We have plenty of help. Go on home." But Buddy insisted on staying, and no one was surprised. He roped calf after calf with unerring accuracy and only when the day's work was finished did he cut off his boot and head to town to get his ankle casted.

I remember a term: major plaster. Minor injuries—a broken wrist, a sprained ankle, a cut requiring stitches—were too insignificant to mention. Major plaster meant serious injury, something that would take months, even years, to heal. A cast on an arm didn't count. One from toe to ass did. So did body casts or almost anything requiring traction. Community gatherings nearly always found someone in major plaster, and Iron Mountain was not a large community. If everyone came together at the same time, including visiting aunts and the Chesers' basset hound, they might have numbered sixty.

Each new badge of plaster met with predictable banter. "You *needed* a vacation." "That's one way to get sympathy." "It's about time you broke something. The doc's youngest son just graduated high school." (Dr. Klein was the bone doctor in Cheyenne and we were convinced our debilities paid for his children's Ivy League educations.)

The quips and wisecracks were a lie, a safe way to say "I'm sorry." Injury meant doctors' bills—huge doctors' bills—often in a time of high interest rates, low cattle prices, and drought. Injury meant one less person to do the work. Injury meant more strain on the marriage. Injury meant new insult to a body already prematurely old. And injury meant pain, acute pain for a while and then chronic pain that flared each time the barometer fell. But injury also promised resurrection. If you were injured, at least you weren't dead.

ANOTHER MEMORY. I am eight years old and wearing a lime-green tutu when Harold, our foreman, comes through the door from the thunderstorm outside to tell my mother that Dad has broken his leg. His horse slipped on a bridge. I am to be in a ballet recital that night in town. "What about me?" I ask.

"We'll try to make it on time," she says.

A hired hand's smashed thumb a few days before has wiped us out of codeine, so she gives my father aspirin before they load him on the door. This time they put him in the back of our station wagon. During the two-hour ride through mud and rain to town, he calls me his ballerina cowgirl and recites Kipling to pass the time:

> *Yes, Din! Din! Din!*
> *You Lazarushian-leather Gunga Din!*
> *Though I've belted you and flayed you,*
> *By the livin' Gawd that made you,*
> *You're a better man than I am, Gunga Din!*

I danced that night, though my father didn't see me. Both bones in his lower leg had been crushed and four hours of surgery left him with a three-inch pin in his calf. The bones had been broken so many times before, they wouldn't knit. He wore a hip cast for a year and a half, and a brace for another year. With the cast, he couldn't ride, he couldn't drive, and he couldn't climb our narrow stairway, so he slept on the Hide-A-Bed in the living room.

He could weld and he worked long hours in the shop, the plastered leg stretched out in front of him. We accused him of welding every piece of metal on the ranch together, and in fact he soon ran out of work. He bought a Heathkit and built an FM radio. Diagrams, tiny wires, and transistors were scattered across the dining-room table for weeks and he soldered patiently. When he finished, the radio worked fine, but we were too far out in the country to pick up any signals.

Once the cast came off, he bought a therapeutic boot to which weights could be attached. Each night he sat in his shorts on the island in the kitchen and strapped it on. He'd straighten the leg again and again until his T-shirt was soaked with sweat. I remember the grind of his teeth as he worked at the weights, and the way tears squeezed out of the corners of his eyes.

YOU DID WHAT you had to and went on. Accommodation, not much talked about, was key. People in Iron Mountain still talk of Mrs. Steele, who ran a nearby ranch by herself after her husband went crazy. A horse fell on her and broke her arm. The arm never bent right after that, and she had trouble combing her hair, so she wore it cropped short, like a man's.

A cowhand's walk, shaped by years of damage and recovery, is a study in accommodation. The body cants forward from the waist, the lower back fuses, the hips stiffen, the walk becomes awkward, the head seems to settle into the shoulders. "It's a kink in the neck," one old-timer told me, trying to describe his own gait, "and a limp in every limb."

Not all accommodation is physical. One night, when my father was rehabilitating his leg and had finished eighty repetitions with fifty pounds, he joked to my mother, "See that? It's almost good enough to break again." Through two and a half years, she had been calm, caring, full of humor. She had chauffeured him to the fields each morning and waited until frustration made him ask to go back home. She had arranged her work in the house around his presence. She had made up his bed on the sofa. She had carted the things he couldn't carry, accomplished the chores he couldn't do. All this without complaint. But that night she turned to him. "Larry," she said without a smile, "break it again and I'll treat you like a horse."

The psychology of accommodation is letting things go. "Sooner or later," one woman told me, "the other boot is going to drop. No sense worryin' until you hear the crash." Then, she might have added, you pick up the pieces. Buddy Hirsig bought a dirt bike to use around the ranch. The first time he chased a cow, the bike hit a rock and he catapulted over the top. He was traveling fifteen or twenty miles an hour when he lit on his hands. They swelled up like hams. He couldn't hold a fork, turn a doorknob, work a button. Glenna, his wife, didn't mind dressing him or feeding him or even attending to his personal needs. What she minded, she said, was helping him smoke. The ability to mine calamity for punch lines may be the most important accommodation of all.

IT NEVER OCCURRED to me that the men and women I grew up with were courageous. Israeli writer and war correspondent Yaël Dayan, the daughter of General Moshe Dayan, once wrote that her father could not be called courageous because he had no fears to overcome. As a child, it seemed to me that my people were similarly fearless, and being fearless, they were invulnerable. I was not alone in this illusion. Carol Horn, a rancher in North Park, Colorado, told me about watching her grandmother get thrown off a hay rake by a runaway team. "Here she was," Carol recalled, "in her sixties, being rolled around under the rake. I wasn't even concerned about it, because it was Grandma. Grandma took care of everything. She had that much control."

In this world of bashed and battered bodies, I felt safe. Injury was real, but it didn't seem to matter much. The injured could rise, phoenixlike, from the ashes of catastrophe, and their feats of recuperation still amaze me. When a horse fell on my seventy-two-year-old Great-aunt Marie and broke her pelvis in three places, the doctors told her she would never ride again. Two months later, she proved them wrong. Merrill Farthing was in his eighties when he fell on a fence spike and punctured his lung. When he finally agreed to go to town, he had double pneumonia and the doctors advised the family to hover near. Three weeks later, Merrill left the hospital and soon returned to the fence line.

With such models around me, I wanted my chance. By the time I entered fourth grade, I had started cutting deals with God. Each night before I went to sleep, I would pray, "Please, God, let me break my leg tomorrow." I dreamed of the kids at school scribbling their names on my cast, but more than that, I wanted the badge of plaster, the proof that the horses I rode were as tough as those of the men, that I wasn't afraid, that I could "take it."

But I didn't break my leg. So I upped the ante. "Please, God. If you'll break my leg tomorrow, I'll be nice to my brother for a *whole year*." And then, when my limbs remained discouragingly sound, "Please, God, break my leg tomorrow or I won't believe in you anymore." And finally, "Okay, okay, I'll settle for a broken arm. Are you up there, God? Are you listening?"

I THOUGHT my people were immortal. Deep down, I had always understood that ranch accidents could be tragic. I knew that Biddy Bonham's father had been killed when his horse tripped in a gopher hole, and that old Mr. Shaffer died when he fell off a haystack. But these deaths were so distant from me they hardly seemed real. Then, when tragedy struck close to home, it had nothing to do with the roughness of our work. "The danger," my mother used to say, "is never where you think it is." Which was her way of saying, "Look behind."

The night my mother died of an aneurysm at the University Hospital in Denver, my father, brother, and I returned to the Brown Palace Hotel. It was ten o'clock at night, maybe midnight, and we called room service. I ordered vichyssoise, my favorite Brown Palace dish since childhood, and when it came, I took the silver covering off the china bowl. I sprinkled the soup with lime, as I always did, and I remember gazing at the perfect little drops of juice, floating on the surface like tiny shimmering planets. I couldn't get any further and my father, too, pushed his dinner away.

"'If you can make one heap of all your winnings,'" he said at last, quoting Kipling, who always seemed to come to him in crisis,

> *And risk it on one turn of pitch and toss*
> *And lose and start again at your beginnings*
> *And never breathe a word about your loss . . .*

And then he put his face in his hands and broke down. I remember the hugeness of him hunched in his chair. I remember a single tear breaking through the dam of his fingers, winding its way down his broad weathered cheek to catch in his quivering mustache.

WHEN YOU WORK with a young colt, there comes a day when you take him up to the bones. In the wide-open spaces of ranch country animal remains are common. A colt will spook at them, even when the bones are decades old. Unless you work to overcome that fear, the colt will always shy away. There will be places in the world the colt can't walk. But if you take time, urge the colt closer and closer, not denying its fear but not turning away from it either, the horse will eventually approach what scares him. He will see that bones are just bones. He will move in the world more freely.

Ranchers walk up to most bones. They look physical danger right in the eye and don't blink. But there are other bones that scare them. For my family, the pile we shied away from was grief. Everything in my background prepared me to deal with physical pain. Nothing prepared me for emotional loss.

When my father worked his repetitions with the leg weight, he let the tears flow freely because he knew, when the session was over, he could turn to us with a wry smile. But he never again shared his grief with us after we left that hotel room. We went through the automatic motions of a funeral, returned to the ranch, and sorted through my mother's belongings. Within days, we had discarded almost everything that might remind us of her.

Long before the pain had started to abate, we declared it over. "It's time," my father said, "to rejoin the human race." I returned to college. My father met and soon married a woman who looked exactly like my mother. The marriage was painful for both partners and ended in divorce. And for years I spent so much energy denying my own longing for the dead that I hardly had energy for the living.

If any of us had broken a leg, we would have taken all the time the leg required. If the bone didn't knit in six months, we would have given it twelve. And if it still wasn't sound, we would have strapped on a brace. We might have asked each other, "How's that leg?" But we didn't ask, "How's that loneliness?" We tried to put our grief behind us, but we had only shied away from it. We started walking before we had healed. For years we hardly mentioned my mother's name. And we soon found there were places we didn't dare walk.

I REMEMBER NOTHING of my mother's funeral, absolutely nothing, until the end when we were leaving the cemetery. A neighbor, Sandy Hirsig, Glenna and Buddy's daughter, came up to me. She was a few years my junior, but I had always felt a particular connection with her—she, too, was close to her mother. She approached me just as I was about to get into the limousine, and she hugged me. I had this curious sense of looking down on the two of us as if from above and thinking: She is the only one who could possibly understand.

And then, when just a few years later Sandy was killed in a brutal accident on the Iron Mountain road, I couldn't sleep for nights. She and her mother had been driving to the ranch, and I could almost hear the intense conversation before they came around a corner and slammed into a snowplow; my mother and I always had our very best conversations on that fifty-mile stretch of road. I wrote the Hirsigs the polite, formal letter of sympathy I had been trained to write, and I never told even the man I was living with about the accident, though he was a sensitive man. I was too afraid that, in the telling, I wouldn't take it well—I would break down.

A few months later, I returned to Wyoming and visited the Hirsigs. I wanted to tell them what I hadn't been able to mention in the letter—how Sandy came up to me at my mother's funeral and gave me the single moment of true solace that penetrated that horrible affair. But I couldn't tell them. We talked for an hour and I never mentioned Sandy's name. Buddy Hirsig had ridden all day with a broken ankle at our branding, but I was afraid to tell either him or Glenna how much their daughter touched me. I was too afraid of making them sad, of challenging their ability to take it, of challenging mine.

≈

When you take a colt near the bones, every muscle in his body is posed in opposition. He may, at your urging, nudge forward, but his energy is entirely consumed by the posture of escape. If fear overcomes him, he will bolt blindly, crashing into a fence or stumbling over a bank. But if he inches up to the bones, bit by bit and soft assurance by assurance, he will smell them, his ears will twitch a time or two and then fall back in bored relaxation. At that point his whole body will relax, visibly and at once, and in a moment he will be focused on the outside world again, anxious to get on with the rest of the journey.

IN EIGHTEEN YEARS of intermittent ranch work, I never had a serious injury: no major plaster. Recently, though, I had a physical and I was asked to fill out a health questionnaire. When I met with the doctor, she started asking about my relationships with men. I answered the first couple of questions perfunctorily, but after the third, I asked her why she cared. "Seven brain concussions," she read off my list of injuries. "A broken cheekbone, a broken rib, bruised kidneys . . ."

How often, I thought later, she must read physical scars for the emotional ruin they hide. How often her questions must probe the deepest shame. But as I explained my own history, I recognized a hint of pride in my voice. I had paid my dues in the world of work. I could "take it." Sometimes, now, physical endurance seems the easy part, but it holds lessons for me if I will only listen.

Almost every ranchstead is littered with bones. The skull of a bull, a deer, or an antelope tacked up over a gate or barn door, a pile of elk antlers by the shed, a cow pelvis in the garden. When you find a bone—a buffalo skull, a bobcat jaw, the precise, tiny foot of a badger—you bring it home. The larger piles you leave alone. Skeletons mark the method of dying, at least until time and coyotes rearrange the evidence. A small pelvis hung up in a larger one: breech birth. Backbone downhill, head flung upward gasping for one last breath: poison weed.

Even to my house in the city, I drag home bones: a deer head for the hearth, a bull skull for the entryway. There's a stark beauty to bones, bleached white by the sun. Bones are as hard as rock and as fragile as rock. They crack, fissure, shatter, and as they wear to dust, they take us with them, both column and conduit of our own evolution. In the bloodline drawn by landscape, all bones are ancestral. Our homage is sincere and yet irreverent, a wry celebration of the fact that we still wrap our own bones with skin.

JUDY BLUNT

LEAVING HOME

As a child I watched my mother's face
like Father watched the sky, those days
the wheat rang hard and red and nothing
slept or left the shade for hours.
I memorized starched lines, her back,
the brief angle of her lap, the quick touch
of hands tempered thin and tough, sometimes
warm, always tired with raising five children
and a farmer. She clicked and snapped
the world to order, raised me believing
the dryland truths, the virtue of storms
that shelled grain yet filled reservoirs,
and she believed that hard lessons last,
that seedlings beaten down by wind and hail
grow back on the strength of one good leaf,
drop seeds with built-in memories of pain,

until generations of plants grow twisted
together, sheltered in some safe spot.

I was 16 the last time my mother went beyond
words, heeled around and swung her hand
so hard my glasses flew against the cupboard
and I came back senseless, one fist rising
to block, the other, punch drunk, pitched
blind, hit with a soft pop and then
nothing. Between us the air hummed
like power lines, thick air that held her
numb against the drainboard, lips
drawn thin over words
that came out noise.
                              At the sink
in that kitchen I have seen my mother
find paring knives buried under plates
with the same sharp suck of breath,
the same hiss of recognition
for rinse water burling red and pink,
for threads of blood set loose.

What comes of winter

mornings, breaking one last
egg into flour, hotcakes, brown
sugar syrup, some blizzard still
pushing forty below at the door,
roads sifted fencepost deep

and phone lines down so long
it doesn't matter. At least
you're warm, the men say, inside
to eat and thaw sweaty
ice off scarves and plaid
Scotch caps, ear tips puffed
wet and black as old fruit
rinds.
    She thinks to kill
another barren hen for stewing
but all afternoon the men are busy
breaking trails to stranded cows.
In the time that plates congeal
and babies nap she pries
the stiff cat, frozen pool
of urine off the front porch
window ledge. She thinks to close
its eyes but can't
calm down for hours, pacing
attic rooms where rows
of women torn and taped
to wallpaper flaps seem
to listen, nodding lips
and long cigarettes
in the draft, and she talks
and shares the final drag
off the last butt scavenged
from the gas man in December
when the dryer broke.
                        But now
the diapers dry for days
on lines strung tight through
rooms with very little air

and two solemn babies draped
in quilts drop clothespins
down the heater vent. Another,
fist-sized, rides her pelvic
bowl like a stoneboat, smug
persistent,
swelling up like wild laughter
that comes of winter mornings, breaking.

AT THE STOCKMAN BAR,
WHERE THE MEN FALL IN LOVE,
AND THE WOMEN JUST FALL

Black Velvet shots and water back,
I tell the creep who tries one sleazy
hand on my ass, but I'll buy my own—
tougher than hammered owl shit fella,
that's me, and he says he hears a Real
Woman calling for him somewhere
down the bar. The shot glass wobbles
in my fingers until I'm safe
at my own back table, transparent
in the crowd. By now they're paired off
and packed to static frenzy, stomping
boots and upraised arms fanning high
clouds of smoke against the ceiling,
foam and ice cubes slung around, so
damn much fun. The lead man's singing
Crackers in Her Cleavage, a love song

I think, and one girl Gets Down Bad,
her own long hair in her mouth,
dancing like a dog shakes a rat.

The man she's with already has his
shirt off, and he whips it over
their heads so hard the pearl snaps
crack and pop like fingers will, but
louder. I look away when Creep
walks by and prods my ashtray. Blow
ten bucks on perfume then waste it
with a ten-cent cigarette, he says,
says he could teach me a few things.
I waltz with someone like my dad,
then grab my coat and find my way
outside, the pull of booze and music
dragging stars down too low and hot
to wish on, lifting the street up
to meet my heels. I smell it first,
Limburger cheese, then see the car
festooned with toilet paper and stupid
shaving cream words that don't make sense.
Balloons bob and weave from the back
bumper, caught like a bride's bouquet.

I could take them all, but I pick
a blue one, break its string, and let it
rise over the street lights, balanced
on the breeze and fat with half-notes
from the Cracker Song, playing somewhere
for the third time, but I hear
Moon River and Bad Moon Rising,
or Once in a Blue Moon and laugh

straight up as far as I can see,
stepping back to watch it,
until something hard jams me down—
a fist, a fence—it doesn't
really matter. I can wedge my mouth
against the chain links and scream
at the couples grinding against
their car doors, but after midnight,
we all need help. The dirt is cold.
The clearest things I see are light-years
away. I can find the Seven Sisters but
I know they're just a part of Taurus,
I know these things. I know so many
useless things, like blood looks black
in the moonlight, and hanging on
the wire I think, I'm only one
more person, and it's only one
hour into Sunday, and I think
if that balloon doesn't come back
right now, and show me how it's done,
I'll never make it out. By God,
I'll never find my way again.

CYRA McFADDEN

FROM *Rain or Shine:*
  A Family Memoir

≈≈≈≈≈≈≈≈

When they were young, my parents believed they were indestructible, so fast and flashy nothing could touch them. Cy was a lady-killer, a small, natty man whose riverboat-gambler good looks struck women down like lightning bolts. My mother, the former Patricia Montgomery, was a vaudeville dancer, the star of the St. Louis Municipal Opera in the late twenties. When she married Cy, she turned trick rider in the rodeo equivalent of halftime shows. You can take the girl out of show biz, but you cannot take a little girl from Little Rock, or Paragould, which is close enough, and turn her into a house pet.

At least not Pat, with her performer's ego, her longing to shine. Tiny-waisted and white-skinned, her black hair slicked to her cheekbones in sculptured spit curls, she was Cy's equal in recklessness, matching him drink for drink, seduction for seduction, irrational impulse for irrational impulse. Together they shot off sparks and left behind scorched earth, and if they ever thought about how their travels might end, they didn't waste much time on sober reappraisal.

They had more pressing concerns, the main one how to get to the next town with little money, a child, and hangovers. My father's schedule took him from Butte, Montana, to Salt Lake City, Utah, from Puyallup, Washington, to Baton Rouge, Louisiana, and sometimes the travel time was a couple of days. We lived in a 1937 blue Packard, spending endless, viciously hot days in it going from Canada to New Mexico and back up to Wyoming, Utah, and Idaho—wherever there were rodeos. We slept in that car, ate breakfast, lunch, and dinner in it, sang along with the Sons of the Pioneers in it, quarreled in it. My parents must have made love in it, when I was asleep and the Packard parked behind the bleachers in some small-town fairground, waiting for daylight and the rodeo. Between them, there was a strong erotic pull. They walked with their hips touching and had flaming fights over each other's real and imagined flirtations.

Raised on a North Dakota farm, one of nine children of a French Canadian family, Cy had been a law student, a self-taught musician who led dance bands and played in movie-theater pit orchestras, a boxer and a radio personality in Billings and Salt Lake City. In both towns, he was a celebrity, known as "The Singing Announcer" because until a tonsillectomy put an end to this facet of his career, he sang with his bands.

The huge leather scrapbooks he kept all his life document some of these successes; but he claimed triumphs in everything he did, telling a writer for a trade paper called *Hoofs and Horns*, early in his rodeo career, that he'd won a Golden Gloves championship when he was boxing and given a recital at Carnegie Hall as a child prodigy violinist.

How much of that interview is true, I don't know, nor do I think Cy did. For much of his life, he was engaged in the game of inventing himself—adding to what was true what was desirable, stirring counterclockwise and serving up the mix. He must have swallowed much of it himself.

What is fact is that after leaving law school with a theatrical troupe, he ended up, in his early twenties, in Great Falls, where he became a radio announcer and moonlighted as a musician. His hillbilly band, reported in the Great Falls *Tribune*, drew 14,600 letters to the local radio station in six and a half weeks. This was roughly the population of Great Falls at the time. It must have been a letter-writing town.

After two months in St. Paul, Minnesota, as "announcer and entertainer," Cy came back to Great Falls, and in 1929 was leading a trio during the dinner hour at the Hotel Rainbow and picking up other band jobs around town. "The Green Mill gardens, dinner and dancing resort on the paved extension of Second Avenue North, will be formally opened tonight. Eddie Stamy will be director of the orchestra that will play for at least four dances a week. Cy Taillon, Minneapolis, who handles the drums, violin, bells, piano, and most anything else, is charged with providing the sweet numbers."

"Cy Taillon and his orchestra will entertain you again at the Crystal Ballroom . . . Featuring 'The Crystal Ballroom Red Jackets.' "

"Tree Claim Park presents Cy Taillon and his 'Rocky Mountaineers.' Master of Ceremonies, Waddie Ginger, Admission 50 cents."

To the list of instruments he played, another ad for a resort added xylophone, banjo, and "relatively smaller string instruments."

The woman who became Cy's second wife got her first glimpse of him during those days. She was a schoolgirl. He was playing one of the twin pianos in the window of a music store.

Their eyes met, she told me, and it was Romeo and Juliet, only more intense. If my mother got in their way for twelve years, that was only because Dorothy was fourteen at the time. My father also had his hands full with other women.

A personal archivist, Cy kept copies of every letter he ever wrote, including one to the city attorney of Great Falls in those years. A woman was harassing him, he complained, accusing him of being the third party in a "spiritual triangle" and fathering her three children by remote control. "Further proof she is hopelessly irrational," he wrote, "is her obsession that I have money."

In my teens, I met a woman who knew Cy in Great Falls. "He was the most beautiful man who ever lived," she said. "You don't look very much like him."

She wasn't rude so much as disappointed. I offered to say hello to him for her.

"He wouldn't remember me. There were too many of us. I'll tell you what, though, say hello for the Willis sisters and let him wonder which one."

The student's pilot license Cy took out in 1933 lists his age as twenty-five, weight 139 pounds, height five feet seven and three-quarters inches, hair black, and eyes gray-green. It doesn't describe the movie-star handsomeness of his regular features, his olive skin, his wavy black hair, and those eyes—as slate green as the ocean, and when he was angry, as cold.

He looked enough like Robert Taylor to double for him, later, in the riding scenes of the movie *Billy the Kid*.

Rodeo stock producer Leo Cremer tapped him for the crow's nest in the early thirties. Cy left radio for what he said was a three months' leave and never went back. Cremer was famous for his Brahma bulls, whose average weight was three-quarters of a ton: Black Devil, Yellow Jacket, Deer Face, Tornado, Joe Louis, Dynamite. He also had good instincts when he signed my father, despite Cy's reputation as a hard drinker and man-about-town.

Because he'd been attracted to it since his childhood, "Roman riding" the horses on the family farm, Cy was a natural for rodeo. He'd mainly swallowed a lot of dust. After he broke a shoulder, he gave up any ambition to be another Casey Tibbs.

He had cards printed, giving his address as the Mint Cafe, Great Falls, and offering "a New Technique in Rodeo Announcing."

A rodeo announcer keeps up a running commentary on the cowboys and the way they fare in the events, calf roping, Brahma-bull riding, bareback and saddle-bronc riding, and, more recently, team roping. Cy was the best, a showman who could play a crowd the way he played stringed instruments, by instinct and with perfect pitch. At the piano, he held to the theory that the more keys you used, the better you played. At the mike, he also used the equivalent of all the pedals. "Ladies and gentlemen, this next waddie broke his wrist and three ribs down in Abilene a few weeks ago, and now he's back in competition. That's called courage in my book. Tiny Rios out of Tulsa, Oklahoma, on a mean hunk of horseflesh called Son of Satan. . . . Let's give him a little encouragement."

From his law school days, when he won prizes in debate, he had a sophisticated vocabulary. He used it, never talking down to his audience of cowboys, stock producers and their wives, ranchers and rodeo-loving kids. Nor did he often forget a cowboy's name, or where he came from, or how he fared in previous rodeos, no matter how chronic a loser the cowboy. So they loved him, even when he borrowed their prize money or their wives. He always paid the money back, and the wives straggled home, moony but unrepentant, on their own.

The reviews began to come in early. Cy never got a bad

one, any more than he ever took an unflattering photograph, or if there were any, they never wound up in his scrapbooks, a researcher's nightmare because he clipped articles without the name of the newspaper or magazine and frequently without the date. Sometimes he clipped only the paragraphs that mentioned his name, which he underlined. The articles described him as silver-voiced, golden-voiced, gold-and-silver-voiced, crystal-voiced, honey-voiced. They talk about his clear, bell-like voice. They run out of adjectives and call him the Voice.

In them, he's also spare, handsome, and hard as nails; lean, wiry, and a natty dresser; suave and dapper; the man who knows rodeo; the possessor of an encyclopedic memory. Said one writer, consigned to anonymity by my father's clipping methods, "Taillon keeps the show going like a golf ball swatted down a concrete highway."

Rodeo was used to announcers who treated the sport as a Wild West show, part vaudeville, part circus. Cy dignified it, with his ten-dollar words, his impeccably tailored, expensive suits, and his insistence that the cowboys were professional athletes. When he intoned "Ladies and gentlemen," women became ladies and men became gentlemen; the silver-tongued devil in the announcer's box, as often as not a rickety structure over the chutes and open to the rain, spoke with unmistakable authority. In a world where pretending to be an insider earns the outsider dismissal faintly underlined with menace, he counted as a working cowboy, though he earned his living with his mouth rather than his muscle.

Like the contestants, he lived from rodeo to rodeo, making just enough money to keep us in gas and hamburgers. He worked in all weather: heat, cold, freak rainstorms that turned arenas into mudholes. If he had extra money, everybody drank, and when we rented a room in a motor court, a luxury, cowboys bunked on the floor with their saddles for pillows. Despite his slight frame, he never hesitated about piling in when there was a fight; you had to get through him to get to somebody bigger, and because he was light on his feet and fast with his fists, few made it. Someone wading into my father also had to take on my mother, not one to sit on the sidelines letting out ladylike cries of dismay. A hundred-pound woman can do substantial damage with teeth, fingernails, and a high-heeled shoe, and Pat had an advantage going in. No man would hit her back, though she was swearing ripely and trying to maim him, because no self-respecting Western man hits a lady.

The bars were my parents' living rooms. We spent our nights in them, our mornings in the Packard or a motor court —with Cy and Pat sleeping off their headaches and begging me to stop that goddamn humming—and our afternoons at the Black Hills Roundup or the Snake River Stampede, rodeos that blur into one.

Pat sat in the bleachers, if she wasn't trick riding. I sat in the crow's nest with Cy, sometimes announcing the Grand Entry or the national anthem for him or testing the p.a. system. "One two three four, testing testing testing." I wanted to be a movie star. Cy said you had to start somewhere.

The high point of those afternoons, for me, was when Cy played straight man for the rodeo clowns, who sometimes railed at him because he wouldn't allow off-color material, the crude jokes that were a staple. Not present just to entertain, the clowns also divert the bulls or horses when a rider is down. The cowboys and the crowd love and respect them. So did I, and when my father bantered with them from the stand, he took on added luster.

Pinky Gist and his two mules, Mickey and Freckles, George Mills, John Lindsay, the great Emmett Kelly, and a dozen others—sad-faced men in baggy pants, absurdly long shoes, and long underwear, out in the arena, and my father aiding and abetting them:

"Eddie, there are ladies present here today. Would you mind pulling up your pants?"

"Sure, Cy." Eddie did a flawless double take, pulled his pants up and doffed his porkpie hat to my father. When he lifted the hat, his pants fell down again, revealing long johns with a trapdoor.

"I'm sorry, Cy. I was asleep in the barrel over there and a train hit me. It tore the buttons off my suspenders."

"That wasn't a train, Eddie," Cy said, kingly at the microphone. "That was a two-thousand-pound Brahma bull, and there's another one coming out of the chute right now."

Eddie screamed hoarsely, stumbled across the arena, clutched at his pants and fell over his shoes. "I wondered why I never heard the whistle."

No matter how many times I heard these routines, they never paled for me. Such is the power of early-childhood conditioning that I still love slapstick; mine is the lone voice laughing at a club act in which the comic gets hit with a pie.

I'm less taken with exhibition roping. The great trick-rope artist on the circuit was Monty Montana, a handsome man who could do anything with a rope, including roping Cy Taillon's daughter. On my father's command, I pretended to be a calf; bolted through a string barrier and into the arena; ran like mad until Monty lassoed me, ran down his rope, threw me and tied me. He never hurt me. The crowd loved it. I hated it.

Not to be upstaged, Pat sometimes followed with her breakneck trick riding—headstands at the gallop, vaulting to the ground from a standing position in the saddle. She was so fearless that the cowboys gathered at the fence to watch her, wondering if this would be the night Cy's crazy wife killed herself.

I still have part of her trick-riding costume, a red Spanish bolero with white scrollwork, silver spurs with tooled-leather straps, and canted-heel boots. The full-sleeved white satin shirt disappeared, as did the high-waisted red pants that would fit a twelve-year-old boy. Pat's life in those years is recorded in a few bits of her rodeo wardrobe, her own mutilated scrapbook, in which she also obliterated the supporting cast, and not much else.

Constants from those countless rodeos: the smell of sweat and horses that rose out of the open stalls, just below the booth; the fine dust that floated over the arena, powdering evenly cowboys, animals, the crowd, my father's suit, and his pointy-toed boots; the haze of cigarette smoke over the stands; the whinnying of horses, the bawling of calves and howling of dogs, left in pickup trucks out in the parking lot.

Always present too were the high voices of women, wives and girlfriends and rodeo groupies, the "buckle bunnies" who were, and are still, the wives' natural enemies. They set the standards of female dress, with their starched curls and their pinkish pancake makeup, ending in a line at the chin. The buckle bunnies wore tight frontier pants and tooled-leather belts, into which they tucked their nailhead-studded shirts. One who was always around, and whom I admired, had a belt with beads spelling out her name, just above her neat rump: "Bonnee."

As for the wives, they were a tight-knit and wary bunch, sitting in the stands afternoon and night, watching their husbands compete and watching the single women through the smoke from their cigarettes. Those that had children left them sleeping in the trailers, and protected their primary interests. Cowboys then, and cowboys now, bear watching.

If the rodeo was in some two-dog town, we might be there for only one daytime and one evening performance, and then it was back on the road again, with a tour of the local bars in between. These had a certain classic similarity—a jukebox playing cowboy songs about lost love and lost illusions, beer signs with neon waterfalls, and on the wall the head of a deer with brown glass eyes.

Such bars did not bother to throw kids out, and so we played the pinball machines, or listened to the bragging and the laughter, or put our heads down on the table, among the shot glasses and beer bottles, and slept. Because slot machines were legal in Montana and Nevada, I liked the bars there best; they weren't legal for children, but who was watching? In Helena, Montana, with money I pried loose from my mother by practiced nagging, I won a jackpot. The quarters poured through my hands and onto the floor, a silver river of money.

No one would have thrown me out of the bars whatever I did, because I was Cy Taillon's daughter, his namesake, a miniature version of Cy in my own handmade boots and my Stetson.

Bartenders served my ginger ale with a cherry in it. Cowboys asked me to dance to the jukebox, and asked Pat if she knew my father had himself another little gal. Expansive on bourbon, Cy sat me on the bar and had me sing "Mexicali Rose." I have no voice, and hadn't then, but what I lacked in musicality, I made up for in volume. I could also imitate my father at the mike, booming out: "The only pay this cowboy is going to get tonight . . ." and other crowd pleasers.

Not only did rodeo people live like gypsies, traveling in an informal caravan from town to town; my father and I looked like gypsies, both dark-skinned to start with and tanned by the sun pounding down on us, both with dark hair and high cheekbones. Mine softened as I grew older. Cy's became more pronounced, until, just before he died, the flesh receded from the bone. Once, when I was ten, and he and I were having lunch in the Florence Hotel in Missoula, Montana, a woman asked to take a snapshot of us. She was from out of town, she said, and we were the first Indians she'd ever seen. We posed for her in front of the Florence's corny Indian murals, palms raised in the B movie "how" sign.

All of which I took for granted, when our family lived on the road, as the way everyone lived, though a social worker might have taken a dim view of it and I already knew at least one person who did. It was normal to have a dapper, charming father whose public self bore little resemblance to the private Cy, the one who drank too much and flared into an alcohol-fueled temper. It was normal to have a trick-riding, ex-chorus-girl mother who still did dancer's limbering-up exercises every morning, sinking into splits and sitting on the floor spraddle-legged, bending her head first to one knee and then to the other. "You better stay in shape when you grow up," she told me as I watched, "because a woman's looks are all she's got."

It was normal to spend days and nights at the rodeo, listening to Cy's molasses voice and the voices of the cowboys, jawing, swearing, and bantering with each other, smelling leather, calves in their pens, and horse manure; to sit high above the bleachers in the announcer's stand and all but melt with love and pride when, on cold nights, Cy took his jacket off and put it around me.

It wasn't just normal to live in a Packard, it was classy. A Packard was still a classy car when it was ankle deep in hamburger wrappers. Some rodeo people pulled trailers and thus had the equivalent of houses, but most drove pickups or the kind of cars which, if they were horses, would have been taken off and shot.

I also believed then that Pat would stay spirited and taut-bodied forever, like a young racehorse, and that my father, whenever he wanted to, could make himself invisible. He told me that he could, but not when anybody was watching, and in the somewhat deflected way he always told the truth, he was telling it then.

DIXIE PARTRIDGE

ENTERING SMOOT, WYOMING
POP. 239

for DAD

We'd come here maybe twice a year
To see old Bill Stumpp.
His house was the brown fake-brick at the bend
Where the gravel lane joined the highway.

I'd mostly sit on his steep cement steps
(Cold on my thighs) and listen to you laugh
With him about the hunting trips
Or the time you camped all over Montana
In his old International.

You'd finally say *let's go;*
I'd watch to see in how much of a hurry
You were, and I'd always say—
Can we go the bumpy road, can we?
You'd never answer and I'd never know

For sure till we backed out the drive
And you turned the wheel in the right direction.

You'd gun it to get a good run;
I'd make my insides take hold
While dust shot up behind us
Like a Yellowstone geyser.
Gravel clattered a million sharp hits
Underneath the car.

Over each rise, one weightless
Instant trilled through me until I was almost
Exhausted when we got to U.S. 89.
You'd have a half-grin on your face
As the smooth quiet of the highway
Settled between us.

Once you turned off again
At the old church-house lane
And we went over it twice.

SEASONS

≈≈≈≈≈≈≈≈

He was typing a letter to his parents. Dear Mom; it said. His wife, Gail, was in the kitchen, it was raining. She was making medium-loud sounds, cleaning out a cupboard or scouring a pan. The whole house smelled pregnant. A yeast, a slight decay, like the vitamins she took. He typed: a fallen womb. He retyped it: bomb, womb. He imagined his mother reading it, straining to read it at the mailbox on a slight rise in the prairie, a wind tore at the corners around where her fists framed it top and bottom. "Gail is what, what has happened . . ." the wind going to tear it away and pull it into the sky where it will disappear into holes she has not seen. He lined his typewriter carriage up on a faint *b*, to darken it; or, to place a *w* on top: behind it the shadow of a *b*, perhaps not clear but a suggestion of darkness and confusion and blood. Bomb, womb, he typed them both. He was no longer certain where terror lay, where a new birth began.

He stood on the concrete; a movement on the horizon became a car. He crossed to the island, clutching a letter; on both sides of him cars hurtled past. He stepped into the street; a car out of nowhere bore down on him, missed him by a breath, he felt it on his face, and was gone. He crossed to the mailbox. Looked down the street for as far as he could see, where it ended for him at the top of a hill. He stepped carefully off the sidewalk back into the street, walked toward home with care. Along the way dirt from a yard was piled against the sidewalk; something for someone had been broken or lost. He had not noticed, and his feet had slipped off the sidewalk, sunk into the dirt as easily as if taking root.

His mother wrote from Montana: how do you turn the soil for a garden. First, get the proper tools. Find the proper ground. Put your foot on the spade just behind the instep and press the spade into the earth to a depth of . . . no, believe me that a spade presses into the ground, dividing north from south, for example; earth boils over with a kind of smell, dark worms dig deeper, seasons change.

Their garden was small and shady. Sometimes, when Gail could not sleep, lay next to him on the bed hard and big and sweating like a melon, he rose to walk outside. There was no moon, the sky was deep and black. He walked carefully around the boundaries of the garden; the edges were straight with sharp corners he rounded as he walked. It was not yet planted: the earth was turned, it lay in broad uneven hills, shafts of straw here and there palely remembering the world this one had replaced.

Gail is doing what she pleases, he wrote. The garden is doing as well as it can. He lifted his hands from the typewriter to look at his garden through the window in front of him. Outside, the wind blew, plants moved slightly, but he heard nothing. Through the glass he was not certain what the plants he looked at were; from his distance they seemed a shifting fluid mass, like a body, an animal perhaps, moving along the boundaries of the garden.

At work the water cooler burst. It stood in the corner for as long as he could remember, like a patient dog or horse. It was about ten yards from his desk, in a corner between some file cabinets and the Xerox machine, making a little stall for it. He would get a drink of water from it every hour or so, using the tiny collapsible paper cup. You would hardly know it was alive, motionless, staring so blankly straight ahead as someone took a tiny drink. But sometimes, he could never calculate how often, it gave a kind of gulp or swallow, and all the water quivered. Then it seemed to be some one-celled animal, that you hardly know is alive it is so simple, it only moves once when it engulfs food, and when it expels it again. One morning it had burst. There were signs, it had been leaking. But nothing like this. Where the glass attached to the spigot, down where he couldn't see, something awful had happened and water rushed out, splattered like blood. Ran everywhere. There was so much water it covered the entire floor. People who thought the disaster was confined to one area were surprised to feel their shoes fill with blood. Wondering what had happened they would look down, it was only water, a broad sea of water had come under their desk, passed on as though it could not be stopped, filled the corners of the room. They were surprised: they mopped and mopped, thought they had it all up, but weeks later they still found tiny stagnant pools in odd corners, as though water sought some place, secret and dark, where it could start to form life, infinitely slow and almost unchanging; still, life would appear, would congeal in the water, make a brief movement all its own.

In eastern Montana, when it rains, it takes your breath away. It can be dry for months, the sun moves through the clear sky like a slow yawn, taking all day, returns again each day like it has forgotten something. The stalks of wheat that were green and moved fluid in the wind dry, turn white, and rattle against each other. His mother stands on the front step and thinks of the children. One hand is balled into a fist in her apron pocket, holding her apron down against the wind. The other arm is flung onto her forehead as if in infinite sorrow, but she is shading her eyes to peer at the horizon. Far away beyond the blank of the wheat fields she sees something begin to move. It is gray and writhes. It is probably the dust of the mailman, but it could be the start of a cloud. She remembers when she had first come to Montana, it was just at the end of the war. The train had dropped her down from the mountains of the west coast onto the plains on the same day the bomb had fallen on Hiroshima. Weeks later, she had seen newsreels of it at the theater. That night, held in her new husband's arms, she had listened to her first thunderstorm in this new country; the sky crashed as though it would break and fall. She imagined the cows and horses in pasture beginning to move at the first sounds of thunder, pressing into a herd, running faster now for shelter . . . but there was no place to run to. There were no trees, no shelters, no mountains where the plain ended where one could lean against and wait it out. She learned later that though they knew there was no shelter they raced anyway, tried to escape, pressed on together in the dark barely sensing in time where they might stumble; leaving behind them all the space that was dangerous, moving into some promise that was slightly ahead of them.

If it rained early enough, the wheat would recover; if not the seeds fell into the ground, in their own tombs, which they would burst out of themselves the next spring. The next morning, there had been floods. She had not seen the differences in the land before, had not recognized the slight rises and dips, but water knew: flowed swiftly by them in a precise course, carrying things for them to watch, old wood and weeds, once a chicken. When it was over they had found a cow, lying on its side where there had been a pond for a few days, now disappeared. The cow, its belly bloated like the best meal it ever ate; its legs not curled but stuck stiffly in the air as though resisting.

Gail had always liked to cook. Since their marriage, four years ago, she had entered a recipe round robin. That meant you received a letter in the mail with a list of addresses; you made copies of a recipe and sent them to the last seven names on the list: you would get thousands in return. It was slow, because she had not yet got thousands; but they came: unexpectedly, pressed between a phone bill and a bank statement, a strange envelope with strange handwriting. Someone who has lived all her life in Oriole Point, Virginia, who has decided that she will join a round robin, that she will send in a recipe that is odd, but it is cheap and she has used it for years. She bravely writes: Mix 3 T cornstarch with 3 T oil . . .

Gail tried all the recipes, at least once. Some they could not eat. Someone in Illinois sent her directions for a dessert made of rutabagas. Someone must have stood outside as the sun set; listening, moving her nostrils slightly, trying to detect the disaster of frost. Something told her it would happen tonight: she gathered in the tomatoes, cucumbers, everything but the rutabagas. The tomatoes would lie under the bed in a box: some would ripen, redden and plump like an excited breast; others just like them would not, would shrivel in the dusty air heavy with the bed above. In the morning everything was gone: the vines were on the ground, and she could see past them the waste of the corral, deep pits where hooves had been, high barren mounds of manure. But the rutabagas survived. Held the horror of that night in their dumb, blind bodies; cooked, they lay on plates bitter and fouled. Someone, in Illinois, with a vision Gail could not imagine, someone out of her time, tried to make a dessert out of rutabagas. She had told her mother-in-law about it in a letter. The typewriter skipped; she wrote "imagine someone making a desert out of rutabagas."

She went to see her obstetrician monthly, then twice a month, and at the last weekly, to be measured and weighed and examined; her stomach like a globe. Everyone was drawn to it, doctors, nurses, placed all ten fingers on it, to hold the span of it in their hands, discovering by presses and probes what life lived here. She pulled on her clothes, left, explored; still it was only a ritual—like a map that was all ocean, there was no way for them to tell what land lay underneath; they could only guess at the secret changes beginning life. She had left the office unsteadily; she was eight and a half months along. She must have taken a wrong door; every month she had gone out the right door, the one that took her to the main entrance that was only a step away from her car that would take her home. But she stepped out into a narrow hallway, dark, and she was not sure it smelled clean. It seemed to be deserted. She followed it along several turns. She knew she had never come down it before but it seemed familiar, even the turns she could anticipate. At the end it broke out into a green lush garden, grass growing thickly and cut close, beds of flowers sturdy and without weeds, the earth cultivated deeply around them. A kind of patio led to the garden, the sliding glass doors were open. She was drawn to it, she thought she could see a little bench beneath one of the trees. As she stepped toward the patio, slam! that whole world hit her in the face. She stepped back: the glass doors to the patio were closed. The baby in her stomach had been hit, too, and she felt nausea. Her face tingled as though she had been reached out and struck; she felt a slight bleeding from her nostrils. Behind the glass it was like another world that now she could not hope to reach. She watched it. She could not see any birds, the flowers and the grass grew, but there did not seem to be anything moving. As though it were an exhibit, or a model, or a world just outside this, waiting to replace it.

She finally found her way back through the hallway and out to her car. She pulled into the traffic, and felt herself begin to cry softly. Tears washed down her face, hung on her chin like raindrops before disappearing onto her stomach. She could not quit crying, each breath brought new moisture to the surface. The steering wheel pressed under her stomach; her stomach, the baby, resisting each movement of the wheel—she could swerve and hit the traffic island once, stabilize herself and be shaken—but the baby might lose the whole world. When she reached home, it was beginning to get dark; the grass beneath her feet was dark, and she could not make out individual plants or blades, she could tell you nothing about the grass—its color, how healthy it grew—it had lost all distinguishing features in the dark so that it was all grass, in pictures and in parks, wherever she had seen it all her life.

For Christmas he had wanted to go home. Gail said no. She was already two months along. He looked at the map: Highway 80 lay like a long root between California and the northeastern corner of Montana, where he was born. The highway like a bindweed root he'd dug at in the garden as a kid; the root stretching in curves that spanned hundreds of miles, another branch reaching down into Colorado, New Mexico, into the gulf. He'd dug at the weeds in the garden till the dirt looked dark and clean, the hacked weeds lying limply along its edges. But underneath, the bindweed roots, making deep and secret links, beginning new life. His mother said there had been bindweed for as long as she could remember; they plowed the garden as deep as their biggest plow would go each spring, but it did no good. You could blast the garden; they never did, but he thought of it: the dirt would suddenly rear like an animal and only as it began its descent, a wave curling and falling, would he hear the huge boom. He might try to anticipate it, imagine it, the hugest sound of all, but it did no good. When it came it was more than he could imagine in his ears, a sound so complete that sound was filled and overflowed: so that it was not just sound, but sensation, something on his tongue and skin, and a feeling in the back of his mouth like a taste. Still the bindweed would live, would crawl to the surface a week later, the shoots white like shock against the bare earth. Instead they spent Christmas at their own home, the California rain rattling at their windows. In eastern Montana it would be silent; fresh snow an inch thick on everything: it seemed like overnight all the things familiar to them were destroyed and useless—the tools turned to something large and soft, so that only someone from another world could use them.

They had named their baby at Christmastime. They had thought to wait till he was born, that just by looking at him, he would somehow name himself. But by Christmastime they had waited two months, and they wanted to wait no more. They decided on Grace if it were a girl, but could not decide what to name it if it were a boy. She had said Justin, but he had argued that it did no good to pick out a name for a boy; he could not imagine what a boy named Justin would look like. In the end they drew names out of a hat—Christopher, Alexander, Gregory, and Thrace—and rejected them all. They had sat dejected, their heads in their hands, facing their Christmas tree, growing more and more certain that their baby would be a boy and unnamable. Gail tried to think of her relatives: remembered tall, stiff men in suits, who had visited her family in her childhood, dead now; she remembered her great-uncle Isadore or Isaac, when he had died the relatives had stripped the little room he lived in bare. She remembered boxes filled and piled high at one side of the room; one had been full of letters. She read one: "Dear Uncle," it read: "It is a devil of a time getting something to grow in this country. It seems like you plant and then before you know it the weather comes along and takes care of it for you. We are all well. We wish you everything. It looks like it won't be long and we will be seeing you." The letter was unsigned. She had not been able to imagine why there was no name at the bottom. The letter was written in a large masculine hand: when he came to the signature was he suddenly rushed, or did a name seem unnecessary?

He lay in bed beside his wife; there was something he wanted to say. He lay with his arm encircling her; her head, turned away from him, rested on his arm. Her breathing was becoming shallower; she was nearly asleep, but there was something he wanted to say. Their baby would be born sometime in the next two weeks. What he had to say was something he had read somewhere, something so familiar it did not seem important. Oh, it had something to do with pain. He imagined Gail would go through great pain to have this baby. He was not even sure where he read it: he lay still, his eyes searching out forms in the darkness that would give him some clues. He was almost certain it was not in something that he ordinarily read; not in a book or a good magazine, so that he read it almost accidentally. What was it: Pain is a great equalizer. No, it was something that Gail might want to hear. "Pain hates with a passion that is profound." That was it, but he did not know why he wanted Gail to hear it. She lay on his arm sleeping. Her belly under her white nightgown taut and rounded; so that her form looked like a mound of snow; of the kind he might find in the spring in Montana: when the prairie was almost dry and new grass blew busily in the wind, he might find hidden somewhere, under an embankment where the sun did not yet reach, a sprawl of snow such as this, silent and white; on the surface it looked like any snow, yet he knew it was leaking, dying, water drawing into the earth, finding tiny narrow chasms just for it to flow. Once as a child he had been under the snow: the drifts that winter were so huge he had dug tunnels. He remembered he had carefully planned turns and curves, but coming upon them again with no landmarks, the turns had always surprised him. The springtime had destroyed the tunnels, filling with water the dips inside that his knees had worn smooth. The melting soaked and chilled him; the warmer weather making him colder than he'd been all winter.

The night Gail had gone to the hospital they had had potato soup for supper. Potatoes from their own garden. She had made it carefully from scratch, brought it to the table in a steaming bowl, a teaspoon of pale butter in the center, sinking and disappearing. At the last minute Gail had not been able to eat. As far as she knew she was not ready to go to the hospital, but she could not eat any potato soup; it smelled funny, she said, as though something had gone bad. Outside, the garden was full of little craters where potato plants had been. It was a good year; the potatoes fat and heavy like cows, leaving large holes: some of the holes they had tried to cover in with dirt, but they'd sunk. She had left him to go to the bedroom. It was an odd, still night. Rain was predicted. He finished his soup and walked outdoors. He stood on his front porch and looked down the street. Back of him was the dark back yard and the garden he had worked in all day. He heard traffic from a long way off; sometimes seeing a car's light before he heard it; their lights a vague brightness on the other side of the hill, like a sun about to rise. The cars seemed to come slower now, or maybe the dark played tricks. A car creeping down the hill with a kind of shyness, a hesitation as though lost. One car, a dark and sleek one, had traveled particularly slowly down the hill, it was all alone on the street. It nearly stopped several times, then sped up again, weaving slightly, the lights reflecting off the mass of dark gleaming trees along the sidewalk. He had watched it, unable to move, feeling danger and anger; then it had pulled up right alongside him and stopped. It was not a stranger at all, it was a man who had visited next door for as long as they had lived in the neighborhood; a man, he could almost feel, that he had known all his life.

As he stands, it begins to rain softly. A drop strikes his face and is warm as a tear. Soon it comes faster, so that he can no longer count. He thinks of his garden behind him, the rain disappearing in the dark, soft earth. From the house, Gail cries out. Rain, he hears her say, it is raining. Pain, she cries. He finds her in the kitchen, one hand wrapped around a large spoon as if in defense. She clutches the counter with one hand; she has a fearful stricken look and he does not dare go near her; it is like an animal trapped: everything is changed, it may be dangerous, it may act like it has never acted before. He goes around the table to get by her; upstairs finds on the bed her overnight bag. When he comes down she is gone; he imagines she is in the bathroom. He goes out to the street to find his car.

She stands in the pantry, clutching the shelves, looking at the food she has canned from the garden. It is so narrow she can hardly turn around; food waits on shelves on either side of her. It has always been dark in the pantry, now it seems light enough that she imagines she can see what is in the jars. In the corner of one of the shelves there is something damp; she imagines one of the jars has begun to leak. She feels tears in her eyes, run down her face; she holds on to a shelf that is as high as her chin; she feels like a child about to leave everything she has loved. Her stomach protrudes hugely, almost rests on a shelf; she knows she is getting dirty. Outside the car honks once, twice; at first it is a sound she cannot place, tries to imagine an animal the size and shape that would make that sound. She hears the motor race like a warning. She feels her way along the shelves out the door of the pantry, imagines the fingerprints she leaves in the dust.

He still believes the traffic is lighter than usual. Travels along the street at a faster and more dangerous speed than usual; the rain has turned the street dark and gleaming, the reflection of the streetlights white vague spots in front of him. Travels in the fastest inside lane, close to the island, sees out of the corner of his eye Gail pull back and away from him as he changes to the inside lane. She has said little. Stares out the window at the scenery going by; the trees are a dark blur on either side of them.

He turns into the hospital complex; the hospital huge and white, set back from the road, lit outside and in, emerging from the dark like an island. The roads are confused; they branch off. He thinks he has found the right one and it branches off again; finally only one road leads to the emergency entrance. When he has parked, someone rushes out to help Gail into a wheelchair. He sits in the car for a moment; Gail is disappearing ahead of him like a blur. He feels hungry; remembers with an ache of pleasure the potato soup he had for supper. Enters the hospital, follows the long corridors to find the cafeteria; he does not ask but searches it out like an animal might, makes sudden unthinking decisions to turn, and finds it at the end of a short hallway that has opened abruptly off another. He sits down at a table; he seems to be the only one there. He has nothing on the table in front of him; an empty coffee cup upside down, white and gleaming, is in front of him. Across the room he hears a sudden loud noise: behind a serving counter is a woman leaning and laboring over something, holding something with her left hand, her right arm making large circular motions; she is scrubbing a huge pot, or she is working with all her might to pull something up from a sink or where it is trying to go down.

He has forgotten he is hungry, he thinks to notify his mother. At his hand is a large paper napkin. He finds his pen, clicks it to a point, holds it above the napkin for a moment. Drops his hand onto the soft white surface. Dear Mother, he writes. We are in difficult times. He wanted to cross it out, instead he continued: There is no way of knowing right now just how things are going to turn out with the baby. Gail is upstairs and I haven't seen her. Well, I am hoping everything will turn out okay, and I will get in touch with you as soon as I know anything. He unclicked his pen, fastened it to the edge of his pocket. Folded the napkin carefully, placed it in his breast pocket; only realized then that time had been lost to him, that mailing a letter to his mother would take days, and the baby would be here in hours.

His mother stands on the front step. She is thinking it will soon be time for the mailman. The sky is blank and it will be another hot day. She can see some of the garden has dried up without rain, the plants disappeared to the ground, the ground crazed by cracks, so that it is no longer solid ground, but pieces isolated, islanded by the deep, dark crevices. She hears a rumble; she doesn't know where it came from, it may even have been in her stomach, she has not yet eaten. She looks off across the fields, raises her arm and it falls back to her forehead, shades her eyes. Sees something familiar forming on the horizon.

SANDRA ALCOSSER

CRY

White legs and pink footpads, the black cat
loved me. It was summer, a perfect flush
of weeds and flowers. Mornings, he'd listen
for my kettle, the screen door snap, and he'd know
I'd come to breakfast in the asters. As I ate
my bowl of red berries, he'd burl and stretch
and claw about my hips.

One night as the cat and I watched the moon eclipse,
amidst the scuttling of bear and mice, there was a cry
from the forest, not seductive, but pained and wailing
like a siren. The next day the cat was gone. I'd heard
that even blackbirds broke veins in their throats
singing love songs. I stood by my window practicing,
trying to shape the feline song, to call him back.

My daughter was no different than a cat,
tapping the window glass over my bed,
crying at night till I rocked her frail ribs
against mine. Her hands on my breast,
dark curls sweated against her forehead,
tell me about the princess, she said, *the way*
she slept in a blue dress, waiting.

It was a month of heatstorms, lightning scratched
like Sanskrit across the valley. A boy came riding
our footpath. He wore black jeans, a sliver of green
malachite at his neck. The breathless afternoon,
the bees laid out on the red eyes of gaillardia.
Before she left my daughter cut off her long hair
and bleached it yellow.

There were years when I too turned from my mother's
cool white arms. First the pale boy, scarred
and silent, then my husband. We cleaned the ditches
together in spring, raking out the silt and dead branches.
He played a silver harmonica. A ring-boned pony
was what I had when we ran away. A field of salsify
and a black skillet.

Stretched out on the porch this noon, resting
my swollen legs, I'm tired of canning tomatoes,
the house thick with red steam and basil.
The bite of salt and vinegar, cucumbers
floating like green bathers in brine.
All that flesh I've tended gone to pulp.
All that mismatched tenderness.

One weed knows another and each animal has its own cry
and when it's right, it's easy. Easy as my husband
behind me now, holding open the black screen door.
He is drinking tea with honey and a halo of gnats
screams about his face. *Let's sneak down to the basement,*
he says, *where it's cool and dark.* He cracks a bead of ice
in his teeth and offers half to me.

TRACKS

There is a man under the wheel of my truck.
I want to pay him, drive off, but he is shivering.
His wife left him weeks ago. He has cut his thumb
and stained his coat. It is the first black ice
of October. I invite him home.

The creek outside my cabin tastes of sapphires and weeds.
A bald eagle feeds there twice a day on deer bones.
The stranger asks if I am afraid to live alone.

We drink rum and hot tea. He shows me photographs
of naked women lying in leaves, black and white slices
of buttocks, spine. I cannot identify one body.
Was this his wife? He never photographed her.
One breast was larger than the other.

And his father was a trapper. Do I know coyote?
It is all lust. Rub badger on leg irons
and bury the traps in moss. Wear soiled buckskin gloves.

The coyote cannot resist green musk. He'll dig down fast,
snap teeth on himself.

I remember what my mother told me about strange men.
When I was ten, one pulled up in a blue sedan
to ask directions. As I pointed west,
he unzipped his pants. My eyes were bad.
I saw nothing but his hand digging.

Fire to door and back again, I want this man to go.
He takes opals from his pocket, a rabbit's tail,
and drops them on my table. I rub fur against my face.
It smells of tar and sage. There is blood on the tip,
still wet.

THE SAWYER'S WIFE

We could go like your grandmother, over
the hogback and down the hill to the village
grocer for a loaf of bread, a sack of lentils
and the Sunday paper. Oh it's pleasant here.
Our boots are waxed. You've stacked the kindling.
There's plenty of wheat to grind and knead, hours
to watch it rise, but I want to go on foot today,
as she would, bored by her bright dishes,
the way eggs sat perfectly in their cups.
I need to check the flumes and weirs, the deer
tufts on barbed wire. I want to know
if the winter nests dismantle.

My husband is patient and charmed by a saw,
the sugary dust that falls in his boots,
the maul that tears red-blond fibers
as little white worms unravel; for him
the epic is home. The ants that leave
their trail markings in cedar are townsmen,
dark running matter, with or without heart.

Let's follow, like the trapper with a sweet
French name, this trail of peeled yellow pine.
See on this day, damp, how lichen plump
chartreuse and spongy on larch branches,
and our hair, wet with melting ice, fattens,
tangles in brambles. Only January
and listen, already the first shy
bargaining of birds.

    They will be disappointed, my husband says,
    we will all be disappointed, like the well
    gone dry for lack of snow cover, the August
    strawberry husking on its runner,
    or the Chinaman who split the wall we walk—
    rock that sparkled not with gold but wandering
    glints of mica. It wasn't even his land,
    but that of a lawyer who liked the word *ranch*,
    the way cattle rumpled in his pasture, black
    and white as newspaper. They celebrated together,
    the fields picked clean, the pleasure of a wall,
    and the rancher called him *Chinaman, Chinaman*,
    as though he were his doll.

We'd come to look at nature, seeps and gorges
full of alder, red osier, blue grouse,

but this is the line between meadow and rock,
or call it failure. Good chicken weather.
Seed peas and apples when there's water.
Little more.

Here, Two Feather Sawmill with timber,
once enough to build a town, all plowed
in slash now, with rusting cans of antifreeze,
a shed of sawyers' gloves tossed down,
thousands of them rotting, open-palmed.

It's hard to live above the timberline
for man or woman. Rocks grinding all night,
sharp cries of animals we cannot name.
There was a ridgerunner behind our house,
a small man with no teeth who wrapped his feet
in dishrags. More than once, half frozen,
he broke into a summer cabin, opened
an abandoned tin of fish or jar
of rhubarb wine. Charmed sometimes by the valley's
false bowl of stars, he'd sneak down, pause
at a window to watch an old woman rocking,
doing recitation to herself. In the grocery
he'd finger the red cans, the ones with the face
of the laughing boy, and always before the town
went to sleep, he'd leave. Afraid of being beaten,
jailed, he'd climb back to the first swale,
bed under a ripped piece of tarp.

And aren't we like that, testing the world
in fits and starts, the bad distilled
and the good? We sit on the hill at dusk
to play out our long shadows. The snow

in the footpath twines two ways, up the mountain
into deep saddles and down through the hayfields.
It's five o'clock. The smell of carrots
and onions rises on an evening thermal,
and how seductive, the dark broth.

CHRISTINA ADAM

FIRES

≈≈≈≈≈≈≈

For over twenty years this memory stayed with me. An afternoon when I was nineteen, lying on my cot at the ranch, a breeze pushing through a window with no screen, no glass—only the flat blue sky and the warm, baked smell of sagebrush. Outside on the line, clean bed sheets filled with white light, and snapped in the wind. I drifted in and out of sleep in a long, empty peace I thought would last forever.

I lived alone up on the Latham homestead for two summers after I left home, washing laundry. By then the Lathams ran a lodge across the valley, but they sent the laundry to the old place for the water.

The last time I came, I worked as a laundry girl again and studied for a test to graduate from high school. In the fall, I started college, just a city college in L.A. But I always wondered what would have happened if, instead, I'd gone with Joe.

It was the summer of the fires. Fires burned in the mountains. By August, the valley disappeared in a thick, brown haze, and overhead, heavy bombers, gleaming like fish in murky water, carried load after load of lake water and chemicals. The town on the other side of the pass filled with firefighters, and a tent city sprang up to the north. I picked Joe up on the highway, hitchhiking into town on a three-day break.

I didn't know until the next day his hair was blond. He'd cooled off under a spigot at the fire camp and his hair was flat and dark. He needed a place to stay, and I let him sleep in an empty line shack. In the morning, I drove him across the valley to the lodge and waited in the truck while he asked if he could rent the cabin. But the Lathams left it up to me.

I was used to stopping on the road for hay crews and fire fighters. But Joe was different. He had hair the color that comes later to children who have been very blond—dark underneath and gold streaked in the sun. His eyes were blue, and on the day I picked him up beside the road, his wide, flat cheekbones were smudged black from the fires. He was tall and broad across the shoulders, but something about the way he moved, not a limp, but an unevenness, made him seem more slight.

He was quiet. In those first days after he moved into the line shack, I passed his open door, glancing in to see him sleeping on his cot, or reading. Sometimes I caught the heavy smell of marijuana.

In the mornings, the girls from the lodge drove into the yard with baskets of dirty laundry and traded them for clean. I loaded two tubs with hot water, let the white linens soak, and guided them through a wringer into a galvanized sink. On most days, I could have it all hung out by lunchtime. I remember the heavy wetness of the sheets and the taste in my mouth of wooden pins. In only a few hours, the dry sheets floated, horizontal in the wind, and I gathered them in against my body, filled with the smell of heat and sage.

Joe's crew worked without breaks, but the fire boss gave him time to rest his leg, four days on and three days off. When he was at the ranch, I sat cross-legged on my cot, the door open, working through the test book, learning geometry by a sheer act of will. But an excitement, a high fluttering energy, took the taste of food away. I could hardly eat.

THAT WAS MORE than twenty years ago. I didn't know exactly why I needed to come back. I'd sometimes gone for years without a thought of Joe. But in the last few months, the memories had been coming, clear and frightening, like dreams.

Only an hour before, I'd driven over the pass and dropped down in the valley. I had called the lodge from town, but a nervousness kept rising. Would the ranch still be there? Would it be the same?

When I finally found it, the place seemed bigger and more desolate, the tired buildings so much smaller and too far apart. The homestead cabin listed sideways, like a house of cards pushed slightly over, the gray shingles on the roof curled up and peeling. Behind it, the old wash shed had caved in, and purple thistles bloomed up through the floor. At the edge of the yard, the leaves of a single cottonwood twirled silver in the breeze.

After so much time, I couldn't bring myself to leave the car. I stared out through the dusty windshield, the quiet buzzing in my ears. Across the irrigation ditch, three line shacks stood in an uneven row. The pale logs had dried and pulled apart, and clumps of sod, the grass parched thin and white, hung from the eaves.

But the car was hot, and I could taste dust from the drive. I climbed out and crossed over on a splintered board. The door to the cabin where I had lived stood open. Inside, the small room had the sweet, damp smell of mice and of rot where the pink-and-gray linoleum, blistered and nearly black with age, peeled up from the corners.

I walked slowly down the line to Joe's cabin, the silence like a stranger watching. A fencing spike had been wedged into the rusty clasp, but I worked the nail out and let the door swing in. The wood plank floor had been swept clean and the cot pushed square into the corner. It was made up with a gray army blanket, spotted with grease, but neat. Somebody lived here.

I turned around and crossed back over the ditch. I didn't know what I should do. Standing in the yard, the sun burning hot on my arms, all I wanted was to climb in the car and drive back to the airport. But the car was packed with camping gear, a week of groceries. I broke a path through the dry thistles, the needles catching in my jeans and prickling my ankles through my socks, and sat down on the steps of the homestead. The rough gray boards were warm.

Below me, hay fields, blooming faintly blue and lavender, carved at the dry hills like a shoreline. On both sides of the valley, the gray sagebrush hills sloped up to knuckled canyons, dark with trees, and beyond them, granite peaks.

High, white clouds stacked up in thunderheads and moved over the pass, casting huge, gunship shadows on the valley floor. I had forgotten how the place could change so fast, be quiet at one moment and dangerous the next. Each summer I had come, climbers had been trapped by sudden storms in the mountains, and twice a man had died.

I knew who had made up the bed in Joe's cabin. It had to be the cowboy hired by the ranchers to watch the cattle on their grazing permits in the mountains. My chest felt hollow with disappointment. Always when I pictured the ranch, I came back by myself. I didn't want to meet up with the cowboy. And if he was an old man like the ones I'd known, he wouldn't want to find me here.

The clouds drifted over the sun in the west and the air turned sharp with cold. I gathered up twigs and stumps of sagebrush and built a fire out near the cottonwood. When the coals flaked white, I roasted a potato and ate it sitting on a rock beside the fire. Afterward, I filled a saucepan at the ditch, boiled the grounds in the water, and drank the thick, grainy coffee with canned milk. The sun disappeared behind the mountains, and shafts of light, falling long across the valley through the canyons, turned the air dusky gold, then blue.

A red pickup truck and two-horse trailer crawled down the highway. In the thin mountain air, I could hear the engine and the sticky whirl of tires on heated pavement, the sound too loud for so much distance. As I watched, the truck turned off the blacktop, and a cloud of dust came toward the ranch.

I had a quick, childlike urge to jump up and drive the car out of sight. Then I tried to will the truck to drive on past. But it rattled into the yard and came to a stop at the ditch. I stood and pulled my jacket on.

The hinges on the pickup door pried open and closed, and a big man, his hat tipped low over his eyes, appeared beside the trailer. He looked in my direction for some time before he started across the yard, walking like an old man. He held his back upright, but bent slightly forward, his white shirt gleaming phosphorescent in the dusk. He stopped a few feet from the fire.

"How're you?" He spoke in a slow, easy voice, but he didn't look at me.

"Good," I said.

His hat was dove colored and new. It gave him the handsome, angled look all cowboys have at first glance. He stared out past me into the sagebrush. His jaw was square, but his face was long, his gray eyes, almost triangular, sloping slightly downward at the outside corners. I wondered why his shirt and jeans had both been ironed, the creases sharp.

"You can't camp here," he said, his lips hardly moving.

"I called the lodge from town." I kept my voice low and steady. "They said I could."

"Well, I guess you can then." He squinted, looking at me for the first time. Then he held out his hand. "Hessie Baker," he said.

"Susan," I said. "Susan Gerton." I shook his hand, startled by how dry it was, and waited for him to say something else, but he only looked down at my fire, then over to the small white car I'd rented at the airport.

"Would it be all right," I asked him, "if I move my things into a cabin?"

He shifted his weight. "Don't ask me," he said. "You're the one that's got authority."

For no reason, I felt the pinch of tears coming. Why? I thought. Why are these men, old ranchers and cowboys, always out to show you what a fool you are?

He looked over at the old shacks. "Take your pick," he said. "I got horses to feed."

He walked across the yard and backed two horses from the trailer, turning them out in a pole corral beside his shack. I watched him pitch hay in quick, neat strokes, his arms and shoulders hardly moving. He finished and disappeared into his cabin. After a while, a lantern glowed inside.

I sat on my heels down close to the fire. The night when it came was black, the white stars touching the horizon. It was very cold. The cowboy always kept a camp up Carmichael Canyon, behind the ranch, and that's where Hessie Baker should have been. With any luck, I thought, he'll be gone in the morning. I dumped my coffee on the coals, and went to the car. I carried a flashlight and sleeping bag to the middle shack and went to bed myself. I hadn't thought to bring a lantern.

IN THE MORNING, Hessie Baker's truck stood in the yard, brick colored under a film of dust, but both horses were gone. The air was damp and cool, but almost as soon as it came up over the mountains, the sun was high. I tugged a towel from my bag and walked up the dry creek bed toward the flume.

I watched the sandy earth at my feet, where small tracks skittered under the sagebrush. I followed a larger, dragging track, a badger I thought, and came to a smooth hole dug under a stump of sage. If it was a badger, I didn't want to be the one to wake him up, but I tapped inside the hole with a stick and rolled out the tiny skull of a mouse. I held it for a long time, weightless in my palm, so fragile the sunlight shone through the bones, before I put it back. It pleased me to know I could still follow a trail and find bones like that.

At the flume, I worked off my shoes and socks, and dangled a leg in the water. Submerged, my skin seemed very white, almost blue, the skin drawn tight in a network of shiny wrinkles. The deep spring-fed water, dammed up by headgates, was so cold it burned like snow. I looked up toward the north.

That summer when the fires had first started, no one paid any attention. The Forest Service brought in firefighters and trucks, but they said the fires were under control. Early in July, I'd seen one plume of black smoke rising straight up from the shoulder of a mountain to the north. Then another fire broke out, and another.

Joe had moved all his gear into the end shack. I went on with the laundry, but I felt his presence, even when he wasn't there. I cooked meals in the homestead cabin, food I couldn't eat. I made stew and soup, biscuits, things I thought Joe would like, but I never asked him to eat with me. We watched each other, but we hardly spoke.

Then one night Joe came to my door and asked me to a movie in town. And afterward, we walked up here, to the flume. The night was warm, but so dark we stumbled over rocks and sage. Joe went in swimming, and later, sat just close enough, I could feel heat radiating from his shoulder. He dropped smooth stones from one palm to another. We talked only a little, the moon rising round over the mountains, and Joe told me he had been in Vietnam.

His friends had gone to college, but he'd been drafted—and his father made him go. I could hear a twist in his voice. He didn't want to hate his father, but he did.

In the darkness, his words were careful and distinct, as if he'd never said these things out loud before. "I thought I was dead. Everything was black. But I woke up in a hospital, in Hawaii." He let the stones drop in the water. "I cried," he said. "When they told me I didn't have to go back, I cried."

A land mine had broken his leg in three places, torn up his back with shrapnel. When they finally shipped him home, he stayed in San Francisco, in an old house in the Mission with his buddies. They'd played music and smoked dope, sleeping late and picking up odd jobs. But something had happened between them, some fight, and Joe started hitching cross country. When he ran out of money, he volunteered for fire crew. He talked about a town on the coast of New England, a big family, but he didn't want to go home.

That night, at the door to my cabin, Joe tipped my face up, and kissed me. He smiled, with something like regret. "I wish," he said, "I could have courted you a long time."

HESSIE BAKER didn't come back, and I had the ranch, the long, slow walks through the sagebrush, to myself. Late in the afternoon, I hiked up the dirt track toward the mouth of Carmichael Canyon, thinking I might look at where the fires had burned, but I turned back. My tongue was dry and cottony with thirst, and I wasn't sure I wanted to see how the canyon looked now.

The morning Hessie finally walked out to my campfire, I hadn't even heard him riding in, or noticed the horses were back. He stood above me, watching the sage stumps burn, and I waited for him to make some remark—how I'd built the fire wrong, or what kind of a fool would want to camp out in the first place.

"Got any extra coffee?" he said. He raised an eyebrow and rolled over another rock without waiting for an answer. He lowered himself down, his long legs stretched out to the fire, and let me pour the coffee. He blew on it and took a shallow sip. "Hell," he said. "You could float a horseshoe in that coffee." He shot me a quick glance. "But not bad."

I wanted to laugh, but wouldn't give him the satisfaction. After what seemed like a long time, he asked if I was going into town.

"I could," I said.

"I've got a letter needs mailed," he said. "To my wife." He looked at me. "You married?"

"Not anymore."

"Sorry," he said. I wasn't sure if he was sorry he asked, or sorry for me.

It turned out he only cowboyed in the summer, just to get away. He owned a big place in Colorado—and Nebraska. He and his wife had split up years ago, but they couldn't divorce. If they divided the land, neither one would make a living.

I promised to take the letter, and wondered why I hadn't told him I was a widow. It would have made things easier, but I couldn't say it. I never thought of myself as a widow. Richard had died in our bed, at home. We hadn't split up or divorced, but we should have.

And my name wasn't Susan. It was Suzy. My father had named me for a gold mine. As a little girl, I pictured the mine shaft, the mountain, the gold in round coins. But after he left, they told me the Suzy had only existed on paper. When I went to college, they wanted my "real name," and so I gave them one.

Hessie stood up, poured the last of his coffee on the edge of the fire and watched it sizzle and steam in the coals.

When the sound stopped, the air was suddenly too quiet. It surprised me, but I didn't want him to go.

"Do you think," I asked him, "I could ride out with you one day? Up the canyon?"

He seemed to consider for a long time, and I wished I hadn't asked. I couldn't tell if he was thinking how to say no, or just thinking. Finally he nodded.

"Don't see any reason why not," he said.

"Do you have another saddle?"

"I guess I could find one someplace," he said.

AT DAWN, Hessie loaded the horses and we drove up into the canyon. I grabbed onto the edge of the open window, braced against the impact of the jolting truck. Hessie drove with his chin tucked in, his hat low over his eyes. He steered with the heel of one hand, keeping the wheels of both outfits riding high over the deep ruts in the washed-out track.

We crossed Clear Creek and pulled over at the cow camp. Where I expected to see a house trailer and a tack shed, there was only a pole corral, one corner built out into the creek. Three horses whinnied at us, and Hessie slipped in through the gate, caught one, and asked me to hold her head while he fitted on panniers and loaded blocks of salt. The pack horse stood nearly asleep, but she made me uneasy. I hadn't been around a horse in so long.

Hessie backed a short, stocky horse from the trailer, and nodded for me to get on. He leveled the stirrup, cupped a hand under my knee, and helped me into the saddle. I felt his touch on my leg, the warm pressure of his hand, for a long time afterward. I couldn't remember when a man had done a thing like that for me.

He rode a tall, black horse and led the pack mare up the canyon into the trees, my horse trotting to keep up. He stopped to lean down and open the drift fence, explaining how it ran for miles along the foothills to keep the cows from drifting home too early in the fall. I knew what a drift fence was, but it was good to hear him talking to me. Beyond the wire, the dry mountain grass was speckled gold and rust, dotted with tiny blue and yellow flowers.

We crossed the first ridge, but I saw no signs of fire. I kicked my horse up next to Hessie.

"The fire," I said, "where was the fire?"

"Which one?"

"The big one," I said.

Hessie reined his horse up. He glanced at me, then pointed all around us. I followed his gaze. Everywhere the trees grew close together in a canopy. For a moment, I couldn't understand it. Then I saw. The lodgepole pines were all exactly the same height.

"Look here," Hessie said. He turned off into the trees and jumped both horses over a fallen log. I found a way around and came to a small meadow where the lush grass had been cropped short. All across the clearing, fragments of bone, shards of ribs and pelvis blades, were scattered, the bones chalky white against the green. It had a strange effect—as if the grass were wet, the bones too dry. They seemed somehow like ancient human bones. Hessie leaned over his saddle horn.

"Hundred head of cattle died here," he said. "Bunched up in the smoke."

"When?" I asked.

"Not the fire you recall," he said. "Must have been two, three years ago. Coyotes dragged the worst of it away. In a year or two, you won't see anything at all." He kicked his horse up.

In the next draw, Hessie unloaded the salt, and we started back. My knees and back began to ache. I kept quiet, but Hessie must have noticed. He turned off at the drift fence, riding up along the wire to a stand of young aspens. On the ground, nearly hidden by tall grass, a tiny pool of water reflected the sky.

"Best water you ever tasted," Hessie said. He dismounted and lowered himself on both knees, lifting a jar from behind the spring. With one hand, he cleared the surface, then dipped the jar full. He stood and carried it to me. When I looked down at his face, his eyes were sharp and blue, not gray.

On the ride back, it began to rain, a light rain but with drops as big as dimes. They splashed hard on our faces and left round pockmarks in the dust. The air filled with the smell of wet sage, clean and cooling, like a sudden drop in temperature.

It was after dark before we drove back in the yard. I sat on the cot in Hessie's cabin and watched him fry steaks in a skillet on his hot plate. He had the room fixed up with a small table and chair, a trailer-sized refrigerator and an extension cord strung over to the wash shed. Everything was neat and clean.

Without his hat, his gray hair damp with sweat and flattened down, Hessie looked old. His broad forehead was smooth, nearly translucent, his cheeks red with broken veins. He'd ridden all day, but his shirt was white, the long sleeves buttoned at the wrist and holding a sharp crease. I looked at the curve of his thumb, dark against the line of his cuff. Outside, I heard dull thunder in the canyon, rolling like a detonation underground.

Hessie lifted my steak onto a yellow plastic plate and handed it to me. His fingernails were broad, flattened at the ends, and a threading scar ran down between the first finger and his thumb. Hessie caught me looking at it.

"Only bayonet charge in the whole damn war."

Hessie cleaned his pocketknife and set about cutting his steak into small pieces. For a minute I thought he was going to reach over and cut up my steak, too. But he handed me the knife and started eating. He wiped his chin with a dishtowel. "101st," he said. "Dropped us in on D-Day."

Because of the movies, D-Day was almost the only battle I knew anything about from World War II. It seemed amazing he had been there.

"It was spring," Hessie said, as if the fact was still a mystery to him. Still a surprise.

I thought he might say more, but he finished his meal and stirred up two cups of instant coffee. He poured canned milk into mine without asking.

"If I'd known you could cook," I said, "I would have let you make the coffee."

He grinned and took my plate. "You learn," he said, "to make do for yourself."

After I'd gone back to my cabin and stretched out in the sleeping bag, the rain stopped and I listened to the coyotes drifting along the ridges, circling the valley. My legs and back ached from the long ride and my hair smelled of dust and horses.

I was exhausted, but suddenly filled with sadness and desire. If things had been as they used to be, I would have gone back to Hessie's warm cabin and climbed in bed with him.

When I was young, things were easy that way. Sex was a simple move from talk to bed. But I knew better. Women in Hessie's world didn't do that.

I thought back to the night Joe and I went to bed, in this narrow cot. How it felt, the first time, to lie down against his body. To open my shirt and feel the shock, the cool surprise of his skin on my breasts. We made love hard, then slowly for a long time, our skin so alive we couldn't sleep. I remembered Joe's hands, his square wrists and swollen knuckles, the place where his smooth arm curved up into muscle. Holding him, I traced the shrapnel scars above shoulder blades, diamond shaped and raised like thick embroidery.

We stayed awake all night, our skin just touching, sometimes sitting up to smoke a cigarette. "I can't get used to how it feels," Joe said, "to light a cigarette and smoke it in the dark."

After that, Joe worked the fires and came back, washed in the flume, and slept around the clock. I passed his door every hour, but I never woke him. When he did get up, I made something for him to eat, and we went to bed. I had never been in love this way, never felt so always wanted. I couldn't keep from smiling at the laundry girls. But I hardly slept at all, even when Joe was gone. I couldn't eat. And I was afraid. I couldn't study for the tests anymore. I sat down on the steps with the books while Joe was sleeping, but I couldn't think.

The tests mattered. It mattered to me to take them and pass. I had already, in so short a time, failed so much. I'd hitchhiked to San Francisco and Chicago, and lived in the slums of New York. I'd left a dozen jobs, and as many friends and lovers. My best friend, Elaine, was a whore, a prostitute. I'd stayed with her in Reno, sleeping on the floor, and watched her come home with black eyes, red swollen bruises on her cheekbones. Elaine, who wore narrow knit suits from the thrift store and was always elegant. She had long, light brown hair, swept up in a bun. It fascinated me to watch her pin it up that way, without a mirror. I'd left home when I was sixteen and I'd seen the sixties, but I didn't want to see them anymore.

THE NEXT MORNING I found Hessie leaning up against the cottonwood drinking coffee.

"Help yourself," he said, and nodded toward the campfire.

I laughed and bent down to pour myself a cup.

"I didn't mean it," I said. "I can make the coffee."

"If we want it for lunch."

"Oh, I'm sorry—what time . . ."

"Forget it," Hessie said, "I'm doggin' it today. Thought I might take a ride into town—tell the government they got a fire."

"What?" I said. He pointed south, to a ridge in the mountains behind us, where a line of smoke rose thin and black until it blew sideways, like smoke from a train, and disappeared.

"Lightning," he said.

I couldn't understand why he wasn't gone already. "Don't you think you better go?" I said.

"No hurry. They might have seen it already—and they might just let it burn."

"I'll go. You want me to go?"

Hessie lowered his cup and gave me a long look. "Come along if you want," he said. He emptied his cup on the ground and started toward the truck.

"No," I said. "I'd better stay here."

"Suit yourself."

I watched him drive out of the yard. I needed to leave that day. I'd meant to tell Hessie, but I hadn't quite told myself. I sat down, facing south. The valley seemed suddenly vast and quiet. I could hear the tick of locusts in the dry grass. On the ridge to the south, I thought I saw a lick of red flame. I couldn't take my eyes away.

DURING THE SUMMER of the fires, there were days when the brown smoke hung so thick in the valley I burned a lantern in the cabin in the daytime. The sun was a dirty bronze glow. It had the feel of something terrible, like the bruised yellow sky before a tornado. I couldn't hang the wash. In the night, dry winds blew ash against the door, and in the morning I found it in perfect, charcoal drifts. When Joe came home, his clothes and hair smelled like wet, burning wool. We hung blankets over the windows and made love in the dark.

Once I tried to pull myself away, spend an hour working through the practice tests. Joe went to his own cabin, but every few minutes I found an excuse to knock on his door—to find a pen, ask him a question. Each time I put my arms around him, sank into a kiss, and had to pull myself away. Finally he looked up and grinned, "You make me feel," he said, "like a sea anemone, waiting for the tide."

I remember nearly every word Joe said, but we hardly talked at all. I never told him where I'd been, where I grew up, what it meant to me to pass the test. In bed, I tried to hold and comfort him, but I never asked him about the war. Joe stopped eating meat, and I thought it had something to do with the war. But it strikes me as strange now that I never asked.

Even when he told me he was leaving, we didn't talk. One day he walked down from the flume, his hair hanging wet and his shirt dark in places where he'd used it for a towel. He sat next to me on the cot and told me he wanted to go home. He hated the heat and the smoke. He wanted to see the ocean.

I couldn't protest, or beg him to stay, because if he stayed I would fail the test. He asked me to go with him, but I didn't believe he meant it. Still, only a year before, I would have gone. In the end he said, "What if it's only sex?" And I didn't know what to say. It hurt me so much I couldn't answer.

I drove him to the interstate, a drive that took all day, and let him off beside a concrete overpass. I didn't look back. In town they told me the fire had jumped a draw and trapped a fire crew. Twenty-two men had died. They talked of calling in the National Guard.

But the fires kept burning. People thought they might as well give up. Only the snow in the fall was going to put them out.

BLACK RAIN CLOUDS churned over the foothills to the south. The rain might put the fires out, I thought, but ozone buzzed in the air. The lightning could start new ones. I looked to the north, half expecting to see the smoke from the old fires rise again. Then, turning back, I saw the fire in Carmichael Canyon.

I searched the highway for Hessie's truck, but I knew he was gone. I didn't know where the fire was exactly. Or what to do. It could be close enough to trap the cattle or the horses. But I didn't know.

I took three running steps toward the car and stopped. My low car wouldn't make it up the canyon. I ran to the corral. When they saw me, the horses spun away to the far rail. I tried to calm down, move slowly. But every time I got close, the horse I'd ridden threw up his head and shied away. "Damn you." I gritted the words out between my teeth. "Damn it, stand still!"

It took a long time, but finally I had the bridle on, the cinch strap buckled down and wrapped. I climbed up on the rail and lowered myself into the saddle. Out of the corral, the brown horse picked his way through the sage. I waited for the trembling in my arms and hands to stop.

Near the mouth of the canyon, I saw the cattle moving

down from the hills. Three white-faced cows were drifting slowly, stopping to eat, but they were moving away from the fire. I looked, but I couldn't see their calves. Maybe they were hidden in the tall sage, but I pushed the horse harder. We climbed up into the canyon, following the fist of black smoke in the sky. I had to get to the pack horses first, then open the drift fence.

The horse lunged uphill, but after the first mile, he began to breathe hard, and his neck glistened black with sweat. I was afraid to keep on. I pulled up and reined him off the trail where the canyon widened into a stand of tall cedars. At the creek, he jerked the reins from my hands and lowered his head to drink.

It seemed so peaceful there, no sign of fire. I stretched my legs in the stirrups, the bones in my knees cracking. A cloud passed over the sun and the skin on my arms prickled with cold. I hadn't stopped for a jacket. I heard the wind shift in the branches overhead and saw the smoke. It twisted dark gray, coming low through the trees. The horse threw his head up and danced in place. I took a grip on the saddle horn and tried to turn him, to get back to the trail, but I felt his back arch under me. Smoke burned in my eyes, and I started to cough. I lost a stirrup. I remember thinking I would just swing out of the saddle and land on my feet. I would just step off.

I THOUGHT AT FIRST I had climbed off the horse and stretched out on the ground. But a dull, hard ache circled my skull from back to front—and an ocean of noise, a high, stinging buzz, roared in my ears. I was on my back in the creek, and the horse was gone.

The water dragged on my jeans, colder than the flume. I tried to stand, but the sound screamed in my ears—like a siren going off, insistent, in the trees, and a needle of pain shot up through my leg. I lay back down. The water felt warmer then.

But I knew I had to get out. Already, my breath came hard and my arms and legs were numb. Slowly I inched my way up on the bank.

My fingers and toes burned hot with pain, and my body began to shake. I tried to sink inside, find one warm place, calm down. But I couldn't stop the shivering. My teeth chattered so hard I thought they might break. I tried to reach my shirt buttons, pull my wet clothes off, but it was as if my arms and hands were baffled in thick padding. I wanted more than anything to crawl back in the creek, where it was warm.

After a long time, the shivering stopped, and it began to rain. The rain struck my face and my arms, white with snow and bits of ice, but I couldn't feel it. It was as if I had no body—as if the rain were pounding on cold earth.

No one knew where I was. I was going to die here—but it didn't matter. I drifted in and out of consciousness. I thought about the day I drove Joe to the interstate. I came back to the ranch and stood in his cabin, looking at the wooden floor, the bare ticking on his mattress, searching for something. A book or a pencil. A wrapper from a razor blade. I found myself kneeling down in the kitchen, going through the trash. But there wasn't anything.

When I came to, the rain had stopped and it was night. I had dreamed my husband's sister called me on the telephone, saying he was coming to see us, coming to her house in Mexico. Even in the dream, I knew she had no house in Mexico. But I felt lifted, floating in a sea of warmth, a sweet euphoria. And I was weeping, "Oh, I thought he was dead. I thought Richard was dead."

I fell asleep again, and dreamed. I dreamed that everybody was alive.

Then I was choking, my heart pounding wildly. Smoke came drifting in the dark, burning in my throat, but I couldn't see it. A deep, animal fear hit like an electric shock. All I wanted was to stay alive. But I couldn't move.

I WOKE UP naked on the ground. I saw myself from up above, exposed, like some hurt dog left lying in the road. But Hessie was there, naked, rolling us in blankets. Slowly, I felt the warmth of his skin seep into mine. I tried to talk, to ask him, Where are the horses? Are the animals all right? But Hessie couldn't understand.

It seemed much later when he shifted to get up.

"Need to get more wood," he said.

"No," I said. I was so warm now, I couldn't bear for anyone to move.

When I woke up again, a campfire burned low close to my face, and the moon was white above the trees. Hessie's fingers pinched into my shoulder, shaking me.

"Look." Hessie whispered close against my ear.

A cow elk stepped slowly toward the creek, her ears pricked wide, and lowered her head to drink. She was so close I could hear her draw up water and swallow. I hardly breathed. The elk raised her head, listening into the dark. Then she backed away. I thought I heard her for a long time, moving through the trees. But I wasn't sure if I had dreamed or seen her.

I HEARD HESSIE's voice and opened my eyes. The campfire was hot, the sky black overhead.

"Talk," he said. "Where do you come from? Who are your people?"

The light from the fire caught in his eyes. He had been awake all night, shaking me and watching.

I was alive. I took a deep breath, the night air sharp in my lungs. And I was awake. Suddenly aware of another body, my face resting on the ridge of Hessie's collarbone, his arm heavy across my shoulder. A hardness pressed on my leg. My whole body tensed up in alarm.

Hessie rolled over on his back. "Don't worry," he said, his voice low and rough with laughter. "The old dog's only barkin'." It made me laugh, too. But it hurt. It hurt my head to laugh.

He got up and threw more branches on the fire. While he was gone, I tucked a blanket around me, but I didn't need to. He came back wearing long white underwear.

"How's your head?" he asked me.

"Hurts."

"Be good if you could keep awake," he said. "Talk to me."

The sky was black above the trees, but the black seemed softer than it had before.

"You never did say what you're doing in this country in the first place," Hessie said.

I started to tell him about Joe. But I couldn't explain why Joe was still with me, after all this time. "Tell me about the war," I said. "Were you afraid?"

Smoke burned again in my nostrils, coming in the darkness. I couldn't see, or move. I fought the urge to thrash out of the blankets, stand up. But Hessie didn't answer. I closed my hand around his forearm, just above the wrist. As if to make a contact there could keep us both from being scared. But his muscles had no give. His arm was hard as stone.

"We almost made it to the last," he said. "There was me, and one of my brothers, Will. You wouldn't think we'd end up in the same outfit—but it was all a mess." Hessie's voice caught in his throat. "He got blown apart. Standing just right next to me. No different from a deer . . .

"It's not a thing you tell about," he said. "Nobody knows."

"I know."

I wasn't even sure I said the words. But Hessie stopped. "My husband died," I said, "at Christmas. I sat up with him in the dark, listening to him drowning in his own breath. The sound of it. The rotting, sick-sweet smell."

My hand went weak, and slipped off Hessie's arm. "For a long time after Richard died, my own breath smelled like his."

Tears welled up behind my eyes. I didn't want this to happen. I wanted to grab onto Hessie, to hold and comfort him. I saw him as a boy in France. With Will. But he circled his arms around me. I buried my face in the wet collar of Hessie's shirt, my mouth wide open, my teeth striking bone. What had I done to be so unwanted? How could I have loved them all so much, Richard and Joe, even my father, and be so alone? I couldn't make the crying stop.

But Hessie held on, his arms hard as wood. He rocked back and forth, his chin pressed sharp on the crown of my head. I gasped for air against his neck.

I was like a baby crying, an engine you think will never stop. But finally, my body gave up. I lifted my head to breathe. It hurt to open my eyes, see the white of Hessie's shirt, the wet bark on the trees around us. After a long time, he reached out and pulled the blankets tight.

That's when I told him about Joe. I thought it wouldn't matter now. But it was hard to say the words to Hessie, to talk about sex and marijuana. Out loud, the story made us seem so young and unimportant. Telling it, I heard the truth. Joe hadn't loved me. Not enough. It should have made me sad, but what I felt was shame. A hot rush of shame burned in my chest and on my face. The lie of hanging on so long to a boy I hardly knew.

But Hessie seemed to think it all made sense. When I finished, he shifted up on his elbow and looked at me. I wanted to hide my swollen face, to look away. But he said something I never expected.

"It's good," he said, "to feel love for people. It's not a thing you give away. It's a thing you have."

He lay back down and pulled my head onto his chest, his broad hand on my hair. I felt him draw in a breath and let it go.

"You could have gone with the boy," he said. "You would have been all right."

THE SUN WAS HOT, but Hessie didn't move. A mist seeped up from the wet ground, glowing iridescent, as if lighted from within. I closed my eyes, curving my cheek into the hollow of Hessie's neck, my arms loose around him. My fingers touched the smooth, raised muscles along his spine, under the steaming blankets, and the damp wool smelled of gasoline and sweat.

I dreamed again, not quite sleeping or awake. In the warmth and sunlight, everybody was close by.

IN MY NEXT LIFE

≈≈≈≈≈≈≈

This is a love story. Although Abby and I were never lovers. That's an odd thing for me to have to say about another woman, because I've never had a woman lover, and yet with Abby it would have been possible. Of course with Abby anything was possible, and I often wonder if she hadn't gotten sick if we would have been lovers: one day our holding and touching and hugging slipping quietly into something more. It would have been beside the point and redundant, our lovemaking, but it might have been wonderful all the same.

That was the summer I was organic gardening for a living, and I had a small but steady clientele who came to me for their produce and kept me financially afloat. I had a trade going with Carver's Bakery, tomatoes for bread, and another with the farmers' market in Salt Lake City, fresh herbs for chicken and groceries. I grew wheat grass for my landlord Thomas and his lover, who both had AIDS. I traded Larry, at the Purina Mill, all the corn his kids could eat for all the grain I needed for my mare. She was half wild and the other half stubborn, and I should have turned her out to pasture like most of my friends said, or shot her like the rest recommended, but I had an idea that she and I could be great together if we ever both felt good on the same day.

Abby had long black hair she wore in a single braid and eyes the color of polished jade. Her shoulders were rounded like a swimmer's, although she was afraid of the water, and her hands were quick and graceful and yet seemed to be capable of incredible strength.

I met her at a horse-handling clinic she was teaching in Salt Lake that I'd gone to with my crazy mare.

"There are no problem horses," Abby said. "Someone has taught her to be that way."

In the middle of explaining to her that it wasn't me who taught my horse her bad habits, I realized it could have been. Abby had a way of looking at me, of looking into me, that made everything I said seem like the opposite of the truth.

"There are three things to remember when working with horses," Abby said to the women who had gathered for the class. "Ask, Receive, Give." She said each word slowly, and separated them by breaths. "Now what could be simpler than that?"

I rode as hard as I knew how that day at the clinic. Abby was calm, certain, full of images. "Your arms and hands are running water," she said. "Let the water pour over your horse. Let the buttons on your shirt come undone. Let your body melt like ice cream and dribble out the bottom of your bones."

My mare responded to the combination of my signals and Abby's words. She was moving with confidence, bending underneath me, her back rounded, her rhythm steady and strong.

"Catch the energy as if you were cradling a baby," Abby said. "Grow your fingers out to the sky. Fly with your horse.

Feel that you are dancing." She turned from one woman to another. "Appeal to the great spirit," she said. "Become aware, inhibit, allow."

At the end of the day while we were walking out the horses Abby said, "You are a lovely, lovely woman. Tell me what else you do."

I told her I played the banjo, which was the other thing I was doing at the time, with a group that was only marginally popular with people my age but a big hit with the older folks in the Fallen Arches Square Dance Club.

Abby told me she had always been intimidated by musicians.

She told me I had medieval hair.

On the first day after the clinic that Abby and I spent together I told her that meeting her was going to change my whole life. She seemed neither threatened nor surprised by this information; if anything, she was mildly pleased. "Life gives us what we need when we need it," she said. "Receiving what it gives us is a whole other thing."

We were both involved with unavailable men, one by drugs, one by alcohol, both by nature. There were some differences. She lived with her boyfriend, whose name was Roy. I lived alone. Roy was kind, at least, and faithful, and my man, whose name was Hardin, was not.

I said to Thomas, "I have met a woman who, if she were a man, I would be in love with." But of course Abby could have never been a man, and I fell in love anyway. It's not the kind of definition Abby would have gotten mired in, but I think she may also have been a little in love with me.

Once, on the phone, when we weren't sure if the conversation was over, when we weren't sure if we had actually said goodbye, we both held our receivers, breathing silently, till finally she had the guts to say, "Are you still there?"

"We are a couple of silly women," she said, when we had finally stopped laughing. "A couple of silly women who want so badly to be friends."

Although only one-sixteenth Cherokee, and even that undocumented, Abby was a believer in Native American medicine. Shamanic healing, specifically, is what she practiced. The healing involved in shamanic work happens in mind journeys a patient takes with the aid of a continuous drumbeat, into the lower or upper world, accompanied by his or her power animal. The power animal serves as the patient's interpreter, guardian, and all number of other things. The animals take pity on us, it is believed, because of the confusion with which we surround ourselves. The learning takes place in the energy field where the animal and the human being meet.

A guided tour into the lower world with a buffalo is not the kind of thing a white girl from New Jersey would discover on her own, but for me, everything that came from Abby's mouth was magic. If she had told me the world was flat, I'd have found a way to make it true.

When Abby taught me the methods of shamanic healing I started to try to journey too. Abby played the drum for me. She shook the rattle around my body and blew power into my breastbone and into the top of my skull. The drumming altered my mental state, that was for certain, but I couldn't make myself see anything I could define. If I pressed my arm hard enough against my eyeballs I could start to see light swirling. But a tunnel? another world? Animals and spirits I couldn't muster.

"People have different amounts of spiritual potential," she said, "and for some people it takes a while. Don't be discouraged by a slow start."

So I would try again and again to make forms out of the shapes inside my eyelids, and I'd stretch the truth of what I saw in the reporting. I wanted to go all of the places that Abby could go. I was afraid she might find another friend with more spiritual potential than me.

"You're seeing in a way you've never seen before," Abby said. "You just don't know how to recognize it. It isn't like cartoons on your eyelids. It's not like a big-screen TV."

Finally, my mind would make logical connections out of the things I was seeing. "It was a bear," I would say, "running away and then returning." Abby's green eyes never let mine falter. "A big white bear that could run on two legs." As I said the words, it seemed, I made it so. "It was turning somersaults, too, and rolling in the blueberries." It didn't feel like I was lying, but it also didn't feel like the truth.

One thing was certain. I believed what Abby saw. If she said she rose into the stars and followed them to South Africa, if she danced on the rooftops of Paris with her ancestors, if she and her power animal made love in the Siberian snow, I believed her. I still believe her. Abby didn't lie.

But it wasn't only the magic. Abby was gentle and funny and talked mostly with her hands. She made great mashed potatoes. She had advanced degrees in botany, biology, and art history. And the horses, Abby loved her horses more than any power animal her imagination could conjure up.

"The Indians don't believe in imagination," she told me. "They don't even have a word for it. Once you understand that fully this all becomes much easier."

We had climbed the mountain behind my house, way above the silver mine, and were lying in a meadow the moon made bright. Abby threw handfuls of cornmeal on the ground. "I'm feeding my power animal," she said. "When I do this he knows that I need him around."

I MADE ABBY batches of fresh salsa, pesto, and spaghetti sauce. I brought her squash blossoms, red peppers, and Indian corn to make a necklace her power animal told her to wear.

She told me about her college roommate, Tracy, her best friend, she said, before me. Tracy's marriage had broken up, she said, because Tracy had been having an affair with a woman, and her husband, Steve, couldn't handle it. They had tried going to therapy together, but Tracy eventually chose the woman over Steve.

"She said she never expected to have an affair with a woman," Abby said, "but then they just fell in love."

I thought about my friend Thomas, about how he gets so angry whenever anybody says that they respect his sexual choice. "Choice has nothing to do with it," I can hear him saying. "Why would I ever have done this if I had had a choice?"

But I wonder if it's not a question of choice for a woman. Aren't there women who wake up tired of trying to bridge the unbridgeable gap, who wake up ready to hold and be held by somebody who knows what it means?

"In my next life," Thomas was famous for saying, "I'm coming back as a lesbian."

"THAT'S WHAT I DID," my friend of five years, Joanne, said, when I asked her opinion, as if her lesbian affair was something I'd known about all along, "with Isabelle. And it was wonderful, for a while. But what happens too often is that somewhere down the line you are attracted to a man and want to go back, and then it's a whole new kind of guilt to deal with. You're hurting somebody who's on your team, who really knows you, who really is you, I suppose, if you stop and think."

"There are so many more interesting things to do than fall in love," Abby said. "If Roy and I split up, I want to live in a house full of women, old women and young women, teenagers and babies. Doesn't falling in love sound boring, compared to that?"

I had to admit, it didn't. We were both fighting our way out of codependency. I wasn't as far as she was yet.

"The problem with codependency," Abby said, "is that what you have to do to be codependent, and what you have to do to not be codependent, turn out so often to be the same thing."

"So what would you do about sex, in this house full of women?" I said. We were sitting sideways on her sofa like kids on a Flexible Flyer. She was braiding and unbraiding my medieval hair.

"Frankly," she said, "that's the least of my concerns."

"That's what you say now," I said, "but I think after a few years without, you would start to feel differently."

"Yeah, maybe you're right," she said, giving the short hairs at the nape of my neck a tug. "Maybe sex would turn out to be the big snafu."

IT WAS ONLY the third or fourth time we were together when Abby told me about the lump in her breast. "It's been there a long time," she said, "about two years, I guess, but my power animal says it's not cancer, and besides it gets bigger and smaller with my period. Cancer never does that."

Even the doctor, when she finally did go, said he was ninety-nine percent sure that the lump was not a "malignancy" (doctors apparently had stopped using the "C" word), but he wanted to take it out anyway, just to make sure.

On the night before Abby's biopsy, I made her favorite thing: three kinds of baked squash, butternut, buttercup, and acorn.

"Sometimes I'm jealous of Hardin," I said. "He lives right

on the surface and he's happy there. Who am I to tell him how to live his life? I should be that happy in all my depth."

"I had a friend in grade school named Margaret Hitzrot," Abby said. "Once on our way to a day of skiing we were the first car in a twenty-one-vehicle pile-up. Our car spun to a stop, unharmed against the snowbank, but facing back the way we had come, and we watched station wagons, delivery trucks, VW buses, collide and crash, spin and smash together. Mrs. Hitzrot said, 'Margaret, do you think we should wait for the police?' And Margaret said, 'If we don't get to the ski area before the lift opens the whole day will be ruined,' so we got in our car and drove away."

"It's not the worst way to live," I said.

"The problem with the surface," Abby said, "is that it's so slippery. Once you get bumped off, it's impossible to climb back on."

Abby's arms bore scars on the white underside, nearly up to the elbows, thin and delicate, like an oriental script. "It was a long, long time ago," she said. "And I wasn't trying to kill myself either. My stepfather had some serious problems. There was a good bit of sexual abuse. I never even thought about dying. I just wanted to make myself bleed."

After dinner we rode the horses up to our favorite meadow. She had been riding my horse, who had turned to putty in her hands. I was riding one of hers, a big gray gelding who was honest as a stone. We kept saying we were going to switch back, now that my horse had been gentled, but I didn't push the issue. I was afraid my mare would go back to her old habits and Abby would be disappointed. It was something I'd never felt with a woman, this giant fear of looking bad.

I was depressed that night. Hardin was in another state with another woman, and it made me so mad that I cared.

"You have given all your power away to Hardin," Abby said. "You need to do something to get it back."

We sat under the star-filled sky and Abby said she would journey beside me, journey, she said, on my behalf. This was accomplished by our lying on the ground side by side. We touched at the shoulders, the knees, and the hips. We both tied bandannas around our heads, and Abby pulled her Walkman and drumming tape out of the saddlebags.

"Don't feel like you need to journey," she said. "I'll do all the work for you, but if you feel yourself slipping into a journey, go ahead and let it happen."

For a long time I watched the white spots turn on the inside of my bandanna while Abby's breathing quickened and leveled and slowed. Then I saw a steady light, and reflections below it. It was my first real vision, nothing about it questionable or subject to change. It was moonlight over granite, I think, something shiny and permanent and hard.

Abby came back slowly, and I turned off the tape.

"Your power source is the moon," she said. "It was a bear who told me. A giant bear that kept getting smaller and smaller. He was multicolored, like light, coming through a prism. The full moon is in five days. You must be out in the moonlight. Drink it in. Let it fill you. Take four stones with you and let them soak the moonlight. This is one of them." She pressed a tiger's-eye into my hand. "It is up to you to find the other three."

I CARRIED FLOWERS with me into the short-stay surgery wing. I saw Abby in a bed at the end of the hall. She was wide awake and waving.

"You brought flowers," she said.

"Store-bought flowers, made to look wild," I said. "How do you feel?"

"Good," Abby said. "Not too bad at all."

The doctor came in and leaned over the bed like an old friend.

"Your lump was a tumor, Abby," he said.

"What kind of tumor?" she said. "What does it mean?"

"It was a malignancy," he said. "A cancer." (Sweet relief.) "I have to tell you, of all the lumps I did today, and I did five, yours was the one I expected least of all to be malignant."

His pager went off and he disappeared through the curtain. It took a few seconds, but Abby turned and met my eyes.

"Cancer, huh?" she said. "My power animal was wrong."

When I had Abby tucked into her own bed I drove home the long way, over the mountain. It was the day that would have been John Lennon's fiftieth birthday, and on the radio was a simulcast, the largest in history, a broadcast reaching more people than any other broadcast had ever done. It was live from the United Nations. Yoko Ono read a poem, and then they played "Imagine." It was the first time I cried for John Lennon.

Abby called me in the middle of the night.

"I know it sounds crazy," she said, "but I can't sleep without my lump. I should have asked the doctor for it. I should have brought it home and put it under my pillow," she said. "Where do you think it has gone?"

BEFORE HER SECOND surgery, a double mastectomy and lymph-node exploration, I took Abby down to southern Utah, to the piece of land I'd bought in the middle of nowhere because I loved it there and because having it seemed a little bit like security. My six acres is in the high desert, where it never rains except too much and more often it snows and freezes cherry blossoms or hails hard enough to make bruises on uncovered flesh. It was sage and juniper mostly, a few cacti.

Abby put her feet into the ground like she was planting them. Two ravens flew overhead in pursuit of a smaller bird, gray and blue. There was squawking, the rustle of wings, and then a clump of feathers floated down and landed at Abby's feet. Three feathers stuck together, and on each tip, a drop of blood.

Abby started singing and dancing, a song she made up as she went along, directed toward the east.

"Why do you sing and dance?" she'd once asked me. "To raise your spirits, right?" She laughed. "That is also why I sing and dance," she said. "Precisely."

She sang the same song to each of the four horizons, and danced the same steps to each with the gray bird's feathers in her hair. The words elude me now, half-English, half-Navajo. It was about light, I remember, and red dirt, and joy. When she finished dancing and turned back toward the eastern horizon the full moon rose right into her hands.

ABBY LOOKED TINY and alone in the giant white bed and among the machines she was hooked to.

"How are you?" I said.

"Not bad," she said. "A little weak. In the shamanic tradition," she said, "there is a certain amount of soul loss associated with anesthesia. Airplane travel too," she said. "Your soul can't fly fast enough to keep up. How are you?" she said. "How's Hardin?"

"He left for the Canadian Rockies this morning," I said. "He'll be gone six weeks. I asked him if he wanted to make love. He was just lying there, you know, staring at the ceiling. He said, 'I was just trying to decide whether to do that or go to Ace Hardware.'"

"I don't want you to break up with him because he would say something like that," Abby said. "I want you to break up with him because he'd say something like that and not think it was funny."

The doctor came in and started to say words like "chemotherapy," like "bone scan" and "brain scan," procedures certain to involve soul loss of one kind or another.

Simply because there was no one, I called Hardin in Canada. "That's too bad," he said, when I told him the cancer was extensive in the lymph nodes. And as usual, he was right.

The nights were getting colder, and the day after Abby got out of the hospital we picked about a thousand green tomatoes to pickle in Ball jars.

"I don't know where I want Roy to be in all of this," she said. "I know it would be too much to ask him for things like support and nurturance, so I thought about asking for things he would understand. I'd like him to stop smoking around me. I'd like him to keep our driveway free of snow."

"Those sound like good, concrete things," I said.

"I love him very much, you know," she said.

And God help me, I was jealous.

We took a walk, up toward the Uintas, where the aspen leaves had already fallen, making a carpet under our feet.

"You know," I said, "if you want to go anywhere, this year, I'll come up with the money and we'll go. It's just credit cards," I said. "I can make it happen."

"I know why my power animal lied," Abby said. "It was the intent of my question. Even though I said, 'Do I have cancer?' what I meant was 'Am I going to die?' That's what I was really asking, and the answer was no."

"I'm glad you worked that out," I said.

"I've made a decision," she said. "I'm going to stop seeing the doctors."

Something that felt like a small bomb exploded in my ribs. "What do you mean?" I said.

"I'm not going to have the chemotherapy," she said. "Or any more of the tests. My power animal said I don't need them, they could even be *detrimental,* is what he said."

The sound of the dead leaves under my boots became too loud for me to bear. "Is that what he really said, Abby?" I faced her on the trail. "Did he open his mouth and say those words?"

She walked around me and went on down the trail. "You won't leave me," she said after a while. "Even if things get real bad."

I leaned over and kissed her, softly, on the head.

"I WANT TO SUPPORT her decision," I told Thomas. "I even want to believe in her magic, but she's ignoring hundreds of years of medical research. This ugly thing is consuming her and she's not doing anything to stop it."

We were walking in the moonlight on our way up to the old silver mine not far above my house. It was the harvest moon, and so bright you could see the color in the changing leaves, the red maple, the orange scrub oak, the yellow aspen. You could even tell the difference in the aspen that were yellow tinged with brown, and the ones that were yellow and still holding green.

"She is doing something," Thomas said. "She's just not doing what you want her to do."

"What, listening to her power animal?" I said. "Waiting for the spirits from the lower world to take the cancer away? How can that mean anything to me? How can I make that leap?"

"You love Abby," he said.

"Yeah," I said. The bright leaves against the dark evergreens in the moonlight were like a hallucination.

"And she loves you," he said.

"Yeah," I said.

"That's," he said, "how you make the leap."

I DON'T WANT to talk about the next few months, the way the cancer ambushed her body with more and more powerful attacks. The way she sank into her own shadow, the darkness enveloping what was left of her hair and skin. Her vitality slipping. Maybe I do want to talk about it, but not right now.

With no doctor to supply the forecasts and explanations, watching Abby's deterioration was like reading a book without a narrator, or seeing a movie in another language. Just when you thought you knew what was going on, the plot would thicken illogically.

When it all got to be too much for Roy, he moved out and I moved in. I even thought about trying to find some old ladies and teenagers, of calling some of the ladies from the Fallen Arches, thinking I could create the household Abby had wished for. It wasn't really as pathetic as it sounds. We ate a lot of good food. We saw a lot of good movies. I played my banjo and Abby sang. We laughed a lot those last days. More, I'll bet, than most people could imagine.

Abby finally even refused to eat. The world had taken everything from her she was going to let it take, and she died softly in her room one day, looking out the window at her horses.

Once I hit a rabbit in the highway, just barely hit it, I was almost able to swerve out of its way. It was nighttime, and very cold, and I stopped the car on the side of the road and walked back to where it lay dying. The humane thing, I'm told, would have been to shoot it or hit it in the head with the tire jack or run over it again. But I picked it up and held it under my coat until it died, it was only a few minutes, and it was the strangest sensation I know of, when the life all at once, it seemed, slipped away.

Abby and I didn't talk at all the day she died. She offered me no last words I could use to make an ending, to carry on with, to change my life. I held her hands for the last few hours, and then after that till they got colder than hell.

I sat with her body most of the night, without really knowing what I was looking for. An eagle, I guess, or a raven, some great huge bird bursting in a shimmer of starlight out of her chest. But if something rose out of Abby at the end, it was in a form I didn't recognize. Cartoons, she would have said, are what I wanted. Disneyland and special effects.

For two days after her death I was immobile. There was so much to be done, busy work, really, and thank goodness there were others there to do it. The neighbors, her relatives, my friends. Her stepfather and I exchanged glances several times, and then finally a hug, though I don't know if he knew who I was, or if he knew that I knew the truth about him. Her mother was the one I was really mad at, although that may have been unfair, and she and I walked circles around the house just to avoid each other, and it worked until they went back to Santa Cruz.

The third day was the full moon, and I knew I had to go outside in it, just in case Abby could see me from wherever she was. I saddled my mare for the first time in over a year and we walked up high, to the place where Abby and I had lain together under our first full moon not even a year before. My mare was quiet, even though the wind was squirrelly and we could hear the occasional footsteps of deer. She was so well behaved, in fact, that it made me wish I'd ridden her with Abby, made me hope that Abby could see us, and then I wondered why, against all indications, I still thought that Abby was somebody who had given me something to prove. *Your seat feels like a soft glove,* Abby would have said, *your horse fills it.*

I dismounted and spread some cornmeal on the ground. *Become aware, inhibit, allow.* I laid my stones so they pointed at each of the four horizons. Jade to the west, smoky quartz to the north, hematite to the south, and to the east, Abby's tiger's-eye. *Ask, receive, give.* I sang a song to the pine trees and danced at the sky. I drank the moonlight. It filled me up.

RED ROCK CEREMONIES

The clear moon arcs
over the sleeping Three Sisters,
like the conchos that string
the waist of a dancer.

With low thunder, with red bushes smooth
as water stones, with the blue-arrowed rain,
its dark feathers curving down
and the white-tailed running deer—
the desert sits, a maiden with obsidian eyes,
brushing the star-tassled dawn from her lap.

It is the month of Green Corn;
It is the dance, Grandfather, of open blankets.

I am singing to you
I am making the words
shake like bells.

Owl Woman is blessing all directions.
This corn—with its leaves that are yellow
In the sun, with the green of small snakes,
with its long leaves, its dark stem,
and the small blue bird that drinks from its roots—
you are shaking purple in dusk,
you are climbing the rims of the world.

Old Grandfather, we are combing your hair
for blue stars and black moons.
With white corn, with cloud feathers
you are crossing dawn with the Dream Runners.

I am closing your blanket
I am making the words
             speak in circles.

Claiming Lives

1

The woman who jumped off Monroe St. Bridge
into the drumming river, left a note
written on an old newspaper:

"My head's full of rippling birds,
my heart is a firmament of water.
My eyes are basalt angels.
Help the small fish I swallow."

They waited days for her to surface,
but her body fell through sun-stringed waters,
down, down, into the deeper calms
she'd always dreamed of.

2

Cold, cold: water ribs protecting hearts
of fin and heron. Water vaulting over
submerged Chevies, drivers still gazing
at veils of windows, their hands stretched forth
as if they were still beating
against the blue-green wings.

Under the bridge, the river's as fervent
as a hallelujah revival. Later, the river
divides itself into rambling duck grass
and mud-plopped pasture. It bursts
into the memories of red-winged blackbirds,
mists over ancient fishing grounds, floods
its waters with rare northern lights.

Deep in the water's veins, its minerals
are human. The water is painted red
by cougar tongues. There is a song
we can hear when it rains on the river:
it is the Song of Consummation.

3

A man is lost under the yellow canoe.
He has a strange memory of sun paddling
deep into his skin. Now he is learning
the language of clear open waters:
grasshoppers clicking inside fish bellies,
the constant belittling of sand.

Soon he will go to the Water Village
whose totem is Salmon and Beaver.
He will see all the water-spirits,
their wispy bodies curling inside
watery holes, skin smoothed down
to rhythms of snow and dam turbines.
Their eyes are as beautiful as the scales
of rainbows in deep pools, their hair
like fishermen's nets of fluid reins.

He will hear them sing about moon spawning
and cattails probing the mud
for drowned children.
He will see the woman whose whole life
was a hollow reed. She will embrace him,
claiming the debt we all owe
to those who die as they were born:
in broken waters.

MOVING DAY AT THE WIDOW CAIN'S

(Rosalia, Washington)

I

Lugging old milk cans, glass
butter churns, pickle crocks,
we dance through the windy dust.
In the kitchen, she cries
at the loss, all of us
too unsure of what to take
or leave behind. The women
want the bedding, the men
want to knock the windows out.
No one's sure it's worth mending:
moss grows deep under the eaves,
stars will drop through the roof.
The barn has shifted
its responsibility
back to the earth, and the clouds,
wind-burnt above the wheat,
are torn in two directions.

II

Forty years ago, these women knew
this house by its births, the men by its fields.
Now we talk about new roads slashing

through the wheat like rusty scythes. The wind slams
into the lean men, stinging their eyes.
In the broad fields, the snakes move slowly in
wider circles. The house is empty;
she locks the door, turning towards the gray
clapboard town and her new husband, caught
like a woman in a prairie of fire.

for ALVINA CAIN

GRETEL EHRLICH

ISLAND

≈≈≈≈≈≈≈≈

I come to this island because I have to. Only geography can frame my mind, only water can make my body stop. I come, not for solitude—I've had enough of that in my life—but for the discipline an island imposes, the way it shapes the movement of thoughts.

Humpbacked, willow-fringed, the island is the size of a boat, roughly eighty-five feet by twenty, and lies on the eastern edge of a small man-made lake on our Wyoming ranch. I call this island Alcatraz because I once mistook a rare whooping crane that had alighted in the lower field for a pelican, and that's what the Spanish *alcatraz* means: pelican. But the name was also a joking reference to the prison island I threatened to send my saddle horse to if he was bad, though in fact *my* Alcatraz was his favorite spot on the ranch to graze.

Now Blue is dead, and I have the island to myself. Some days, Rusty, my thirteen-year-old working dog, accompanies me, sitting when I sit, taking in the view. But a view is something our minds make of a place, it is a physical frame around natural fact, a two-way transmission during which the land shapes our eyes and our eyes cut the land into "scapes."

I sit to sweep the mind. Leaves, which I think of as a tree's discontinuous skin, keep falling as if mocking my attempts to see past my own skin, past the rueful, cantankerous, despairing, laughing racket in my head.

At water's edge the tiny leaves of wild rose are burned a rusty magenta, and their fruit, still unpicked by birds, hangs like drops of blood. Sun on water is bright: a blind that keeps my mind from wandering. The ripples are grooves the needle of memory makes, then they are the lines between which music is written—quintets of bird song and wind. The dam bank is a long thigh holding all restlessness in.

To think of an island as a singular speck or a monument to human isolation is missing the point. Islands beget islands: a terrestrial island is surrounded by an island of water, which is surrounded by an island of air, all of which makes up our island universe. That's how the mind works too: one idea unspools into a million concentric thoughts. To sit on an island, then, is not a way of disconnecting ourselves but, rather, a way we can understand relatedness.

Today the island is covered with duck down. It is the time of year when mallards molt. The old, battered flight feathers from the previous spring are discarded, and during the two or three weeks it takes for the new ones to grow in, they can't fly. The males, having lost their iridescent plumage, perform military maneuvers on the water, all dressed in the same drab uniform.

Another definition of the word "island" is "the small isolated space between the lines in a fingerprint," between the lines that mark each of us as being unique. An island, then, can stand for all that occurs between thoughts, feathers, fingerprints, and lives, although, like the space between tree branches and leaves, for example, it is part of how a thing is shaped. Without that space, trees, rooms, ducks, and imaginations would collapse.

Now it's January, and winter is a new moon that skates the sky, pushing mercury down into its tube. In the middle of the night the temperature drops to thirty-two below zero. Finally, the cold breaks, and soon the groundhog will cast a shadow, but not here. Solitude has become a reflex: when I look at the lake no reflection appears. Yet there are unseen presences. Looking up after drinking from a creek, I see who I'm not: far up on a rock ledge, a mountain lion, paws crossed, has been watching me.

Later in the month, snow on the lake melts off, and the dendritic cracks in ice reappear. The lake is a gray brain I pose questions to. Somewhere in my reading I come on a reference to the island of Reil. It is the name given to the central lobe of the cerebral hemisphere deep in the lateral tissue, the place where the division between left and right brain occurs, between what the neurobiologist Francisco Varela calls "the net and the tree."

To separate out thoughts into islands is the peculiar way we humans have of knowing something, of locating ourselves on the planet and in society. We string events into temporal arrangements like pearls or archipelagos. While waiting out winter, I listen to my mind switch from logic to intuition, from tree to net, the one unbalancing the other so no dictatorships can stay.

Now snow collapses into itself under bright sun with a sound like muffled laughter. My young friend Will, aged nineteen, who is suffering from brain cancer, believes in the laughing cure, the mango cure, the Molokai cure, the lobster cure— eating what pleases him when he can eat, traveling to island

paradises when he can walk, astonished by the reversal of ex-
pectation that a life must last a certain number of years.

In the evening I watch six ravens make a playground of
the sky. They fly in pairs, the ones on the left, for no reason,
doing rolls like stunt pilots. Under them, the self-regulating
planet moves and the landscape changes—fall to winter, winter
to spring, suffering its own terminal diseases in such a way that
I know nothing is unseasonal, no death is unnatural, nothing
escapes a raven's acrobatic glee.

NEIDY MESSER

THE FORCE OF ONE VOICE

In small towns you become acquainted
with everyone. It happens like this.
You go to the Sears catalog store,
place your orders, pick them up
in a week. The woman behind the counter
remembers your name, apologizes
if your order is late, asks
after your children, your allergies,
your harvest of apples.
Then one day
someone tells you three boys drive drunk
into the river, and only two make it out.
The lost one, you hear,
is the son of the Sears lady.
You wait every day for news
of his drowned body,
seeing week after week

the map of grief on her face.
All winter her voice calls his name
across the frozen water.
He churns to shore in spring
covered with fine silt
among tangles of pine branches.
Now, you sigh, begins
the long archaeology of mourning.

LEGEND IN A SMALL TOWN

One day she ran off, left
a husband, three sons
and a note. Simply packed
two bags, shoved the front door key
under the mat, and took off
with some man from a smoke-jumper crew.
Even a stranger passing through town
will hear this story—at the café
or maybe Bud's Chevron—how
a local girl went bad.

I heard it, of course, buying groceries
just after moving in, how she
headed for Alaska with her new man
and how, somewhere along the Alcan Highway,
things began to curdle.
Six months later she came back,
knocked at the door of the home
she'd left, told her ex

he could take her back or
shut the door.

One day we stood in the shade
of an ancient oak, and she told me about
that moment, standing at the door,
marked with the scar of her mistake. He
took her hands, pulled her slowly
inside. Still, she said, it's between them,
between her and everyone. No matter what
comes before or after, leaving's the only thing
people remember.

≈≈≈≈≈≈≈≈

M yra sat in her trailer in a park on the banks of the North Platte River on the outskirts of Douglas and thought she'd stay a while. There was something comforting and enclosing about Tom working for Arlen. Years ago the family had been close-knit, and they'd had reunions once a year on Memorial Day or the Fourth of July.

They'd played baseball in the horse pasture on Memorial Day. She remembered looping fly balls and splendid catches and the novelty of the men at play. They all played together, the children and the men, and sometimes one of the women would be pulled protesting to bat, and if she hit the ball she'd run, giggling and jiggling, bosom flapping, for first. The men moved in when the children batted, and pitched slowly, burlesquing outrageous fumbles until the batter was safely on first, or all the way around the bases on errors, joyously proclaiming a home run. But against one another they were serious and concentrated. Myra remembered playing first base and the power of the men hurtling toward her, boots thumping, grunting with exertion, the smell of their sweat and their shade overwhelming her, enclosing her in their aura, and she stood, small and solemn, in hallowed space, her hand lost in the glove. The sun burned down, the grass curled, and Myra thought of foreign shores, dead soldiers, lilacs, and baseball.

There had been a lot of Dyers in that country back then. There still were, but many had moved away, gone to California. Her family had, back in the sixties, after she'd married Gene and was over by Rock River. They'd raised chickens north of Sacramento, Quinn and Eva Mae, on a ranch Myra never saw, with a palm tree in the yard (oh, symbol of exotic ease), until her father died of emphysema and her mother went back to a sister in North Dakota.

Baseball and firecrackers—and Arlen, kissing her out behind the chicken house, his mouth wet and hard on hers, and him enough bigger to make her believe that he could make her do it, and she'd better not tell. But she knew, and had to admit to herself, that she'd liked it too, and had liked knowing, even thirty years ago, that he could make her let him kiss her but he couldn't make her like him, and that was what he really wanted. She did like him, but she didn't let him know.

A poor-cousin feeling infiltrated her pleasure in the family gatherings. Her family had a place outside of Wheatland—a poor place with a few head of cows and a few hopeless reminders of her father's unversed passion for quarter horses, long-limbed and narrow-chested, whose descendants years later still defined the look of a Dyer cow horse, but a piece of ground of their own. Arlen's folks were in south Laramie then, across from the cement plant, breathing dusty air, selling gas and sundries, and even so they'd thought of themselves as a cut above, with saucers under the cups and ironed pillowcases with tatted edges. Her Uncle Ferris believed that Leona and his own backbone raised him above his true nature and the extravagant, sentimental boozing of his brothers.

Myra knew that for all his liking her and wanting to kiss her, she was something vulgar that Arlen didn't want his family to know he wanted. He didn't want to want her himself and was shamed by their kinship as though she were struck from a disgraceful rib of his own. He was the brass ring to her, forever out of reach, and she assumed a careless air to keep him from knowing how much it mattered to her.

The reunions fell off with time but the kids saw each other in the towns and at the dances and rodeos in the summer. The parents visited and danced on a calm plane above the turbulence of the children's encounters. The cousins fought among themselves, taunting and scuffling between parked cars, locked in combat but united against the threat of adult intervention. When they weren't fighting they were tense and watchful, and egged each other on to smoke sooner, drink more, ride rougher events. Myra was always there, watching, tagging along, sworn to secrecy on pain of all sorts of imaginative torment, comprising their audience and mediator, medic and second to them all.

When she was thirteen she let Arlen make love to her on top of a saddle blanket in a horse trailer out behind the chutes at the Guernsey rodeo. It was the Fourth of July and he was home from college for the summer.

He pulled her by the hand out among the pickups and trailers behind the chutes as though to show her a secret, and then, as she had thought he might, he pinned her against the side of a horse trailer and slid his hand up under her blouse, kissing her all the while. Then he was inside her jeans with searching fingers and she sailed along on the current of his desire. He unbolted the tailgate and pushed her down on top of a saddle blanket on the straw.

The pain of his penetration was no more inexplicable or

unexpected to Myra than the sting of an Indian rope burn administered and endured as a boy's demonstration of ascendancy, no more outrageous than the tongue thrusting against her child's teeth while he held her arm bent up behind her back. More quickly than she had imagined, it was over, and he knelt above her and buttoned his pants.

"Come on, Myra, let's go," he said. He put on his hat and waited.

Myra had no sense of loss or shame. She sat up in the dim light, dewed by the heat, and grinned at him. Her breasts were low cones rising from the furrowed plain of her rib cage, divided by the flat rift of her sternum, white except for nipples small and flat as pennies. She was happy to be there, but with his passion abated Arlen saw her in another light—now she was an unaccountable kid, his cousin, and he was suffused with remorse. If only she would hurry. He was afraid of discovery and wanted to escape the reproach of her presence, and there she sat in nothing but her jeans and boots, gilded by the angled light, perversely languid. He shook the straw from her blouse and slid it over her arms and buttoned it down the front, enhancing his awareness of her as a child.

As they wound back among the vehicles toward the arena he wasn't holding her hand but striding ahead, eager to lose her. He merged with a group of friends perched on the chutes and from the sanctuary of their company turned and lifted his hand to her.

"See you later," was all he said.

That afternoon she sat in the stands and watched him rope.

ARLEN WENT BACK to college in the fall without seeing her again and stopped coming home for weekends. Myra heard that he was going to Denver, courting Florence Mayer. She hadn't known how dependent she'd become on the conviction that there'd always be a next time she'd see Arlen and he'd always be in pursuit. Without knowing it she'd disregarded their kinship and linked her future to his, and when he and Florence married her world fell away.

Myra hadn't seen Arlen in years—not since Rock River days when she had run the hotel in blue jeans and a plaid shirt and her hair tied up in a handkerchief to discourage the roughnecks, Tom dragging on her belt loop. It was more a boardinghouse than hotel, a two-story frame in need of paint with its back against the tracks, catering to transients working on the highway or railroad or moving north to the oil fields. By then Arlen had a place on La Bonte Creek near Douglas and he joined the Rock River Grazing Association for summer pasture. He trailed his steers over in the spring and promenaded through town in their wake, knowing that Myra watched from the hotel doorway. He came in later for dinner with his spurs still on to strut before her, scandal and reputation having long since allowed him to shift the guilt for the Guernsey rodeo to her. That was the first time he miscalculated her effect on him. He walked into the hotel with the world by the tail and Myra grinned and said, "Well, hello," and Arlen found a lot of reasons to spend time in Rock River that summer. She poured him coffee and chicken-fried his steaks but he never slept overnight at the hotel. He had no glimmer of insight into the impact his abandonment had had on her.

Myra wondered what he'd think to see her now. She lit a cigarette and watched her reflection flare up in the window.

She wanted to stay. Anything else seemed more than she could bear. She wanted to turn back and tunnel into the comfort and familiarity of the past, to be enfolded back into the circle of the family.

She wondered if Arlen would put her on. Tom had said they were shorthanded, but she'd never worked on a ranch and couldn't remember chores from her childhood beyond feeding the chickens and gathering eggs and submerging her fingers in a pail of milk to encourage a bucket calf to suck.

Driving down the hill that evening and seeing the lights of the house in the surrounding blur of cottonwoods, and the roofs of the barns and sheds, and the corrals spreading toward the creek, she'd felt a lurching desire to be coming home. She would be thirty-six in a few months. Old, she thought, older than she'd ever thought of being, and not a whole lot to show for it—her car and her trailer and the place out by Rock River that an old man had left to her. She'd had that leased out ever since and the buildings were just tumble-down by now. The land never had been much use for anything except summering. And Tom. Child of her childhood. But the connection had snapped, stretched to breaking by separation and neglect. He'd resisted her drifting at an early age, digging in his heels one fall and refusing to go. She'd left him in Wheatland with Wells cousins for school, and after that had only seen him from time to time in the summers and at Christmas. He was always a surprise to her—that he was hers, and how much he wasn't hers at all.

She had flagged traffic on road crews until a dare from the men boosted her into an apprentice program that graduated her to heavy equipment. The summer Tom was sixteen he spent with her near Rawlins, both of them working on the highway. She had liked that. They drank beer together after work, sitting on the step of the trailer, then she grilled antelope steaks for supper and they listened to the radio and fell into bed before the light was gone from the sky. It was a peaceful time for her, with his silent companionship. She'd been sorry when he was laid off in September and drifted on. He didn't go back to school, but worked for one outfit or another, preferring ranch work to the mines or oil fields despite the low pay.

Myra thought about the years when he was little as though they had happened in another lifetime. She recalled the black-and-white border collie that Gene Wells had had, a good cow dog with its eyes constantly on Gene's face in anticipation, ready to spring with a rubbery bound to the back of the pickup, and when he rode it trotted at his stirrup in his shade. But when Tom was born the dog completely gave over its responsibilities and would slink around and hide from Gene when he called, and jump out of the pickup at gates and trot home to a fretful vigilance at the side of the baby. Gene fumed at this ruination of his best dog but was powerless to break its obsession. Myra was amused and let it inside and fed it under the table.

Tom and the dog spent countless hours in the pickup together, in front of bars and feed stores, in the dark at dances, feeding in the winter and fencing in the summer. More than anywhere else a pickup is home to a dog and a boy in the West. Myra wondered if Tom remembered that dog. Its name had flown her memory.

LESLIE RYAN

THE OTHER SIDE OF FIRE

≈≈≈≈≈≈≈

I have heard it said that storytelling starts with the body and ends with the body. That's what gives stories the ability to snag the mind by its ankles from behind and land it face down in something: life if the story's good, blandness if it's not.

But as a woman I worry about this. For most women, the body, like the story, is not a simple thing. It's a battlefield where lies and truths about power go at it. A woman's mind might wander from skirt to skirt in that smoky place like a dislocated child, looking for some grounded legs to stand by, or on, for years. The woman might end up knowing herself only as a casualty, or recognizing herself only by her scars. While there may be some truth in such an identity, it is only a partial truth, and a potentially destructive one.

I want a different story.

I NEVER THOUGHT much about fire until a few years ago, when I began teaching survival in the Great Basin desert of southern Idaho. I worked in a wilderness therapy program for troubled youth. The idea was that direct contact with the natural world could help students gain a more healthy sense of identity and empowerment.

We instructors taught the kids how to make backpacks from their blankets and string, how to find water in the desert, how to dig coal beds, how to construct debris huts and other shelters, how to identify and gather wild edibles, and basically how to keep themselves alive in difficult terrain. But the hardest thing we taught out there—the thing that made the students cry in frustration—was how to make fire with sticks.

Some of the teenagers who ended up walking around the desert like hunter-gatherers had been court-ordered to do so. A few of the boys arrived in cuffs, with their hair shaved down to the rind on one side and left to seed on the other. On their forearms they displayed homemade logos of heavy-metal rock bands, scratched in with sewing needles and flooded with blue fountain-pen ink. They wore the tales of their crimes like dog-tags, and we called these narratives "war stories."

But most of the boys didn't come that way. In spite of a few shocking tales, the boys' toughness hung on them uncomfortably. The manic energy they used in comparing transgressions made me smile, because beneath it they seemed to writhe like grubs set down in unfamiliar terrain, glistening and blinded by their recent emergence from childhood but as yet unsure of how to burrow into the next phase.

The girls came to the desert differently. Their fear wasn't just a thing to guess at beneath layers of toughness and tattoos; it was as evident as the black lace panties and see-through underwire brassieres they wore for twenty-one days of rigorous hiking. Their stories, shared in secret with the other girls, were less war stories than love stories—or, more specifically, sex stories—but they were stories of power and identity just the same.

I have been questioned about the relevance of bow-and-drill firemaking to everyday life, and I have been challenged on the social structuring of wilderness therapy programs, which mostly benefit rich white children. Wouldn't these kids feel a lot different about survival if they *really* had to do it—if they had to make fires on the floors of their freezing city apartments, rather than in this fabricated game of survival?

I can only answer that question from my own experience, with a story that also takes place somewhere between war and love.

WHEN I WAS TWELVE, my younger brothers and I were abandoned for over a year in an apartment on the southside of Richmond, Virginia. Mom was wherever Dad had left her, probably back in the old house, where she had been struggling with mental illness for years. After repeated complaints from our neighbors, who thought we children were being hurt and neglected, the court had ordered our father to remove us from the old house. We went to the other side of town, where no nosy neighbors knew us. At first I thought we would all live in the apartment together—the four children and the father—and start a new life. But it didn't work that way.

We still don't know where Dad lived during that time. At first it was every few days that he came back, bringing what we needed to survive. Some groceries: Spam, milk, and a case of Bisquick boxes. Then every week he would come. Then there was no pattern, and we couldn't tell when we would see him again.

Somewhere in there the phone got disconnected. The power got shut off. Water too. It was a husk of an apartment, with no resources. The dishes in the sink had been crusted for so long they began to flake clean. The toilet hadn't been flushed in what seemed like months. We just kept using it until it began to overflow, and after that we shut the bathroom door and went in the new construction site under a pile of boards. Some of the windows in the apartment were broken out—one from my head, one from my brother's fist, others from things we threw. My brothers were aged ten, eight, and four. We fought.

We also made a pact. If anyone found out we lived alone, Dad had said, they'd break us apart. Mom was too sick to take care of us, so we'd all have to go live with different families, and we'd never see each other again. The four of us had gathered in the kitchen one day by the dry sink, and I scraped the crud from a sharp knife with my teeth. We sliced a blood pact into our hands never to tell.

The neighbors on the left had evidently abandoned their apartment in a hurry. We went in there a lot at first, eating the food they had left and looking at the bloated fish floating in the tank. There were parts of a broken waterbed, some lava lamps, clothing, and a bunch of empty boxes. All their wallpaper was swirled with bright metallic patterns, like our kitchen paper, but patches of it were torn down and left hanging. No one ever came in or out of there, and after the food was gone we stopped going there too, because it was a creepy place.

The neighbors on the right acted like we didn't exist. I think they knew that we had gone into their apartment and stolen food, because they got double-bolt locks and began to talk loudly about calling the police if they saw any delinquents around. We stopped taking from them, in case we got caught and separated.

My brothers learned from an older boy how to steal from stores. They could walk to the 7-Eleven in about half an hour. They stole food from there, since there was no electricity to cook the Bisquick and everything else was gone. They refused to eat Bisquick raw. Mostly they stole small food, for safety. Candy bars were usually the biggest they got from the 7-Eleven, because the clerks could see down the aisle pretty easily. From Safeway, though, they could get more, like peanut butter; it was easier, because the clerks changed more often and didn't expect kids to be stealing there. Sometimes they'd get extra for the baby, who couldn't come. I don't know how long this went on. Nine months, maybe a year.

Then finally one day I was standing in the kitchen. It was coming on winter, dusky in the house. A wet wind blew through the broken windows. I lifted my bare feet up and down on the cold kitchen floor. I was staring at the stove, scooping dry Bisquick from the box with crooked fingers. I wanted to turn on the stove. I wanted to wave my hands over the fiery concentric circles of the working heating element. I wanted there to be power in the house.

"I am twelve years old," I said out loud.

Bisquick floated out onto the air as I spoke. In summer I had mixed the Bisquick in a bowl with sprinkler water and eaten it wet like that. Now the sprinkler faucets were off. The boys had shown me where they drank from the creek, which was oily and bright orange-brown. I wouldn't do it.

"Bisquick should be cooked," I said.

When was the last time he came? I couldn't remember. He might never come back. Could we actually freeze there?

Something about the stove started to infuriate me. It was supposed to give us something.

"Damn thing," I said.

Big and useless. How it made these promises and never kept them. I spit chunks of Bisquick at it, but they were too dry to stick. They fell all over my arms and chest, making a pattern of white dusty splats.

I pulled the burner control knobs from their sticky prongs

on the stove and hurled them one by one across the kitchen at the orange metallic wallpaper peeling from the wall. They left the paper dented like bent foil.

I grabbed a big metal spoon from the dish pile and banged on the steel edge of the stove. I wanted sparks. I wanted gouges. It was the cheap kind of spoon and the bowl just bent back perpendicular.

"Damn you," I said, with the Bisquick on my teeth like plaque.

The baby was four and he still couldn't talk. He did know to poop in the lumber. I was still getting good grades at school, because I had learned to read at a young age and was placed in the gifted classes, but my brothers were not doing so well: they had missed over one hundred days of school each. We had received a letter about it, addressed to Dad. I had to do something. I surveyed my options.

The only books we had were old *Scientific Americans* and the ones under the mattress where Dad used to sleep on his rare visits. *Scientific Americans* were all men. The mattress ones were women: *Penthouse* and *Playboy*. Dad liked their articles best. We all had read them.

I read them again. There were women who had sex with all their best friends, their bosses, delivery people, and pets, with everyone watching everyone else, and it seemed to make things better. "Dear Xavier," they wrote to their friend Xavier, a woman who was pictured only as a pair of red lips with a penis-shaped lipstick going in. They told her all about it.

I read about all the special techniques women could learn to please men, like mouthing unwaxed cucumbers. Men took women to cooked dinners for this, and gave them promotions. They'd provide apartments, heated, for the whole family.

I walked to the bathroom doorway and stood outside. No one ever went in there. Stuff had actually flowed onto the floor.

We could smell it all over the apartment. But it had the only mirror. I stripped off my pants, shirt, and underwear. I held my breath, opened the door, and climbed onto the sink counter.

In the murky light seeping in from the hall, I looked at my legs in the bathroom mirror. There were three triangles where the light came through, just like Xavier said men liked: one between the ankles, one between the knees, one between the thighs.

A stiffened orange towel lay on the small bathroom counter. I wrapped it around my mouth and nose like a gag so I could breathe. I turned around on the bathroom sink to look at the backs of my legs and butt.

If I swayed my back I looked curvier. I bent down with my butt stuck out and my hands on my knees to get the side-ways picture, checking the curve of dim light along my spine and the flatness of my stomach. I was still holding my breath for as long as I could because the towel smelled almost as bad as the bathroom.

I squatted above the sink and looked into my pupils, wide and black above the bristling cloth. I said aloud through the mask, "You have one thing."

I REMEMBER A TIME not long after that stove day when I was being hit by a jealous man. He had six motorcycles, a punching bag, and a seemingly unlimited supply of drugs. I couldn't leave; he was giving me the drugs I sold for money. I wish I could say I sold them for food money, for food I would share with my brothers. This did happen sometimes. But not often. I wasn't a good mother.

What I really wanted was to be someone. What I really wanted was power, and the only way I could get it was to take it from someone who had more than enough. Drugs were the currency that allowed my body to be exchanged for money, and money is a poor person's idea of strength and possibility. So I just clamped my teeth, stood there, and let my friend hit me.

As he got madder, one zigzagged vein began standing and pulsing in his forehead like lightning. He was hot, coiled up red with his fury.

I, on the other hand, felt like a block of ice. Each blow to my head seemed to break off little pieces of my mind; they would go floating up into the corner of the room and stick there like ice chips behind a river rock.

Soon my body was standing alone in the bedroom, being hit.

But not me. He couldn't get at me. I was hovering alongside the brown ceiling stain from the upstairs toilet. I could watch my head lolling around as he cuffed me.

Do whatever you want to my body, you jerk, I said to myself. That's not *me*.

It was the same way having sex with him, and with the other men who, as I see in retrospect, had no business being sexually involved with a twelve-year-old girl. When I was with them, my mind would slip out the back of my head and go look out the window, if there was one. My mind became more and more a body unto itself—in time, when it left me on the bed, I could feel its dry, bare feet shuffling across the floor. One time it made it all the way to the door, and paused there with its delicate spirit fingers on the knob. When it looked back to say goodbye to my body on the bed, something—compassion, necessity?—made it pop back inside.

AFTER THIS WENT ON for what seemed to be a long time, I began to worry about my brothers. One night my eleven-year-old brother and I sat in the living room of the apartment watching TV (the power was on at that time). We were both stoned, and the vertical hold on the TV didn't work, so we were watching Captain Kirk's head and torso being severed and lifted by a constantly rising black line. My brother told me that some of the men I'd been sleeping with had given the baby pot to smoke with them, and maybe other drugs.

This, I said to myself, is not what I want our lives to be. I quit doing drugs then and didn't allow any of those men in our apartment again. All my friends disappeared.

I made another plan. My body had gotten me into this trouble; my mind would get me out. I had good grades, but they weren't useful yet. In order to be a good mother to these boys I'd need a job.

But a girl of my social class couldn't get a job, I knew; my clothes were embarrassing, my hair greasy, my shoes fake leather, with unglued soles that slapped the ground as I walked. I was thirteen. I still couldn't work for three years. I did look sixteen already, though; someone might be fooled into hiring me if I had the proper attire. Even if I couldn't work yet, it was best to steal my wardrobe now, because as long as I was under sixteen, it wouldn't go on my permanent record and expose us if I did get caught.

I hitchhiked downtown to a fancy department store called Miller and Rhodes. I told the salesladies my father had asked me to come look for something nice for my mother—she was about my size, I said—and he'd be back later with me to see what I'd found. In the dressing room, I opened my big Naugahyde purse and stuffed in a gray wool business suit: tailored skirt, vest, and jacket, completely lined. I broke the hanger in half and stuffed it in, too, and left the rest of the clothes there.

From that department I went to lingerie. I picked out a peach-colored Christian Dior teddy, pure silk. It snapped discreetly at the crotch; one hip was cut out and flounced with pleated gauze. I stole that too.

I see now that my faith in my mind was skimpy. My body

was still the bottom line for power. I resented the fact, but I was a practical girl. Even if I was lucky enough to get a job with my suit and my grades, I'd need to be high class underneath too—for my boss, and for the real work that women do.

When I got home, I went up to my room and found my suitcase full of Barbies, which I was ashamed about still having anyway. I had written my name in pen all over the plastic luggage a long time before, in big curly handwriting with exclamation points and flowers. I took it into my father's closet and dumped the Barbies on the floor, so no boss would see Barbies in my room. I cleaned the little Barbie shoes out of the side pockets, folded the gray suit and the silk teddy into separate piles in the suitcase, and hid the suitcase under my bed.

As time went on, I added to the suitcase a tan pantsuit, some oxford shirts, a pair of leather sling pumps stolen right off the rack, red lace bikini panties with bows on them and a matching bra, and the sexy kind of nylons that need a garter belt.

BEFORE THE SUITCASE was full, though, my father had come back to live with us. When he came, it was late at night. He had a woman with him.

He called us one by one to where she sat at the three-legged kitchen table. Most of the lightbulbs were blown out, so only half her face was visible in the dim light from the hall fixture.

The woman was young, twenty-seven or so. She was twenty years younger than my father, but she had three children of her own. By the time I stood rigidly beside the boys, the woman was crying. We were embarrassed by her emotion, and by the way she swore she would marry my father and save us from the stinking apartment and our motherless lives.

She did marry him, but she couldn't save us. She could

make sure we had shoes and meals and schooling, for which I am grateful. But she couldn't protect us from our father, who was violent and who owned her love. She couldn't even protect herself.

The skirts she wore, and the power they signified, offered no refuge to a child. They were too much like the ones I had stolen. All the pretty garments underneath, which were supposed to lead my stepmother somewhere better, actually only dragged her farther into my father's control, like bridles and bits. In a landscape of boys and men and lies about power, though, they were the only skirts she and I knew. A year later, when the nine of us lived in a three-bedroom apartment, my own suits and panties still lay tucked in the suitcase under my bed, waiting there like passwords.

THERE ARE OTHER lies about power and identity, more subtle than the ones told by pornography. When I first learned, not long ago, that being abandoned in a house without utilities or food is called "child abuse," I smiled. When I learned that a twelve-year-old girl is a child, and a child's being molested by anyone—an adult or another child—is called "sexual abuse," I grinned. Suddenly I had a strange, different kind of power over the men who had hurt me, and it lay in my scars: if I had been wronged, then I was on the side of the good, and the men were on the side of the evil. Although I might not be stronger, or richer, or better in any other way, I was morally superior to them. And the moral superiority of the victim brings her power.

Like the virtue of victimization, the promise of pornography—that a woman's body is her identity and her source of strength—wasn't entirely wrong. But the way in which both of them *were* wrong no person alone would ever teach me. The desert had to do that.

In my midtwenties, I was led to the desert less by a decision of intellect than by a response to blood urgency. Going there was like picking up a baby who's face down in a puddle.

Through all those years after middle school, my mind and body had stayed as distinct from one another as the wool suits and the garter belts. My mind, the gray suit, had helped me get a job and go through college on scholarships. But as time went on it grew more and more controlling, until it became tyrannically disdainful of my body. By the time college ended I was living almost completely in my head: the intellectual jargon of modern philosophy rang in my brain all night like an alarm, and I hardly knew if or why I was alive.

Fortunately, my body still had some sense. She spoke up from under the bed, where I'd kept her locked up like a caged animal and had fed her only scraps for years. She said, "Get outside."

I went west, to the desert, to a state where I knew no one, and took a job for which I had little preparation other than backpacking.

I've heard the Great Basin described by one survival student as "Nature's Worst." It's sage and basalt country: gray and brown and fairly nondescript at first. The hunting-and-gathering Paiutes who lived there in early times were disparagingly labeled "Diggers," because they ate roots and grubs rather than something charismatic like buffalo.

In the rain, the Great Basin ground—where it's not rock —turns to slimy mud. If you have to walk when it's wet, the mud will grow on your boot soles in bricklike platforms, your quads will cramp with the weight of them, and your ankles will roll above the boot blocks like they're broken. When the sun sucks the moisture out of the mud again, the ground will crack into miles of dusty pieces.

In some places, a six-foot-tall person can lie in the dirt and make dust angels without knocking into anything but basalt gravel and stickers, so people call the desert barren. But the desert isn't barren. It's alive, and it tells the body stories that are true.

When I began teaching survival, wandering for several months through the basalt-pillared canyons and the expansive plateaus of the Great Basin with some blankets, knives, cooking cans, and personal items, I underwent a transformation.

My hands twisted wet bark into cordage, carved firesticks, and dug holes for coalbeds; the fingers and palms hardened into dark, basaltic chunks of flesh. Wind and sun made my hair spiny as the wild wheat we gather near old homesteads; the nomadic days chiseled a landscape of calluses and cracks into my feet. My dung shrank like a coyote's, and my breath came slow and reptilian.

I came to know a little about the creatures who passed their lives out there. Snipes would swoop above us at dawn like bats. Grouse would do the unthinkable—eat sagebrush, puke most of it back up in pellets, pass the rest through in slimy wads like black slugs—and live healthy, normal lives in the process. Golden eagles would fly over with their writhing meals in tow—rabbits or snakes. Badgers would excavate holes big enough for twenty-gallon drums overnight; they'd put a shovel to shame with their bare hands, plowing through cementlike earth in the dark. And the sun ignited both ends of day with what looked like fire; morning and evening would never tire of being burned that way.

My mind and body began separating less and less often, mostly because I was learning to survive out there, and doing so did not require that my mind float up in the air watching bad things happen to my body. In fact, the desert required just the opposite: in order to survive there, I had to be fully present. When the summer heat seemed intent on vaporizing my scalp as I walked, my senses would tell me where to locate shade.

They'd show me which cranny was safe for crouching in during a rainstorm. They'd let me know which plant was wild carrot and which hemlock.

In the desert, a mind that wanders far from the body can land a person in strange territories, far from water or cover. If I stopped listening to my body and to my lived experience at any time, I might become lost. I found myself realizing that power does come from my body, after all, but in a very different way.

ON THE FIRST winter survival trip I led, I met a student who brought some things together for me. Dawn was fourteen years old. Her face was tinged with a solemn and unnerving coldness, like the blush on frost-nipped fruit. On that trip, she was the only other female. For some reason, I wanted her to be the first to make bowdrill fire.

On the trail, Dawn was a quiet girl, and distant. Like so many other students, she triggered in me the sense that something had been lost. I didn't know why she was there.

On Day Ten of the trip, we awakened to a low dawn in the mouth of a wide canyon. We'd each built a fire the night before in a rock-lined coalbed pit, and then buried the coals. Eight hours later, the earth beneath me was still as warm as hands. Four teenagers and another instructor lay around me in their snowy pods, each tight in a sheet of plastic and two blankets. Three boys snored out of time with each other; one had come unhatted. His hair stuck out in a unicorn spike.

Later that day, I was working with Dawn on her bowdrill fire. I had already let the boys quit trying; they were cooking lentils a short distance away. Big sagebrush stood around us, seven feet tall, on an unlikely patch of fertile riparian soil. Twenty degrees, plated sky, pre-weather stillness. Serviceberries were shriveled on the bushes; the wild onions, yampah, and nettles we'd gathered had dried to bony stalks and blown away. Loose strands of gray-brown bark ribboned the tall sage; they scraped in a brief breeze.

Dawn knelt on a thin layer of granular snow. Her left hand, blistered and ruddy from carving, cupped a bone handsocket, which served as a pivot point for a sage spindle. Dawn worked wood considerately, and her spindle was just right: like a stout pencil, it was a little longer than her hand and thick as her index finger. She'd sharpened the upper end of the spindle to fit into the handsocket. The lower, blunt end was black from friction.

When the blunt end was newly carved, before it had begun to burn, it had shown the sage's concentric growth rings. The wood grain moved out from them like the linking strands in a spiderweb. I told Dawn I hadn't seen many things prettier than that pattern. She gave me a sideways, suspicious look.

The thong of a half-moon bow girdled Dawn's spindle, and by stroking the bow back and forth with her right hand, Dawn could drill the spindle down into a plank of sage. The friction between this fireboard and the spindle would rub off clouds of smoke and charred wood fibers called "punk."

The punk would drop down through a pie-shaped notch in the fireboard. Hotter and hotter punk would accumulate there, and it would eventually weld itself into a small coal. Then the firemaker would gently lift the coal into a nest of well-rubbed sagebrush bark, and her long, steady breaths would turn it into flame.

Theoretically. But Dawn still stared at her bowdrill set as if she were illiterate in fire, even though she had cut the set herself. Technically, she was fine. Perfect form. I stayed after her about it, keeping her up later than the boys almost every night, trying to figure out what was wrong. Her light hair whipped back and forth above the fireboard, her bowing arm cramped tight, and her breath came hard, but each day ended the same: no punk, no fire.

She'd say quietly, "I'll never do it."

None of the other students had made this type of fire yet either. Everyone could make sparks by striking a quartz or flint rock against their carbon-steel knife blades, and they got fires at night this way, even Dawn.

But something about bowdrill spooked them. It seemed so old, like magic. There was nothing but their own bodies and the body of the sagebrush, twirling together, and the result was fire.

The boys had a bowdrill-related superstition. The one with the unicorn spike, George, would shake a crusty ash cake at Dawn and say, "Dude. You gotta believe."

On Day Eleven, the group had hiked the usual distance of about seven miles. We made camp near a shallow basalt cave. It was "don't get your hair wet" weather, but Dawn and I wanted to wash up. We heated two billycans of water on a small fire, grabbed our bandannas, and retreated to the shadowy cave where we could undress away from the boys.

White-owl splats looked like paint along the head-high inner ledges of the cave. Dawn and I shifted our cold barefoot weight on the basalt gravel and tried to give each other as much bathing privacy as possible, but then an echoing crack and rush snapped along the walls and we both jerked to the sound. Rock and ice from a ledge outside.

I saw then in the half-light that the girl had a secret. Low on her breastbone, where no one would see, a lattice of rippling white scars ran over Dawn, like someone had thrown a net on her. Unlike the superficial heavy-metal logos the boys flaunted, her grid was a private and permanent statement from herself to herself; white and geometric as a chain-link fence, the pattern was more certainly the sign of her own neat hand than the cramped signature she made on paper.

LATER, when I talked to a supervisor on the radio, she said Dawn was cruel at home. She was cruelest to what was most vulnerable: her younger sisters and the pets. Helpless animals called forth a meanness in her, and trapped creatures flipped something inside—she became vicious.

The supervisor also told me a story about Dawn. She had been seeing a bad therapist not long ago.

He had told her this: "Listen. If you can't get along at home, you'll end up on the streets. You'll need food. You'll need shelter. You'll need warmth. And to get those things, you'll need money. You're a fourteen-year-old girl. You have no marketable skill. You have nothing."

I imagined him pausing and scanning her.

"Well," he'd continued, "you do have a nice body. You could use that."

He had showed her magazines, how the girls—eleven, twelve, sixteen—had found their pimps and set up their survival strategies.

He was trying to scare her into behaving at home, but when I asked her about it Dawn said, "He didn't tell me anything I didn't already know."

ON DAY TWELVE, I was leading, so I called a silent hike. I'd woken up in a funk; I wanted some time to think. We had a five-mile jaunt up and down scree slopes, through icy sage and over frozen coyote turds. I kept turning around to find the group shrinking on the near horizon. Dawn was farthest back, straggling forlornly.

I realized I was stalking the desert like a madwoman,

clamping my teeth and pounding my digging stick on rhyolite blocks without noticing it every time I had to wait.

I thought of the untold stories that had caused Dawn to carve a grid on her chest and to torment helpless things. I imagined what had compelled her to shut her body in a cage of scars. I read once that two-thirds of all people jailed for abuse have been victims of it themselves.

There is something pathological about inhabiting victimhood, and about living off its skewed sense of power and identity. It's like being in a high basalt tunnel. It's all right to hang out there for a while, when the actual storm of abuse is occurring; the true victim doesn't have much choice. The high walls are protective, and "moral superiority" offers an overhang of some dignity. But moral superiority itself can become an abusive trap, and there's not much to sustain a person in that place, where the floor is a sharp cushion of dark gravel. Like anger, victimization is a place to move through, and the next step is survival.

I don't know what comes after that.

Dawn wasn't moving; she was fenced into one of those partial truths that quickly become lies. The pornographic therapist told her to separate her mind and body and peddle the body part; her role as a victim told her that power lay as much in being scarred as in scarring. Both lies make battlefields of women's bodies: they require that we keep hurting our bodies somehow, because our power and our identities depend on it. But these lies are based on an incomplete assumption: that strength lies only in our having power *over* ourselves or others.

DAY THIRTEEN marked Dawn's turn to lead the hike. Overnight, the temperature had dropped from 20 to 0, and the wind shot up over the mesa rims in a wall of velocity. We began walking over a major plateau at sunup, and by midday it was at least 15 below in the wind.

At one point we set our eyes on a big chunk of basalt three miles away, which appeared periodically through the whipping granular snow. We planned on crouching there for a minute of rest, but when we arrived, the wind crashed around the rock like icy surf. It knifed through the blankets we had wrapped around our sweaters, and when George stopped there to pee, his zipper froze open.

By dusk we had reached a system of shallow caves and overhangs in a sheltered basalt canyon. We made camp there.

Squatting on the ground, chipping away pieces of frozen earth with my digging stick to make a coalbed pit, I realized why I had been so anxious for Dawn to be the first to make bowdrill fire. I'd wanted her to have power over the boys, so she'd believe in herself. But the desert doesn't teach power over. It teaches something else.

Standing in front of a dead electric stove is nothing like kneeling beside a smokeless fireboard. Regardless of her race or social class, unless the stove girl is a master electrician who can illegally tap into power from a faraway source, she is bodily helpless before the cold metal cube. All she can do is break it apart and throw it around. The stove teaches her that her body can't bring her power, unless she uses it to take power from someone or somewhere else, at the expense of her spirit.

When she's kneeling by her fireboard, though, the cold girl is free to choose another identity. In fact, she can identify with the world through the bowdrill set. After all, she chose the tall, dead sage plant, cut the branches from it, and shaped the parts herself. In choosing and shaping her tools, she has created a sense of autonomy. If the tools don't work, there are things she can do about it, with her mind and body together: push down harder, go faster, examine the set, smooth out the parts, try again.

Fire by friction requires something more than turning a knob on a stove. It requires spirit, or at least, in Dawn's case, the belief that mind and body can go safely together in the world. It requires the faith that a woman's power does come from within her body, but not separately from her mind.

Even though the girl feels an empowered individuality making friction fire, she never does it entirely alone. As anyone who has tried to make fire from sappy or sodden wood will tell, she makes flame only through her surroundings, by the grace of the fire that exists already in the sage and in the natural world at large.

In some spots in the Great Basin, basalt towers spewed as fire from the recesses of the earth just three thousand years ago. In these spots, firemaking seems less individual than collective: it's an invocation of an ever-present, hidden power.

The attentive student comes to tell which plants—like sage, clematis, and cottonwood—are full of fire, and which are not. The fire in her own arms shifts with her physical or psychic state. In this sense, friction firemaking enacts mystery and provides a link with a different sense of identity. The woman has power within herself and through her connection with the natural world, not power over them.

This was a sense of identity I could never force Dawn to accept. She'd have to choose it herself or find a different one on her own, probably through a long chain of experiences. Her story might end up sounding nothing like mine, or the other girls' love tales, or the boys' war stories.

Dawn's flint-and-steel-firemaking skills were good enough for safety, and she had hiked well in the lead. I wouldn't keep her up bowdrilling any later than the others from now on.

After finishing my firepit, I went and sat beside Dawn under her overhang, out of the wind. She looked small, sitting back on her heels rubbing tinder. I got out the map and measured the day's route with string.

"Fourteen and a half miles, Dawn."

She quit rubbing and looked up. "What?"

"You led fourteen and a half miles without a break."

Dawn stared at me. I heard the irregular sounds of the boys breaking up wood.

After a while she said, "Either it wasn't fourteen and a half miles, or I didn't lead."

We were silent.

"You led fourteen and a half miles without a break," I said again. I cut the string and laid it over the knee of her wool army pants, across the long strands of sagebrush bark tinder, which spread around her like a dress. The Paiute Indians, Diggers, used to weave their clothes, boots, and blankets from such bark—the same bark they blew into flame.

"You must be tired," I said. "You can skip bowdrill tonight."

DAWN'S CAMP stayed quiet until after dusk. I was about to go check on her when the sound of grinding firesticks echoed out from under her ledge. I sat for a while wondering whether or not she'd want company for this attempt.

After a few minutes the good smell of sage smoke traveled out toward my camp. I was on my feet heading toward Dawn's spot when I heard the bowdrill stop and saw a glowing pile of punk moving slowly through the air on her knifeblade.

The cherry coal disappeared into the dark tinder. She lifted the bundle to blow. The tinder nest began to glow orange, and its dim light revealed Dawn's uptilted face as she sent her breath through the fibers.

I walked up just as the bundle took flame. The fire lit the ceiling of her overhang for the first time, and she still held the bundle aloft. But she wasn't watching the fire; she was looking up. Chiseled into the rock overhead was a petroglyph, left by the Paiutes or the Shoshone: a series of concentric half-circles like a sunset, or like half the pattern of a pebble thrown in water. Dawn didn't smile, but I saw the reflection of the fire in her eyes.

A COYOTE IS LOPING ACROSS THE WATER

≈≈≈≈≈≈≈

I studied him at a distance as though he were a man in a photograph, caught in a moment that was never meant to last longer than a breath: the way he walked through the green, shivering wheat in June, his deliberate steps, the strength suggested in his slowness, his arms muscled heavily, tanned. He would take off his straw cowboy hat, grimace at the sun, then wipe the sweat off his forehead, the hat now a moon eclipsing, shadowing his face.

The way I would hear his buckskin, Peco, when they were chasing a stray, the blasting, snorting exertion long before I saw the black mane and tail streaming, before I watched the huge muscles gather in his chest and explode down his legs, before I saw the rider, 6 feet 4 inches, 230 pounds, his gray Stetson scrunched low, his huge thighs hugging Peco's ribs—their easy rocking rhythm.

The way he used to hip back in the saddle, searching the horizon, gazing across the maze of summerfallow, planted fields, scab patches, down the clawed-out canyons, off to the Blue Mountains as if for an answer to some philosophical question he had been turning over in his mind. I would stare at his squinting blue-gray eyes, his body as tense, still, and intent as when he scanned a hillside for deer or elk. Then I would look off into that landscape, too—looking for Dad's questions.

My father was the hardness of basalt; he weathered, he endured, and he was as elusive as a handful of dirt spurting rivulets through my clenched fist. I used to sneak out to the laundry room at night, find one of his clean flannel workshirts, western cut, the pearled snap buttons, and slip it on for a nightgown. It still smelled like him. I imagined I was sliding into his skin. I would know what he knew.

≈

August 18, 1991. 6 A.M. Quit Drinking. A family ultimatum. We each read letters, first telling him how much we love him, then listing times we have seen him drunk. The interventionist with us makes me read my letter last. "Dad, I remember walking on the beach with you when I was a little girl. I will never forget the sound of the ocean, the mist, the cold, and the warmth of your hand. . . ." The room is dead silent as though time is moving very slowly, except for the quiet crying of Jake and Bruce, my brothers, and Zoey, my sister. Dad drills his stare into me. I use the letter as a shield. Near the end, I break down, and stare at the ceiling while I regain control. When I finish, Dr. Campbell asks him if he will go to a three-week treatment program we have set up for him. Dad says he can do it himself. I close my eyes and take a deep breath, preparing myself for what I have been dreading all summer; his refusal means we must now read the postscripts of our letters: we all will refuse to talk to him, and my brothers will dissolve the ranch partnership. We read our brief statements. He refuses again, gets up, and walks to the bathroom. We exchange panicked looks. Yesterday, Jake told us he knew a pistol was hidden in a bathroom cupboard. Dad's dad committed suicide with a pistol when Dad was only twenty-one. I tense my muscles, bracing for the recoil.

I force myself to look out the cabin window. Big pines and cedars, blue jays screaming, the lake. Sunrise wind is pushing small gusts across the water. On the far side, there are now more clear-cut patches than when I looked through this window on my wedding day, eight years ago. Has it really been that long since I moved away? I try to imagine my life without talking to him or seeing the ranch. This might be the last time I see this lake.

Finally, I hear the door open, hear a muffled conversation between Dad and Dr. Campbell, and then feel the shaking of the hallway when Dad strides past us into the kitchen. He doesn't even seem to see us. He pours what is left of a half-gallon of V.O. down the sink, then whispers he will go. He heads for the door. Jake blocks him. Dad might get in his truck and drive away. He also has another pistol underneath the seat of the pickup. They both stand coiled. "I need to go out to my truck," Dad almost snarls. Jake holds his stare for a moment longer, then stands aside. Dad returns with a fifth and pours that out, too. In his bedroom, I try to keep my mind carefully numb as I help Dad look for matching pairs of socks. We do not look at each other.

The hour and a half out of the hills to Seattle then up to Ballard Community Hospital is an endurance run. We are driving in Jake's van. Dad already has the shakes. Every so often I see him studying a tree, a ridgeline, as though he can't believe this is happening. His shoulders sag. There is more gray in his hair than the last time I saw him. Every so often he wipes away tears with his big red handkerchief. Mom, Zoey, and I try to make small talk. Mom asks me how my flight was. She still can't believe I have flown a thousand miles to do this without telling her. I describe how my flight blew a tire on landing, how we had to sit on the runway while the emergency crews surrounded the plane. Jake and Dad are speaking quietly about what needs to be done on the ranch. I think about flying over it, how I could follow the river, the road from thirty-five thousand feet, how I could pick out the grain elevators and the house. I had wondered if she were at home, even perhaps working in the garden and looking up at the contrail overhead. At Ballard, they take his clothes away, give him a flimsy hospital gown and slippers. We are told to make our goodbyes quick. When I go into his room, he is lying on his side, his back to the door, crying so hard his shoulders shake. I walk up to him and put my hand on his muscled arm, stare out the window into the brick of the next building until he can talk to me.

Ten minutes later, I walk out of the hospital. The streets and waterways of Seattle look unreal. Time has stopped for us. We stand on the sidewalk for almost an hour; none of us knows how to leave. Finally, Jake walks to his van, and heads for the ranch. The rest of us take the Bremerton Ferry. Mom and I stand outside on the deck; the wind and spray give us a small chill. We pass the time watching sailboats. It seems that more than water separates us from them. The bright sails, the way they cut through the water belong to another life, another world, a grace and ease I will never have again. We watch Seattle slide away, try to pick out where Ballard must be. I give her a hug, and suddenly her shoulders are the small, fragile bones of a sparrow. We might be a long way into the future, when she might be a widow, her steps small and slow; we might be on a trip together, my father committed to memory. I have to grab the railing.

≈

I am eleven years old. It is hot. Dust and the sharp smell of animals hang in the air. Out across the Horse Heaven and eastern Oregon, noon stillness makes the world seem about to explode. I am bored, lonely, so I walk out to the corral to spend time with Peco, my best friend in the world. Dust devils like ghost tornadoes swirl in the distance.

Peco is asleep, a back hoof raised in total relaxation, his tail swatting flies. I slide through the corral and walk into his chest. He opens his orange, knowing eyes and nuzzles my neck before he latches onto the shoulder of my shirt. He goes back to sleep. I rest my head against the hardness of his jaw, absorbing the sharp sweat smell, feel his skin ripple, and scratch the gray scar on his shoulder. We stand in the afternoon heat for a long time. Finally, he shifts, stares past me. I turn around and discover a young coyote playing in the other corral.

He is ignorant of us. He keeps leaping over the Powder River gate, back and forth. He is just playing like a puppy, so full of energy he can't contain it. He snaps at a rock on the ground, leaps again, snaps the air—effortless. I am fascinated. I have heard about the evils of coyotes for years, seen what a pack of them will do when they find an unguarded calf's hiding place. I know I should go back to the house, where my Dad is eating lunch and listening to the noon commodity report. I stand there, watching him play, not wanting that moment to end, but my guilt finally wins out.

Dad jumps from the table, strides down to the den, and slams shells into his rifle. A sick feeling starts in the back of my throat. "Where is it?" he whispers as he opens the door.

I point to the corral gate. He crouches and works his way to the edge of the yard, then past the shop, to the corrals. I can't help following. Suddenly Dad stands, shoulders his rifle, shoots. My head snaps back with the recoil. The coyote takes off running across the field, digging in with his shoulders, toward a set of old seed drills, the rusting metal shafts curving down into the earth like bones. Dad fires again. "Run," I urge him to myself. The third shot slams him into the ground, end over end. On a ranch there is rarely such a thing as a quick kill. He is kicking weakly. Dad ends it with the butt of his rifle.

I have done my duty. Dad killed one of the bad guys. I expected to feel good about this, that I have in some small way won Dad's approval. Instead I have turned that coyote in. Pat Garrett. I am still staring at the body, his bared teeth, the stillness of the afternoon broken by gunfire, and now a small breeze is lifting the brown-gray fur, exposing the red undercoat.

"Good eyes," Dad says.

"Thanks." I look at his face—the grimness of dirty but necessary action—then quickly away, afraid he will see the traitor.

I keep walking out to the red seed drills in the fall when I think no one will notice. I watch the weather wear him away, first his ribs cave in, then he becomes just fur and bones, and finally tufts of fur blow away leaving me with a skeleton and still those teeth bared and gleaming.

≈

Oh, the party was good while it lasted. My twenty-first birthday: my Dad and we sisters are supposed to drive to town and buy groceries for dinner. Mom and the younger men stay at home. Instead we drive to the Tillicum Room and drink tequila with salt and lime, then get back into the truck, fish out the V.O. from under the seat, and drink from the bottle the forty miles it takes to get to Yakima, to a rundown Chinese restaurant-bar on First Street where the western-wear stores are and the prostitutes. We drink more whiskey, and finally Dad and I get up and dance the Cotton-Eyed Joe, "Bullshit, one, two, three . . ." around the tables. There is no band, no jukebox. I remember the feeling of being in his arms, how easily he guides me through the steps: his feet, his hands a separate way of knowing—like wading into swift water, my father is a river surrounding me, holding me up, talking to me without language. Other patrons applaud us when we are done. We are having a high time, howling at the moon, damn straight.

Work hard, play hard. Tomorrow, your horse may be spooked by a rattlesnake, crowhop, and break your neck in the fall; your combine may roll down a hillside; a hailstorm may wipe you out; the bottom may fall out of the commodity market; a cow might kick you in the head. You're not getting out of this world alive, so you may as well enjoy it while you're here. Which is all a very long explanation of one word: denial.

≈

Three days after we leave Dad to the Ballard CARE unit, Mom and I drive back to the ranch to water the garden, take Dad's pickup home, make sure Janine-the-Banker has all the figures she needs to approve next year's $700,000 operating loan, see if there's enough moisture in the ground to seed. Dad's truck has been washed; it no longer smells of field dirt, chaff, his Stetson cologne, peanuts. It's a four-hour drive, so we stop in Roslyn for a cold drink and to shift drivers. On a whim we see a sign for the pioneer cemeteries and drive into the woods. We spend the late afternoon walking among the immigrant graves, sun filtering through the pines, memories of babies, mining disasters. On a few there are pictures nearly a hundred years old. I stare into those long-dead faces. Investigating old pioneer cemeteries is a ritual for us, and today strangely soothing. I understand why when we finally drive into the Yakima Valley: neither of us really wants to go back. We drive to Mabton, population one thousand, the closest town to the ranch, and turn off the highway. Desert sage flats spread out all around us. I have always loved this road; the narrow track seems to be heading for the edge of the universe, to absolute space. As we approach the edge of the valley, the foothills of Horse Heaven suddenly rising, Mom points east, to a few lone wheatfields carved out of the desert ground. Dad wants to lease it, three thousand more acres. I look at the stubble fields. Where will the extra hours it will take to farm that ground come from? The ranch seems to be endless seasons of work: seeding, plowing, hauling wheat, weeding, harvest plus the worry about the weather and the price of wheat in any season. She glances at me, and her eyes tell me she is thinking the same thing.

As we wind our way up into the hills, we try to figure out when Dad's drinking ran out of control: my twenty-first birthday comes up. For me, a rite of passage, for Dad, another drunk. I remember seeing him drink an entire fifth in one day eleven years ago. How many times had I sat with him, a bottle of V.O. between us, and solved the world's problems? How many times had I dismissed that fifth a day because he had to worry about operating loans, rain, the depth of ground moisture, government programs, dismissed it because he was that western man who could hold his liquor, a fifth and not slur, and still make his point? Why did we keep drinking with him? How long ago was it when he replaced singing "Oh, bury me not on the lone prairie," while he was making coffee in the morning, with silence, and the squeak of the closet door where the liquor cabinet was, the scrape of the bottle across the shelf, the sound of the whiskey slipping into the coffee cup like water over polished stones?

We make the top of the grade, the valley gone now, then turn onto Alderdale Road. The truck follows the curves up the ravine like a salmon moving upstream. We crest the ridge, Horse Heaven slopes gently before us, the Columbia River, the Oregon plains, the Blue Mountains, and the home place.

I don't want to be at the ranch right now. Everywhere I look I see Dad: the plowed fields, the granaries (four bins with ten thousand bolts each, raised that spring between weeding and harvest), the semis, the combines, the tractors, all lined up outside the new shop (raised that year between seeding and hauling wheat to Roosevelt), and the house he built for Mom thirty-nine years ago, that same landscape, the fields harvested down to bare yellow wheat stalks—the hollow bones of birds—the blue sage of scab patches, canyons, the Blue Mountains he was always looking off to.

He is not here.

Sometimes, in the night, I have nightmares: he has died, I have seen him with his eyes closed in his coffin, I have just come from his funeral, the heavy scent of chrysanthemums, I am looking for him for a long time before I realize he is dead. I wake up with the weight of grief on my chest. I have to make myself breathe. Now, I feel like I am caught in that nightmare again, only the sun is shining hard, pushing my shoulders back. I have to concentrate on the details of the hospital (sound of elevator, nurses talking, Dad's crying) to make him alive.

Mom frowns as we drive into the yard. Her eyes are watery. I follow her out past the windbreak, through the gate of her garden. She walks up rows, inspecting the radishes, potatoes, carrots. Her back is rigid. I look at the fence she put around it to keep out gophers and badgers, the wire cages around the tomatoes and roses to protect against birds, the irrigation lines to make ashy soil produce, the cans of high-powered pesticides and fertilizers. She turns to me on the last row, away from her prized, now wilted, flowers. "My zinnias," she says, quietly. "I worked so hard to get them to grow here."

After I moment, I say quietly, "They'll come back."

The next morning, I sit talking with Jake in the shop. He still looks like he can't believe what has happened. "I haven't had a beer all summer," he says, shaking his head. Although I have heard it before, he needs to tell me about the summer, about harvest: Dad driving the combine drunk, running the header into the ground like a green kid, the evening a neighbor called to say he was passed out in front of the fertilizer truck, a drive to Pasco when my brother almost called the state patrol. And then this morning Jake found seventeen V.O. bottles in the dump that hadn't been there last time, which wasn't all that long ago. When I tell him I felt like we had come from a funeral, he suddenly starts crying. Something twists inside me, but this morning I don't have any tears left. I am too tired. I just sit quietly with this thirty-eight-year-old man with the weathered face and hands, the wide shoulders, the oldest son, the younger version of my Dad.

≈

For years while I am growing up a mysterious black coyote runs through the country. I hold my breath when I hear the stories, waiting to hear the end. Dad and my brothers see him sitting on hillsides while they are driving tractors. In pickups with the gun racks behind the seats, they see him out of the corners of their eyes loping over a ridge. By the time the rifles come down he is just out of range, or the bullets whine over his head. Other ranchers tell the same stories, report seeing him with mates, denned up with puppies. Stories about the ranch dogs he lures away, plays with, those dogs who are never seen again. He is half again as big as a regular coyote. And, of course, he is every rancher's dream. Often, my dad goes out with his rifle, looking for him. No bullet ever rolls him.

Much later, I discover Spil'yay, the trickster of Northwest Indian tribes, a god who appreciates a good joke, who holds grudges. He can assume the form of any creature, but usually chooses the raven or coyote.

≈

A week after the intervention, we return to Ballard Hospital. Saturday is family day. We sit through lectures, films, group sessions aimed at keeping the alcoholic from taking that first drink, and even an Al-Anon meeting for relatives and friends to talk about how they feel. But there are no tips for what I really want: how to talk to him. We smile at each other warily, but have nothing to say. None of the patients look like alcoholics to me. Dad doesn't look like an alcoholic. They are only allowed decaffeinated coffee, which everyone keeps offering me all day. I feel bad about turning down their only form of hospitality, so before the day is over I will drink about ten cups of the stuff. Dad's counselor tells us Dad has to put the ranch second to his sobriety. Later, I hear Dad corner Mom in the patients' kitchen, hear him try to convince her of all the sound financial reasons for taking on that extra three thousand acres. He is asking for four more weeks of work a year. I sip my decaf in the next room, thinking, how? He would have to add them to the calendar; he pushes the fifty-two. In Mom's tight one-word responses, in her tone, I hear all the unsaid, unsound emotional reasons. I realize he may be sober, but he still can't see the exhaustion around Mom's eyes, my brother's, his own. Dad is still driven by what every man in his family has done: move west, buy more land, keep moving, keep growing. What is it in their collective pasts that drives so hard they can never stop to look back?

During a ten-minute break he invites me into his room. There are stacks of A.A. literature by his bed. He has me read a letter he is writing—goodbye to his best friend, the one he has played with, worked with, gone to bed with, and who eventually became more important than his family—V.O. The letter says he has been drinking hard for twenty-plus years. I am only twenty-nine. Just who is this man sitting slouched on the edge of a hospital bed? I recognize the lines I have come to know on his face, the way the ends of his blond-brown hair curl, those familiar western shirts, Levi's, tennis shoes. I think of him looking out over the land when I was trying so hard to find out who he was, who was behind that stoic face, the man I have been trying to figure out all my life. "What do you think?" he says, guardedly.

I shake my head. I have no idea. We both start crying. He stands up and hugs me for a long time. I feel safe for a minute, the way I felt in his arms dancing, but then I realize again the deception of this centeredness, this calm.

≈

There is a room with sloping ceilings on the second floor of my grandmother's house. You can stand up straight only in the very middle. Klickitat baskets, cases of arrowheads, beaded leather bags, and a small library of very old books. This used to be my father's room when he was a boy. I spent hours there growing up, trying to see with his boy's eyes, exploring the Indian artifacts hidden in the musty, deep closets, and reading those books. In one of them, the creation story of the Klickitats, how a god during a river flood took up great masses of mud from the riverbed, molded it, then gouged out eyes and carved out mouths with his hands. I remember looking out the window to the Columbia and imagining the feel of that muddy thumb, the salty taste of mud as he parted my lips. Was that god's name Spil'yay?

On the hottest days at the ranch, out to the horizon, heat waves shimmered, swelled, rolled like the ocean. Once when I glanced out over the fields, I saw a coyote loping across the water. That illusion has stayed with me: getting away, ghost of the land, trickster who laughs in my dreams.

≈

I am sitting in Little Nell's, a bar I can't afford, sipping a glass of Dewar's straight, feeling guilty as hell. There seems to be some truth in that slow burn in my mouth, down my throat, and a welcome numbing. I can't believe, seeing what happened to my father, I am still so compelled. Perhaps this is what keeps us in a little wildness, afraid of looking too hard, the search may end before we find the answer. Land is still everything to me. Without the ranch, that land, to center me, how will I navigate through the stars? It is my homeplace, my identity, but I haven't invested my life into it as Dad has. Dad hasn't been off the place for longer than three weeks at a time, ever. His house is a half-mile from where he was born. On a trip to Chicago, he couldn't bring himself to walk in the city more than five blocks from his hotel. He was convinced he would get lost. This man who has walked through blizzards at night, in the middle of the Blue Mountains, and always found elk hunting camp. I stop drinking when my scotch is only half empty because I am unconsciously asking that amber, beaded glass the question that I have asked of Dad, and of myself, and of the

land. The question that has haunted me, will haunt me until I
hit the floor: "Quién es?" Who is it?

≈

I love summer nights at the ranch, the moon so large and yellow
it seems to hang just out of reach, the stars unimaginably bright
and thick. But I find that I am holding myself stiff, away from
the night, from the moon-shadowed ridges and fields. I am
frightened down to my bones, like the childhood fright I felt
when coyotes howled close to the house. When I was nine, a
cold October afternoon, snow threatening, Dad, Jake, and I had
to go up to Kimball Ridge. Earlier in the day Dad had pulled
a calf so large it paralyzed the mother. He had returned to get
Jake to help him move the dying cow so they could milk her.
And they needed me to hold the flashlight. By the time we
reached the rim of the canyon, dusk was creeping. We walked
down the canyonside, the sharp smell of sage and dirt, coyotes
already yapping, so close I thought I could hear them slinking
through the brush. They were circling.

The calf lay small and quiet, the white on its face brilliant.
Dad and Jake wrestled the cow until full darkness blanketed
us. The yapping and howling increased. Complete night washed
out to every horizon, my flashlight the only light. I heard the
restless padding animal feet, the grunting of the men, and finally the sound of milk squirting into a jar. When the calf had
been fed, Jake scooped it up in his arms, and we climbed back
to the rim. Jake laid the calf on the floor of the cab and switched
on a floodlight. Everywhere coyotes milled like sharks swarm-
ing. My throat was completely dry. Later that night, the calf
gurgled strangely, then died. Although I knew it wasn't true, I
couldn't shake the belief that the coyotes had something to do
with its death, a foreshadowing.

But tonight, this gentle August night, this moon, I know there are bigger fears, like the one I have just discovered: my father and the landscape are inextricably linked. My love for the land is the love for my father. When I feel acutely lonely, lost, small, I have to go back to the ranch. Sometimes I stand in a field watching the green wheat sway, and I feel the hardness of furrows carved into the ground. Sometimes I stand on a canyon rim watching a dry creekbed flow to the river, and I feel the hardness of basalt under my feet. That hardness and strength move through my body like shock waves. And when he is gone, will I be able to see the land without the wash of my father over it? Will grief for him make this place unbearable, like the thought of holding one of his shirts next to me, the grief of his scent?

PAULINE MORTENSON

THE HUNSAKER BLOOD

≈≈≈≈≈≈≈≈

That spring in 1955, the floor in my parents' bedroom suddenly dropped out, just gave way one day when the old man was walking through, and then there it was, the truth we had all been avoiding—the orange, acrid smell of dry rot.

We had all been sidestepping the issue, the issue of the dry rot and of building the new house. We had known that something was the matter with the floor because of the way it felt when you walked across, like walking on cracked ice. But we didn't like to think about it. And besides, the old man said he needed a new truck, and Mother said, "So that is that." So we had all been waiting, letting things go because someday we were going to build.

And then that spring the floor dropped out when we least expected it, dropped out on our father after he had been ill for so long and we thought that he was getting better.

And that's when I became head nurse, my father's own

little Florence Nightingale, the one who would bring him candy pills in the medical kit that came from the grocery. I was the one who would feel his pulse and take his temperature, while he would say cooing things, how's-my-little things, and he would tell me how everyone was against him and try to get me on his side.

So I was on his side, more Sanderson than Hunsaker. And that was a good thing because you didn't want to have anything to do with Hunsakers, if you could help it—one of them Hunsakers who took everything they could lay their hands on. Like the Hunsaker brothers who came to the wedding on foot and left on the old man's best horse. Bloodlines always showed. You could count on that. You could follow it back on your own genealogical chart, two lines traced back to Adam, one through the Sanderson line by way of William the Conqueror and the other through the Hunsakers by way of Attila the Hun.

Mother was a Hunsaker. And the old man would sit there in front of the television in the summer of his growing paralysis, polishing apples, rubbing them on the bib of his overalls, sizing them and knocking off little quips about Attila. Things like "Where's your axe? Where's your horse? Seen any good Hunsackers lately?"

It was all funny as hell until your mother said, "Just what do you think we are going to live on? Just what do you think we are going to eat?" which suddenly drained all the blood from our veins. Because we knew what that meant, that she had spent the entire winter asking him for money, coaxing last year's logging money out of his savings through the narrow funnel of his pocket, getting it out five dollars at a time.

And he'd say, "Battle axe. Money grabber. This here's money that I earned. And nobody's getting one red cent until they come around." He would say it, and his face would turn red, and he would shake his cane at her for emphasis, and she would walk out the door for $1.25 an hour and leave me home to fetch apples and make scrambled eggs.

And that was the big thing back then. Nothing to laugh at. I mean we had spent an entire winter of the old man swinging his cane to get our attention, and then in the spring when we thought that he should be getting better, the floor dropped out, and we were left pushing in cinder blocks and laying down plywood. Because for the first time in five generations of faithful women, our mother had gone to work. Not that she hadn't milked cows and delivered pigs, cleaned house, and fed crews of lumbermen and sons for twenty-five years. But she had never done it for money before, never gone outside the boundaries of home, never crossed over that line of his will.

But everyone had to go to work back then. It was the beginning of the end. Everyone with their own assigned job, everyone who was still in the family and wasn't off married or in the marines. And I was the head nurse. My brothers, Harlo watering at the golf course, and Gary setting pins at the bowling alley, and my sister Eileen, recepting for a dentist and trying to save money for dental-assistant school. And Mother cleaning houses and bringing home laundry, to the old man's tune of "I'm keeping this money that I have. That's money I've got to retire on. And not one of you is getting a penny until you all stay home where you belong."

And where did we belong really? At the end of his arms? Everyone was beyond arm's length but me, everyone going in his or her own direction, instead of being there when he needed them. Six sons that had farmed and logged for him, since they were ten and useful, but had been marrying off and leaving home about the time they were just beginning to amount to anything. Until he was down to three, just Harlo and Gary and Jarvis, and then Jarvis running away from home the year before, and now only two left, only two left to take his orders, and there they were beyond his grasp, his failing extremities, the last two to disobey.

And what do you have left with a house that drops out from under you like that, changes on the spur of the moment, makes you hesitate just to put your foot down? What do you have left after the orange, acrid smell, the smell that you get when you lean in close for a hug?

But then, it was money we had all earned, especially the boys who had skipped school to skid logs. But it was money we couldn't touch, money held over our heads. And Mother would say, "We have to go on living. What do you expect us to do?" And she would pave the way for everyone else, open up a hole in the wall of possibility. "This is what all of us have to do," she would say. "We have to go on living."

And everybody was working, only me and the old man at home whiling away our time. Trying to think of things to do to keep ourselves out of mischief, watching "Rin Tin Tin" and "Howdy Doody," and "I Led Three Lives." Switching the channel back and forth, arguing over Clarabell the clown and the guy saving the world from communism. Whiling away our time trying to think up things that would break the monotony—like saddling my horse. And the one day when he tried that, when he went out and threw a blanket and saddle on Old Coalic, and cinched the saddle down tight, he forgot about the bloat, forgot about how a horse that's been cinched up too tight once will remember and bloat up after that when you are cinching. Then when you go to get in the saddle, he relaxes. And the old man forgot about that, forgot and put his foot in the stirrup and started up and the saddle flipped 180 degrees under the horse, and there was my old man upside down under the belly of Old Coalic, hanging on upside down for a split second, before he let go and fell on his back. And that was the end of riding, and we went back to polishing apples and saving the world from communism and Howdy Doody.

And then after it had been a long spring, after everyone had been doing their jobs and everyone was getting used to the idea, it suddenly all came back to the floor. Not the bedroom floor this time, but the kitchen. It all came back to the floor just after breakfast, after I'd fixed my best scrambled eggs with bread like the old man liked. And he started in on the floor, after eating the scrambled eggs, walked across the floor toward the living room and discovered the latest evidence, another soft spot getting ready to go. Another place where we had been holding our breath. We had all noticed it except for the old man, and then he discovered it like he was the first one. And he began to play with it with his feet, putting on his full weight and bouncing just a little. It gave you a sick feeling because you knew that if anyone was going to fall through, it would be the old man. Because he was the one who did it before. It gave you that sick feeling because you didn't know how far the dry rot had spread, and you could see that the old man was getting interested.

"This here floor's got to be fixed," he said. "Rotted clean through." And he stepped on it and stepped back. A kind of gingerly step that you hadn't seen for a long time, and then you knew he was remembering something. Remembering how he was the one who used to do the work of ten men. Nobody could keep up with him, sawing timber, driving a team. That was Alton J. Sanderson, they would say, the toughest SOB in the country. It made you proud you had Paul Bunyan blood in your line.

"This here floor's got to be fixed. And who will fix it if I don't?" he said. And that's how it started, the whole mess with the floor that we had to live with for the rest of the summer and through the winter. First the testing of the floor with his foot, and then the old man going outside to crawl under the house to see how bad it really was. That's how it started. When he came back inside he was covered with black dirt and cat hair.

Next came picking at the corners of the worn linoleum, peeling little chunks off like puzzle pieces. And then he got serious and his mind took hold, and he began ripping the linoleum up like it was shelf paper. The pine-wood flooring glared white underneath. And when he'd cleared a good spot over where he said it was worst, he went at it with an axe and wrecking bar, splintering away and prying up the good wood, and crushing through the bad until you began to get whiffs of the mildew smell, the sour smells of rotting lumber under your feet, and you breathed in with the rhythm of the old man's axe. "I'm going to fix this floor," he'd say. "I'll be damned if I'm not." And there he was hacking and hacking, and wheezing between swings, the sweat rolling down his face since the pulling up of the first board. And then, all of a sudden, there it was, the underneath of the house, the black, hard soil smelling of cat urine, cat urine smell coming up through the floor into our kitchen.

He hacked a space the size of a rug, then jumped down and started poking around with his bar. And you could see the dry rot in the beams and the splinters, and see how shrunken and lightweight the wood had become. The uneven hole in my mother's kitchen floor looked like a mouth full of cutting teeth. And there the old man was down in this mouth talking about getting a saw to finish the job, when Mother came home. Came home and caught him down in the hole in our kitchen floor.

"What do you have to say for yourself?" she said to the old man like she was saying it to me, said it like it was time for him to go to bed. And then she said to me, "What did you let him do a fool thing like that for?" And that turned the tables on everything. And I felt like hell about it, and the old man felt like hell about it, and for the rest of the summer we walked a wide path around the plywood they laid across the hole, laid across the hole he tore up but couldn't finish. "Don't nobody touch that hole," he would say. "Don't nobody touch that spot I'm working on, or there will be hell to pay." And the rest of us walked carefully around that spot, felt the kitchen move up and down whenever we walked across, but none of us touched that spot. And we all felt the turn of events, the updraft of change, and knew then that the old floor was gone for good.

And then that fall—"You're not going anywhere without my say. Nobody is going anywhere," he said to Eileen when she was leaving for dental-assistant school. Said this to her back as she was walking out the door. "Horse thief. Pickpocket. Bitch! You're not getting any of my money. Not one red cent!"

And the smell of cat urine lingers with me still. But the following spring, when it finally came to tearing down the house, after the old man had died, there was much that was left unexplained. The house, in its dismantling, became a maze of boards and lumber squared off in unfamiliar configurations. There were new piles of lumber where formerly solid walls had been, boards nailed across dangerous conditions, and prohibited comfortable old places where you used to walk. And even though you couldn't walk there anymore, there were confined spaces opening up—holes in walls, holes in closets where you could stretch yourself right through like a ghost, like Super-woman. The house was a new maze.

And Harlo and Gary worked all summer wrenching away with crowbars, their backs bared to the sun, the dust and chips of the house freckling their skin. And inside on the walls, there were wall drawings, wall games, condemned-wall graffiti. Every day, walking through to inspect the progress taking place on the house, you would see the artwork taking shape—happy faces, angry faces, stick people in crayon. People in a landscape, people in trees, people hanging out of the windows of houses. The place where someone had written, "Don't write on these walls." And then more writing and games, tic-tac-toe, dot-to-dot, and "Follow this line!" You'd walk in the front door and read, "Follow this line," and you were compelled. And you would follow the stupid line around one room and into the next, into closets and through the holes in back, around windows and up stairs, and then behind some door you would follow this line where it ended in some depraved picture of a naked lady.

And a day later, you would come in and there would be another line in some other color, and you would have to follow that too, another line longer and better than the first, that took you into corners of the house that you had never known before, an interesting line that gave you little notes of encouragement, "Watch where we're going now," "Wasn't that fun," and "We're almost there." Notes in strategic places that kept you going, until there at the end you discovered the ineffable, the quintessential four-letter word, that put you in your place.

And still another line on another day, a line that incorporated the previous lines, continued on after the naked lady, joined in with the unspeakable word in crayon. And this third line was a superior and exceptional new line that took you all the way to the wild attic and back, a line that circled the living room twice and went across the ceiling, a line drawn by some invisible long arm. And then finally, when you thought that maybe it would never end, the line led you to the inscribed words under the stairs, the words drawn like a picture of a note stabbed with a bloody dagger to the wall—"Bless this house!"

And here's the thing. You had followed the line expecting

some great revelation, some new word about sex, but all you got was a prayer. A prayer that made no sense. It was more disgusting than the naked lady or the four-letter word. And there that stupid line was where you had to look at it day after day until they pulled it apart and burned it in the field. And you've been thinking about that line for a hundred years. But also about the naked lady. And everything else about the old house.

How they tore down the maze, the graffiti walls, the dry rot floors. How they tore down the maze and slowly transformed it into two piles—lumber reusable and lumber to burn. And the lumber to burn was thrown into the field in one pile, one huge pile for a bonfire, a bonfire that burned hot and high, that ignited your clothes halfway to the house, left little circular burn holes that you didn't notice until the next day and realized you could have burst into flames, spontaneous combustion. One huge bonfire that burned your clothes and singed the hair off both your arms.

A bonfire that burned for days after they got it going, a bonfire bigger than any you would ever see again. A bonfire that burned away the walls and floors of where you lived, the dry rot and the putrid smell, while you moved with your mother and your one brother left, Gary, to a two-room shack across the field. A measly little shack heated by the flame of the kitchen stove and the unshared warmth of your three bodies. A shack that was not half the house that your first house had been. A bonfire that burned into a white heat that left, when it was done, gray smoldering ashes and heaps of red bent nails.

And they tore down the first house, your mother out giving orders to your two brothers (she was in on it, too), and your brothers bashing in the walls with a crowbar. They were all in on it together. You knew it had to go, but for all these years you remembered the way they did it to the house, not taking it apart logically, systematically, as you would to remedy the question of dry rot, to solve the problem of where you would live, but angrily, brazenly, like finally getting their way.

And finally your mother, in on the thick of it, pulling out the cupboards with a wrecking bar, doing things that you never thought were in her. And then that one time, that one time when you were passing through on your way to the woodpile, there she was in her kitchen with the axe, and you couldn't tell why she was doing it, and you couldn't predict where it would all end, but there was your mother swinging an axe at the last of the black hole. You saw her raise the axe, saw it hesitate in midair, saw it fall. Saw the splinters flying up like before with the old man, and again you felt the rhythm of an idea, felt the rhythm of leveling a house with your will, felt the mixed blood vibrating, ready, in your fingertips. You felt the rhythm, and it all became a part of you then, even at six years, especially at six years. And you felt the changed space, felt the pinpricks of heat upon your arms that were slowly burning you away. And even though you couldn't predict where it was all going, you wanted to go along, too. You wanted to take the axe yourself, wanted to swing it high and let it fall.

And all you really remember remembering is the confused state, a maze of confusion that left you burnt and dry and unknowing. You were miles away from any real knowing. You were so blind you couldn't analyze anything. But there was something that flashed behind your eyes, something in the anticipation of the perpetual question that even your mother would put to you years later, put to you after your sacking some sacred cow, after doing some unspeakable prohibitive thing, put to you by a woman who should have known better than to say to you on the very brink of adolescent discovery, "When are you going to straighten up and fly right?" The perpetual nagging question designed to ruin the rest of your life. But put to you, and here is the nasty taste in your mouth, put to you by the same woman who was forever opening up the space of being and then trying to shut it down, the woman who still lifts the axe high at night in my dreams and lets it fall. A woman like that, who said to her old man, "We have to go on living. What in hell do you think we intend to eat?" A woman with Attila's blood in her veins, our veins, one with the visceral motion of the axe, one with the exposed bloodline, the one exceptional line. A woman like that—with the Hunsaker blood.

HOW I CAME WEST, AND
WHY I STAYED

≈≈≈≈≈≈≈≈

I t was a long, strange trip, over frozen plains and rivers and into the mountains, but when the going got really tough, I'd close my eyes, and I'd see them: Lisa, in camouflage pants, stalking bears; Debbi, in blaze orange, wheezing out mating calls until huge bull elk stampeded down the hills, ready to perform.

Now I stood outside the Silver Dollar Saloon, the wind whipping around my collar, my hands like two lumps of ice even in my Thinsulate-lined mittens. The sky was cluttered with stars, but I couldn't stand there staring at them all night. I took a deep breath and pushed my way through the swinging doors.

My glasses steamed up, but I could tell everyone was looking at me, because dead silence dropped over the room. I took off my glasses and wiped them clean on my neckerchief. Then I put them back on. I'd been right; every head in the bar was turned toward me, and the faces were sort of orange, and puffy-looking, in the light from the video games.

I cleared my throat. "I'm looking for cheerleaders," I said.

They looked at one another and then back at me.

"How's that?" said an old geezer at the bar.

"I said, I'm looking for cheerleaders," I said.

"That's what I thought you said," the old guy said. He guffawed, and suddenly the whole room erupted in laughter, people pounding one another on the back, slapping their thighs, rolling in the sawdust on the floor. I smiled, glad the ice was broken.

I walked over to the bar and sat down beside the old guy. He said I could call him Ol' Pete. "You cain't never find 'em, not in this weather," he said. The snow had stopped, but the night air was bitterly cold. The roads up the pass were closed, with drifts over twenty feet high.

"Haw!" Ol' Pete suddenly guffawed again, and the rest of the heads—hoary, bewhiskered, grizzled—turned back in my direction. "On'y a fool!" he said, and the others grinned and nodded, and chanted, "Fool, fool."

"Buy 'em a round," the bartender whispered, as she wiped off the bar in front of me.

"A round on me," I said, and an excited hum swept the room. After the third round the hum broke out into singing, and in the middle of ". . . deer and the antelope play . . ." someone sat down beside me.

"Why you want to go up there, anyway?" she said. I turned and looked her in the eye. She was dark, of indeterminate age, and she wore a buffalo-head helmet, complete with gleaming horns. "They wanted you up there, wouldn't they a' took you with 'em?"

I nodded. "I can't explain it," I said. "It's just something I have to do."

She nodded too. "I can understand that," she said. "It's big—bigger than you, maybe. What's your name, stranger?"

"Most folks call me Whitey," I said.

"It won't be easy, Whitey," my companion said. "I can coach you some, but it'll be hard work."

She said her name was Buffalo Gal, and that I could bunk with her. On one wall of her cabin she had a USGS map, all squiggles, with red-headed pins marking the cheerleader near-sightings. I stared at it but could find no pattern in the scattered red dots.

"They come and they go," Buffalo Gal said. "They might as well be bigfoots."

"Bigfeet," I said.

"Whatever," Buffalo Gal said.

She worked me hard. She never let up, never let me slack off. "Hit 'em again," she'd say, time after time. "Harder, harder." But she was generous in her praise, too. "Go, go, go!" she'd shout, as I telemarked through the aspens. I worked harder for Buffalo Gal than I'd ever worked before; something about her made you want to.

And then one evening, as we skied through a narrow canyon, Buffalo Gal stopped so fast that I crashed into her. "Listen," she said.

"Give me an *A!*" The voice came, faint as starlight, distant as the sigh of a bear in a snowbound cave. It was followed by a wailed response from a dozen throats: "*A!*" It echoed down the hills and canyons, and up under the trees around us.

"It's them," Buffalo Gal said.

SATURDAYS WE MADE the long trek down to the Silver Dollar, just to be in contact with human beings, and to have a drink.

"Sure, I heard 'em," Ol' Pete said when I asked him. "Hear 'em all the time."

"Have you seen them?" I said.

"Hell," Ol' Pete said.

When he didn't say any more, I had to ask. "How can I find them, Pete?"

"Haw!" he guffawed, and nods and slow grins spread across the other faces in the room. "Where you from, Whitey?" he asked.

"Veedersburg, Indiana," I said.

"Well, then, I'll tell you," Ol' Pete said. "Them cheerleaders is like a poem. You don't go lookin' for a poem; it sort of comes to you, iffen yer in the right place, doin' the right thing." His rheumy eyes got rheumier, dripping a little, as he watched Lu, the bartender, wiping up some spilled milk. "You cain't predict. You can be out there for days, huntin', trackin' 'em across the range, countin' the buttercups, and you won't see hide nor hair. And then one day yer building a fire, or you just washed yer hair and yer mebbe smokin' some weed you saved up from yer last southern trip, and there she'll be, standin' afore you, smilin' down at you, her hand stretched out, whisperin' 'Score, Pete, score.' "

"Wow!" I said. "That happened to you?"

"Nope," he said.

Buffalo Gal and I skied home, heading back out of town and up the canyon through the moonlight. I looked around for shooting stars, and my nose twitched at the smells that skidded across the moonscape toward us: a last whiff of tobacco from the Silver Dollar, the sweet, flowery smell of someone's anti-static sheet from a dryer vent, the mucus-freezing smell of cold air rushing off the mountains. It was just the sort of time I might have seen them, if I'd only known.

In the mountains, in Montana, in winter, time loses its substance; it becomes meaningless. Night runs into day like the Ovaltine that Buffy stirred into our milk in the morning. I knew time had passed by the way the moon grew and shrank; I knew a week had gone by when we headed for the Silver Dollar on Saturday night. But that's all I could tell you.

"That's how it is here" was all Buffalo Gal would say.

ONE DAY, up in Avery Pass, we came upon a single dainty footprint, clear as day, left by a size-seven ripple-bottom gym shoe. I flung myself into the snow beside it. "How could she leave just one?" I cried, and when I put my face next to it, I sniffed the faintest of odors—rubber? Anti-fungal medication?

"You tell me," Buffalo Gal said. With her ice ax she chopped the footprint out of the frozen snow and laid it gently in her helmet. I pulled it along the ground behind me, the horns serving as runners across the snow. We flew down the mountain, down to the lower pass and back to the cabin, and the speed of our passage created a wind that freeze-dried the footprint, sucked the moisture right out of it. It was frozen so solid it would never melt.

We hung the footprint above the front door, hoping it would bring us luck.

I WAS BEGINNING to understand how important the presence of the cheerleaders was to the local people. They were part of the mountain mythology, feral fauna as significant as the mountain lion, the grizzly, the Rocky Mountain bighorn sheep. And they were not a recent phenomenon, nor were they exotic visitors. The history of cheerleaders in Montana went back for many, many years: as far back as the reach of local memory.

Ol' Pete had given me a hint of what they meant. What the manatee is to the naturalist in the mangrove swamp, what the race car is to the Hoosier, what the tornado is to the Kansan—that is what the cheerleader is to the Montanan.

Cheerleaders are Possibility, they are Chance, they are Fate; they are beauty, and grace, and poetry.

Many had learned the hard way that Ol' Pete was right: you couldn't find a cheerleader. You had to wait, and be ready. Many an expedition, hunters in their red flannel, stocking up their mules or their llamas or their ATVs with two or three weeks' worth of food, had set out determined—come what may!—to find the cheerleaders. They carried guns, too. "Hell," they'd say, if you asked why. Would they shoot a cheerleader? Would they hang a pink-cheeked, freckled face above the fireplace, among the furry heads of grizzlies and mule deer and moose, and the iridescent bodies of stuffed dead pheasants?

The truth was—the truth was that nobody really knew how he or she might react, if he or she actually found them.

And in all the years the cheerleaders had been in those parts, no one *had* found one. They'd found tracks, and signs: bits of pompon here and there, and of course my frozen footprint, and once an old, well-used megaphone, standing on its wide end under a spruce tree.

But many a hunter had returned cold, frostbitten, disappointed. And many a hunter had hung up her gun, and taken up, say, jogging, or tai chi—something that would get her outside, in the woods, on a hilltop—and in solitude, maybe whispering, she'd chant, "S-U-C-C-E-S-S." Just in case, someday, the cheerleaders came to *her*.

"OKAY, B.G.," I said one evening, as we stretched like lazy cats before the glowing wood stove, each with her own bowl of popcorn—Buffy liked garlic powder on hers, but I stuck with melted butter. "What gives?"

"Ah," Buffalo Gal said. She smiled, and gazed dreamily at the stove. "Impetuous youth."

"Youth?" I said. "Buffy, I'm forty-two years old. I'm not exactly youth."

She shook her head and gave me a look I couldn't interpret. "Whitey," she said, "do you know how long I've been up here?"

"No," I said.

Buffalo Gal leaned over her popcorn bowl and put her face close to mine. "Neither do I," she said.

"But, Buffy," I said, "how do I find the cheerleaders?"

"How the hell do I know?" Buffy said. "I've been up here lo these many moons, and I haven't found them yet."

When Buffalo Gal said that to me—when I realized that, by golly, she never had said she could help me find them—I had to ask. "Why are you up here, Buffalo Gal?" I said.

She smiled. "Whitey," she said, "I used to be a jock. I did every sport you can imagine—field hockey, tennis, jai alai. Seems like every time I turned around, there they were, supporting me all the way. Go! Go! Go! Yea, rah, Buffy!" She shook her head. "Guess I just didn't want to go on through life without 'em. Even if they're not cheering for me anymore, I just want to be near 'em, hear 'em, once in a while in the night. Just want to know they're there."

I nodded, and stood up. "I'm off," I said.

"See you around," she said.

That's the way it is in Montana. When the time comes to go, you go, and there are no hard feelings.

I don't know how far I skied that night, or how long. I was thinking as I went, and that's a dangerous thing to do. Thinking distracts you. You can get lost, thinking of something other than where you're going. You can ski right up the mountain and over the top, and get going so fast that, too late, you realize you've gone too far, that you have taken off into pure, crystal-clear Montana air. Every now and then in Montana you see someone who's done that, a skier, flying across the moon like a deformed Canada goose.

I DON'T KNOW how far I skied, but when the trail ended, I was right where I knew I'd be: at the door of the Silver Dollar Saloon. I went inside, and when I'd wiped off my glasses, there was Buffy, nodding at me, and Ol' Pete lifting a finger from his glass in greeting.

I sat down at a little table and ordered a glass of milk. Then someone spoke. "What are you up to up there, anyway?" she said, across the crowded room.

I knew who it was: Renee, a lean, grim-faced ranch hand, not much older than I was. She'd ridden the rodeo circuit for a while and then come back to Montana to work Ephraim P. Williston's sheep ranch. Somewhere along the line she'd lost her left hand—caught in a lasso and squeezed right off when she was roping a steer—and most Saturday evenings she sat in the Silver Dollar with a chamois rag, rubbing and polishing her elk-antler hook until it gleamed. She was a tough customer, Renee; even the feral dogs stayed away from her flocks.

The bar was so still you could hear the chamois rubbing against her hook. She stared at me, her eyes in the shadow of the Stetson she never took off. Her hand, polishing, never stopped moving.

I swallowed the last of my milk. I put down the little glass, and then I looked up and across the room straight at where I figured her eyes were.

"Nothing," I said.

She took off her hat then, and I found myself looking into the hardest eyes I'd ever seen. They were as cold as ice, and dry ice at that; I had a tough time believing they'd ever cried, or looked at anything but bleak and windswept sagebrush desert.

I'd said the wrong thing.

"Sister," she said, "you just said the wrong thing. You come up here, from God knows where—"

"She's from Veedersburg, Indiana," Ol' Pete interrupted. "She never made no secret of that."

I threw him a grateful look, but Renee shook her head.

"From God knows where," she repeated. "You sit in here and drink with us; you follow Buffalo Gal around the woods like a goddamn puppy dog, sucking up everything she knows; you pry, and eavesdrop, and then you go out and harass our cheerleaders; and when I ask you, in a friendly, innocent manner, what you're doing, you say *Nothing?*"

The silence was so thick you could have cut it with a Bowie knife. I didn't know what to say. She was right about part of it: I did come in and drink with them, I did ask questions, I did follow Buffy around. But that part about harassing the cheerleaders was way off the mark.

How could I explain that I was doing this for *all* of us?

"All my life," I began, and I prayed my voice wouldn't shake, "I wanted nothing more than to be a cheerleader. All through my childhood my parents held up cheerleaders as role models for me. 'My dream,' my dad used to say, 'is that someday you'll be just like them.' We went to every game. And then when they started broadcasting games on TV—oh, I burned with the desire to be out there with them, leaping and bending and rolling on national television, and flinging my arms out to embrace the whole world!"

I paused for breath. I looked around the room, and I knew I'd struck a chord. No one was saying a word: all eyes either were on me or were dreamy, looking back to their own youthful aspirations, remembering the cheerleaders from all those little towns—Moab, Hammond, Rockland, Kennebunk. These ranch hands came from all over the country, and I suspected they'd come for much the same reason I had.

I took a deep breath. "I guess it's an old, old story," I went on. "For years I practiced, twirling my baton, getting in shape with tap lessons. I did so many splits that my legs would hardly stay closed. I memorized the chants, the yells, you name it."

They were nodding; they'd been there too.

"I never made the squad," I said quietly. "Not even the B squad. I just wasn't good enough."

A sigh rippled across the room; some of those dusty eyes were a little damp.

"You know," I said, "I wanted to be a cheerleader more than anything else in the world. I would have sold my soul." I laughed softly, sadly. "I guess it's still for sale."

"Hell," Ol' Pete said, "so's mine!"

"Whitey," Renee said, standing up and crossing the room to where I stood, "I misjudged you. I'm sorry." She did a forward lunge and stuck out her hand.

I took it. "Renee, Renee, Renee," I said. "You were right about so many things."

She punched me on the arm with her hook. "Hows-about a turn at the cards?" she said.

"Yeah! Yeah!" The crowd roared its approval, and Ol' Pete actually did a herkie. I grinned with pleasure; this was another Montana tradition. In many a saloon heated discussions came to an end when the cards were pulled out, and would-be pugilists resolved their differences with a hand or two of this traditional game of the Old West. It had saved the glassware and bar mirrors of a good many drinking and gaming establishments.

Eight of us sat down around a table, and Ol' Pete dealt the cards. Carol Ann, another shepherd from out at Williston's, held Renee's cards for her—she had trouble managing them with her hook.

The game wasn't a long one—these games never are—

and one after another the players matched their last card and dropped out. Finally, as fate would have it, Renee and I were face to face. And, friendly as we now were, I was sweating.

I held two cards, and one of them was Her. Carol Ann was holding one card for Renee, and it was her draw. If she drew the matching card, she'd be out. But if she drew the Old Maid, I still had a chance.

Renee kept her eyes on my face and reached. Her hand hesitated above my cards; the tension—friendly tension—in the room was palpable. And then, as Renee's hand descended toward the Old Maid, she stopped. She lifted her head. "Listen," she said.

I'd heard it too. A rhythmic clapping, the soft patter of sneaker-shod feet. And then voices.

"H-O-W-D-Y! Hey-hey! We say hi!" And through the swinging door burst the first cheerleader the Silver Dollar had ever seen. She popped those doors back and bounced into the room, her hands rolling in front of her, her blond curls cascading over her shoulders. She bounded across the room, right over to our table, and dropped to one knee, one arm flung out to her side and the other straight over her head. "DeeDee!" she cried.

Another cheerleader leaped through the door and sprang over to kneel beside the first. Flinging her arms exactly the same way, she cried, "Kristi!"

And they kept on coming, the door swinging and banging against the wall, their little rubber-soled feet tap-tapping through the peanut shells that littered the Silver Dollar's floor. "Debbi! Suzi! Lori! Heather! Patti! Mindy! Lisa! Darlene!" They climbed on top of one another till their human pyramid reached the ceiling. They jumped up and landed in splits on the bar.

And in the dim light from the bar we saw that they had

changed. Gone were their pleated skirts, the snowy white ten-
nies, the matching panties. Their sweaters were black from the
smoke of a thousand campfires and stiff with the arterial blood
of dying elk. The dimpled knees were hidden in layers of wool,
of heavy-duty twill, of camouflage-patterned neoprene. Their
sneakers were gray, worn; their little socks showed through
holes in the toes.

And their faces. No longer pink and shiny, their skin was
rough from winter winds, wrinkled from the brutal western
sun. Their blond hair was stringy and sort of greasy, unwashed
for what must have been years.

But their teeth! One after another they smiled; again and
again the gloom of the Silver Dollar was broken as their teeth
flashed little reflections of the neon beer signs in the windows.
Years of fluoridated water, decay-preventive dentifrices, and or-
thodontia had worked their magic. Whiter than new snow,
more uniform than kernels of hybrid corn, brighter than Venus,
Jupiter, and Mars in alignment, their teeth alone would have
revealed them as the cheerleaders they were.

They stood, and knelt, and sat splayed before us in splendid
formation, and then they windmilled their arms and all at once
leaped into the air, spread-eagling their limbs toward the four
corners of the world, and screamed, "Yea! Rah! Team!"

Something warm surged through my body; I looked at
Renee, and she was smiling right into my eyes. She reached out
and took the matching card.

I was the Old Maid.

The crowd went wild, and the cheerleaders bounced and
hugged each other, tears rolling down their leathery cheeks, and
they all clustered around Renee and wanted to pat her, and
touch her, and have her sign their sneakers. It was Renee's
moment of glory.

I might have felt really bad if something hadn't happened

that warmed my heart all the way to the mitral valve. As everybody pushed over to the bar, the cheerleaders spontaneously stopped, and they all came back and stood around me, in a circle, and each one put her left hand on the right shoulder of the next cheerleader. And then they bent their knees, and they stuck out their right hands, and in unison they bobbed up and down, as if they were shaking my right hand, and they chanted, "YOUR'RE OKAY. YOU'RE ALL RIGHT. YOU PUT UP A DARN GOOD FIGHT! Yea! Rah! Whitey!"

There wasn't a dry eye in the room. "A round on me!" I shouted. And they cheered me again.

IN THE DAYS that followed, I knew something had changed. I had achieved a goal, a major one, and now—temporarily, anyway—I had nothing to strive for. I was happy, but I felt a little empty, too.

On about Wednesday, I was sitting listlessly in the sun, contemplating the bleak future that stretched ahead of me, when I heard someone coming. I looked around and saw that it was Buffalo Gal, and behind her was Renee.

Buffy got right to the point. "We've been huddling," she said. "We want you to stick around."

"I don't know," I said. "I'm not sure I can do this anymore."

"Not this," Renee said. "The Williston ranch has an opening for another shepherd. Carol Ann's getting hitched."

"I don't know anything about sheep," I said.

"You don't have to," Renee said. "They mill around, and you stand there. Or you sing to 'em, sometimes."

"Surely there's others more qualified," I said.

Renee gazed off at the horizon and rubbed her hook with her mitten. "The thing is, Whitey," she said, "most of us, we haven't seen a cheerleader since we've been here. It's what we came out here for, and we tried to do everything right, and we waited. But they never came until you got here. It's got us hoping again."

"Hoping?" I said.

Hard-bitten, rugged, dry-eyed as she was, she blushed. "We've started practicing again. It's all we really want, still. And we've realized that even if we'll never be varsity cheerleaders, we can still do the work, learn the new routines. And who knows? Someday they may need a substitute."

I looked at her. Something was in her face that I hadn't seen there before, but I recognized it. It was spirit: team spirit. It's something that's hard to find in the West, in Montana, in the wide-open spaces, where women spend most of their time alone. I thought, maybe that's it. It's not the adulation, the cheering, the popularity, that we want; it's team spirit.

"I guess I could learn," I said.

So I stayed. I'm still just an assistant shepherd—sort of on the B team—but I'll tell you something: sheep are the best pep club in the world to practice on. You can be out there in front of them walking on your hands, doing triple back flips, and they don't even look at you. They keep on munching the grass, ripping it out of the ground and chewing it up.

But it's in the nature of sheepherding, and of cheerleading, to stick with it, to keep on trying. You realize how hard the cheerleaders have worked to get where they are. That makes you work harder.

Sometimes, of a summer evening—oh, yes, summer finally came—I'll be out there on the range, practicing in front of my sheep. "Give me a P!" I'll shout, and the only response is from a border collie, who obliges on a nearby fence post. And then the warm summer wind picks up, just as the sun sets, and the sky is all red and purple and pink, and I hear, from miles away, "Two bits!" And maybe a distant figure cartwheels across a hilltop, silhouetted against the place where the sun just disappeared.

And then, from the east, where the sky is already dark, I hear "Four bits!" And I know it's Buffalo Gal, calling down from her lonely vigil on the mountain. And from up at the ranch house, where Renee is maybe loading supplies to bring out to us the next morning, comes "Six bits!" And I jump up and shout, "A dollar!"

And the next voice is so far away that the words aren't quite clear—it's up in high pastureland, where the sheep are chewing grass in the dark, and the little lambs are jumping around, or nursing on their moms, and the dogs are lying in the dust after a hard day, sleeping with one eye open, always on the lookout for coyotes. But we all know it's Ol' Pete, yelling, "If you got spirit, stand up and holler!"

And wherever we are, we leap into the sky and holler for all we're worth. Down in town they probably think it's thunder, but it's us, practicing, ready for when the snow flies in the fall and the cheerleaders come down from the high mountain passes. We'll be ready to go with them, hunting for the Big Game.

DEIRDRE McNAMER

FROM *Rima in the Weeds*

≈≈≈≈≈≈≈≈

Margaret had just gotten her first pair of eyeglasses, perfect cat-eyes, and she was amazed at how much she could see. She lay in the scrub grass beneath a stand of cottonwoods, took them off, and watched the branches turn gauzy and familiar. Then she put the glasses back on, bracing a little for the barrage of detail. Thousands of leaves leaped out, trembling and hard-edged. The narrow river, a few yards away, turned crunchy-looking again. Bird sounds attached themselves to small shapes on high branches.

She didn't know when her vision had started to go seriously bad. It had been so gradual, this nearsightedness, that she hadn't noticed it for a while. At first, it seemed only that a luxurious vagueness had come into her life. Then it had begun to make her uneasy. But this sudden return of all the details was more than she really wanted. It was unnerving. It gave her the same feeling she got when someone explained how something scientific works—osmosis, say, or photosynthesis. The ex-

planations crowded out her imagination and made her feel
bleak with information.

The day after she got the glasses, she saw Woody Blank-
enship, leaning against the wall of Bledsoe's Drug with his hand
in his jeans pockets, looking as if he were waiting for someone.
She was walking along the sidewalk and couldn't avoid him.
She said hi, he said hi. She speeded up and walked right in
front of him and on down the sidewalk, head tilted back to
make her hair look longer.

As she walked on, she felt a strange twinge of loss. It had
been too easy. Maybe it was the glasses. She had felt almost
nonchalant when she saw him standing there, so sharp and
clear. He seemed to wipe out the fuzzier Woody, the one in
her dream, the one who stretched along her body and breathed
in her ear.

NEAR THE RIVERBANK, upstream, MaryEllen and her best
friend, Julia, and Julia's brother from Philadelphia were spreading a picnic blanket and setting up a few lawn chairs on its
edge. Julia's children, a two-year-old and a four-year-old, were
home with a babysitter because they were in the last phase of
chicken pox.

The tailgate of the station wagon was covered with ther-
moses and Tupperware containers and fried chicken. With her
glasses on Margaret divined almost every detail of the lunch.
Squinting, she saw the pattern on the Dixie cups.

Julia wore loose slacks and a billowing blouse the color of
cotton candy. She transferred food from the tailgate to the picnic
blanket with oiled, backward-leaning movements. Her baby was
due in two weeks, and Margaret was grateful for the possibility
of crisis that Julia brought with her. She had a feeling the baby
would be born here at the Rising Wolf rodeo, an hour's drive
from any town. It wasn't impossible.

She imagined all the chaos and urgency if the baby came. She would have to help. They wouldn't be able to ignore her, because she already knew about babies from her job wheeling Sam around town. Now that summer was here, she sometimes wheeled him to the swimming pool and parked the buggy near the wire fence so they could watch the swimmers. Rita Kay was always there with her new friends, blue-lipped from the un- heated water, racing down the concrete walk to dive again from the medium board. Margaret still couldn't dive. Wheeling Sam was a small relief from having to think so often about trying.

As she approached the adults, Margaret scrutinized herself briefly in the car window. She noticed very little except the new glasses. It was as if a hidden, sober part of her was emerging. The fully adult Margaret. The Margaret who would be able to explain osmosis, who would be tall and explicit and solemn.

She took her chicken and potato salad and sat down on the grass next to her mother. MaryEllen ran a hand through Margaret's long, buff-colored hair, so different from her own, which looked, at the moment, like the pelt of a small animal, short and alive. Margaret's was like a different species of hair, more languid and distant.

MaryEllen and Julia and Julia's brother, whose name was Aden, sat in the sun, munching, talking lazily. Aden looked a little like Robert Kennedy. He was explaining himself to MaryEllen, who listened, head cocked to the side, as she cracked a hard-boiled egg.

"I'm thinking about the Peace Corps," he was saying. "That's one possibility."

In the near distance, beyond several rows of cars whose roofs glared in the sun, Margaret could see the small split-rail arena where the rodeo would soon start. A buoyant announcer tested the tinny sound system. "Test, two, three, four . . . Can you hear me over there, Bob? Raise your hat if you can. . . . Test, two, three, four." Some of the contestants galloped their horses around the arena, warming them up, kicking up little twisters of dust.

Margaret's father, Roy, and Julia's husband, Red, were riding around in the arena. Roy was entered in the calf-roping and team-tying. Red was entered in the team-tying and bulldogging.

"Or the Forest Service," Aden said, looking appreciately toward the mountains. "No one told me you people had this at your back door."

Margaret wished Dorrie and Sam were here, so she would have something to do, someone interesting to talk to. She had thought about bringing Midge, her old mare, to ride around on so she'd seem like part of things. But she didn't actually like to ride Midge that much. She liked the way horses looked and acted, more than she liked to ride them. Maybe it would be different when Señor Roja was trained. For now, she just liked to look at him and imagine what it was like to be so fast and brave.

Between MaryEllen and Aden sat Julia, a big-bellied queen, her square face flushed. Margaret wondered why Aden looked so relaxed when he was so out of place. She felt embarrassed for him: for his slacks and white sport shirt; for his canvas shoes that weren't even sneakers, much less boots; for the fact that he was probably the only man around who wasn't at the arena. His forearms were covered with black hair, a soft layer that reached down to the tops of his hands. That was strange, too, though it might be ordinary in Philadelphia.

He stretched his long legs and let them rest a few inches from MaryEllen's neatly crossed ankles. MaryEllen told them a little about the history of the place where they sat, how it had been a Blackfeet summer camp a century earlier. "And you can see why," she said, making a wide circle with her hand.

It was, indeed, a gentle spot, with its small, clear river, the tall trees on either side of the water, the little breeze that skittered through, lifting a corner of the blanket, rustling the summer-dried leaves, then stopping so the leaves could bake drier. Margaret munched potato chips. No one seemed to need to speak.

At that moment, Roy and Red—pink-cheeked, dusty, excited—clattered up on their tall sorrel horses. The rodeo would begin in a few minutes, so they didn't even get down to eat. MaryEllen handed up sandwiches and beer. The men ate rapidly. Their horses, Pokey and Boone, stepped softly in place, as if they too were anxious to be off.

"How're you feelin', sport?" Red said to Julia between munches.

"Fine," she said softly, rubbing her hand over her big belly. She was a tall, big-boned woman with an ordinary face that changed entirely when she smiled because her smile was so wide and white-toothed.

Red spit on the ground. He was large and freckled, with eyes like a nice dog's, earnest and thoughtless. You looked at him and thought of something that crashed through bushes and underbrush, something that thought about one thing at a time. He liked to tease Margaret—called her stringbean and, now, four-eyes. She liked him because he was loud and real and made the world seem like something anybody could handle.

Roy was quieter and smaller. He had a smart face that looked a little tense under his broad cowboy hat. Sometimes he looked as if he wore a costume when he came to rodeos because, most of the time, he wore his doctor's clothes—slacks, starched white shirt. Margaret could tell that he wanted something Red had. Rudeness, maybe. Because Red was very rude. He drank too much and stayed away from home. Once, Julia had come over to their house, red-eyed, late at night. She and MaryEllen

sat in the kitchen and talked in low, sad voices about something
Red had done when he went to the livestock auction and stayed
four days. Margaret had listened to them through the grate in
her bedroom floor.

Pokey nickered softly. Julia kept her hand on her belly and
closed her eyes. Aden lit a cigarette and leaned forward, toward
her, his hairy hands clasped.

"What does it feel like when the baby turns inside you?"
he asked his sister. Everyone looked at him. Margaret blushed.

"When the baby does what?" Red asked loudly, looking
around for clarification.

"Turns," Julia said. "In the womb."

Red rolled his eyes, swallowed the last of his beer, and
lobbed the empty can at a paper sack, making the shot. "Let's
go, Roy. Girl talk." But Roy was watching MaryEllen, who
studied Aden in a completely unguarded and curious way, as if
someone had just told her something amazing she never expected to hear. Her face was flushed. Margaret took off her
glasses and cleaned them rigorously with her shirttail. She didn't
like this moment.

"When the baby turns?" Julia smiled her lit-up smile. She
cocked her head to the side and thought for a minute.

"It feels like falling in love," she said. No one responded.

"You know. Like the inside of you is doing an underwater
somersault." She laughed ruefully at her inability to explain
herself. But Margaret understood her, because of the Woody
dream. And so did Aden, she thought, because he smiled in a
satisfied way. MaryEllen still looked curious, as if the question
hadn't been answered. She smiled at Julia, willing and uncom-
prehending. Julia shrugged again.

Red turned his horse briskly and trotted off to the arena.
MaryEllen stood and handed Roy a candy bar for quick fuel

later on. "Gotta go," he said unnecessarily. And she patted Pokey's nose, and he was off.

MARGARET FOLLOWED the men on foot, heading for the crackling loudspeaker. "Merlin Chatham is our first roper," it quavered. "Buddy Connell on deck and Joe Whiteman in the hole." It was an island of tinny sound amid the calm swish of the river, the hot breeze through the trees, and the faint, sharp sound of children playing among the parked pickups on the far side of the arena. Margaret crawled up on the splintery fence near the busiest end of the arena, where the chutes were and the pen that held the bucking horses. It was very hot now, and the heat wavered up from the pickup hoods and the tin roof of the little hot-dog stand.

In Madrid, the mountains were small, two-dimensional points that marched along the western horizon. But here, at the Rising Wolf rodeo, they were near and gray. They had a hunched, big-shouldered look, like thunderclouds or buffaloes.

Margaret watched her father and Red team-tie a big steer. They raced behind the animal on their tall horses, Red reaching forward to rope the neck, Roy scooping his lariat across the ground to snag two feet. They stretched the steer out flat, and all the men and animals panted while horns honked and the people in the bleachers clapped.

She watched the barrel racers with their straight, pretty backs, their brilliant blouses and short whips. She watched a huge steer come charging out of the chute, horns wide and aloft, and Red galloping his horse behind it, then alongside. Then he was hanging off the side of his horse, then leaping through the air, grabbing the horns, planting his heels in the ground, twisting, twisting, the massive leather neck until the animal thudded dustily to the ground.

Margaret sat on the fence and watched. It all repeated itself. The first go-round. The second go-round. Horses dashed out of chutes, calves speeded down the arena, men circled their long lariats in the air and leaped onto horned steers, dust devils skittered across the dirt, car horns honked.

As the afternoon wore on, a sense of distraction and driftiness entered the crowd. Kids with Popsicle mustaches and small cowboy boots ran around in packs, darting between parked cars. A baby wailed. The arena filled with short, intense engagements, but the overall feel of it was timeless, full of the smell of river trees and dust and the dry whir of grasshoppers.

Young bucking horses with names like Thunderbolt, Staircase, So Long, and War Paint milled around a holding pen. Then one of them, a splashy pinto, did something very strange, even for a raw young bucking horse. He reared up and raked his hooves against the old rail fence, drumming it with his hooves, trying to make it break.

This spooked the other horses. They began to run around the narrow enclosure, whinnying. The rearing horse pawed at the rails.

Red appeared. He had a stiff leather strap in his hand. He climbed up on the fence, leaned over, and hit the rearing horse, hard, on top of the head. *Crack!* Margaret could hear it plainly. At the same time, her father rode up to the fence on his horse. "Where is your mother?" he said quietly.

"At the car."

"She's missing everything."

MARGARET RAN BACK to the car. Aden had a Kool-Aid pitcher in his hand and was pouring the Kool-Aid into three Dixie cups. They were all laughing softly.

Margaret interrupted loudly, rudely.

"The rodeo's half over, Mom." Her voice was accusatory and shrill, even to her. "When are you coming over?"

MaryEllen looked sleepy. She gave Margaret a gentle, satisfied smile. "Coming, sweetheart," she said. Her hair had become a mass of wild ringlets. There was a challenging lilt in her voice, and Margaret knew it wasn't meant for her.

Her mother turned back to Aden. "And what makes you think that I would think something like that? What gave you that idea?" Her face was alive and unruly, like her hair.

Margaret tugged at her hand like a very young child and pulled backward as hard as she could. She knew she was acting like a brat, but she didn't care. She felt trapped and hysterical, like the bucking horse Red had smacked on the head.

She pulled backward, trying to raise her smiling mother to her feet. Then her sweaty hand slipped out of MaryEllen's, and she crashed backward into the side of the station wagon. Her glasses flew off and landed in the potato salad. And when she saw them there—sunk into the lumpy mess—she burst into tears.

Aden scooped them out of the salad and cleaned them off with his handkerchief. But Margaret didn't put them back on.

"Come on!" she screamed at her mother, her voice shaking.

"Margaret," her mother said sharply. "Stop it. Calm down." Margaret walked off toward the trees and sobbed, but she felt as though she had gotten through the worst part. She had managed to wake her mother up, so that she was talking again in an ordinary, familiar tone of voice. She didn't mind that it had taken some screaming and tears. It had to be done.

She put on her glasses, which smelled faintly of mayonnaise. Then she and her mother walked together toward the arena.

"That Aden guy has hair on his hands like a monkey," Margaret offered. "And he's a wimp."

"No, he's not," MaryEllen said briskly. "You're wrong." And they found places to sit on the rickety bleachers.

ROY SAT WITH two other cowboys on the fence rail, across the arena. He waved widely at them, and Margaret felt another burst of anger at her mother. This was where MaryEllen belonged. She should have been at the bleachers long ago. MaryEllen waved back serenely. Everything seemed to be fine. And then it occurred to Margaret that she was the one on the outside. That, although she was the person who was keeping everything smooth, they were oblivious of her efforts.

A few clouds had bunched together directly above the arena and were taking on a blue-gray tinge, but most of the sky was still a clear hot blue. The announcer's voice wavered onto the air. He kept up a jovial stream of patter that sounded intimate, like a card player in the next room.

"Touch luck for that cowboy," the tinny voice said when a bronc rider landed hard on his face.

"Hey, Lorraine!" This was too loud, and the loudspeaker screeched. "You sure you clocked that cowboy right?"

"Hey, Rosco," he called down to the clown, who was twirling dizzily beneath the announcer's platform. "Keep your shirt on."

He never stopped. It was as if he couldn't bear to leave the airwaves empty. He had to keep talking, up there on his frail little perch, had to keep hearing his ordinary voice come back at him from somewhere else, enlarged.

Red was holding court at the far end of the arena near the chutes. He stood at the center of a half circle of cowboys. They all spit a lot in the dirt. A few had cans of beer. They stood with their feet apart on their high-heeled boots. They took furtive-looking drags on their cigarettes and threw them curtly away. They wore Levi's, and brightly colored shirts, and leather hand-tooled belts with enormous buckles that flashed in the sun.

A small dog, a border collie, ran between the men, ducked under the holding pen, and nipped a bucking horse on the heels. Red picked up a rock and lobbed it at the ragged dog, which yipped away, tail between its legs. But it came back a few minutes later, as if it had no memory. And this time it darted straight into the pen and stirred up the horses so that they ran in circles.

When the dog ran out of the pen, Red lunged at it and gave it a kick, a kick so hard that the dog flew into the air and landed, rolling, in the dust. Then Red picked up a stick and lobbed it at the animal, which ran yelping out of the arena. He returned to the group of men, popped open a beer, tossed his head back, and roared with laughter at something someone said.

Margaret kept her eye on Red, monitoring him. She felt in her bones that he had started something rolling. She looked at her mother to see if she saw the danger, but MaryEllen was folding a bandanna, tying it around her wild curls, putting on sunglasses to watch the rodeo. The timekeeper, the lanky woman the announcer called Lorraine, leaned over the rail on the announcer's perch to say something to a man on the ground, and Margaret felt another small flutter of dread, as if it were she who was high above the ground.

MaryEllen's head was tilted back, receiving the sun. Then the clouds covered the sun for a minute and her mother's face went into shadow.

"I feel kind of sick," Margaret announced. "I don't feel right."

"You didn't get enough sleep last night," MaryEllen said, putting a hand on Margaret's knee and waving with the other at Aden, who was mounting the bleachers. He had pushed his shirtsleeves farther up his arms. There was a sheen of sweat on his face. His teeth, when he grinned at them, were as white as Julia's.

He stood in front of them, blocking the view. "Julia is taking a nap," he said. "I thought I better see what this is all about." He sat down next to MaryEllen and looked out on the men and horses.

"It's almost over," Margaret said sullenly.

The three of them watched together. Roy rode past—he was one of the men who helped riders off their bucking horses—and looked sharply over his shoulder at them.

Something was going on in the chutes. Margaret saw a wild-eyed horse's head above the wooden gate. It was the pinto again, the one who had tried to break the fence. Then the head disappeared and there was shouting, and the rider leaped for the side of the chute as the horse crashed to the ground and flailed its hooves against the narrow enclosure. Red leaned down from the side of the chute and pulled the horse upright. The white-faced rider eased back down on the animal, and the gate flew open and they were out.

The pinto ran out fast, then stopped, put its head down, and kicked its hind feet almost straight up. The rider, leaning far back, stayed on. Margaret was silently cheering the horse. He reminded her of what Señor Roja would do if someone cinched leather around his flanks and raked him with spurs.

"Here's a tough customer," came the echoing voice from the announcer's box. "This critter tried to crash out of the holding pen earlier this afternoon. Whoa! Look at that!"

The horse had stopped and stood stock-still. It didn't move. The rider raked it with his spurs. Nothing happened. Then Margaret saw her father climb down from his horse, pick up a rock, and lob it at the horse's feet, as if he were skipping a stone across water as hard as he could.

"Don't! Stop it!" Margaret's voice was piercing. It seemed to follow the horse, which had broken into a straight gallop and was running around the arena crazily, like a fly in a bottle.

It ran toward the fence and reared high. The rider fell over backward and lay for a few moments in the dirt before picking himself up to run. The horse continued to attack the fence. Its hooves crashed through the brittle rails, and then the rest of its body followed, sinking heavily into the broken wood. The big animal rolled forward and sideways, and when it came up again a large stick protruded from its neck.

The horse staggered across the arena as if drunk. It stopped and stood in place, head almost to the ground, the stick like a buried sword.

MaryEllen tried to cover Margaret's eyes. "God help us," she moaned. Aden stared.

A clump of men ran out and stared at the horse. Then one of them trotted back to the chute area and came back with a gun. They all stood for a moment, looking at the wound and at the blood that now flowed from the ears and nose. Then the man with the gun, a fat man in a pink shirt, stepped back, raised the pistol, and shot the horse once in the head.

Margaret wailed.

MaryEllen took her arm firmly and steered her down the bleachers and away from the arena. Margaret turned once to see her father and Red bent over the dead young horse, putting ropes on him to pull him away.

THEY DROVE HOME in the rain. Through Heart Butte, past the abandoned boarding school, across the Two Medicine River, on home. Margaret rolled down her window to smell dust being tamped down by moisture, that particular smell that is more like dust than dust. Her parents were silent.

A week later, a baby boy was born to Red and Julia. A week after that, they all gathered at the church: Red, Julia and the baby, their other two children; Margaret and her parents; Aden.

Aden was going back to Philadelphia that afternoon. He wore the suit he would travel in, and his hair was slicked down in a way that made him look very young. His clothes fit badly.

Julia handed the baby to Aden while they waited for Father Malone to get ready. The baby whimpered a little, and Aden jiggled him back and forth, awkwardly. He looked uncomfortable. Father Malone thumbed through his black book and checked the water level in a small crystal pitcher at his side.

MaryEllen and Roy stood close together. Ever since the Rising Wolf rodeo, they had been different with each other. Margaret had noticed something new in the way they said good-bye in the morning: a longer touch of MaryEllen's fingers on Roy's fresh-shaved cheek, a softer sound in their voices. Roy looked like a doctor today in his gray suit and white shirt. He held his arm lightly around MaryEllen's waist, and she leaned into it a little. She wore a crisp linen dress and a straw hat.

Julia looked tired and a little puffy. The four-year-old and the two-year-old, Mitzi and Jake, rustled and poked each other. Red looked restless too. His face was sunburned and his receding hairline, usually covered with a hat, was dead white. His corduroy sport coat was too small to button. His cowboy boots were dirty and unpolished.

Aden jiggled the baby tentatively, and it began to cry. Red reached for the baby, and it cried louder. Red's big freckled fingers splayed across the gauzy blanket.

Margaret knew she needed to speak. "Why don't you let

the mom hold him?" she said to Red, trying to sound cute and whimsical. It was the wrong thing to say. Everyone looked at her. But Red did pass the baby to Julia.

The prayers began. Margaret closed her eyes for a few seconds, opened them. Then the baby's fuzzy head was tipped back over something that looked like a giant birdbath, and Father Malone called him in Latin from limbo into the world.

CIRCLE OF WOMEN

Like an ambush, the forest
rose around the circled trailers.
Wooden and straight and scrubbed
to the splintered floors, they stood stilted
on tamarack and pine. The men every day
off to the woods, the smells of heart-
rot and chain oil, the diesel breath
of machinery. And the women, in days
of long summer and snowed-in winter,
each morning rose to put on
make-up before the bacon and biscuits,
before the gooey-eyed children came
stumbling across the numbing linoleum
to lick the sweet crust of jam jars.
Men gone, children to school,
they nursed the babies and smoked
carefully. They painted their nails,

mending each tear with tissue
and glue. Siren Red and Playfully Pink
flashed like trout through the dishwater.
Wedged in highchairs, the women cut
one another's hair, Sears models
for inspiration, and numbed their ears
with ice before piercing the lobes
with needles fire-blackened.
Denim stained their wash. Pitch
ambered their furniture. Hot mornings,
in meadows of camas and yarrow,
they tanned while brown children in the near
creek clacked stones, and cicadas
whirred away the sound of metal teeth
cutting the fir, the cedar, the very air
the women breathed. Nights, husbands
home and fed, the next day's lunches
packed, they slept in the clean silence
of mountains. My mother, my aunts, acting
as though the men were not intruders
but the very reason, painted
and sweetened their days for greasy touches,
sweet sap kisses, and sawdust sifting their beds
like sand. The men must have thought themselves
lucky then, finding them waiting,
golden-shouldered, hungry for more.

CALLING THE COYOTES IN

Dark green ravines run like lava
through the canyon's fissured humps,
and it is here they come, late
in winter's good cold, to find
the seventy-dollar pelts.
Crouched in a shadowing hedge
of sumac and sap-leeched syringa,
she waits. Five nights
they have worked the ridges, calling
the coyotes in. From the camouflaged recorder
cries of a dying rabbit play
again and again, a chant
she rocks to, feet numbed to stone.
Beside her, the man squats trigger-ready,
the white orbit of his eyes blueing
in half-moon light.
He's been in Nam, and though she won't say it,
there's an enemy somewhere. Even his breath
seems cloistered, the way his jaw slacks
to quiet the rush of air.
This time, two split
from the tangle of brambled cottonwood,
trot forward, high-stepping the snow.
He signals for her to take the right one.
Raising the rifle, liquid from knees to cheek,
she shoots easy, good at limiting damage:
behind the ear, a finger-sized hole.
The man stands, the blue flame
he holds to her blinding

as she draws the smoke deep.
Kneeling at the first belly, he begins
the skinning, cigarette clenched
between his teeth.
She'll take her time with hers,
slip the knife between muscle
and hide, follow the leg's curve
to cobbled spine.
There's a moment when he'll call her, in his hands
a bundle rolled tail to nose, and she'll see
how his lips have tightened to hold
the last biting fire, how he hasn't moved
to stop the calling, and neither has she,
knee-deep in dark dappled snow,
feeling all around them the closing eyes.

THE SMELL OF RAIN

I've read the obituary of a woman
I once knew: Dead of cancer, a lingering
illness, and for a moment I am glad.
Her photo is unfamiliar, a face
already hollowed by pain and decay,
not the face I remember from years
before when I sat in her sixth grade
class and marveled at the gold of her hair.
Mrs. Eisenhower, young then, sure
of her control and nothing to stop her.
We sang Christmas songs all year, each morning
a chorus of Handel's *Messiah*, her soprano voice

rising in hallelujahs until the windows chattered.
She drove ignorance from our heads like demons,
pacing the room's four corners, while we
listened and watched the red of her lips,
perfectly painted to match her nails,
which clicked against the backs of our chairs
like beetles. The day we studied clouds,
I told her my mother could smell coming rain.
She called my mother a fool. Does your mother
watch cows lie down in the fields? she asked.
Or maybe she expects company when her nose itches.
No one laughed but sat wondering how she knew
our private lives, now ridiculous, our parents'
wisdom nothing but nonsense. Listen, she said.
Close your eyes and see the lightning
of your own brain. The salt of your mouth
is the makeup of oceans. Tides ebb and flow
in your blood, you will see, you will see.
That day she raged and tore Bonnie Hanson's
newly pierced ears, still swollen with the heat
of the needle, pulled the small gold rings
through flesh and cast them against the wall
like dice, I remember only our silence and red
drops pearling onto the pages of an open history book.
I wondered then how nothing changed, no parents
demanding resignation, no apologies, just the daily lessons.
It is all pleasure or pain, she said. Our bodies know
only these two things. In sixth grade, we thought we knew
both. What we didn't know came to me later,
behind the church one Sunday when Bonnie confessed
her brother loved her, and she loved the way
his older body hardened in the bed she slipped to
each night. The earrings he had given for her

twelfth birthday were gone, and only the lightest
scars creased the fullness of her lobes. This knowledge
has stayed with me longest, how we resist what we know
to be true and blame the makeup of our bodies
in their endless beauty, reminders
of what we must leave and come to, the ivory
and roses of flesh bringing us to hallelujahs of ecstasy
echoing long after decay has begun.

Terry Tempest Williams

The Clan of One-Breasted Women

≈≈≈≈≈≈≈≈

Epilogue

I belong to a Clan of One-Breasted Women. My mother, my grandmothers, and six aunts have all had mastectomies. Seven are dead. The two who survive have just completed rounds of chemotherapy and radiation.

I've had my own problems: two biopsies for breast cancer and a small tumor between my ribs diagnosed as a "borderline malignancy."

This is my family history.

Most statistics tell us breast cancer is genetic, hereditary, with rising percentages attached to fatty diets, childlessness, or becoming pregnant after thirty. What they don't say is living in Utah may be the greatest hazard of all.

We are a Mormon family with roots in Utah since 1847. The "word of wisdom" in my family aligned us with good foods—no coffee, no tea, tobacco, or alcohol. For the most part, our women were finished having their babies by the time they were thirty. And only one faced breast cancer prior to 1960.

Traditionally, as a group of people, Mormons have a low rate of cancer.

Is our family a cultural anomaly? The truth is, we didn't think about it. Those who did, usually the men, simply said, "bad genes." The women's attitude was stoic. Cancer was part of life. On February 16, 1971, the eve of my mother's surgery, I accidentally picked up the telephone and overheard her ask my grandmother what she could expect.

"Diane, it is one of the most spiritual experiences you will ever encounter."

I quietly put down the receiver.

Two days later, my father took my brothers and me to the hospital to visit her. She met us in the lobby in a wheelchair. No bandages were visible. I'll never forget her radiance, the way she held herself in a purple velvet robe, and how she gathered us around her.

"Children, I am fine. I want you to know I felt the arms of God around me."

We believed her. My father cried. Our mother, his wife, was thirty-eight years old.

A little over a year after Mother's death, Dad and I were having dinner together. He had just returned from St. George, where the Tempest Company was completing the gas lines that would service southern Utah. He spoke of his love for the country, the sandstoned landscape, bare-boned and beautiful. He had just finished hiking the Kolob trail in Zion National Park. We got caught up in reminiscing, recalling with fondness our walk up Angel's Landing on his fiftieth birthday and the years our family had vacationed there.

Over dessert, I shared a recurring dream of mine. I told my father that for years, as long as I could remember, I saw this flash of light in the night in the desert—that this image had so permeated my being that I could not venture south without seeing it again, on the horizon, illuminating buttes and mesas.

"You did see it," he said.

"Saw what?"

"The bomb. The cloud. We were driving home from Riverside, California. You were sitting on Diane's lap. She was pregnant. In fact, I remember the day, September 7, 1957. We had just gotten out of the service. We were driving north, past Las Vegas. It was an hour or so before dawn, when this explosion went off. We not only heard it, but felt it. I thought the oil tanker in front of us had blown up. We pulled over and suddenly, rising from the desert floor, we saw it, clearly, this golden-stemmed cloud, the mushroom. The sky seemed to vibrate with an eerie pink glow. Within a few minutes, a light ash was raining on the car."

I stared at my father.

"I thought you knew that," he said. "It was a common occurrence in the fifties."

It was at this moment that I realized the deceit I had been living under. Children growing up in the American Southwest, drinking contaminated milk from contaminated cows, even from the contaminated breasts of their mothers, my mother— members, years later, of the Clan of One-Breasted Women.

It is a well-known story in the Desert West, "The Day We Bombed Utah," or more accurately, the years we bombed Utah: aboveground atomic testing in Nevada took place from January 27, 1951, through July 11, 1962. Not only were the winds blowing north covering "low-use segments of the population" with fallout and leaving sheep dead in their tracks, but the climate was right. The United States of the 1950s was red, white, and blue. The Korean War was raging. McCarthyism was rampant. Ike was it, and the cold war was hot. If you were against nuclear testing, you were for a communist regime.

Much has been written about this "American nuclear tragedy." Public health was secondary to national security. The Atomic Energy Commissioner, Thomas Murray, said, "Gentlemen, we must not let anything interfere with this series of tests, nothing."

Again and again, the American public was told by its government, in spite of burns, blisters, and nausea, "It has been found that the tests may be conducted with adequate assurance of safety under conditions prevailing at the bombing reservations." Assuaging public fears was simply a matter of public relations. "Your best action," an Atomic Energy Commission booklet read, "is not to be worried about fallout." A news release typical of the times stated, "We find no basis for concluding that harm to any individual has resulted from radioactive fallout."

On August 30, 1979, during Jimmy Carter's presidency, a suit was filed, *Irene Allen* v. *The United States of America*. Mrs. Allen's case was the first in an alphabetical list of twenty-four test cases, representative of nearly twelve hundred plaintiffs seeking compensation from the United States government for cancers caused by nuclear testing in Nevada.

Irene Allen lived in Hurricane, Utah. She was the mother of five children and had been widowed twice. Her first husband, with their two oldest boys, had watched the tests from the roof of the local high school. Her husband died of leukemia in 1956. Her second husband died of pancreatic cancer in 1978.

In a town meeting conducted by Utah Senator Orrin Hatch, shortly before the suit was filed, Mrs. Allen said, "I am not blaming the government, I want you to know that, Senator Hatch. But I thought if my testimony could help in any way so this wouldn't happen again to any of the generations coming up after us . . . I am happy to be here this day to bear testimony of this."

God-fearing people. This is just one story in an anthology of thousands.

On May 10, 1984, Judge Bruce S. Jenkins handed down his opinion. Ten of the plaintiffs were awarded damages. It was the first time a federal court had determined that nuclear tests had been the cause of cancers. For the remaining fourteen test cases, the proof of causation was not sufficient. In spite of the split decision, it was considered a landmark ruling. It was not to remain so for long.

In April 1987, the Tenth Circuit Court of Appeals over-turned Judge Jenkins's ruling on the ground that the United States was protected from suit by the legal doctrine of sovereign immunity, a centuries-old idea from England in the days of absolute monarchs.

In January 1988, the Supreme Court refused to review the Appeals Court decision. To our court system it does not matter whether the United States government was irresponsible, whether it lied to its citizens, or even that citizens died from the fallout of nuclear testing. What matters is that our government is immune: "The King can do no wrong."

In Mormon culture, authority is respected, obedience is revered, and independent thinking is not. I was taught as a young girl not to "make waves" or "rock the boat."

"Just let it go," Mother would say. "You know how you feel, that's what counts."

For many years, I have done just that—listened, observed, and quietly formed my own opinions, in a culture that rarely asks questions because it has all the answers. But one by one, I have watched the women in my family die common, heroic deaths. We sat in waiting rooms hoping for good news, but always receiving the bad. I cared for them, bathed their scarred bodies, and kept their secrets. I watched beautiful women become bald as Cytoxan, cisplatin, and Adriamycin were injected into their veins. I held their foreheads as they vomited green-black bile, and I shot them with morphine when the pain became inhuman. In the end, I witnessed their last peaceful breaths, becoming a midwife to the rebirth of their souls.

The price of obedience has become too high.

The fear and inability to question authority that ultimately killed rural communities in Utah during atmospheric testing of atomic weapons is the same fear I saw in my mother's body. Sheep. Dead sheep. The evidence is buried.

I cannot prove that my mother, Diane Dixon Tempest, or my grandmothers, Lettie Romney Dixon and Kathryn Blackett Tempest, along with my aunts developed cancer from nuclear fallout in Utah. But I can't prove they didn't.

My father's memory was correct. The September blast we drove through in 1957 was part of Operation Plumbbob, one of the most intensive series of bomb tests to be initiated. The flash of light in the night in the desert, which I had always thought was a dream, developed into a family nightmare. It took fourteen years, from 1957 to 1971, for cancer to manifest in my mother—the same time, Howard L. Andrews, an authority in radioactive fallout at the National Institute of Health, says radiation cancer requires to become evident. The more I learn about what it means to be a "downwinder," the more questions I drown in.

What I do know, however, is that as a Mormon woman of the fifth generation of Latter-day Saints, I must question everything, even if it means losing my faith, even if it means becoming a member of a border tribe among my own people. Tolerating blind obedience in the name of patriotism or religion ultimately takes our lives.

When the Atomic Energy Commission described the country north of the Nevada Test Site as "virtually uninhabited desert terrain," my family and the birds at Great Salt Lake were some of the "virtual uninhabitants."

ONE NIGHT, I dreamed women from all over the world circled a blazing fire in the desert. They spoke of change, how they hold the moon in their bellies and wax and wane with its phases. They mocked the presumption of even-tempered beings and made promises that they would never fear the witch inside themselves. The women danced wildly as sparks broke away from the flames and entered the night sky as stars.

And they sang a song given to them by Shoshone grandmothers:

Ah ne nah, nah	Consider the rabbits
nin nah nah—	How gently they walk on the earth—
ah ne nah, nah	Consider the rabbits
nin nah nah—	How gently they walk on the earth—
Nyaga mutzi	We remember them
oh ne nay—	We can walk gently also—
Nyaga mutzi	We remember them
oh ne nay—	We can walk gently also—

The women danced and drummed and sang for weeks, preparing themselves for what was to come. They would reclaim the desert for the sake of their children, for the sake of the land.

A few miles downwind from the fire circle, bombs were being tested. Rabbits felt the tremors. Their soft leather pads on paws and feet recognized the shaking sands, while the roots of mesquite and sage were smoldering. Rocks were hot from the inside out and dust devils hummed unnaturally. And each time there was another nuclear test, ravens watched the desert heave. Stretch marks appeared. The land was losing its muscle.

The women couldn't bear it any longer. They were mothers. They had suffered labor pains but always under the promise of birth. The red-hot pains beneath the desert promised death only, as each bomb became a stillborn. A contract had been made and broken between human beings and the land. A new contract was being drawn by the women, who understood the fate of the earth as their own.

Under the cover of darkness, ten women slipped under a barbed-wire fence and entered the contaminated country. They were trespassing. They walked toward the town of Mercury, in moonlight, taking their cues from coyote, kit fox, antelope squirrel, and quail. They moved quietly and deliberately through the maze of Joshua trees. When a hint of daylight appeared they rested, drinking tea and sharing their rations of food. The women closed their eyes. The time had come to protest with the heart, that to deny one's genealogy with the earth was to commit treason against one's soul.

At dawn, the women draped themselves in Mylar, wrapping long streamers of silver plastic around their arms to blow in the breeze. They wore clear masks, that became the faces of humanity. And when they arrived at the edge of Mercury, they carried all the butterflies of a summer day in their wombs. They paused to allow their courage to settle.

The town that forbids pregnant women and children to enter because of radiation risks was asleep. The women moved through the streets as winged messengers, twirling around each other in slow motion, peeking inside homes and watching the easy sleep of men and women. They were astonished by such stillness and periodically would utter a shrill note or low cry just to verify life.

The residents finally awoke to these strange apparitions. Some simply stared. Others called authorities, and in time, the women were apprehended by wary soldiers dressed in desert fatigues. They were taken to a white, square building on the other edge of Mercury. When asked who they were and why they were there, the women replied, "We are mothers and we have come to reclaim the desert for our children."

The soldiers arrested them. As the ten women were blind-folded and handcuffed, they began singing:

> *You can't forbid us everything*
> *You can't forbid us to think—*
> *You can't forbid our tears to flow*
> *And you can't stop the songs that we sing.*

The women continued to sing louder and louder, until they heard the voices of their sisters moving across the mesa:

> *Ah ne nah, nah*
> *nin nah nah—*
> *Ah ne nah, nah*
> *nin nah nah—*
> *Nyaga mutzi*
> *oh ne nay—*
> *Nyaga mutzi*
> *oh ne nay—*

"Call for reinforcements," one soldier said.

"We have," interrupted one woman, "we have—and you have no idea of our numbers."

I CROSSED THE LINE at the Nevada Test Site and was arrested with nine other Utahans for trespassing on military lands. They are still conducting nuclear tests in the desert. Ours was an act of civil disobedience. But as I walked toward the town of Mercury, it was more than a gesture of peace. It was a gesture on behalf of the Clan of One-Breasted Women.

As one officer cinched the handcuffs around my wrists, another frisked my body. She did not find my scars.

We were booked under an afternoon sun and bused to Tonopah, Nevada. It was a two-hour ride. This was familiar country. The Joshua trees standing their ground had been named by my ancestors, who believed they looked like prophets pointing west to the Promised Land. These were the same trees that bloomed each spring, flowers appearing like white flames in the Mojave. And I recalled a full moon in May, when Mother and I had walked among them, flushing out mourning doves and owls.

The bus stopped short of town. We were released.

The officials thought it was a cruel joke to leave us stranded in the desert with no way to get home. What they didn't realize was that we were home, soul-centered and strong, women who recognized the sweet smell of sage as fuel for our spirits.

Breathing the Snake

≈≈≈≈≈≈≈≈

The river rocks me. Lifts me until my feet hang plumb from my body, lowers me between swells, heel and toe touching sandy bottom. I've biked the thirty miles from home. I know this stretch well enough to ride it blind, and it seems I have—for I don't remember the ride or the road. I've left the bike at the top of the cliff at my back, dropped it in the roadside gravel, walked out into this river clothed and intentional. The stepped hills across the way were fired last night, by lightning, and though by chance, in the height of the storm, I'd actually seen the distant smoke, at this moment, with the scorch still stinking and the charred slopes black against the blue sky, I don't see it. I've come to a place in my life that I thought I'd never see. I am middle-aged and having waded my way out of the debris of a reckless youth and a failed first marriage, I'd come finally, again, to believe in myself, in the orderliness of work, in the solace and passion of a good marriage. And even though in summer this valley wilts at the mouth of Hells Canyon like the opening of a brick oven and the high desert rims one side of it encouraging prickly pear, puncture weed, rattlesnakes and drought, I believed most in the kindnesses, and that the basalt hills would shelter me as they did this valley, and this valley with its river dammed to slack water, its clement winters encouraging a luxury of dogwood and roses, wisteria and grape, its forgiving fall after the hot, dry summer, would encourage this same accommodating grace in the willfulness of my own heart. I believed my life good, my course set. But in the span of an afternoon, it has all disappeared. All I see is the river, wide and fast and true—that thing to which I have come, to trust with my life.

It is the Snake River, flowing out of Hells Canyon—deepest gorge in the country—and this part of the river marks the boundaries of western Idaho from eastern Oregon and Washington. For two years now, summer, spring and fall, I have been biking a small stretch of this river. From my home in Lewiston, Idaho, I cross the river into Washington and upriver to Buffalo Eddy, about 40 miles one way. Although I bike almost daily, it is not always the full distance—depending on time and weather—but it is always this route, *this* river.

I don't know rivers. They're not in my nature. I am a Wisconsinite where water mostly stands still—lakes, sloughs, wetlands. Rich, rich in water. We used to joke about Minnesota, "land of ten thousand lakes," how poor, to be able to count the number of lakes. I am still new to the West, a short ten years, and even newer to Idaho. The larger, riverless part of my life, thirty-seven years, I lived within a twenty-five mile radius of the place where I was born—farmlands tuck-pointed in fences. My parents, brother and sister, aunts, uncles and cousins still occupy that rooted sphere.

Out here water rushes away, propelled down slopes in freshets and avalanches, pours off the face of the land in harrowing channels, forms and reforms the earth, a series of changes that frankly terrifies me. So much inconstancy.

I am buoyed by the river, lifting and falling, following the current with my eyes, how it snags the spit of land in the near distance, diamond chop that for once fails to glitter. I cannot begin to think of how my life has become a sustained wreck, how I want to go back to the early morning and wake to a different day, a different landscape. Or not wake. The current is a broad stroke away. I can feel its pull, but my body is strong, as I'd fought to make it these past two years, and I hold my ground even as it's shifting from under my feet.

THE FIRST TIME I bike along the Snake it's two years earlier, summer. Biking is an old love I take up again to shed these middle years' indulgence, the writer's sedentary days and nights, my secession to the fusing bones in my feet. It's a capitulation of will to age and appetite that has taken place over a period of five years, giving in, giving out. Up until recently I was still smoking three packs a day. Even walking had become a chore—breathless on stairs, I'd get to the top and light up. This is age I'd say. But now I'm pushed out of myself, out of my house by some deeper urge.

This was a spring of flooding. A one hundred years' flood and all the dikes, dams, levees and spill ways couldn't keep the waters back. Although amid the destruction—roads blown out, towns abandoned to the National Guard, houses submerged or unmoored to float down the spring tide—Lewiston was spared, an island in a national disaster zone. By now, the worst of the floods are long done, but the effects are still visible. The Snake River is brawling and muddy. I bike the levy and the river is uncomfortably close with its cargo of logs and boards, spin drift and the occasional carcass—a deer with its rack shimmied into the branches of a tree. Renegade logs stack in

Program Total 18

2013-2014

Интересно. когда мужик хочет уединения, —
— он "художник", "философ" и "творец".
Когда женщина хочет того же, — она социопат и чудачка

colliding rafts against the Memorial bridge, grind a curious complaint under water and work their way loose to float down the confluence of the Snake and Clearwater on down to the Columbia, ocean bound.

I keep to the levy and its safe asphalt path, though parts have been closed off because they're still under water, and I stop a cautious distance above the blockades. The surface foams and bubbles like a pot set on simmer. It's a sticky brew that stinks of high timber and snow, pulp wood, fish, the first vegetation, and mud.

The surrounding hills are a clean green and I spend a better part of that first month with my eyes raised to them. I avoid looking at the water. God only knows what might come boiling down the current. There's always the car wreck, the capsized boat, the drunken man who stumbled away from his friend's wedding. There's always a body in the river, some gone to pieces over years and under logs. It's in the relentless nature of big waters, to subsume whatever the landscape offers itself, be that canyon rock or careless people, suck them under, wear them down to gravel and sand, pitch it all up in mid-channel spits, or sandy beaches. It's a deeply black view I have of this river with its grinding hydraulics, its hidden currents, its lore of the dead. An untrustworthy thing, a thing I cannot look at head on, but must keep in my peripheral vision, as if it might change course midday, midride and sweep me over the levy rocks, as if it might rise in a tidal wave and take me, along with this entire valley.

I grow stronger, and bored. By late summer the levy has lost its challenge, the treeless hills are burnished brown and the rows and stacks of houses nesting the cliffs shimmer in waves of heat, bake to bleached colors. Here is the Clarkston Heights subdivision, over there the Elks' cement-and-glass bunkered clubhouse. Here a subdivision, there a subdivision.

Hells Gate park with its RV caravans and chained poodles. The river has dropped, and the center, where it holds the sky, has turned a clear blue. The valley temperature hovers in the nineties. I've gained muscle in these daily rides, regained my wind. I pedal the entire levy there and back and back again. More than ever I'm restless, on the road and at home. My husband, Dennis, dislikes biking, can't understand my compulsion.

It is an early afternoon, and I am on the back porch, unchaining the bike. Dennis leans against a pillar. His blond hair sticks up in quills under the nervous combing of his fingers. His careful distance seems almost natural now. And when did that happen? I can tell he wants to say something, but hesitates and this too is new, this awkwardness. When I thump the bicycle down the steps he follows. I feel chased and stop in the yard, turn to him.

"You're not riding this bike for the same reason as in Mukwonago, are you?" he asks. He ducks his head, his neck exposed—how white his skin is, how nearly translucent with light. We both know what he means. The last time I took to the bike was just before I separated from my first husband, when I lived in Mukwonago, Wisconsin. He was a big man, six foot two to my five foot three. I was getting strong, riding thirty to forty miles a day. Readying myself for battle.

I laugh, is that all? "Of course not," I say, and I believe I mean it. "I'm just getting fit," and this is true, the old me, the body I am most acquainted with is reemerging; thirty pounds lighter, I begin to recognize myself when I catch glimpses in store-front windows. I reach over and brush his arm, feel the tightness in the muscle under my palm. I say, "The novel's in New York and I can't sit still," and this too is true. When I ride away, it's with a light heart. I tell myself it's because his worries are unfounded. I tell myself it's because I'm reassured he still loves me. I tell myself I still love him. We are, I believe, who we have always been.

It's Hells Canyon that I aim for—that sketchy gap in the distant hills. Dennis and I have driven up it a couple times in the truck. A narrow, twisting, ill-bred little road that's dangerous at the best of times, even in a vehicle. I'd ooh and aah, plant my feet on the dash and sweat against the vinyl seat until we'd come to Buffalo Eddy where we'd get out to look at the petroglyphs roadside. Then my husband would turn the truck for home and I'd feel this immense relief to be out of the constriction of basalt walls.

And now here I am biking out of Asotin, with the towns and ranches falling behind me, heading out on a road that's hardly safe for biking, up a canyon that by mid day will be a slow cooker, and I'm level with the river for the most part, a short hop away from the water, eye to eye with that thing I've avoided.

The Snake.

This is not the slack water I have become cozy with—that deeply pooled backwater with its swimming beaches and teenage angst beating out of boom boxes, coveys of jet skis, wild Canada geese turned domestic, rock chucks grown fat on Danish and sweet rolls. This stretch above Asotin is the Snake still fresh from Hells Canyon's steep walled gorges, with rapids and riffles, drops and eddies. I bike close to the cut banks, the eroding islands, the miles of rocks piled high and dry—the clutter of floods. *This* river is a winnowy thing, slippery in its casual destruction, its lack of intent. I head for Buffalo Eddy, an ambitious ride and I keep my eyes raised to the hills soaring above, hosts to the swallows' nests—mud wallows abandoned to the heat of the season—the cliff-side spiders—great fleshy dollops in a crosshatch of webs—and the columnar basalt outcroppings—home to bighorn sheep.

On bike, I insert myself into this landscape. I pause to study and explore. I drift, alternately mindless and aware. I meditate. I breathe it. I take it into my body. The sun blisters the

back of my neck and the tops of my legs. I push on. At Buffalo
Eddy I let out a whoop and scale the rocks down to the river.
I find a shallow pool and step in up to my knees, ladle water
over my breasts and back, face and neck. The river is a white
noise beneath the grousing of magpies, the heckling jays. Back
on shore I stretch out on basalt, look up the canyon, always up
to where the sky collides with the cresting hills. In a contest of
wills between river and land, I say, *Do your worst, river. The
hills will always be here.* What I do not know is that over the
course of this next year the river will cut a channel as deep in
me and as irrevocable as it has the canyon.

THE OLD RIVER CAPTAINS argue whether the river is 130
feet deep or bottomless at Buffalo Eddy. It's a narrow squeeze
between basalt outcroppings, and the score of whirlpools on the
river's surface are just a suggestion of the turmoil beneath. It's
said that at times, at this point in the river, and for unexplain-
able reasons, it rises like a person lifting from his seat, up and
up and over the rocks with a great roar of rushing water. I
have never witnessed this. It's one of a multitude of stories
about this spot. I've no doubt this portion of the Snake is one
of the more dangerous. Before the river was dammed, when it
was still in its wildest youth, whole logs were scooped into
whirlpools, and upended, churned like wooden spoons in batter before being sucked from sight. The occasional boat went
the same fatal route. A quarter mile down river some of them
resurfaced with a boom, others are said to still be down there,
stirring, endlessly stirring. Even now, people navigate this
channel warily. White crosses mark spots where unfortunate
swimmers found the current.

It is spring, my second year biking. Always I aim for
Buffalo Eddy. I don't understand what draws me, frightened
as I am by this river, to this place, to the heart of chaos. Water

is high again this year—double the average snowcap—but flooding is localized and the rains helpfully hold off. I'm determined to know the canyon in all its stages. I believe, since last year, that I've struck an uneasy peace with the river.

Early on, the levy is closed again. This time it doesn't stop me; I detour onto the highway and bike above the flooding. It's curious to know that beneath the murky water is the bike path, that even now blunt-headed carp are wallowing in the shallows, mouthing the asphalt surface in a long, muddy kiss.

I'm starting out with an advantage, my wind and weight good, my legs strong after the mild winter, from taking long walks with Dennis. Although walking is not comfortable—the bones in my feet are fusing and painful—nor is it easy to keep up with him—my stride as short as my legs—I believe we're both trying to find some way back to each other. Still, we inevitably end up walking apart, his step ahead of mine. He is abstracted. His gaze never settling on any one thing longer than a few moments. We talk about work. We talk about pulling my book from New York for revision. We talk about teaching. We spend great blocks of time not talking about much more than the weather. It never occurs to us to admit out loud that in the past four months we haven't said anything more or less to each other than a stranger might.

Always he is that pace or two, five feet, ten feet ahead of me, not a conscious abandonment, rather it's a reflex, an impulse like the one that keeps his gaze from mine, sets him pacing the house, a jumpiness that's driving him away faster, and further until, finally, even a pair of roller skates I purchase from the local Goodwill can't catch me up. I get back on my bike. If I must be alone, I prefer it to be of my own choosing.

I pass beneath Swallows Nest—an enormous cliff that juts out from the rolling hillsides like the prow of a ship. The swallows have mudded the rock face—river bottom mud—a thousand and more hollow-bodied nests piping in the wind. The river flows, hard to judge its speed. I watch a log, one of many, hurtling down the current, and it takes my breath away, hits me like a rush of adrenaline. I pedal beneath Trees of Heaven—spindly, skyward things—and past a locust grove where the grass is always greener. I spin away down the highway, through the tiny town of Asotin with its ball park, school, gas station and rumored serial killer.

Outside of town, although the hills steepen abruptly, the river commands the view with elegant serpentines, a broad greeny swath that buckles the willow stands, scrubs a dirty foam from cottonwood roots. Magpie startle out of the cut bank, pennoned wingtips flashing, and there's the stench of something dead. Something large. While I'm surprised by the smell, I become aware of the undercurrent in the air, an infusion of decay—loess, bones, leaf marl, flesh—sweet and bitter all at once, released from the reliquary snows. A vast purging, an outpouring of old regrets.

I pedal on, paralleling the river, counter current, finding my way upstream like some unlikely fish. It's a struggle, so early in the year. I pace myself, and three quarters to the eddy I already know I will make it there and back. It will be a six hour day, away from cares, home, husband. It is the first of many that spring. The first of a growing number of hours.

THE RIVER BREATHES. I discover this early summer. June, I think. I'm averaging 210 miles a week, mostly on this river road. The temperature is in the high eighties mid canyon and I stop often to swim, and this is new to me, the ease with which I now step into the water. Although the river is never really warm, as my childhood lakes were, the air is so hot, so dry, my skin so beaten by the sun that I relish the cold that stings even the breath from my lungs. The waters are still unusually high, but have cleared so that I can see the five or more feet to rocky bottom. The surface is opaque with color from shoreline trees: bright aspen, the early green of dagger leaf willow, a deep spray of cottonwood. It is umber with the rocky hills, and in the bowl of the current where the choppy spume of rapids levels out it is a bright wash of sky. All color and movement.

I am happiest out here these days. I find a quiet I can't locate in my home, filled so often as it is now with friends or activity, TV or stereo, as if the two of us can't admit silence. We fall to sleep in grudges, but Dennis still ladles me into his lap so that I can drift to sleep spooned against his belly. My bike rides have become lengthy meditations. I pedal the long hours and my thoughts wheel. I contemplate the new novel I'm hard at work on—all about a woman whose marriage is unraveling in ways she cannot begin to comprehend. How the destruction of her life blind sides her.

I think about marriage, how difficult it is, the days of easy drifting, the turbulence, and at its hardest—that most ordinary eddying of passion—the time all couples come to when they bank on their accumulated years and history to tide them over, to carry them safely through to the next great flooding of heart. I love knowing a man so well that I recognize the sound of his step among many, or coming down a corridor, out of sight. I love that my heart still jumps and calms with the recognition, even after all these years, or perhaps because of it. For this deep knowing is like coming to understand some inarticulate part of myself, some capacity to respond outside of reason, the way water finds its own level.

I venture further into the river, duck my head under through an act of will, for I have never trusted total immersion, giving it over so completely, eyes and nose and ears closed off from the known world. I open my eyes and in the murky underwater light I fight the panic—fearful I will see the things

I consciously avoid thinking of when treading water, those great toothy creatures: sturgeon, pike, or the latest dead caught in a tangle of logs, or that thing out there I can never really know, that has chased me up basement stairs since I was three. Immersion for me is, like marriage, a question of faith, of trust in its possibilities, in my husband, and more importantly in myself, believing that should I finally see the sturgeon at my heels I will prove strong enough.

Cooled off and on my bike again, I pass the brace of rocks where a wild mink resides. Bold little creature. He stands on hind legs, ears pricked forward and watches as I slow. He bounds along the rocky shore a short distance, keeping parallel, keeping me in sight. When I stop, it is he that studies me and when satisfied dips from sight and is gone. It is a ritual we have developed these last several weeks.

I ride beneath an osprey nest, the adult pair screaming overhead from opposite ends of the river they circumnavigate. They are cunning fisher birds, and it is not unusual on these rides for me to look up and see fish torsioning, a snake coiling in their talons.

I reach one of my four favorite views, where the hills form a gap and the river disappears in a bend. It is, I realize, the texture of this place that engages me, the overlays of hill against hill against distant mountains, the slender thread of river working its will.

When I reach the eddy, I clamber down to a jut of rocks freshly revealed this past month by the river's fall, part of the basalt archipelago that cinches the river's waist. I hop across a small side rivulet, step over a stone bulwark to perch on top a likely boulder—the tip of a much larger rock mass, perhaps the original wall the river weathered through all those thousands of years ago. I face downriver, the water rushing by on my right. It takes a while to hear it—the steady sound of the

rapids so easily consigned to white noise—the lapse I gradually become aware of, those few moments when the call of the
gray jay bells down the canyon and the drone of bees nestling
into the blossoming Lamb's Ear takes on a singular clarity. I
hear a moment of silence, and then the continuance of river,
and shortly thereafter yet another hush. Pivoting on my rock
as the rushing sound reappears, I become aware of the water
forging around my perch. The water is rising, subsumes the
small rapids, and I become an island. It's a paltry channel that
separates me from the mainland rock and over the next half
minute it dribbles into nothing. And so it is the river rising and
falling, rising and falling—sound and silence—like an intake
and exhalation. I wonder what law of physics plays into this. I
imagine the spits of land that form the eddies, the bends and
bottlenecks that suspend the river's momentum until the
weight and rising mass carry it in a surge to the next bend, the
next eddy. Up river, downriver, it's all an interconnected system
of checks and release.

Or not. It is more than that. A long, sustained, intake of
breath. And release.

I am transfixed to the rock, holding on. I am giddy with
discovery—as if I've stumbled on some great secret.

But what the secret is I'm still unsure, and when I finally
start the long ride home, it is not with the usual dread—the
logginess that settles into my limbs as I angle back toward town,
toward the slackwater, the canyon vistas closing shut behind
me, the half-hearted pace I usually set—this time I travel with
the current, pace myself with a brash of logs bucking their way
down stream. I set my back to the wilderness and focus on the
road ahead. I lose sight of the logs while climbing, gain on the
downside. I swing past isolated homes, no time to wonder about
their lives, what these couples speak of when they turn lights
off. I pass fenced horses drowsing in the late afternoon light,

cattle foraging in the sage. I speed by empty beaches, ride the gravel shoulder too close to a hundred foot drop. I have been gone almost seven hours. I wing the last miles to tell Dennis of my discovery. I arrive downstream with the logs, and we part at the confluence. I chain my bike to the back porch and enter an empty house. I wait for Dennis. Showered and refreshed, I sit on the front stoop, a glass of ice water against my cheek. The hills take on a bruised hue. I wait, and wonder what it was I actually saw—the breath of rivers?

Or perhaps, as likely, the breath of God.

MIDSUMMER. The day starts in an eddy. All the affairs I have put off for biking need to be attended to—summer school, preps, revision on my book, a new short story, conversation with my husband. He's surprised I'm staying home. I take it for granted that he won't argue, or try to dissuade me from leaving—all the hours I'm logging alone on the road. I've stopped wondering why. I take it as a sign of love, his willingness to give me the space and distance I seem to need these days. But like that great mass of river in the eddy, building its own slow momentum, the everyday matters threaten to spill over unless I see to them. Today, I'm housebound, but it's all right. I feel charged. My body is in fighting trim and I'm focused in a way I haven't been in years. I have energy to spare. I'll ride later, I say. Tomorrow.

Dennis is staying close. When I look up he is there, hovering, and I think of the evening before, how restless he was, turning in sleep, turning, pulling me and the blankets to him again and again. "Was it a bad night?" I ask, although I already know, having wakened with his fits and starts.

He nods. He opens his mouth to speak, closes it again. Paces off. When he comes back, he carries his distraction in his hands—fingering the counters, hands in and out of pockets, fingers raking through his hair. I wait.

"Bad dreams all night," he says.

I think of how he held me when we woke. How tenuous it felt. I want to sympathize, but I sleep well these days. Sheer exhaustion.

≈

I am suspended in the river. My feet firm on the sandy bottom. My bike is still roadside in the gravel. I don't hear any traffic and the motorboat that caused the wake has long passed. I don't hear or see any of it. I can still feel though, how the water rocks me, and marvel at the stubbornness, the strength with which my legs and feet hold me in place. I look down the river. I feel the current so close at hand, and it becomes clear to me that I could let go.

That easy.

I could let go, give myself over to this river as I have given myself over to the events of an afternoon, the sudden unraveling of a marriage, riding the momentum of the last two years. I could let it take me where it would. There is no greater harm this water can do to me.

Earlier this morning, Dennis had suggested a walk. A short distance from home, we stood under spreading elm branches, the bright sunlight dappling the grass and concrete sidewalk. He talked—anxious patter that took a sudden serious turn, and then a dark turn and darker still, stripping away our lives together, our marriage, like flesh from bone. I stumbled where I stood. A black Lab launched himself along a picket fence, and children bolted past with backpacks slung from arms, but the day had lost all familiarity—the hills flattened beyond the trees, and the trees became a weedy tangle in air turned watery. My limbs were weightless. Though I did not believe I had closed my eyes, I felt them open. I saw my husband a stranger. I stepped back. I saw who we had been—the couple

I believed in—become unrecognizable. A bird swam upward, between leaves and branches, was gone. We waited in silence, having said all we needed. Having put our twelve years of marriage to rest in the span of those bright, brief moments. I left him standing there and I made my way home alone.

I found my bike, and then I found myself here. Immersed in the Snake.

It's curious. There are no questions. No blame. I stand emptied. I hardly know myself anymore. I study my body through the wavering water, the arms that float out at my side as though they were a stranger's. I become aware of how thoroughly this river has reshaped me, how deep this new channel cuts through my heart.

I tread water. The sound of blood rushes through my ears like the hum of katydids. In a world gone out of true, I search for something *certain*. I know this river. There is comfort in that. I know how the hills fold against each other. I know how quickly the canyon cools once the sun fails the other side of the hills. I know the cry of a magpie slicing through the air. All of this—like a blessing. I cup my hands in the water, rinse my face. What I cannot know is what awaits me once I step out of this river. I cannot yet imagine the ride home, the angry days ahead, or the dark evenings when Dennis and I will sit at a careful distance, determining our courses, together or apart. I cannot know how we will struggle to understand the forces that undermine us—what we bring upon ourselves, what is wrought upon us. We are steeped in undercurrents, riffles and slackwater, bottomless pools and eddies. It seems I have always known this. It is the immersion, the act of will, the transcendent leap beyond the limitations of flesh and fear—call it faith—that I must learn and relearn continuously. This is a river as old as memory, older. I feel the water rise, and fall. And rise. I breathe.

Christina Adam

Christina Adam's stories have appeared in a number of magazines. "Fires" was selected for inclusion in *American Fiction #3*.

She writes, "I grew up with my brother and sister playing in the swamps and vacant lots of Florida, barefoot or on horseback. We stayed out after dark. No one summoned us for dinner or for baths. Recently, a friend referred to us as feral children. I went to high school in southern California, a place I hated at the time and now miss for its dry hills (where I first saw fires) and cool lawns, the safe smell of alyssum in the garden.

"In 1984 I bought part of an old ranch at the base of the Teton Range in Idaho. Even my father's sweet cousins who live near the Adam homestead in Anamoose, North Dakota, think *this* is the middle of nowhere. But I've sold the cows, and things are tame—no bears, no wolves, no killer bees.

"The trouble comes from weather. This winter, snow covered the first-story windows through March. Here in zone *one,*

I have to struggle to grow roses. On summer evenings, I pull on my brother's worn ski parka and work in the garden. I've looked up to see the big ears and old faces of all the baby foxes, watching me. I am deeply happy in the falling light, listening to the solitary calls of cows and cranes across the field."

Christina Adam lives in Victor, Idaho.

SANDRA *A*LCOSSER

SANDRA ALCOSSER has been selected by Daniel Halpern and The Writer's Voice Project as a poet in their New Voices of the West series. Professor of poetry, fiction, and feminist poetics at San Diego State University, Alcosser will be a Writer in Residence at the University of Michigan, Ann Arbor, in 1994. Her poems have appeared in *The American Poetry Review, The New Yorker, The North American Review, The Paris Review, Poetry*, and many other magazines and anthologies. She is a recipient of numerous awards, including two National Endowment for the Arts fellowships, a Bread Loaf fellowship, a Pushcart Prize, a Pen Syndicated Fiction Award, and The American Scholar's Mary Elinore Smith Poetry Prize. Her second book of poems, *A Fish to Feed All Hunger*, was selected by James Tate as the Associated Writing Program's Award Series Winner in Poetry.

Sandra Alcosser lives on glacial till at the mouth of Carlton Creek Canyon near the Selway Bitterroot Wilderness Boundary, where many of her poems (including "Cry" and "The Sawyer's Wife") are set.

ALISON BAKER

ALISON BAKER is the author of *How I Came West, and Why I Stayed*, a collection of short stories. Her fiction and nonfiction have appeared in *The Atlantic, Orion, ZYZZYVA, The Gettysburg Review, The Kenyon Review*, and other magazines, as well as in *Best of the West 5* and *New Stories from the South: The Best of 1992*.

She describes her new home as a difficult place: "I have lived in many parts of the United States, from Maine to Indiana to Utah to Oregon, and I find that the West is not an easy place to love. The western landscape is not a kind one, and its sense of humor is less than gentle. When I first moved to Utah its wide-open treelessness fed my incipient agoraphobia, and I could only move out into it sideways, in incremental steps. It took years for me to begin to feel comfortable in the West's glaring sunshine, exposed under its brilliant sky. Western air is so dry that I found breathing it very difficult for a long time. I am still not completely at home here. At heart, I feel that I still belong in the civilized part of the nation east of the Mississippi."

Alison Baker lives in southwestern Oregon.

KIM BARNES

KIM BARNES's stories and poems have appeared in numerous journals, including *The Georgia Review* and *Shenandoah*. Currently she is working on *In the Wilderness*, a memoir.

Descriptions of her childhood evoke both sound and atmosphere: "When I was a child, living in northern Idaho, my father often worked so close I could hear voices over saws and shifting machinery. It was a comforting mix of sounds: the little creek burbling a few feet from the porch; the thrum of logging trucks gearing for the hill, headed for the North Fork; the whine of metal teeth through larch and cedar; the loader my father operated clanking with the balanced weight of logs. Perhaps because I'd spent years unaware of distance, I never felt any need to see beyond the dark saw-toothed horizon, and I've never felt safer, more protected, than I did in that hollow, with the forest so close pine needles tatted our roof with the slightest breeze."

Kim Barnes lives with her husband and children above the Clearwater River in Idaho.

Mary Clearman Blew

Mary Clearman Blew is the author of several books, including *All But the Waltz* (Viking Penguin). Her memoir, *Balsamroot*, appears concurrently with *Circle of Women* from Viking Penguin.

Montana, her childhood home, elicits a mix of ambivalent emotions: "I grew up on a ranch in central Montana, on the site of the homestead my great-grandfather filed in 1882. I feel as though I have been imprinted from birth by that landscape. Often I can see its low mountains, grasslands, buttes, and river against the backs of my closed eyes like the lingering effect of looking at the sun. But I also feel a kind of aversion, in that the human cost of that landscape, in terms of hopes and lives, displacement and loneliness, has been so high."

Mary Clearman Blew lives with her youngest daughter in Lewiston, Idaho, beside the Snake River.

JUDY BLUNT

JUDY BLUNT spent her first thirty years on cattle and wheat ranches in eastern Montana, exploring, and eventually crossing, the fine line that separates solitude from isolation. She moved to Missoula in 1986, earning degrees in creative writing and journalism at the University of Montana. In 1991 she was awarded a Jacob K. Javits fellowship by the U.S. Department of Education. She is currently working toward her master's in creative writing at the University of Montana. Her first book, *Not Quite Stone*, won the Merriam Frontier award and was published in 1992. A book of essays is forthcoming from Little, Brown.

She lives in Missoula with three teenagers and a large black cat.

MADELINE DEFREES

MADELINE DEFREES is the author of six poetry collections, the most recent being *Imaginary Ancestors* (Broken Moon Press, 1990) and *Possible Sibyls* (Lynx House Press, 1991). Born in Ontario, Oregon, she grew up in Hillsboro. As a sister of the Holy Names of Jesus and Mary for many years, she taught elementary and secondary school in Oregon before transferring to college teaching, most recently at the University of Massachusetts, Amherst.

" 'In the Hellgate Wind' was written a little more than twenty years ago," she writes, "and now seems quite alien. But I still remember the fear I experienced each time I crossed on foot Missoula's Higgins Avenue Bridge. The height created an impulse to jump—perhaps a symbolic 'suicide' involving the life I was about to leave for another."

For DeFrees, the western experience is first and foremost a coastal experience. In spite of many years spent inland, her truest inspiration is allied to water—preferably oceanic—and even the poems written while in the interior frequently go in imagination or memory to the edge—the border between land and water.

Since retiring, Madeline DeFrees continues to write in Seattle, Washington.

DEBRA EARLING

DEBRA EARLING is a member of the Confederated Salish and Kootenai tribes of the Flathead Reservation. She is an assistant professor with a joint appointment in Native American Studies and English at the University of Montana in Missoula. Her work appeared in *The Last Best Place: A Montana Anthology*.

As she describes it, "The stories I write are stories of the land, stories of how the land reclaims us after all we grow to love has disowned us or forgotten us. The land *is* the knowledge that we all belong and that we are always returning. In remembering the land through stories I remember all my ancestors. I remember my place. I write in some ways to go home again."

GRETEL EHRLICH

GRETEL EHRLICH's most recent book is *Lightning Strikes Twice* (Pantheon). Her books of essays and fiction include *The Solace of Open Spaces*, *Heart Mountain*, and *Islands, the Universe, Home*, all from Viking Penguin.

Ehrlich found a home in Wyoming through a sense of distance from her urban environment: "Beginning in 1976, when I went to Wyoming to make a film, I had the experience of waking up not knowing where I was, whether I was a man or a woman, or which toothbrush was mine. I had suffered a tragedy and made a drastic geographical and cultural move fairly baggageless, but I wasn't losing my grip. . . . What I had lost (at least for a while) was my appetite for the life I had left: city surroundings, old friends, familiar comforts. It had occurred to me that comfort was only a disguise for discomfort; reference points, a disguise for what will always change.

"Friends asked when I was going to stop 'hiding out' in Wyoming. What appeared to them as a landscape of lunar desolation and intellectual backwardness was luxurious to me. For the first time I was able to take up residence on earth with no alibis, no self-promoting schemes."

Gretel Ehrlich presently lives in California.

ANITA ENDREZZE

ANITA ENDREZZE received her B.A. in teaching and her M.A. in creative writing at Eastern Washington University. Her poems have appeared in numerous magazines, including *National Geographic* and *Yellow Silk*, and in several anthologies, including *Dancing on the Rim of the World* (University of Arizona, 1990). Her paintings have been widely shown, and they have appeared on book covers in the United States and in Europe.

Endrezze is of half-Yaqui and half-European heritage. She is a professional storyteller as well as a poet, fiction writer, translator, and artist. She has taught classes for elementary, high school, university, and community college students, as well as for various community groups, and she has presented her work in France and Denmark.

Visions of loss, of failed dreams, fill her natural landscape: "The poem 'Moving Day at the Widow Cain's' was based on a real experience. The many abandoned homesteads speak of lost dreams and failure of some sort. The West is famous for its promise of a better life, but the harsh realities of weather, isolation, misjudgment, escapism, and hard work have defeated many people. Seeing an old house, battered and gray, with windows empty and black, the chimney bricks littering the mossy roof, the front door open or half-unhinged, all of it speaks of lives lost. Around an abandoned house, or even where there's no house, you can see the mountainous lilac bushes and scabby-barked trees that some woman had watered carefully, each pail of precious water carried in one hand, perhaps a baby in the other."

Anita Endrezze currently lives in Spokane, Washington, with her husband and two children.

TESS GALLAGHER

TESS GALLAGHER's previous publications include *Amplitude: New and Selected Poems, A Concert of Tenses* (essays on poetry), *The Lover of Horses and Other Stories*, and *Portable Kisses* (Capra Press). She has recently completed the introduction to *No Heroics, Please*, the first of two volumes of *The Uncollected Work of Raymond Carver*, edited by William Stull.

In *A Concert of Tenses*, she describes the influence of light on her poetry: "Growing up [on the Olympic peninsula], I thought the moss-light that lived with us lived everywhere. It was a sleepy predawn light that muted the landscape and made the trees come close. I always went outside with my eyes wide, no need to shield them from sun bursts or the steady assault of skies I was to know later in El Paso or Tucson. The color of green and gray are what bind me to the will to write poems."

Tess Gallagher lives in Port Angeles, Washington.

MOLLY GLOSS

MOLLY GLOSS is the author of several books for children. Her novel, *The Jump-Off Creek*, won the 1989 Pacific Northwest Booksellers' Award and the 1990 H. L. Davis/Oregon Book Award for Fiction. It was nominated for the 1990 PEN/Faulkner Award for Fiction.

Her novel was partly written in response to a void in western fiction—an account of a woman's experience of the frontier: "*The Jump-Off Creek* was written out of my lifelong familiarity with and affection for the western novel in all its forms, Ernest Haycox to Willa Cather. It was very much a piece of writing that, as a reader, I'd been looking for without success—a western novel with a woman holding up the center. It is, among other things, an exploration of women's experience of the frontier, an experience of home and community and peaceable, authentic courage, set alongside what is primarily a male mythology of conflict and conquest. As J. D. Salinger has said, 'It was a piece of writing that in all the world I most wanted to read, and I shamelessly sat down and wrote it myself.' "

Molly Gloss is a fourth-generation Oregonian living in Portland with her husband and son.

MARY GOLDEN

MARY GOLDEN received an M.F.A. in creative writing from Colorado State University. She has published fiction and nonfiction in *The Northwest Review, The Seattle Review, Mid-American Review,* and other journals. She has been the recipient of a fellowship from the Colorado Council on the Arts and Humanities.

Land, to her, has always been a source of both terror and comfort: "I grew up on a wheat and cattle ranch in the Horse Heaven country of eastern Washington. From my earliest memories I have had this dichotomous relationship to the land—at once terrified of its strength and absolute indifference to me and comforted by that strength. Sometimes I imagine the land as an old woman, her hands spotted and swollen with age, comforting like a grandmother, but not a grandmother, a combination of all the generations who have lived or wandered here."

Mary Golden teaches writing and literature courses at Colorado State University.

JANET CAMPBELL HALE

JANET CAMPBELL HALE, a member of the Coeur d'Alene tribe of northern Idaho, grew up on the Coeur d'Alene reservation and graduated from the University of California at Berkeley, where she also studied law. Her first novel, *The Owl's Song,* was published in 1974 in the same month and year she was graduated from college. Her second novel, *The Jailing of Cecelia Capture* (1985), was her master's thesis at the University of California at Davis and was nominated for a Pulitzer Prize. *Bloodlines* (1993) is a collection of essays.

For Hale, the region is a connection with her history and the land of her ancestors: "My tribe has been in this region, The Palouse—what is now called the Spokane–Coeur d'Alene Area—for thousands of years. The reservation, where my father and all my siblings were born, where I grew up, remains in ancestral land. It is the first country I remember. I recently drove to southern Idaho to visit my college-student daughter, down through Nez Perce country, beside the Snake River. I hadn't seen that country for thirty-five years, but it was so, so familiar. I've dreamed of it often, along with Coeur d'Alene. I remembered my father taking me to watch the beavers at work on their dams in this place. I remembered the little town of White Bird where the Nez Perce War began. I remembered the great vistas and canyons, even the rock formations. I 'make my home' (as they say) in New York City now and am quite content there. I don't see myself leaving anytime soon. But if I don't ever see the West again, my heart and soul will always belong to its dramatic terrain. It is my own inner landscape."

Janet Campbell Hale is married and lives and writes in New York City.

PATRICIA HENLEY

PATRICIA HENLEY's two collections of short stories—*Friday Night at Silver Star* (1986) and *The Secret of Cartwheels* (1992)—have been published by Graywolf Press. She is working on a novel, *Bright Praise*, set in Guatemala.

Living in the heartland has made Henley keenly aware of her longing for the wilderness. To her, it is both teacher and healer: "When you meet someone who has ranged where you have ranged, slept beside Image Lake in the North Cascades in a lightning storm or climbed down into a thousand-year-old kiva in Grand Gulch—that person knows your secret self, the Original Face of who you were before you were born, as a Buddhist might say. In wilderness we discover who we are in relation to fire, creekwater, snowfields, thunder, sunlight. And other animals. If you stare long enough into the eyes of a bighorn sheep, you know yourself as just another traveler on the planet. Wilderness teaches us that our cravings are not all there is; at best, I think, each time we return from the wilderness we are healed, and perhaps, in slight and almost imperceptible increments, less attached to the things we desire."

Patricia Henley teaches in the creative writing program at Purdue University.

PAM HOUSTON

PAM HOUSTON is a part-time river guide and hunting guide and a frequent contributor to such magazines as *Mirabella* and *Mademoiselle*. Her collection of short fiction, *Cowboys Are My Weakness*, was published by Norton in 1992. She is at work on a novel.

Houston evokes the connections between the western landscape and her writing: "More than any other single thing, I believe it was the western landscape that taught me how to write, specifically the canyons, mountains, and rivers of the Colorado Plateau. It was those buttes and mesas, those undefinable shapes and constantly changing colors that opened my imagination, that said, 'Okay, writer, describe this.'

"Without the time I spend hiking, rafting, sleeping, sitting, breathing in the West's remaining wild places, I'd lose not only most of my metaphors but many of my characters and almost all of my stories; I'd lose the very connection that gives my work and my life its energy. I'd lose my self-definition, and the most important reason why I write."

Pam Houston currently lives in Park City, Utah.

VICTORIA JENKINS

A SCREENWRITER as well as novelist, Victoria Jenkins has been twice selected as a fellow at the Sundance Film Institute. Her novel, *Relative Distances*, was published by Peregrine Smith in 1990.

For Jenkins, discovering Wyoming was like finding herself: "I was born in Texas, but most of my childhood was spent in Massachusetts, much of it alone on horseback, going nowhere in particular, displaced and closed in, lost in a fantasy world, longing for another landscape, which I found, finally, on the high plains of Wyoming."

Victoria Jenkins presently lives in Seattle.

TERESA JORDAN

TERESA JORDAN is the author of *Cowgirls: Women of the American West* (Garden City Press, 1982) and *Riding the White Horse Home: A Western Family Album* (Pantheon, 1993). She has edited *Graining the Mare: The Poetry of Ranch Women* (Peregrine Smith, 1994), and is coediting an anthology of nonfiction—*The Stories That Shape Us: Twenty Women Write About the West.*

Storytelling, even though most of the storytellers were male, was a way of life to Jordan: "I was raised as the fourth generation on a cattle ranch in the Iron Mountain country of southeast Wyoming. We were isolated, living fifty miles from town with no phone or TV (these came in the mid-1960s). Stories were everything—our social life, our entertainment, how we passed the time on long rides to distant pastures. I always loved these stories, and I was well into adulthood before I realized that the storytellers were almost always male, and that even when women told stories, they generally revolved around events in the outside world. The more interior stories of family, of grief, of loneliness, of emotional trial, survival, and even triumph were not spoken of at all or told only in truncated form—"they were hard years, but we made it through." Lately, these hidden stories have interested me most: how did they "make it through," and what did it cost?

Teresa Jordan lives on a hay meadow in eastern Nevada with her husband, folklorist and musician Hal Cannon.

CYRA McFADDEN

CYRA McFADDEN has written for *The New York Times, The Nation, Smithsonian* magazine, and many other publications. Her biography of her father, *Rain or Shine*, was published by Alfred A. Knopf in 1986.

In *Rain or Shine* she describes eastern Montana as "vast expanses of sagebrush, sand cliffs and emptiness. The landscape is dun-colored except for white spots on the horizon, the tails of grazing antelope. Alongside streams, cabins with no roofs stand abandoned, swallows their tenants. The cold winters, or the loneliness, proved too much for the homesteaders who built them."

Cyra McFadden writes a biweekly column for the *San Francisco Examiner*.

Ruth McLaughlin

Ruth McLaughlin grew up in eastern Montana. Her stories have appeared in small magazines and in *Best American Short Stories*.

"My grandparents were homesteaders," she writes. "I would trail around the farm with my grandmother, who often stopped me in the windbreak to gesture at a spot of ground unmarked and only long ago disturbed. 'These are my babies,' she would say. I would want to hurry on, always embarrassed by her suffering—babies born at home who didn't survive; a body bent from years of killing work. I much preferred the stories of my grandfather, whose daring and flamboyance had caused him to move West, bringing my grandmother with him.

"Only after their deaths and decades away from eastern Montana have I wished I hadn't hurried my grandmother past her stories."

Ruth McLaughlin lives in Great Falls, Montana, with her family.

Deirdre McNamer

Deirdre McNamer has been a reporter for several western newspapers and the Associated Press. She periodically contributes short pieces to *The New Yorker*. She has written two novels, *Rima in the Weeds* (HarperCollins, 1991), which won the Pacific Northwest Booksellers Award, and *One Sweet Quarrel* (HarperCollins, 1994).

She grew up on the high plains of Montana, a landscape which she says encourages simultaneous feelings of puniness and possibility. The resulting unease, for her, encourages dark laughter and the telling of stories.

Deirdre McNamer lives in Missoula, Montana, with her husband, the essayist Bryan DiSalvatore.

NEIDY MESSER

NEIDY MESSER's collection of poems, *In Far Corners*, was published by Confluence Press in 1990. She was Idaho's 1990–91 Writer in Residence.

Her father's family came west to ranch in 1842, before the great gold rush. Land, she says, was their idea of gold, and land keeps them bound to the western way of life today.

Neidy Messer lives in Boise, Idaho, with her husband and two sons.

PAULINE MORTENSEN

PAULINE MORTENSEN's collection of short fiction, *Back Before the World Turned Nasty*, received a Utah Arts Council First Book Award and was published by the University of Arkansas Press in 1989.

She was born in Coeur d'Alene, Idaho, and spent the first years of her adult life logging and planting trees in Idaho and Montana. She has spent the last twenty years, she says, being married, in Utah, where she acquired one son and several superfluous degrees from various universities, published a few odd stories in literary magazines around the country, and now works for "real money" for a computer software company— "and Thoreau made pencils, so give me a break."

Like so many of the writers in this book, Mortensen draws

strong connections between her writing and the landscape: "I tried striking a transcendental pose once in the middle of an icy spring runoff (as in flashbacks of Walden Pond), and excuse me but I just didn't get it. So part of me writes to set the record straight. Another part writes in the hopes that some psyche-centered landscape metaphor will play around in my head long enough to make sense."

Pauline Mortensen lives in Salt Lake City.

DIXIE PARTRIDGE

DIXIE PARTRIDGE grew up near Afton, Wyoming, on a farm first settled by her great-grandfather in the 1880s. She received a degree in English from Brigham Young University in 1965. Her poetry and essays have been published widely in journals and anthologies. Her first book, *Deer in the Haystacks*, was published by Ahsahta Press in 1984 as part of its series Poetry of the West. Her second book, *Watermark*, won the Eileen W. Barnes Award in 1990 and was published by Saturday Press in 1991.

Words, to Partridge, were bridges to things one couldn't name: "When words started to come from me—unstoppable—they came for my mother, who had little way to develop her interest in music or writing because of farmwork and family. They came to bridge the silence my father set between himself and us, to name his frustrations and affections for the land, animals both wild and domestic, and us—his family. And they came for me, for the unrealized parts of myself that could come to light only if I could name them, put weather around them, connect them to the ice skies of deep winter, the spring rock-picking, the horse-drawn leveler, the itchy skin of hayfields, and that endurance of my mother's will, staunch against and for it all."

Dixie Partridge lives in Richland, Washington, with her husband and their six children. When not writing, she teaches workshops and enjoys books, gardening, and annual family treks back to western Wyoming.

INEZ PETERSEN

BORN BEFORE the Indian Child Welfare Act could protect her family rights, Inez Petersen was removed not only from her mother but also from her extended family of the Quinault tribe. She survived the foster-care system and was chosen as a 1991–92 Kidd Scholar at the University of Oregon, where she received her B.A. in 1992. Her work has appeared in *The New England Review, The Kenyon Review*, and in *Earth Song, Sky Spirit*, an anthology published by Anchor Books in 1993.

Petersen writes poignantly of finding her voice: "I recognized how close I came to being one of those silenced by birth: gender, race, social standing, and education. My circumstances changed. Now I am blessed with the fortunate combination of opportunity, of community, of belief and desire to speak my turn."

Inez Petersen is currently working toward an M.A. at the University of New Mexico in Albuquerque.

DIANE RAPTOSH

RAISED IN NAMPA, Idaho, of Italian and Czechoslovakian descent, Diane Raptosh received her M.F.A. in creative writing from the University of Michigan in 1986. Her work has appeared in the *Mid-American Review, Michigan Quarterly Review, The Malahat Review*, and the *Kansas Quarterly*, as well as a variety of anthologies. Her book of poems, *Just West of Now*, was published by Guernica Editions of Montreal in 1992.

"The one dictum that I've perhaps unwittingly set for myself when it comes to writing about place, about the West, is that all landscapes, in order to engage, must be peopled," she writes. "I will borrow the words of Colorado poet Thomas Hornsby Ferril, in his 1930 essay 'Rocky Mountain Metaphysics': *Landscape is simply a static stage; it requires the movements of people, clouds, storms, the coming and going of vegetation, and most of all, human experience applied to these movements, if it is to be interesting in literature.*"

Diane Raptosh returned to live in Idaho in 1990. She teaches English at Albertson College.

MARILYNNE ROBINSON

MARILYNNE ROBINSON is the author of the highly acclaimed novel *Housekeeping* (1981), which is set in the northern Idaho region of Robinson's birth. She has also published an environmental study, *Mother Country* (1989), which was nominated for the National Book Award. Her reviews have appeared frequently in *The New York Times Book Review*.

Images of ranch-living abound in her account of her childhood years: "I remember the evenings at my grandparents' ranch, at Sagle, and how in the daytime we chased the barn cats and swung on the front gate and set off pitchy, bruising avalanches in the woodshed, and watched my grandmother scatter chicken feed from an apron with huge pockets in it, suffering the fractious contentment of town children rusticated. And then the cows came home and the wind came up and Venus burned through what little remained of atmosphere, and the dark and the emptiness stood over the old house like some unsought revelation.

"It must have been at evening that I heard the word 'lonesome' spoken in tones that let me know privilege attached to it, the kind of democratic privilege that comes with the simplest deserving. I think it is correct to regard the West as a moment in a history much larger than its own."

Marilynne Robinson is now a faculty member in the writers' program of the University of Iowa.

LESLIE RYAN

LESLIE RYAN's work has appeared in *Northern Lights*. Respect for the land as a healing, protective force has influenced much of her work: "One morning I awoke alongside a stream in central Idaho: sunlight jingling the poplar leaves, blue air behind, water applauding the light. I lay very still on the ground. A snipe was diving in the sky; it escaped the corner of my ear when I listened for it. Two garter snakes slid through the brush. The red ladders patterning their backs were dull with summer dust. I was twenty-three years old. I was two thousand miles away from the years before. I hadn't felt safe before that day, or had so long ago that the memory had gone by, like fruit that farmers speak of sadly with acceptance.

"Seven years later, I still sleep outdoors, work with troubled youth, and draw water from a pure stream, but now I also support the Northern Rockies Ecosystem Protection Act and teach a semester course on poetry and ecofeminism in an experiential program. I want to help women heal and grow, and to help protect the lands that so kindly rejoined me at the neck—to keep us all from being further fragmented and injured."

Leslie Ryan lives in Missoula, where she is completing a degree in environmental studies at the University of Montana.

DENNICE SCANLON

A BUTTE NATIVE, Dennice Scanlon received her M.F.A. degree in creative writing from the University of Montana in 1984. While she has written freelance articles and stories for outdoor magazines, poetry is her first and main interest. Her work has appeared in *The Last Best Place, McCall's, Outdoor Life, Montana Outdoors, Poet & Critic, Poetry Northwest, Seattle Review, A Trout in the Milk, Montana Poets' Anthology, Chiaroscuro, The Malahat Review, Writers' Worksheet, Intro II, Wild Sheep Magazine, Yokoi, Cutbank, Urthkin*, the *Missoulian*, the *Montana Standard*, the *Bozeman Chronicle*, and *The Montana Review*.

The emotional drawing power of the western landscape is an inner force to Scanlon: "When I'm not flyfishing Montana streams or hiking to mountain lakes, I'm writing about my long love affair with the land here—how it seeps inside to fill up a lifetime; how its valleys and rivers have a way of winding around me and turning me slowly home."

Dennice Scanlon lives and teaches elementary school in Anaconda, Montana.

RIPLEY SCHEMM

RIPLEY SCHEMM is the author of *Mapping My Father*, published by Dooryard Press in 1981. Her work has been anthologized in *The Last Best Place*.

She says, "Once I wrote, 'There were heroes / each side of the road.' The high plains country I belong to shaped the men and women I was raised with, learned from, and keep discovering. These people, who live in terms of water level and weather, good breaks and bad, are the ones who make my poems."

Ripley Schemm teaches in the Montana Arts Council's Poets in the Schools program. She lives in Missoula, Montana.

ANNICK SMITH

ANNICK SMITH was born in Paris, raised in Chicago, and has lived since 1964 in western Montana. She is a freelance writer and filmmaker, coproducer of *A River Runs Through It* and executive producer of *Heartland*. She coedited the Montana anthology *The Last Best Place* with William Kittredge. Her essays have appeared in *Outside, Modern Maturity, Travel & Leisure,* and other magazines. "It's Come to This," her first published story, was included in *Best American Short Stories: 1992* and has been widely anthologized.

She describes her story as "largely autobiographical": "My husband, Dave, did die of a heart attack on our kitchen floor; I heard Ernest Tubbs play one of his last gigs at the Turah Pines bar; one night at the Top Hat in Missoula I danced with an old cowboy whose right hand was shriveled and deformed; and my companion, Bill, and I saw a rainbow at midnight over the Clark Fork River, near its junction with Rock Creek, where I lived with my young family on a small ranch owned by a woman named Mary Del, who was in love with horses."

Annick Smith still lives on that small ranch.

Melanie Rae Thon

Melanie Rae Thon was born in Kalispell, Montana, in 1957. She is the author of two novels, *Meteors in August* (1990) and *Iona Moon* (1993), and a collection of stories, *Girls in the Grass* (1991).

The haunting quality of the West is as much an effect of the people as it is of the land to Thon: "I started writing about the boy Matt Fry in 1975—his story haunted me, but I never knew how to follow it. In 1986, I discovered his life collided with others I wanted to explore, and I made the stories 'Iona Moon' and 'Snake River.' Later still, Matt Fry's name became the first words of the novel *Iona Moon*. For me, Matt's insistent presence is part of what it means to write from my western experience. I lived in Boston for twelve years, in Michigan for six years before that. Now I live in Syracuse, New York. But the people I knew as a child are like the huge rocks left by glaciers—only a force as slow and strong as ice could move them out of me."

Melanie Rae Thon teaches in the Graduate Writing Program at Syracuse University.

Irene Wanner

Irene Wanner was born in New York in 1949, but has lived in Seattle—except for stints in Greece, Ohio, Iowa, and Idaho—since 1951. Her collection of stories, *Sailing to Corinth*, won the Western States Arts Federation fiction award in 1988. She is completing a novel, tentatively titled *White Roads*.

"In the early 1980s, the *Seattle Post-Intelligence* gave me several travel assignments in the West," she writes. "Like Abby in my story, a visit to a Hutterite colony with a friend who lived in Shelby, Montana, proved especially memorable. One young girl's intelligence and curiosity chafed her community, her family, her own desires, and the two of us who dropped in without having considered the effect of our freedom to come and go as we pleased. My characters tend to travel a lot. They're interested in trade-offs between freedom and security. The Montana landscape, beautiful even as it also denies many people an adequate living, embodies a common dilemma for survival in the West."

Irene Wanner reviews books for the *Seattle Times*, serves as features editor for *The Seattle Review*, and teaches at University of Washington Extension.

MARY ANN WATERS

MARY ANN WATERS was born and raised in Missoula, Montana. Her book, *The Exact Place*, was published by Confluence Press in 1987.

For Waters, the elemental Western landscape was the inspiration for her poetry. She wrote "Though I've traveled a great deal, I'm never happier than when I'm behind the wheel of my car, heading over Lookout Pass toward the Flathead Valley. It has a lot to do with being able to breathe deeply and smell trees, or with sitting on the bank of the Jocko River, transported by the water on the rocks, the sunlight on the water. Many of my poems come out of this elemental experience."

Mary Ann Waters lived most of her life in Spokane, Washington, where she died from breast cancer in early 1994. A new collection of her poems is forthcoming from Confluence Press.

TERRY TEMPEST WILLIAMS

TERRY TEMPEST WILLIAMS is the author of several books, including *Refuge: An Unnatural History of Time and Place* (Pantheon, 1991).

Williams describes the intensity of the landscape: "Everything about Great Salt Lake is exaggerated—the heat, the cold, the salt, and the brine. It is a landscape so surreal one can never know what it is for certain.

"In the past [several] years, Great Salt Lake has advanced and retreated. The Bear River Migratory Bird Refuge, devastated by the flood, [has begun] to heal. . . . I sit on the floor of my study with journals all around me. I open them and feathers fall from their pages, sand cracks their spines, and sprigs of sage pressed between passages of pain heighten my sense of smell—and I remember the country I come from and how it informs my life.

Terry Tempest Williams currently lives in Salt Lake City.

CLAIRE DAVIS

CLAIRE DAVIS teaches fiction writing at Lewis-Clark State College in Lewiston, Idaho. Her first novel, *Winter Range*, won both the Pacific Northwest Booksellers Award and the Mountain States Booksellers Award for 2000.